ticket out

traffic warden mysteries
book one

Michelle Diener

Cover design: Creative Paramita

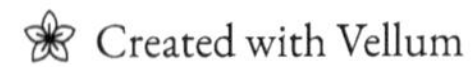

about ticket out

It's the summer of 1963 and Gabriella Farnsworth is a newly-minted London traffic warden. She's used to temper tantrums, swearing, and threats, but finding a dead body is an entirely new low.

She isn't interested in getting more involved than she already is in the investigation into the man she found's death, but when, a few days later, she stumbles over a second body lying feet away from where she found the first, she can't avoid it.

She knows the streets of her route, knows the people on them, but she is absolutely astonished when New Scotland Yard discovers the art gallery near where she found the bodies is a front for mixing up a new psychedelic drug.

Suddenly, the reason for the killings starts to make sense, but what neither she nor the New Scotland Yard detective assigned to the case understand is that the killer's agenda is more complex than a drug turf war, and by the time Gabriella works it out, it just might be too late . . .

chapter one

London: Summer 1963

IT WAS EARLY.

Not early enough that Gabriella had the streets to herself—not that that was possible in London. The city seemed to always be humming, no matter what time you stepped out into it.

But most of the traffic, both on foot and by car, was light.

She didn't mind the early shift.

She'd worked in her mother's bakery in Melbourne, and sometimes that meant being up before four am. Starting the day at seven was a luxury.

It also meant less interaction with the public.

She preferred to write parking tickets and fix them to windscreens without ever having a face-to-face with a real life person.

Most of them weren't very happy to receive what she had for them, and they took one look at her, in her neat black uniform and black satchel, hair pulled back in the regulation bun under her cap with its yellow band, and thought they could intimidate her.

Gabriella had a philosophical objection to being intimidated. She didn't like it. She always pushed back.

She had a feeling that was why Mr. Greenberg had decided to put her on the early shift.

He couldn't fault her for standing her ground, but he seemed to think there was a polite way to deal with someone screaming obscenities in your face. Gabriella had asked him what that way was, and he had looked at her for a long beat, and then put her on mornings.

Kensington this time of day was just stretching awake, what with the sun already up.

It was summer, and the faint stink of rotting food scraps puffed out of narrow alleys as she walked past them. It was still cool enough, this early, but yesterday had been a scorcher, and she wrinkled her nose at the smell, aware that as the day heated up, it was only going to get worse.

She turned the corner, into Clematis Lane, with its upmarket collection of boutiques, restaurants and cafes.

The boutiques had names like The Cat's Meow, and Glamour Girl, and Gabriella enjoyed looking at the dresses she couldn't afford in the windows.

There was no one parked in the few spaces available, not at this hour, but up ahead, like a deliberate insult, she saw the yellow Ford Sunliner parked once again in the loading zone outside the Horatio Gallery.

"Never make it personal," Mr. Greenberg said to all of them, a reminder each morning before he sent them out from the Kensington and Chelsea Traffic Warden Centre. "It will feel personal, sometimes, but be professional. Be the bigger person."

Johnny McLad, as she had chosen to name her nemesis, was making it very difficult to be the bigger person.

She was walking at a fast clip as she approached the car, feeling her cheeks heat, even with the cool morning air on them.

He had refused to give her his name, had ripped up all three FPNs she'd issued, each one for the very same infringement—parking in a loading zone. She'd caught him in the act of destroying the second one and he'd laughed in her face as he'd shredded the ticket and then thrown it on the road and ground it under his booted heel.

He was crass, dressed like some kind of wannabe cowboy—if cowboys wore every crazy pattern and color on the spectrum—and he was a sexist pig.

This was the fourth time he'd flouted the rules.

Four times too many.

She already had her ticket book out by the time she reached the car, but she slowed when she noticed the passenger door was slightly ajar.

Maybe he'd just stopped quickly to drop something off, and hadn't even bothered to close the door.

Although it was the passenger door that was open, not the driver's side.

And he had always claimed not to have anything to do with the gallery. She'd asked him politely, the first time, in case he was genuinely using the loading zone for its correct purpose, and he had sneered at her, told her he had never set foot in the gallery in his life, and for her to feck off and mind her own business.

Well, this *was* her business.

She began to write the ticket, but a strange dark streak along the door made her take a closer look.

She slotted her pencil back into its holder on the side of the ticket book and took a step closer.

It was blood.

It had dried and it looked as if someone had trailed a bloody hand across the door and then grabbed the handle.

Clutching her ticket book with both hands, she peered through the passenger side window.

Johnny McLad lay twisted around in the bucket seat as if to face her, one hand flung out and propped up by the gear lever, palm up. The palm was dark with blood.

She let her gaze travel from his hand, up his arm, to his head. The face that had smirked at her only two days earlier was covered in blood down the left side. His blue eyes stared at her, the left one all the more blue because of the dark red surrounding it.

She took a shuddering breath and a sharp step back. Her hands shook, and she shoved her ticket book into her satchel and leaned back against the gallery wall to steady herself.

When she was calmer, she looked up and down the street for some kind of official help.

No bobbies in sight.

A little way up, at the Italian restaurant she'd noticed on her rounds, a door creaked open and she saw the end of a broom sweeping dust onto the street.

"*Mi scusi!*" she called.

The broom stopped, then an old man stepped out, a white apron tied around his short, barrel-chested form. "*Sì?*"

"Phone the police," she called in Italian. "There is a dead man here, and I don't want to leave the scene unattended. Tell them to hurry."

He stared at her, then propped the broom against the wall and walked toward her.

She said nothing, allowing that in the same situation, she would probably want to see for herself before phoning the police, as well.

The café owner was looking at her, rather than the car, suspicion in every line of him, but when he got closer his gaze flicked to the window and he stopped with an exclamation.

Then he gestured back to the café, and she gave a nod in response.

He turned on his heel and moved away at a fast clip, and Gabriella hunched a little, arms crossed over her chest.

It felt like a long time later that the café owner came back out, this time with a small espresso cup and saucer in his hand.

He held it out to her and she took it gratefully, drinking the strong coffee in small, appreciative sips.

"Good," she told him.

"You aren't from the old country," he said. "Your accent is wrong."

"I'm from Australia. It's my mother and her family who are from the old country."

"Ah." He nodded sagely. "Where in Australia?"

"Melbourne."

"My cousin Luigi went to Melbourne. He tells me it is paradise."

Gabriella gave a snort. "It's not bad."

"But you are here. Not in Melbourne."

"I wanted to have a look at the world." She handed him back the cup and saucer. That wasn't her real reason for being in London, but it wasn't completely untrue.

"A young, beautiful girl like you. You should be settling down and having babies." He said it in a way that made her sure he knew he was being provocative.

She said nothing in response. It wasn't the place for an argument. She was horribly aware of the eyes staring blankly from the car, a silent watcher to them both.

At that moment two bobbies rounded the same corner that she had ten minutes earlier. One must have just made the height cut off, the other was massive, head and shoulders taller than herself.

"You with Kensington Traffic?" the smaller one asked in surprise.

"Morning rounds," she confirmed. "Approached the car as it was illegally parked in a loading zone. Found him."

The café owner had stayed to watch the proceedings, although he had taken a few steps back as if to distance himself from them. He wanted to be an observer, not a participant.

The bobbies studied the body in the car.

"I'll go back to the station, shall I? Get someone out?" the shorter one asked.

"Go on, then." The bigger one turned to her and the café

owner as his partner loped off and took out a small pad and a pencil. “Name?”

“Gabriella Farnsworth.” She gave her badge number. “Can I be off now? I’ve got rounds.”

He thought about it. “All right. We can find you again easily enough.” His gaze flicked to the café owner. “And you, sir?”

The café owner burst into a flood of Italian, and Gabriella had to work to keep her face neutral at the nonsense he was spewing.

She eventually cut him off. “He works up the street. I asked him to call the police for me, so I didn’t have to leave the body unattended.”

“Right. What café is it?” The bobby looked grateful for her interruption and craned his neck to try and see the café name from where he stood.

“Gennaro’s,” Gabriella said.

The bobby wrote it down. “Do either of you know who the victim is?”

“No.” And that was the truth.

“And you, sir?”

Gennaro threw up the hand not holding the cup and saucer, as if the world itself was a mystery.

Gabriella just caught the sly glint in his eye before he turned and walked back to his broom and his café, muttering darkly the whole way.

“That’s foreigners for you,” the bobby said, cheerfully. “You all right, though? Can’t be nice, finding this.”

“No. Not nice.” She drew a deep breath. “Worse for him.”

“Got that right.” The bobby turned to look down the street, and Gabriella saw his partner was coming back, looking animated.

“Well, cheers.” Gabriella turned on her heel and walked away before she got caught up in it again.

She had targets. Rounds.

And a deep, abiding wish to not see those eyes any longer.

She had a feeling they’d haunt her for a while.

chapter two

"WHAT'S THIS ABOUT A BODY, Ms. Farnsworth?"

Gabriella had just stepped out of the changing room, and she'd hoped to have a clear run at the door. She turned to Mr. Greenberg politely. He was standing in the doorway to his office, his age no drag on his bearing or smartness of dress. An elderly sentinel at the gates.

"Yes, Mr. Greenberg. In a car parked in a loading zone."

"Bad?"

She gave a tight nod.

"I used to be in the Met," Mr. Greenberg said suddenly. "When parking control moved out of policing, some of us retired beat coppers were asked to come back to manage the traffic wardens."

"You were a bobby?" Now he said it, she could see it, plain as day. He wore a suit and tie now, but it was in the way he stood. She could see him helping old ladies across the street without any difficulty.

"Aye. And I know the shock of your first body."

"I'll be all right, sir. Thank you for the concern. The bobbies came quickly, and I wasn't there long." She looked up sharply in dismay. "I started issuing a ticket, before I noticed the body. I wasn't supposed to finish it, was I?"

"What? No, girl." Greenberg shook his head. "The City might want every ha'penny out of the car-driving public it can get, but we aren't that far gone."

She nodded, taking a step toward the door in escape.

"Someone's been on the line from Scotland Yard, said they want to speak to you."

"Oh?" She couldn't hide her dismay. "I really just found the body and waited with it until they came."

"It's like that sometimes," Mr. Greenberg said with a shrug. "When there's nothing else, they go back over the same ground, hoping to find something new. Just tell them what happened again, and hopefully that'll be the end of it."

"When do they want me to go in?"

"Now, I think." Mr. Greenberg checked his watch. "If you don't have any appointments, I'd get it over with, if I was you."

She gave a reluctant nod.

"Ask at reception for Detective Sergeant Archer."

She ducked her head. "Thank you, sir. Good afternoon."

She escaped out into the afternoon sun onto Kensington Church Court and walked in the direction of Kensington Palace. It was a couple of miles at least to New Scotland Yard from here, and she wondered grumpily if the detective sergeant had considered that when he'd requested her presence.

She was just in time to catch the bus that came to a screeching stop on Kensington High Street, and spent the twenty minute journey to Victoria Embankment trying to settle her nerves.

The bus dropped her close to the entrance, and she looked up at the large red and white brick building. New Scotland Yard made her think of a fortress and she steeled herself to enter.

While she dithered, someone bumped her from behind as they pushed through the door and she forced herself to follow them in.

She was directed to wait for DS Archer on an uncomfortable wooden bench, and passed the time watching the line of people approaching the desk with complaints and reports.

She was so engaged, DS Archer had to clear his throat to get her attention.

"Miss Farnsworth?"

She twisted round and looked up at him. "Yes?"

He seemed to be taken by surprise at the sight of her. "I'm Detective Sergeant Archer. Thank you for coming in. Do you want to follow me?"

She stood and straightened her skirt before walking to the door he held open for her, surprised by his curt manner. Hopefully that meant he wouldn't keep her long.

He said nothing more, leading her up the stairs and into a narrow office on the second floor.

"Have a seat." He rounded his desk and waited for her to settle into the hard visitor's chair.

He was Welsh, she realized. She was getting to know British accents slowly, and she finally recognized the gentle lilt in his voice.

"When you spoke to PC Longmore, you did not say that you had dealings with the murder victim in the past." He leaned forward, eyes fierce, eyebrows arrowed down in a frown. He tapped a finger on some papers on the desk, and she glanced at them.

Copies of the FPNs she had issued Johnny McLad.

"I only found out about them when we ran the car license. Why is there no name on these tickets?" His tone was not pleasant, and she leaned back slowly in her chair and crossed her arms over her chest.

"Most FPNs have no name, because the person is often not there when we issue them. The fine is attached to the car registration by design, not the person." She stared at him, eyes cool.

"So you never interacted with him?" He seemed startled by the idea.

"As it happens, I did interact with him. Twice." She tucked her legs primly beneath the chair, angled to the right with feet together.

He raised a large hand and ran it through his sandy hair. She noticed his tie was askew, and he looked harried. He could be a farmer, with his rugged good looks and his sunburnt cheeks. He had the broad-shouldered build of someone who worked hard lifting heavy things, and his gentle accent made her think of shepherds on green hills, surrounded by sheep.

"But there is still no name." He spoke more calmly this time. As if he had checked himself—was prepared to take a more amicable tone.

"That's right. The first time I found him in the loading zone, I asked him if he was delivering something to the gallery, and he told me to get lost, but in ruder terms, and that he had never set foot in the gallery in his life. He refused to give his name, and when I issued him a ticket he ripped it up in front of me. The second time was a similar encounter, and the third time I never saw him, I just left the ticket on his windscreen."

"So this morning was the fourth time you'd seen his car there in the loading zone?"

She gave a nod. "Got right up my nose, to tell you the truth."

Archer's lips turned up in a quick smile. "Can't say I blame you."

He leaned back in his chair, as if he had finally relaxed. "Notice anyone hanging about when you were issuing your tickets?"

She shook her head. "I'm on the early shift. There usually aren't that many people about."

"What about what he was wearing? Was it similar to what he had on this morning?"

She lifted her shoulders. "I didn't pay any attention to what he was wearing this morning, but previously he was wearing what I think of as psychedelic cowboy."

"You thought he was on drugs?" Archer leaned forward again.

She shook her head, then paused. Lifted her shoulders. "It was more to do with the crazy colors and the blue cowboy boots, but maybe." She thought back to their interactions. "He was certainly unreasonably angry at getting the tickets."

They lapsed into silence for a few moments.

"I just realized why you didn't pay attention to his clothes this morning."

Gabriella was looking at her hands, which were on her lap, fingers entwined. She lifted her gaze to find Archer watching her with steady gray eyes.

"The blood," she said.

"I'm sorry. I hope you're alright."

"What happened to him?" She suddenly realized she didn't even know. "Was he shot?"

His gaze sharpened on her face. "I'm afraid I can't tell you that."

She gave a nod, and rose to her feet. "I have to be going."

Archer got to his feet and opened the door for her. "I'll walk you out."

When she got out on the street, she stood in the late afternoon heat and thought about Detective Sergeant Archer.

He had mellowed between meeting her and wishing her a good afternoon in front of the duty sergeant on the desk a moment ago.

There was an intensity about him, a calm focus that made her think he was probably a very good detective.

And, most likely, she would never see him again.

She hitched her bag higher on her shoulder, and went to join the queue for the bus.

chapter three

JAMES MADE it back up to his office in time to see Gabriella Farnsworth board the bus, disappearing inside in her brown and pink flowered skirt and pink top.

He had expected her to be in uniform, so he'd been thrown when the duty sergeant had pointed out the slim-limbed beauty, lost in thought, ringlets framing her face, her elegant bun emphasizing her high cheekbones and her large brown eyes.

She had the thickest, longest eyelashes of anyone he'd ever met.

A quick knock at his door forced him to step back from the window, and Detective Inspector Whetford strode in. "You speak to the traffic warden?"

"I did." James picked up his notebook, glancing down at it as if he needed the memory prompt. Which he did not. "She interacted with him twice, just left the ticket on the windscreen the third time without seeing him."

"Why didn't she get his name?" Whetford's tone was irritated.

"She says he refused to give it to her, and she couldn't compel him. It sounds as if he was belligerent and obstructive. He ripped up the tickets in front of her both times she had direct dealings with him."

"Is that so?" Whetford rocked back on his heels. "That's interesting. Like he had something to hide?"

"Or he didn't want a fine and thought not giving his name would make it harder for her to issue one." James could see both as likely scenarios.

"True enough. So it's a dead end."

"Not completely. We know he was in the area, parking in that same spot, at least four times in the last three weeks. It makes it more likely we'll find someone who knew something about him."

"Right. Well keep me up to date, will you?" Whetford took a step toward the door. "I'm dealing with another matter, so you'll have to fly this one more or less solo."

James nodded, standing by his desk until Whetford left.

He didn't like his boss. There was a slick, smarmy way about him that rubbed him up the wrong way and the occasional sly cracks about his Welsh heritage didn't help.

James gathered his papers neatly into piles, locked them away, and then shrugged into his jacket. He'd go back to the scene, talk to whoever was hanging around.

Uniform had already done a door-to-door, but the victim seemed to have used the loading zone as a parking spot at night, if he was reading the fines Gabriella Farnsworth had issued correctly.

She'd caught him returning to his car in the early morning each time, as if he'd spent the night somewhere nearby.

The car's number plates had been false, but the engine number was linked to a car purchased by a company that they were still trying to track down. There was only a post office address on record for it, and James had a strong feeling it was going to turn out to be a shell company or a front.

The pathologist hadn't found anything in the car except the blood of the victim and a knife under the seat.

He'd been stabbed in the chest, but not before someone had made a nasty slash across his forehead.

It looked to James as if he'd been attacked outside the car, had tried to get away by getting in on the passenger side, and then was stabbed in the heart once he was inside.

Gabriella Farnsworth thought he'd been shot. He supposed it was a logical enough assumption given she hadn't had a good look at the body, and all the blood on his face could be explained by a bullet to the brain.

He walked to his car and then regretted his decision to use it as he turned out of the Yard and hit the afternoon city traffic.

The drive to Kensington took twice as long as it had taken this morning, and he felt hot and out of sorts by the time he pulled up in the same loading zone where the victim had parked. He put his police sign on the dashboard, and as he began to look for likely witnesses he wondered with a smile if Gabriella Farnsworth would track him down for his sins.

The nearby Italian café was busier than it had been this morning. They were playing Italian opera on a turntable and people were sitting at red and white check tables on the pavement, sipping red wine.

It was the kind of place that James thought he might enjoy, but had never tried. He was more comfortable in a pub, or at teashop.

A man shifted in the gloom of the doorway. "You are the policeman from this morning."

James stepped closer, nodding to Gennaro Moretti, the café owner who he'd interviewed earlier.

"Yes, Detective Sergeant Archer."

"You here to ask more questions?"

"Just looking for people who might have noticed the car or the man before. He was here quite often in the last three weeks at least. And more likely in the evening or late afternoon than the morning. So I'm hoping someone who's around this time of day might have something to tell me."

"Ha."

James wasn't sure if the exclamation was an excoriation or agreement with the logic. The bobby from this morning had been surprised the man had understood any English—he'd been under the impression he couldn't speak a word.

That was clearly incorrect. James wondered if the misunderstanding had been deliberate.

"You have a picture of him?" Gennaro asked. "I couldn't see well this morning—there was a lot of blood."

"Yes." James took out the photograph the pathologist had sent over of the victim with the blood washed off.

Gennaro held it, frowning. "Yes. He comes in maybe two or three times."

"Did you catch his name?"

Gennaro shook his head. "He orders wine and drinks with his friend, then goes."

"His friend?" James felt the surge of adrenalin, the start of the hunt.

Gennaro gave a shrug. "Not so interesting, that one. Brown suit, slicked-back hair."

"Light hair, dark?" James asked.

"Brown." Gennaro said. "I think."

"If you remember anything else, you can phone Scotland Yard and leave a message for me."

Gennaro gave another snort. "The little girl, she was all right?"

"Little girl?" James asked.

"The parking fine girl." Gennaro's tone was impatient.

"You called us for her," James remembered. "She was upset?"

Gennaro shot him a pitying look. "Of course. She is young girl. Looking at dead body."

James thought he was probably underestimating Gabriella Farnsworth. "I spoke to her this afternoon. She's holding up."

Gennaro gave a snort of disgust. "Such a one should not be walking streets in that horrible uniform. She should be making beautiful babies." He gestured his hands, as if to indicate the world had gone mad, and turned back into the café.

His words caused James to do what he'd been trying to avoid doing since he'd met Gabriella Farnsworth.

Think of her and sex.

The sensation was heady.

He tried to shake it off. Gabriella Farnsworth was a material witness, and therefore off-limits until this investigation was over.

He started walking toward the still-open clothing boutiques, hoping to find more fruitful hunting grounds. Hoping to get the picture of Gabriella Farnsworth, naked, hair loose around her shoulders on the pillow, out of his head.

chapter four

GABRIELLA LOOKED THROUGH THE POST, stacking it into piles on the narrow table in the foyer.

The letter she had been hoping for since she'd gotten her bedsit and begun sending out enquiries was not among the pile.

She took the few letters that had come for her from home, along with Mr. Rodney's post, and began to climb the stairs with her groceries.

It was still beautifully light, even though it was after five, and she liked the way the sun shone through the stain glass to pool in colorful puddles of light on the landing.

She and Mr. Rodney were on the third floor, and with the way the stairs creaked, he could hear her coming from about the first floor landing.

He was waiting for her outside his door, expression amused, as if her very arrival was cause for delight.

"Letters!" he exclaimed as she held them out to him. "And from home!"

She had noticed the letters were from Trinidad, and she hoped this time it wasn't bad news. Once or twice he had received word an old friend or relative had passed away, and she could tell it wore on him that he couldn't go to the funerals, or spend time with others who had known the departed, and honor their memory.

"You look sad today, Gabby." Mr. Rodney may be old, and not very mobile, but he was sharp.

She lifted her hands. "Bad day at work."

"Someone shouted at you? Threatened you?" He was always outraged when she told him stories of how people reacted to getting a fine.

She hesitated, then decided to tell him the truth. He wasn't a child, and he would be more hurt to find out she had kept something from him. "I found a man dead in a car."

"Dead, how?" He stepped closer, shocked.

"I don't know. Violently. The police won't say what happened to him. I just saw lots of blood."

"You have had a shock." He studied her closely. "They didn't let you go home?"

She shook her head. "I didn't think to ask. I just carried on with my rounds."

He clicked his tongue. "You need to take care of yourself, girl."

"I will, Mr. Rodney. I'll get an early night tonight. Are you off to the club for dinner?"

"I am. Solomon's coming to fetch me at six." He already had his coat over his arm, and his hat in his hand.

She thought about joining them. She had an open invitation from Mr. Rodney to attend the Calypso Club in Notting Hill, she loved the music, and the spicy Caribbean food they served was reasonably-priced and delicious. But she had bought groceries, and she was looking forward to a quiet night.

She set her paper bag of groceries down, and was getting out her key when Solomon came bounding up the stairs.

Mr. Rodney's nephew was as tall and broad as Detective Sergeant Archer, she thought as she turned to him. His dreadlocks spilled over the colorful jacket he wore, the opposite of the dark suit DS Archer had been wearing.

"Gabby! Looking good!"

She laughed. Felt even more tempted to go with them to the club. "Not as good as you, Solomon."

"True, that. But then, I am who I am." He spread his hands out and sent her a wicked grin.

He was involved in something illegal.

She knew it.

Both because Mr. Rodney worried his nephew would get into trouble with the police, and also because she had seen him with his group of friends at the club, talking quietly together, clearly planning and organizing their business.

If she were to guess, she'd say he was selling dope to the party boys and girls in the West End, using his friends who worked for British Transport to deliver the goods.

And looking at the expensive leather shoes he wore, he wasn't doing badly out of it, either.

Solomon was good to his uncle, good to his mother, and had never been anything but friendly to her.

If he was a crook, he wasn't a vicious one.

"I'll let you two get on to the club. I'll try to join you tomorrow. I can bring Mr. Rodney, Solomon."

The club served meals Tuesday to Saturday, and Mr. Rodney never missed.

"That would suit me fine," Solomon said, taking his uncle's key to lock his door for him. "You don't want to join us tonight?"

"Gabby found a dead man in a car today. She needs an early night." Mr. Rodney tugged on his jacket, making sure it was straight.

"I heard the coppers were all over Clematis Lane. That's why?" Solomon's face was still friendly, but his eyes had gone hard.

Taken aback, Gabriella gave a nod. "I found a man dead in his car outside the gallery there."

"Shot?" Solomon asked, voice low.

Gabriella lifted her shoulders. "The police wouldn't tell me.

There was a lot of blood on the one side of his face, so I asked them if he was shot and they refused to say."

"Bastards," Solomon said, suddenly cheerful again. "Never want to part with information, but want you to spill everything to them."

"What do you have to do with the police, that they want information from you?" Mr. Rodney asked, voice a touch querulous.

"Nothing, Uncle Eric. Nothing at all." Solomon gave her a wink over his shoulder as he helped the old man down the stairs, and Gabriella lifted a hand in response.

A bad boy. No doubt. And a little more scary than she'd realized.

But still, she liked him.

And he was right about the police. They wanted it all one way.

Theirs.

chapter five

"YOU BITCH!"

Spittle from Mr. Bottle Green Jaguar hit Gabriella's cheek as she finished fixing the FPN onto the jag's windscreen.

She stepped back, always a wise move when they got this worked up, this quickly.

She had noticed him storming out of the smart, white Georgian row house while she was sliding the FPN into its thin plastic sleeve, and had moved just a little bit faster.

"You're illegally parked on double yellows, sir. Instructions are included on the fixed penalty notice on how to pay, or if you want to contest the fine, when and where to do that."

She eyed him. An old rugger player from the Home Counties, she guessed, now gone to seed, but still trying to pretend he was in his prime.

"I want to contest it here and now," he shouted. "Cancel it, you little witch." His face was almost purple, and he seemed to be struggling for air.

"If you're unable to pay the fine, you can request a payment plan," Gabriella said, sweetly. She actually didn't know if people could do that. She would ask Liz at end of shift. She only said it to shame him into backing down. "There is a hardship allowance . .

." She let her voice trail off. "Have a good day!" She half-turned, trying to keep him in view as she moved away.

He gave a roar, like a gravely wounded bull in full charge, and came at her.

She had just decided to give running away a serious go when lights and sirens suddenly broke the calm of the street, and a big black Wolseley leapt the pavement, cutting between her and the irate jaguar owner.

He stumbled to a halt, mouth slack as Detective Sergeant Archer swung out of the car.

"You all right, Miss Farnsworth?" the sergeant asked, putting himself bodily between her and Mr. Jaguar.

She pulled herself together and gave a nod. "Thank you, Detective."

He turned to Mr. Jaguar. "Name?" He pulled out a pad and paper as he spoke.

"I say, why do you need my name?" Mr. Jaguar was all bluster now.

"Because I witnessed you attempting to attack a traffic warden while she was discharging her duties."

There was a short silence.

"Name?" DS Archer's tone was cold and impatient.

"Now, no need for that," Mr. Jaguar said, backing away, hands up. "Let's just call it a misunderstanding, shall we?"

"That might be convenient for you, but it's hardly accurate, is it?"

Gabriella saw Archer was writing down the car's registration number.

"I didn't mean the gal any harm." Mr. Jaguar looked over Archer's shoulder at her. "Not really. Just didn't think a fine was fair, is all. I wasn't parked here long."

"You meant me harm," Gabriella said. The adrenalin was still coursing through her, and her hands were shaking. She hated that. Hated that she was close to tears.

She had been closer to tears all day, at every encounter, and she put it down to the nightmares she'd had last night of blue eyes set in dark, bloodstained faces, staring at her.

"Look, let's just chalk it up to a mistake, all right?" Mr. Jaguar had continued to edge back as he spoke. He had already yanked his door open earlier, and with a surprisingly nimble leap, he jumped into the car, slammed the door and started it up.

Archer watched him stonily as he reversed, clipped a bollard with his bumper, and then roared off.

Gabriella guessed from the tight look on DS Archer's face that Mr. Jaguar was not as free and clear of trouble with that move as he thought he was.

"Do you get that a lot?" Archer asked as he turned back to her.

"A couple of times a day, but usually just shouting. Not imminent attack, like Mr. Jaguar."

Archer's lips twitched. "Mr. Jaguar?"

"He was even worse than Johnny McLad in the yellow Sunliner," Gabriella said. "Johnny McLad only swore and tore up the ticket. Mr. Jaguar was going to throttle me." She glanced at the townhouse. "One day, you'll find his wife strangled in there. Or his mistress." She turned back to him. "If he claims a burglary gone wrong, don't believe it."

"I won't." Archer wrote down the address she'd indicated.

"Well, I'm grateful you happened to be driving along." Gabriella guessed she was a little more nimble than Mr. Jaguar, but he had been pretty motivated. It was a toss up if she would have gotten away.

Archer's ears turned pink, and Gabriella wondered how a hard-nosed detective could be so embarrassed by a simple expression of gratitude.

"I was driving back to the crime scene," he said. "I'm glad I came along when I did."

"Well, thanks again." Gabriella glanced down the road, saw at least two other cars that were parked on the double yellows. "How's the case going?"

Archer made a face. "As well as it can. If you can think of anything else, please get in touch."

She nodded. "I really have told you everything I remember, though."

"Look, I'm going on to Clematis, would you like a lift?"

She shook her head, pointed down the street. "I've still got cars to ticket here."

He pocketed his pad and pen and walked back to the Wolseley. "Have a good day, Miss Farnsworth."

She waited for him to start the car, reverse back into the street, and drive away, waving as he headed toward Clematis Lane.

Taking this street was a strange route from Victorian Embankment to Clematis, but perhaps he'd been coming from a different direction. Whatever the reason, she really was grateful.

She made sure her cap was still in place after her encounter. Then she turned toward the two cars parked further down the street on the double yellows and got on with her job.

chapter six

SHE DIDN'T KNOW if she kept seeing bottle green jaguars because she had had a run-in with one, but she thought she glimpsed one at least three times over the rest of her shift. She had gone so far as to check the registration number in her ticket book so she could know for sure if it was the same one next time she saw it.

Mr. Jaguar probably lived somewhere close to her route, though, and it was logical she'd spot him around. It didn't necessarily mean anything, although she didn't think he'd cry if he ran her down.

She thought about it as she returned to the Traffic Warden Centre and came to the conclusion Mr. Jaguar wouldn't have anything to gain from following her.

The ticket was written, and there was a witness, a police detective no less. Anything he did to her would only make things worse for himself, not better.

But he had not seemed very logical or reasonable to her.

Maybe he was a man fueled by spite.

The thought of it made her shiver, and as she pushed her way into the center through the big wooden doors, she decided she would take extra care that no one followed her home.

Liz was in the change room, getting out of her uniform, and

Gabriella joined her, carefully hanging her skirt and blazer up, and then slipping into something altogether cooler and more comfortable.

"If someone can't pay their fine, can they work out a payment plan?" she asked.

Liz glanced at her, then went back to brushing her long blonde hair. "No idea. Why?"

"I told someone today they could, as a way to get them to back down."

"They were saying they couldn't pay?" She lifted both eyebrows.

"No, but his reaction was so extreme, I said it to make him embarrassed at how much of a fuss he was making. He was driving a great big jag, coming out of one of those fancy town-houses on the edge of Chelsea."

"You wanted him to back down by suggesting he was objecting because he couldn't afford it?" Liz hummed. "Not a bad ploy. But be careful who you use it on. Some might take even more offense at that."

Gabriella lifted her shoulders. "I had to do something. And even so, he came at me, hands out to throttle me."

"Really?" Liz put her brush down, and turned to give Gabriella her full attention. "What did you do?"

"I was going to run, but the detective that's dealing with that dead man I found, he was coming past, and he ran his lights and siren. Stopped the attack dead."

"He a looker, this copper?"

Gabriella grinned at Liz. "He's a looker."

"Ooh. Asked you out, has he?"

She laughed again. "No. I'm a witness in his case." She slipped on her espadrilles and stood, pulled her hair out of its bun and massaged her scalp in relief. "I'm off. I'm taking my neighbor to his club for dinner tonight."

"Is *he* a looker?" Liz asked.

"He was, fifty years ago." Gabriella lifted her bag over her head, setting it across her chest. "And he's still charming."

"Aren't you the one with the hot night life?" Liz zipped up her platform boots, wiggled her legs. "I'm just going to Dance-A-Go-Go tonight."

"Have fun." Gabriella gave her a wave and left her applying more mascara.

She took the back entrance, which she'd never done before, but the green jaguars had spooked her a bit. She made her way through back alleys and narrow lanes to get to the other side of Kensington Gardens.

She wasn't familiar with the buses on this side, but she decided to treat it as an opportunity, rather than an inconvenience.

She was pleasantly surprised to find the bus was a little quicker than her usual one, dropping her in a parallel street to her usual stop. She got home around the same time as usual, and washed up and was ready to knock on Mr. Rodney's door at six on the dot.

"Ms. Gabby." He pulled the door open as if he'd been waiting just in the hallway.

"Ready to rumba?" She admired his carefully pressed suit and the jaunty angle of his hat.

"Not at my age." He held out an arm, and she slipped her own through his. "But I hope you are."

She helped him down the stairs, and they took the walk to the club slowly.

It was a small building that had been painted with beautiful murals depicting Trinidad and Tobago, and the sound of calypso met them before they stepped through the door.

The musicians were up on a stage, and women worked at the tables set along the far wall, getting the supper ready.

A small desk was placed near the door, behind which sat a thin, young man who Mr. Rodney greeted as Jerome.

"Solomon here yet?" Mr. Rodney asked Jerome as he wrote his name in the book.

Gabriella handed over her supper fee and looked around the room.

A lot of the usuals were here, as well as a small group of white boys in the corner, shooting looks at everyone and whispering to themselves.

"Dopeheads," Mr. Rodney said. "Or that's what they want to be. Thinking the Calypso Club is the place to score some dope."

He sat down, angry and upset.

Gabriella shot the boys a dirty look and sat so that she blocked Mr. Rodney's view of them. "They'll learn their lesson."

Solomon would not like these boys pointing anyone in the direction of the Calypso Club. It was where the elders of the community came for companionship and to keep the ties of family strong.

Solomon was probably a strongman on the streets, but here, he was protective and patient, generous and thoughtful.

She'd seen it in the Italian Clubs in Melbourne where she'd grown up. Men who ran smuggling operations from the old country to the new, who would cut a stranger on the street but protect their own with their lives.

A flurry from the back, where the small, old-fashion kitchen was situated, had her turning her head.

Solomon stepped out, a friend on either side of him. He approached the table with the white boys, greeting them with friendly handshakes. Gabriella twisted in her chair, saw him lean down to talk softly to one of the boys.

She saw the boy's face freeze, and then he swallowed, his Adam's apple bobbing. He rose to his feet, his gaze going to his mates, and he jerked his head, to get them to stand up.

Solomon's smile never slipped. He kept hold of the boy's hand, as if he'd forgotten he still had it clasped in his own. When he eventually let it go, the boy flexed it, and they left, amid jocular shoulder slaps and friendly goodbyes from Solomon and his friends.

Gabriella turned back to Mr. Rodney, saw his nod of approval.

"Now we can relax," he said. He got to his feet as Solomon came up to them.

"Uncle Eric." Solomon held out both arms and enveloped his uncle in a hug. "And Gabby. How are things at?"

"Doing fine, Solomon." She'd felt herself relax as she'd walked with Mr. Rodney to the club. There hadn't been a green jag in sight.

"Good, good. I have to make it a quick one tonight. I've got to work."

"Overtime pay?" Mr. Rodney asked.

Solomon nodded. "We'll make good money tonight."

Gabriella heard the laughter in his voice and glanced at him, saw him looking at her. It was a thoughtful look, nothing she would call alarming.

She tipped her head at him in response, and he went off to get them each a plate of food before he left.

They had just started eating when a young woman swung into the chair beside Gabriella.

"You doin' all right, Mr. Rodney?" The woman leaned forward on her elbows.

"I am, Catherine. Have you met my neighbor, Gabriella?"

Catherine turned to look at her, and Gabriella wondered if she had ever seen anyone as beautiful as this woman.

"Very pleased to meet you." Gabriella extended her hand.

Catherine gave her hand a firm shake, her eyes watchful. "You got your sights set on my Solomon?"

Mr. Rodney made a sound of surprise, but Gabriella ignored him. She shook her head. "I don't."

"True?"

"True," Gabriella confirmed.

"Well then, very pleased to meet you, too, Gabriella. Have a good evening." She slipped out of her chair—wide, colorful skirt swirling around her knees—and disappeared into the crowd.

"That girl." Mr. Rodney shook his head. "Her mother was a tear-away, just like her, back in Trinidad."

"She's very beautiful. And she knows what she wants." That was probably a very good thing if she had picked Solomon for her own. He would need a strong personality to stand up to him.

After dinner, when the two of them were walking home, Mr. Rodney told her stories about some of the regulars at the club she had danced with after dinner. Men who were in their sixties, who'd served in the war or had come over from the Caribbean after the war to find a better life.

She noticed none of the younger men had stayed after their meal, all slipping out in ones and twos.

All hands on deck, indeed.

Gabriella wondered what they were up to, but guessed she would never know.

They reached the house just after nine, and Gabriella could see Mr. Rodney was tired. She walked him up, settling him in with a cup of tea, and then remembered she'd forgotten to check the late post.

Mr. Higgins, who lived on the ground floor, was in the hallway doing the same as she skipped down the stairs.

The look he gave her was unfriendly as he tossed letters into the pile on the table, holding a few in his hands. "I saw you come back with Mr. Rodney."

Gabriella didn't like the way he said it, as if he was accusing her of something.

"Yes." Her answer came out short.

"Maybe you Australians don't have a care for your reputations, but here in England, it matters." Mr. Higgins clutched his letters to his chest, and his hands were shaking.

Gabriella didn't know if it was with rage or nerves at the confrontation.

A confrontation created by him, and him alone.

"What do you mean, my reputation?"

"Not that I mind his sort, but others do," Mr. Higgins said.

"Have a care for yourself, missy." With that, he darted down the short passage and into his flat.

She stared after him, eyes narrowed, feeling grim.

"Limey bastard." She said it softly, but she could hear the venom in her own voice. "Racist limey bastard."

"What was that about?" Solomon seemed to coalesce out of the darkness, and Gabriella only just suppressed a shriek of surprise.

She clutched at her throat and he winked at her in reassurance.

"Where did you come from?" She didn't like how breathless she sounded.

"Back door," Solomon said. "Uncle Eric gave me a key to the garden entrance that lets out in the alley." He tossed the key in the air, caught it with a flourish. "Now, what was that about?"

His voice was steady, calm, but Gabriella could see his eyes were hard again. Impenetrable.

"Mr. Higgins is a bitter, unpleasant old man," she said. "He isn't a patch on your uncle, and he knows it."

Solomon inclined his head. "He's on the ground floor?"

"Yes, he's got the only ground floor flat, with a little garden on the side."

She walked toward the stairs, waited with her foot on the first one, expecting Solomon to join her. "You coming up?"

He shook his head. "Just remembered, I've got things to do." He gave a wave and disappeared back into the shadows, and she heard the back door open and close softly. It led into a small courtyard with a shared washing line and a few pots of rhododendrons, then out through a high wooden door into the back alley. Which would be a handy way to come and go without being seen.

As she climbed the two flights of stairs to her bedsit, she gnawed at her lip.

Mr. Higgins had chosen the wrong moment, and the wrong man, to vent his bigotry on.

Solomon would not let it lie.

chapter seven

"THE KILLING BLOW was this stab wound to the chest." Dr. Jandicott pulled back the sheet over the victim and showed James the neat incision. "Nicked an artery and he bled out internally. The cut to the scalp bled a lot, but it wasn't fatal."

"You have a name for him yet, Archer?" Detective Inspector Whetford asked. "When was he found? Tuesday? It's already Thursday."

James shook his head, wondering why Whetford had insisted on attending the post mortem. He'd had no interest in the case until now. "I've got an appointment later to look into the paperwork for the company that owns the car he was found in, but there's been no missing person report come in fitting his description. We might have to go to the press with it."

Whetford grimaced. "All right. Try the other avenues first, then talk to the media liaison officer about a press release. Maybe use the police artist to draw a picture of him, rather than put the lad's post mortem picture out."

"Yes, sir." James agreed with that.

"And the murder weapon? Did you find that, at least?"

"Under the car seat," James said. "A stiletto knife, which Dr. Jandicott confirms fits the wound."

"That's right." Jandicott pulled the sheet back up. "Perfect match."

"Any dabs on the handle?" Whetford asked.

"Wiped clean." James hadn't expected anything else.

"I had his blood tested for alcohol or drugs." Jandicott picked up a clipboard with some notes attached. "He'd had a pint earlier in the evening of his death, but otherwise, nothing. He'd had fish and chips for his dinner."

"Like half of London, then," Whetford said. "A pint down the pub, then a fish supper."

"That's about the size of it, sir." James knew the longer this languished, the harder it would be to solve. "If that's all of it, Doctor, I'll be off to check the company records."

He walked out with Whetford.

"You good to keep going with this on your own?" Whetford paused at the top of the stairs and drew out a cigarette.

James shook his head as Whetford offered him one. "That's fine, sir."

"Good. I'm still involved in this other thing. If you need a few more hands, let me know and I'll see if there are any constables available for the leg work." He blew out a stream of smoke and strode off.

James watched him go.

His guv'nor wore a very nice light summer suit, and the car he slid into was the same type of jaguar driven by the man who tried to assault Gabriella Farnsworth the day before, except Whetford's was maroon.

He was on the take.

James had worked it out with a slow dawning of awareness over the last ten months, since he'd joined the Met.

He'd come in from Cardiff, not totally green when it came to corruption, but hopeful that the Met was more clean than dirty.

Maybe it was, but Whetford wasn't.

There was no other 'matter'.

James had looked into what his boss was working on. Found it was nothing.

Just as there hadn't been a string of other 'matters' Whetford had used as an excuse for not being actively involved in the cases that landed on James's desk.

James didn't know who Whetford was getting his money from, or what he did day to day to earn it, but it wasn't policing. Or not much, anyway.

No wonder he'd been so eager to have a newly minted detective sergeant from Wales. It was handy to have someone who hadn't come up through the ranks in the Met itself. Who didn't know how things worked.

But James was a quick study. He'd started collecting evidence on his boss from the first day it had dawned on him he didn't have a lazy superior, but a corrupt one. There was no doubt in his mind that if Whetford was ever caught, he'd point the finger at his new sergeant, the outsider, faster than you could say Jack Robinson.

At least this current case didn't overlap with any of the criminals Whetford spent his time protecting, or James wouldn't have control of it.

And even Whetford needed a few wins, a few closed cases, to stop the slow and half-blind eye of the Met's anti-corruption arm from looking his way.

Whetford would not actively give him any help, but he wouldn't obstruct him, either.

That was the best he could hope for.

As James ran down the steps and headed for his Wolseley, it pained him how low the bar had been set.

chapter eight

THERE WAS another car parked in the loading zone outside the gallery. A powder blue Ford Prefect.

Gabriella approached it with sinking dread and stopped a car's length away, giving it a good look before she approached.

There was no one inside.

She expelled a breath, feeling a little queasy in her stomach. She took out a notepad to write down the time, in case it was still here when she came back, and had just started to put pen to paper when the door to the gallery burst open.

"I say, don't write a ticket. They're just here unloading some paintings for me." The man who called out was smartly dressed in a suit, his hair thinning slightly on top, his mouth curving down in temper.

Gabriella lifted her pencil. "This vehicle is delivering goods to your business?"

"Yes, yes! The driver's just stacking them in the back. I came out to get the last few from the boot." Impatience and condescension saturated his tone. He was tall and had the thin, aquiline features she associated with the upper class.

Gabriella had begun to get a real feel for reading people over the last month she'd worked as a traffic warden, and she reckoned this one would have liked to hit her.

Instead, he opened the boot of the car and took out two wrapped canvases.

"You don't need to hover," he said as he slammed the boot shut. "There's no rules been broken here."

Gabriella gave a nod and moved along, wondering at the vitriol. He seemed strangely panicked at her presence and desperate to move her along.

She continued down the street, issuing a few FPNs to cars parked on double yellows, and then worked her way up the other side of the lane.

She was approaching a white van when she noticed the car outside the gallery was still parked in the loading zone.

She checked her watch. It had been over twenty minutes since her encounter with the owner. He was back outside, standing beside the car, and another man was standing with him, dressed in drab work clothes, with a beret on his head.

They were talking in low voices. A few doors up from where they stood, three girls came out of The Cat's Meow, laughing together, one holding a shopping bag. A shop girl followed them out, watching them for a moment before she turned and walked toward the two men.

She looked angry.

The gallery owner caught sight of her bearing down on them.

"Patty." It wasn't a greeting so much as a warning.

It had an effect.

Patty adjusted her stride, making it less vigorous, and when she reached them, her voice was low.

Gabriella would guess she hadn't planned on being quiet initially.

It was surprising more because Patty clearly felt entitled to give the gallery owner a piece of her mind.

Even in Australia there was a discernible class structure, but she'd found it was far more obvious in England. Her beat was the affluent boroughs of Chelsea and Kensington, and toffee-nosed prats tried to put her in her place on a daily basis.

The gallery owner was clearly educated at a public school and came from money. Gabriella guessed Patty came from a very different world, yet here they were—on first name terms, and even with the warning to keep things quiet, Patty stood toe to toe with him.

They spoke for a few moments.

"No!" Patty's voice at last lifted up to an audible level.

At her exclamation, the gallery owner glanced around, and the man in the beret took Patty's hand, murmuring to her. He looked over her shoulder, said something, and she glanced back.

There were two women approaching, and Gabriella guessed he was telling her she had customers.

With a tight nod, Patty extracted herself and disappeared back into her shop.

The men stepped even closer to each other, heads bent together.

The butt of a cigarette flew out of the passenger side window of the van Gabriella was standing behind, and a man inside cleared his throat softly. Gabriella took a step back as the van started up.

Since she'd last looked across the road, the man in the beret had gotten into the car and was driving off.

The van did a tight u-turn and drove after it.

Gabriella watched it go, wondering if it was following the car or simply a coincidence that it left at the same time.

She glanced over at the gallery again and found herself looking straight at the owner. He was watching her from the other side of the street, staring at her with an intensity that lifted the hairs on her arms and the back of her neck

Then he turned away, walked into the gallery, and shut the door.

When she got home, she saw a removal van parked outside, and furniture being packed inside.

"Who's moving?" she asked one of the men carrying a rolled-up carpet over his shoulder. He was a small man, with a cigarette hanging from the corner of his mouth. He looked as if he should be bent under the strain. He gave her a cheeky wink as he slung his burden into the back of the van.

"Geezer on the ground floor."

"Mr. Higgins?" She hadn't realized he was moving.

She went in, got her and Mr. Rodney's post, and walked up the stairs. Mr. Rodney was waiting for her at the top. He looked a little jumpy.

"Mr. Higgins is moving out," he said.

"I saw the movers downstairs," Gabriella said. "I didn't even know he was going."

"Me, either. But Solomon's arranged for me to have his flat." Mr. Rodney's hands twisted around each other.

"That's . . ." Gabriella found herself speechless for a moment. "That makes sense, Mr. Rodney. I'll be sorry not to have you opposite me, but you'll be far more able to go about if you don't have to take the stairs, and you'll have that sweet little garden out the back."

"Do you think so?"

"I do. Solomon must have spoken to Mr. Higgins about it in advance and kept it as a surprise." And she had a good guess as to when that had happened.

"That lad." Mr. Rodney shook his head. "He does so much for me."

"No more than you deserve." Gabriella handed him his post. "I suppose I won't need to get your letters brought up anymore. You let me know when you're moving your things down, and I'll give Solomon a hand."

"Gabriella." Solomon appeared at the top of the stairs, and Gabriella realized she hadn't heard him walking up. He said her name in four syllables, and there was a warning in his voice.

"Solomon." Gabriella repeated the cadence. "What a lovely surprise for your uncle."

"He shouldn't have to go up and down stairs at his age, eh?" Solomon smiled his delightful smile. "Want to come down and see the flat? Mr. Higgins is out now, and gone."

"I would." She was always nosey about looking through other people's houses and flats.

She followed the men down, and when they entered Mr. Higgin's old place, she noticed Mr. Rodney went straight through to the lounge and out the double doors into the garden.

"This is a good thing," Gabriella said, voice low. "But how did you manage it?"

"I found a new place for Mr. Higgins." Solomon said. "Persuaded him he would be happier elsewhere." He paused. "And that stays between ourselves, Gabby."

She mimed buttoning her lips, and he laughed softly.

She wondered how he'd managed to pull this off in three days, but if money talked, money and muscle probably talked even louder.

Then she wandered into the kitchen, and came to a stop in the doorway, mouth agape.

"Quite something, isn't it?" Solomon came to stand directly behind her. "This was the original kitchen of the house, back when it used to be a posh Victorian home to a rich industrialist."

"The bread I could make in that," Gabriella said, eyeing the oven.

"Bread?" Solomon asked.

She moved into the room and crouched in front of the oven, opening it up to have a look inside.

She would give Mr. Higgins points for keeping it spotless.

"My mother is a baker. I've nursed my sourdough starter all the way from Melbourne. It got a good workout on the ship coming across to London, because I worked as the bread maker in the ship's kitchens in lieu of my fare, but all I've done is feed it since I've been here, due to lack of an oven."

"I'm sure my uncle would enjoy a fresh-baked loaf. Why don't you do a deal with him? Use of the oven in exchange for some of the bread."

"I'll take that deal," Mr. Rodney said, stepping in behind them. "I wouldn't know what to do with an oven like that."

"I do," Gabriella said. She rose to her feet. "Let me know if I can help with the move, but right now I have to get ready."

"Going out for a Friday night on the town, Gabby?" Solomon asked.

"My friend Liz persuaded me to go to Dance-a-Go-Go." In fact, she had insisted. And given what she'd dealt with in the last week, Gabriella had decided a night out might just take her mind off everything else.

Solomon gave a slow nod. "Well, mind how you go."

As she ran up the stairs, Gabriella realized she spent more time than she should trying to analyze what Solomon really meant when he spoke.

Or maybe she didn't spend enough.

chapter nine

THERE WAS a small crowd gathered near the entrance to Dance-A-Go-Go, but they were smoking, not waiting in line.

Liz stood to one side, sucking on a cigarette, and she gave Gabriella a wave as she approached. "You look smashing."

"So do you." Gabriella took in the short blue satin dress and white knee-high boots Liz was wearing. She felt a pale shadow in comparison, in her dark green drop-waisted dress with its prim white collar.

"Come on, then." Liz hooked her arm through Gabriella's and pulled her toward the door.

Once they were through, Gabriella saw a counter where people could leave their coats, although on such a warm evening, she hadn't needed one.

Two bouncers stood near the door, and one turned to her as they entered.

She recognized him immediately as one of Solomon's friends from the Calypso Club. Melvin.

He was wearing a maroon suit with the arms and chest stretched tight over his muscles—by far the most formal she had ever seen him dressed. He gave her a nod, and she nodded back.

His partner—who looked like a former boxer, complete with crooked nose and scarring on his cheeks—noticed the exchange.

He bent closer to Melvin, and they exchanged a quick word. The boxer ran a hand over his dirty blond hair, which lay slick against his skull, flicked her a quick look, and then turned to the next person who came in.

She and Liz reached the edge of the dance floor. There was a crowd, all dancing, and Gabriella had to admit the sight of it cheered her up.

"I love this song!" Oblivious to the little exchange between the bouncers, Liz dragged her deeper into the room, where the buzz of conversation was drowned out by the sound of Lesley Gore singing she would cry if she wanted to.

Liz went straight to the dance floor and flung herself into dancing.

Gabriella followed after her, taking the time to get the lay of the land. It was her first time in the club, but Liz was a regular.

A few people called a hello to her friend, and she gave a cheerful greeting in return. Her blond hair was in a jaunty pony tail on top of her head, and she made it swing from side to side as she did the twist.

With a laugh, Gabriella hitched her handbag a little higher on her shoulder and joined in. A few men wandered over, and Liz clearly knew them, making room for them to dance.

Later, the two of them settled in to a small table near the bar, both sipping their shandies.

"Some of the fellas are all right, aren't they?" Liz said. "I like Luke, he's the one in the white trousers."

Luke had danced with them a few times through the evening, but Gabriella thought he was less interested in Liz than she was in him.

"Ooh. I like that girl's dress." Liz nodded over to the bar, and Gabriella turned in her chair to look.

It was the shop girl from The Cat's Meow. Patty, the gallery owner had called her. She was wearing one of the gorgeous dresses that Gabriella had admired in the window—a white sleeveless dress with a black stripe down the front and another across the hips.

"It's from a boutique on my rounds," Gabriella said. "I've admired it a few times on my way past." She watched Patty order a drink and then sip it while she stood near the bar, facing the dance floor.

She looked as if she was waiting for someone, or looking for them in the crowd, brushing off a few men who sidled up to her, asking her to dance.

Her strawberry blonde hair was cut short and curled up around her ears, and her earrings dangled almost to her shoulders, balls of alternating black and white.

She turned suddenly, and Gabriella saw a man had come up behind her. It was hard to get a good look at him in the dodgy lighting of the club, but she thought he looked like the driver who'd been parked in the gallery loading zone, delivering paintings.

They disappeared off together.

Gabriella finished her shandy and allowed Liz to persuade her to dance some more, but as the night had gone on, she had the sense some of the dancers around her were less and less inhibited. The mood had turned strange. Not violent, but frenetic.

She realized she was done.

The club was stuffy, the music over-loud, and the crowd had swelled considerably, making it hard to dance.

"I'm heading home, Liz. Do you want to walk with me to the bus?"

Liz hesitated, her gaze going to Luke, who was dancing to Gerry and the Pacemakers. He caught sight of her watching and crooked his finger.

Liz gulped a quick breath. "I'll stay a little longer. You sure you don't want to dance some more?"

Gabriella shook her head. "I'm done in. It's been a week. I'll see you Monday?"

Liz waved in answer, dancing her way over to Luke, who

watched her with what Gabriella thought were calculating eyes.

She let it go.

Liz was a year older than she was, and knew her own mind.

She headed for the door, having to push through the crowd in the middle of the room, but things were less of a crush near the entrance.

When she stepped out she saw Melvin and his boxer friend had moved outside and were doing some crowd control—only letting a few in at a time.

She gave a quick smile as she squeezed past him but didn't speak to him as he clearly had his hands full. Still, he found the time to lift a hand in goodbye.

She broke free of the crush and came to a stop a little way down the street, drawing in a big lungful of cool air. The perspiration she'd worked up inside chilled on her skin and she shivered.

She got her bearings, and wondered which bus would be more reliable at this time of night. The sound of a voice made her glance right, and under the street light up ahead, she saw Patty standing on the pavement, stooping slightly to talk to someone through the open window of a white van.

Her expression was serious, and she suddenly stepped back with a nod, opened the door, and got in.

Almost immediately, the van pulled off, driving slowly toward Gabriella.

She tried to see the driver as they passed, but Patty had wound up her window by the time they reached her, and the reflection of the streetlight obscured whoever was inside—Patty and the driver both.

It made Gabriella uneasy.

She couldn't say for sure if it was the same van she'd seen outside the gallery earlier. It certainly looked very similar.

Even if it had been the same van, there wasn't necessarily anything sinister about Patty accepting a lift. Still, she followed after it, aware it would most likely be long gone by the time she reached the main road.

She saw no sign of it when she reached the bus stop, although just as the bus pulled up she thought she caught sight of a jaguar driving toward Kensington. The light was bad, though, and it could have been black or dark blue just as easily as bottle green, and when she caught a glimpse of the number plate, it didn't match the one she was worried about.

She sat up front near the driver, avoiding the giggling lads in the back. They seemed to have been drinking, despite the fact that they couldn't have been more than sixteen.

She let herself into the house just after midnight, and when she reached the top floor, she stopped in astonishment at the sight of Mr. Rodney's door standing open.

"Wotcha." A man leaned out into the hall, and then stopped short, his eyes wide in surprise.

"Jerome?" Gabriella recognized him from the Calypso Club.

"Gabriella, is it?" He inclined his head. "I'm your new neighbor, looks like."

"You've already moved in?" She glanced past him into the flat, which looked very sparsely furnished. "Has Mr. Rodney moved already?"

"Solomon got the lads round, and we did it inna couple o' hours," Jerome said. "Quick as you like."

"Well, welcome to Rose Court," Gabriella said. "Have a good evening." She unlocked her door, and sensing he was still watching her, turned back to him.

He was studying her closely. "Have a good evening yourself," he said at last, stepped back, and closed his door.

She would miss Mr. Rodney being right opposite. He had been the first friend she'd made in London after she'd arrived off the ship from Melbourne.

A laugh came through the door, and she realized Jerome wasn't alone. He must have friends helping him move his furniture around.

She stepped through her own door and realized things might not be so quiet on the top floor any more.

chapter ten

THE WEATHER HAD TURNED.

Sunday had been cool, although still sunny and bright, but it started raining as Monday dawned.

Gabriella made her way to her patch with a black umbrella over her head, shivering at the sudden change in temperature, and for once wishing she didn't have the early shift.

Liz didn't look like she minded, though.

She'd given Gabriella a cheerful wave and swung off to Chelsea with a spring in her step.

The dark sky made it seem even earlier than it was, and gusts of wind kept catching Gabriella's umbrella and trying to rip it out of her hands.

She walked past the townhouse Mr. Jaguar had come out of with a wary eye, keeping a watch for his car, but there was no sign of a bottle green jag. There were plenty of cars illegally parked, though. The rain did that, Liz told her this morning at the meeting. People took chances to park closer to where they needed to be.

She moved down the street, sticking FPNs on windscreens as she went, then turned into Clematis Lane. The loading zone outside the gallery was empty, and it was telling how relieved she felt at the sight.

The narrow alleyways she passed no longer stank like they had last week in the heat, but she heard rats fighting with each other down one of them and stopped to have a closer look.

A bare foot stuck out from behind the bins, its shoe a little way away.

Gabriella stood still, focused on the sling-back, with its black heel and white front.

The shoe Patty had been wearing at Dance-A-Go-Go on Saturday night.

Gabriella forced herself to walk into the narrow alley, which lay between the gift shop which shared a wall with the gallery on the left, and The Cat's Meow, where Patty worked.

She pressed up against the wall on the other side of the bins and took careful sideways steps until she could see around them.

Patty lay half-propped up against the wall.

One leg was bent at the knee, the other stretched out, its foot the one she'd noticed sticking out from behind the metal bins stacked along the gift shop wall. She was still wearing her smart black and white dress, but blood soaked down the side of it, pooling below her body.

The rain had formed puddles, and the blood had swirled and seeped into them, so it seemed to Gabriella that she was lying in an ocean of blood.

The rats had run as she'd approached, but she could see bite marks on Patty's hands, and she suddenly felt lightheaded. For a terrible moment she thought she was going to throw up.

She staggered away, moving back to the street and leaning against the corner, head bowed, waiting for the dizziness to recede. She had lowered her umbrella to her side without realizing it, and rain hammered her head, running in rivulets from her hair, under her collar, and down her back.

Finally she got a hold of herself and stumbled toward Gennaro's, hoping the old man would be there early like he had been last Wednesday.

The door was closed, probably because of the weather, but

when she knocked, she heard him shuffling through to the door. He paused, looking through the patterned glass to see who it was, and then pulled it open.

She almost fell in, and he moved back.

"What is it?" he asked in Italian. "Not another one?"

"Yes."

As she said it, he swore, throwing up his hands in shock as she stood, water dripping off her to pool around her sturdy black shoes.

"I must phone the sergeant."

"I have his card." Gennaro went behind a wooden podium from where she guessed he greeted his customers. He pulled out a small card and handed it to her. "The telephone is in my office."

She followed him, pushing her hair out of her eyes, and when he offered her a chair, she almost fell into it as her knees gave way.

"I call for you," he said.

She shook her head. "I'll do it."

He nodded, but dialed for her, at least, and then held the receiver out when Scotland Yard got Detective Sergeant Archer on the line.

"Yes?"

"It's Gabriella Farnsworth." She paused, suddenly at a loss, wondering what to say.

"You have information?" he asked.

"There's another body." The words burst out of her. "The girl from the clothing boutique near the gallery, Patty. I think . . ." She swallowed. "I think she might have been there since Saturday night."

"I'll be right there. Where are you calling from? The gallery?"

"Gennaro's."

"Stay there," he said. "Don't move."

She was happy to obey that order.

Gennaro had stayed with her as she'd spoken, but as she set the receiver down he disappeared and she heard the grinding of beans, the whoosh of steam, and then smelled the aroma of espresso.

Her hand shook as she took the cup he presented to her, and her teeth bumped against the rim with a click.

She sipped slowly, still remembering how close she'd come to throwing up.

"Patty is the one you found? Where is she?" Gennaro sat on the corner of his desk, and seemed to transform from the barrel-chested café owner into someone more dangerous.

"In the alley between the gift shop and the boutique. I only found her because I heard the rats fighting . . ." She had to put the cup down or spill her coffee. She looked up at Gennaro. "The rats were fighting over her body."

He swore again, and walked toward the door. "Should I go stand by her? To stop the rats?"

Gabriella nodded. "Please."

With a nod he snatched up her dripping umbrella, which she hadn't even remembered putting down, and strode out.

She slowly drank the rest of her coffee, then forced herself to move out of the office to the front door to wait for DS Archer. She walked slowly, stiff with cold and shock, and sank into a chair near the entrance. She jumped in shock at the rap of knuckles on the glass of the door, and then fumbled to open up.

DS Archer stared at her for a moment. "Where is Gennaro?"

"Guarding the body." She lifted a trembling hand, tucked a lock of hair behind her ear. "I found her because I heard the rats . . ."

He took a step back. "Wait here."

He disappeared, and a few minutes later, Gennaro returned. He shook out her umbrella, set it in the stand near the door, and clicked his tongue.

"Bad sight," he said. "Very bad sight."

She nodded. "Are the bobbies there, too?"

"The big ones in uniform? They are there." He patted her shoulder. "You want more coffee?"

She shook her head. "Thank you, but no."

With a grunt of acceptance, he moved off, and she heard him moving around in his office and then the kitchen.

The café door opened, and DS Archer stepped in. He pulled up a chair and sat opposite her.

"What time did you find the body?"

"Two minutes before I phoned you." She clenched her fists. "I was walking my route, and heard rats fighting. I just looked down the alley to see what they were doing, and I saw her shoe. Her . . . foot."

She swallowed.

"You said you thought she'd been there since Saturday night? How could you know that?"

Gabriella heard an edge to his voice, and looked up to meet his eyes. His suspicion grounded her, strangely. Gave her the backbone she needed.

"Because I was at the same dance club as her on Saturday night. I didn't speak to her but I saw her leave. And she was wearing the same clothes she's got on now."

Archer leaned back in his chair in surprise. "Which club?"

"Dance-A-Go-Go. I left just after her, and I saw her accept a lift in a van just outside the club."

"Who was driving?" Archer asked.

She shook her head. "I didn't see him. Or her."

"What can you tell me about the van?" Archer leaned forward, intense and focused.

She hesitated. Wondered if she should say something about the incident in Clematis Lane she'd witnessed earlier. "It was white. I don't know the make, but if I was shown some pictures, I might be able to point it out."

Archer leaned back with an explosive exhale. "That's not much to go on."

That wasn't her fault. She forced herself to her feet.

"You bothering the girl?"

She looked over, saw Gennaro standing in the doorway of his office. She wondered how long he'd been there.

"Just questioning my witness." Archer got to his feet, as well.

"I need to do my rounds." Although it was the last thing she felt like.

Archer studied her. "You look like you're about to collapse."

That made her stiffen her spine a little more. "I'll walk it off."

She stepped around him, reached for her umbrella.

"Give me your home address, please, Miss Farnsworth. I might need to speak to you later."

She gave it to him reluctantly, something he picked up on, if the quirk of his lips was anything to go by.

"Call me if you remember anything more." He opened the door for her.

She stood just under the awning, then turned back to look past him to Gennaro. "*Grazie di tutto.*"

She gave a small wave, and forced herself back out into the rain, lifting her umbrella and fighting to open it in the wind.

This was going to be a hard day.

chapter **eleven**

JAMES LOOKED after Miss Farnsworth in surprise.

Her Italian had sounded completely fluent.

He put her first name and her dark hair and eyes together suddenly. "She's half-Italian?" He swung toward Gennaro, who was also staring after her.

"*She* says she's Australian. It is her mother who's Italian."

He sounded almost affronted.

"Sir." Detective Constable Hartridge hailed him from the right, and James flicked up the collar of his coat against the rain and stepped out from under the awning.

"Thank you again for your help, Mr. Moretti. Much appreciated." He tipped his head and strode back to Hartridge and the alley.

He'd brought Hartridge with him from the Yard to help at the scene. The young detective was three years or so younger than he was, but almost painfully keen.

"The pathologist wants a word, sir." Hartridge gestured in the direction of the alleyway, and then fell into step beside James as he walked back to the scene.

"Was that the witness? The girl in the traffic warden uniform?"

"Miss Gabriella Farnsworth. She heard rats fighting over the body on her way past the alley and looked in to see what was going on."

"Oh, God." The horror of the situation was clear in Hartridge's voice, and James liked him more for it.

"Quite."

The pathologist was Dr. Jandicott again, which James was glad of.

"Likely the same killer?" he asked, stepping over a puddle tinged with blood.

"Same as the man in the car, you mean?" Jandicott asked. "Yes. Could be. Our killer likes stiletto knives, so that's a commonality, and there is the fact that the bodies were found mere feet from each other." He gave a slow nod. "Stab wound is in the same general place, too. Though there wasn't any other mark on her, not like that nasty head cut we had on the other one."

"He was bigger. More able to fight back, maybe?" James said. "This girl is five foot two if she's an inch."

"Any sign of the weapon?" Jandicott asked.

James glanced over at Hartridge, who shook his head.

"Not yet. Maybe he has a limited supply. Decided to keep this one."

James didn't like the assumption implicit in that statement. "Keep it for next time, you mean?"

There was a moment of silence.

"You think this is a madman?" Jandicott asked. "A homicidal maniac?"

James shook his head. "If you mean someone killing for the sake of killing, no. I think there's something going on in this street, and everyone who's been killed so far is mixed up in it."

"Like what?" Hartridge asked.

"I don't know."

But he was going to find out.

"There were coppers all over Clematis Lane again," Solomon said from behind her.

Gabriella had heard his cheerful call hello from the front door as he'd come in, and she turned from the stove and gave a tight nod. "Another body." She turned back and lifted the lid off the roasting tin. "A young girl."

Solomon blinked. "How'd she die?"

Gabriella lifted her shoulders, feeling unbelievably weary. "I don't know." She carefully put the bread back in the oven, set the timer for thirty minutes, and leaned back against the counter that ran next to the oven range.

"You don't look too good, Gabby. You don't have to bake if you're not feeling it."

"No, I like making bread. I feel better now than when I got home." She straightened, realizing that was true. Making the bread had soothed her. "You want some tea? I told Mr. Rodney I'd make some after I was done with the bread."

"Sure, 'n' all." Solomon sent her a laughing look. "Melvin said he saw you at Dance-A-Go-Go on Saturday."

She nodded. "The girl who died, Patty, she was there the same night. I think she was killed just after, because she was still in the same dress she was wearing when I saw her in the club."

Solomon had gone still. "What'd she look like, then?"

"Blonde. In a white dress with a black stripe down the front and across at the hips."

"You told the coppers she was there?"

She nodded.

"I'll just give Melvin the heads up. They'll no doubt be round." He turned to the door.

"Solomon." She didn't know she was going to call him back so vehemently, but he turned, eyes narrowed in surprise. "Please tell them to cooperate. I found her body." She drew in a shuddering breath. "She was lying in that alley for over a day. I found her 'cause the rats were fighting over her. She deserves some justice."

He hesitated. Gave a tiny nod. "I'll tell Mel, but I don't control the others. That's not my playground."

She was grateful for anything he could do. She gave a nod. "I didn't like the man who was murdered in the car, though I didn't think he deserved to die. But Patty . . ." She shook her head. "Someone has to pay."

"Don't hang your hopes on the coppers," Solomon said. "Believe me when I say they can be bought." He left with a friendly call out to his uncle, and Gabriella set about making the tea.

She brought it out into the garden which Mr. Rodney had made almost his permanent home since he'd moved in. The rain had eased off at lunch time, and the sun had made an appearance since the early afternoon. There was a cast-iron table and two chairs which Mr. Rodney had toweled off so they could sit, and she set down a pot and two cups and saucers, then went back in for the milk and sugar.

The smell of fresh-baked bread wafted out with her as she returned.

"You're happy," she observed as she poured the tea.

"I never thought I'd have a patch o' garden," Mr. Rodney said. "And Mr. Higgins took good care of it. Jerome says he'll help me keep it up. I told him to be respectful of you, Gabby. No loud noises or funny business in my old flat."

The timer went in the kitchen, and Gabriella left to take the bread out. It was crisp and golden brown. Perfect.

She stared down at it. She had spent every day churning out dozens of loaves onboard the ship that she'd taken from Melbourne, but this was the first loaf she'd made since she got to London.

It felt like a turning point.

She was settling in here, for as long as it took.

She had received a letter from her mother just the other day, begging her to come home, to give up her search for her father.

But her mother and Gino wanted to marry, and there was no way they could until her mother had a death certificate.

Her mother was sure her father had to be dead or he would have come back to her, or at the least let her know where he was.

But the more Gabriella enquired, the more she had to face the possibility that her father was not dead at all. That he had left Melbourne for London, and had simply decided not to come back.

He'd gone over to help settle his father's estate. That's what he'd told her mother. Whether that was really so, Gabriella had no way of knowing. But whatever the truth of it, from what she had managed to find out so far, her father, under the name her mother had known him, did not seem to exist.

Which—given she had her parents' marriage certificate and her own birth certificate with her to aid her in her search—was clearly impossible.

chapter twelve

SHE HAD JUST GOT BACK to her room and was in her tiny kitchen, about to cut into the half loaf she'd brought up from Mr. Rodney's for her supper, when a knock came at the door.

Thinking it was either Solomon or Jerome, she opened it without asking who was there.

Detective Sergeant Archer stood, hand raised to knock again.

"Oh." Surprised, she took a step back.

"You were expecting someone else," he said. She didn't know why he sounded disappointed.

"No. I have a new neighbor. I thought it was him, needing something. We're the only two on this floor." She took another step back to give him room. "Come in."

"Thank you." Archer closed the door behind him and sniffed the air. "Fresh bread?"

"Just baked. Would you like a piece with strawberry jam? I was about to cut a slice." She lifted the bread knife. "And have some coffee? I make it on the stove because I don't have an espresso machine."

He hesitated, then gave a nod. "I'd like that." He took off his jacket, hanging it on one the hooks behind the door, and she noticed him studying her little bedsit as she added an extra teaspoon of coffee to the pot on the stove. He made no comment, but she liked the way she had done up her space, and she wasn't self-conscious about it.

She sliced the bread with the ease of long practice working in a bakery, and pushed the butter and jam toward him.

He looked up in surprise when he bit in.

"Sourdough," Gabriella said. "I was only able to make it because my old neighbor moved down to the ground floor flat a few days ago and his place has the original kitchen with a big oven."

"You made this?" Archer held it in front of him, looking at it in surprise.

"My mother has a bakery in Melbourne. I worked there my whole life."

He took another bite, and they sat for a while in silence, sipping strong coffee and chewing bread.

"You hesitated while you were telling me about that van earlier. What did you leave out?" Archer asked the question straight after he swallowed his last bite of bread.

He didn't sound accusing, just curious, and she gave a slow nod.

"I only hesitated because I honestly can't say for sure, but I might have seen the van before. Outside the gallery."

Archer set his coffee cup down and leaned forward. "When, exactly?"

She couldn't help notice the way his biceps bunched under the white cotton of his shirt as he rested his elbows on her table. The impression she'd had the first time she'd met him, of a man capable of hard physical labor, struck her again.

"Saturday morning. I work a half day."

"Go on."

"I had a little set-to with the gallery owner."

"Devenish?" Archer asked.

"Is that his name? There was a car parked in the loading zone, and I . . ." She felt like an idiot saying it, but forced herself to forge on. "I was afraid, walking up to it. But it was empty, and so I noted down the time, because they're only allowed to park there for thirty minutes. Devenish came boiling out of the gallery, thinking I was writing a ticket. He said the driver was there dropping off paintings, and he took a couple of canvases out of the boot himself. He was rude."

"You thought that was strange?" Archer said.

"I thought it odd that he took such offense, but then just the sight of my uniform seems to bring out some people's temper." She shrugged. "So I kept on down the street, then came back up the other side. The car was still there, and Devenish and another man were standing beside it, talking quietly. I stopped behind a white van and checked the time, although I didn't really notice the van."

"Was the car there more than thirty minutes?" Archer asked.

She nodded. "Almost. But I guessed the man talking to Devenish was the driver and about to go, so I wasn't going to issue a fine. But while they stood there, talking, Patty came out of her shop and she looked pretty steamed. She stormed toward Devenish, like she was about to have a go at him, and he called out her name, like he was warning her to be careful what she said in public."

Archer leaned back, the look on his face thoughtful as he sipped his coffee. "Did it stop her?"

Gabriella nodded. "She slowed down, and when she got to him and the other bloke, I couldn't hear what was being said."

"Nothing at all?"

"She said 'no' loud enough to be heard at the end."

"What did Devenish do about that?" Archer asked.

"He looked around nervously, but the other man took her hand and said something to her. I think he was telling her she had more customers, because she turned and then went back into her shop."

"So he took charge of the situation? The delivery man?" Archer's surprise was clear.

Gabriella nodded. "It felt like there was something going on between them. And I thought I saw him with her at Dance-A-Go-Go. She looked as if she was waiting for someone, and then a man came up behind her and they disappeared into the crowd. It was hard to see for sure, but I thought it was the delivery driver."

"You think he could have been driving the white van?" Archer asked.

She lifted her shoulders. "He wasn't the one driving it earlier. When Patty left Devenish and the delivery man on the street, the delivery man got into the blue car and drove off. Whoever was in the van threw out their cigarette, started up, and did a u-turn. It looked to me like he was following after the car, but it really might have been coincidence."

Archer studied her. "And you're sure you can't say it was the same van that picked up Patty?"

She shook her head. "I thought it was very similar, or the same, but I honestly couldn't say for sure. And there are a lot of white vans in London."

He gave a grim nod. "Unfortunately."

"Did you speak to the people who work at the dance club?" she asked, thinking of Melvin. He would have seen the delivery man, but he most likely wouldn't have noticed who he talked to once he was inside the club.

"They were surprisingly cooperative, but it was their busiest night of the week, and they didn't notice anything off."

She glanced at his empty plate and nudged the bread toward him. "Would you like some more?"

He looked torn, as if he'd like to say yes, but instead, he pushed back his chair and got to his feet. "I have to go. But thank you. What you've told me helps."

She got to her feet, and felt suddenly shy.

He drew her.

There was something clear and straightforward about his manner, and his face was open, his height and his strength very attractive.

"Be careful when you go about," Archer said when he got to

the door, his gaze locking with hers. "If the driver of that white van was responsible for Patty's death, he might have seen you."

She hadn't thought of that. She didn't like it.

She gave a nod.

"If you feel like someone's following you, or you're in any way uncomfortable, go into a shop or something, and get them to call me." He handed her another card, and she took it, careful to make sure their fingers didn't brush.

"Thank you." She leaned against the doorjamb as he stepped into the passage.

He gave a nod, looking like he wanted to say something more, but then he tipped his head and disappeared down the stairs.

chapter thirteen

GABRIELLA FARNSWORTH'S bedsit was small, but it was neat, and it had a warmth about it that James didn't know how to create himself.

His flat was larger—he had a separate bedroom, not a little nook hidden from view with what seemed to be a Chinese-style folding screen like she did—but his place looked unfinished somehow. The fact that he lived in a new block of flats built out of the rubble of the war, and she lived in a cramped, converted Victorian, didn't seem to matter when it came to style.

He'd wanted to stay—he had really wanted to stay—but it had been too tempting.

He had found himself on her doorstep after coming from Patty Little's parents. Her father had gone very quiet when he gave them the news, pacing the front room, while her mother had sobbed in loud, heart-wrenching bursts.

They had been trying to contact her friends since Sunday mid-morning, looking for her, and James could tell they wished they had gone to the police immediately.

"She were a good lass," her father said, when James asked to see her room, and had followed him up the tight stairs to a small bedroom at the top of the landing. "She loved fashion, and such. Pleased as punch she were, getting a job in that fancy clothes shop.

Were ever so particular, she was, in what she wore. She wanted to be a designer. She were going to night college, to study for it."

Patty's room was an explosion of color compared to the heavy Victorian style of the rest of the small row house. It looked neat, although there were two dresses laid across her bed, as if she had been choosing what to wear.

He'd done a thorough search, and had taken away a dark red diary to study later, and a current photo of her, leaning against a tree out in the countryside, with the sun shining on her hair.

"That were our holiday last year," her father said, hand trembling as he held it out to James. "Down Brighton way."

James had driven away from their house feeling the weight of time passing, the frustrating lack of any direction. He needed something to break.

He had checked on where Gabriella lived before he'd left to see Patty's parents, and he didn't even try to excuse why he went to her before he headed home to his empty flat.

Despite his reasons, though, it turned out to have been a good idea. She'd given him a lead he wouldn't have had.

As he pulled into the main road traffic, he faced the fact that he needed to keep a professional distance from Gabriella Farnsworth, because his thoughts where she was concerned were so plainly unprofessional.

He stopped at a chippy on the way home to get some fish and chips, as the slice of bread he'd eaten had only just touched sides, but it had been delicious, for all that.

Sourdough.

He didn't think he'd ever had it before.

He burned his fingers as he lifted hot chips out of the bag to eat as he drove, scorching his tongue as he tried to chew, and knew he would picture her in her small, pretty bedsit, sipping strong, Italian coffee and nibbling on jam and bread whenever he thought of her.

It was a better picture than her, white-faced and head bowed, in Gennaro's café, trying to talk about finding Patty's body.

As he swung into his reserved off-street parking, he thought about what she'd told him about the car outside the gallery.

He didn't know if it was reasonable for someone to take longer than half an hour to drop off paintings, but what interested him more than that was that Devenish and Patty Little had known each other. From what Gabriella had told him, the delivery driver had known her, too, and if it was him who'd met her in the club, then he'd known her more than just in passing.

Had the conversation in the street that Gabriella had witnessed been the reason why she'd been killed later that night?

As he walked up the wide stairs to his second floor flat, he thought back to his original interview with both Patty and Devenish. Neither had given any indication they knew each other.

Devenish would be getting a visit from him and Constable Hartridge tomorrow morning.

It kept coming back to Clematis Lane. Whatever was going on there seemed to be worth killing for.

"Something's up with you." Ben had to lean in close to speak to her over the general mayhem of the pub. "What is it?"

Gabriella hesitated, then glanced over at Dominique and Trevor, walking back to them with drinks for everyone in their hands. She didn't want to drag her friends into this. She had pondered going out to meet them at all after DS Archer had left her flat, but they had arranged this get-together two weeks ago, and she didn't want to sit alone in her flat, brooding.

"What's going on?" Dominique scooted in next to her, forcing Gabriella to move a little deeper into the booth.

"Not here," she said at last. She couldn't bear the thought of shouting about dead bodies over the laughter in the King's Arms. "When we walk home."

Ben looked like he was going to push it, then he took his Guinness from Trev and gulped down a sip instead.

He would never have even considered pushing her when they'd first met. He'd been too quiet, and Gabriella had the sense he kept waiting for Trevor, Dominique and herself to tell him to get lost.

He'd shared a cabin with Trev the whole way across from Melbourne, and he always gave Gabriella the impression that he didn't think himself cool enough for a friend like Trevor.

But slowly, as the journey had unfolded, he'd gained more and more confidence.

It made Gabriella very angry when she thought of his family. He never spoke much about them, but she knew they were the reason he was so timid and self-effacing.

She was glad he'd had the courage to leave them and go off to find a new life for himself.

He caught her watching him and she gave him a cheeky grin and tipped her head toward Dominique. "So, are you running Terrific Teens yet, Neeky? I look out for it when I walk past the news stands on my route."

"Not yet." Dominique shook her head. "I'm still just answering the phones. But give it some time. I've only been there four weeks."

"My cousin reads it," Trevor piped up, setting down his pint of bitters with a sigh of satisfaction. "She's forever saving up for the makeup recommendations."

"How're things going at your aunt's?" Ben asked.

Trev gulped down another sip of bitters. "They're all right. A little too clingy, but I can't complain, and my uncle's got me in with a good construction company. I've been in work since two days after I got here."

Trevor had been the envy of their little group of working passengers on the way over to England. He had family expecting him, a place to stay, and a promise of a job.

The rest of them had landed hard, by comparison.

"And you, Gabs? How's life as a traffic warden?" Dominique asked.

Gabriella quirked her lips. "Surprisingly few people like getting tickets. Or FPNs, as we call them in the trade."

"And they what? Shout at you?" Dominique asked.

"Mostly. If I have to deal with them at all. Fortunately, a lot of the time they aren't near their cars. I just stick the ticket on the windscreen and that's it. But sometimes I have a face-to-face."

"Has anyone tried to do anything other than shout?" Ben asked.

She hesitated.

"They have!"

"Once," she admitted. "But a policeman stepped in. I wasn't touched."

"At least tell us the pay's good," Dominique said.

"It's not bad," Gabriella said. "Better than a secretary. Not as good as a master baker, but I couldn't get into a bakery anywhere before my money ran out, so I had to take what I could get."

"Keep looking," Dominique said and flicked back her hair in an exaggerated way. "I had that poxy job at an insurance company for a few weeks before my French name and my blonde hair got me in the door at Terrific Teen. Ooh-la-la, don't you know?"

Gabriella laughed. "I'll keep my eye out. But I actually quite like it. The hours are better than a bakery would be, and it's nice being out on the streets. I'm getting to know London well."

"What about you, Ben?" Dominique asked. "You're looking good. You obviously found something better than checking contracts at that real estate office since we last saw you."

"Definitely," Gabriella agreed. "You're looking like a proper London lawyer."

Ben smoothed a self-conscious hand over his tie, tugged a little at his collar. "I got a position as a pupil in the Temple."

"Ben!" Trev gave his shoulder a thump. "Wasn't that your dream position?"

Ben ducked his head. "I was lucky. The money isn't very good, but I've got my foot in the door."

"Look at us, all established." Gabriella realized she'd missed her crew. They had been inseparable onboard the *SS Oriana*. All of them had gotten jobs on the ship to pay for their fares, and they had eaten their meals together in the kitchens, shared a bathroom, and relaxed together when they'd had time off. "I must admit, it's good to hear a proper accent."

Dominique grinned at that. "God, you clearly don't live in Kangaroo Valley."

"Kangaroo Valley?" Trev almost spat out a mouthful of bitters on a laugh.

"Earl's Court. My lovely neighborhood is full of more Aussies than you can shake a stick at."

Trev gave another chuckle. "That'd be nice. My aunty's family claim they can't understand me. But I can hardly understand *them*."

"What about you, Ben?" Dominique asked. "You still living in that boarding house?"

He grimaced. "My landlady is a busybody, but the house on Victoria Embankment is close enough to Chambers that I can walk to work easily." He sighed. "She's very put out I've opted not to eat meals with her and her daughter, but I just can't bear the sniping between them. It reminds me too much of home." He pursed his lips. "I think she's going to find an excuse to give me the chuck at the first opportunity."

"I doubt it if you're a good tenant. But I recommend finding a bedsit, like me. There's more independence." Gabriella had never regretted taking the tiny bedsit in Notting Hill.

"A few of the other pupils working in Chambers were talking about a flat share," Ben said. "There's a few I think I'd get along with, so maybe I'll go in with them."

The noise in the pub began to get to rowdy levels, making it impossible to have a decent conversation, and they eventually gave up, collected their things, and stepped out into the balmy summer air.

It was a relief.

"The smell of spilt beer and sweat mingled together is god-awful," Dominique said, wrinkling her nose as they moved to the other side of the road.

The pub was on the Thames, and by unspoken agreement they all leaned against the wall to look down at it, breathing in the briny scent of the water.

The lights of the pubs and the street lights reflected in the flowing river, and in combination with the warmth of the evening air, made Gabriella feel very fond of her newly adopted home.

"It's quiet now," Ben said. "Tell us what's wrong, Gabs. Is it your dad? You've found out what happened to him?"

Gabriella thought he'd have forgotten about her promise to explain, but she should have realized he wouldn't. He wasn't the forgetful type.

She hesitated again, but Ben gave her a look that said he wasn't going to drop it. She sighed.

"It's nothing to do with my search. I found a dead body on my rounds last week, and then another one today."

Dominique audibly drew in a breath, and Trev and Ben's faces registered shock.

"Are you alright, love?" Dominique put an arm around her and drew her close.

Gabriella wound her own arm around Dominique's waist and gave her a squeeze to thank her for the sympathy. "I'm doing okay."

"The police are on it?" Ben asked.

She gave a nod. "Look, I'd rather not talk about it."

"You sure?" Dominique studied her face carefully.

"It was grim, and I'd prefer not to think about it more than necessary." She hugged herself, turning away from the river, and saw a green jaguar pulling away from the curb.

She frowned after it, relieved to see she didn't recognize the registration number, but as it disappeared into the traffic she thought she glimpsed a dent on the rear left bumper. Just where Mr. Jaguar had hit the bollard the day he'd roared off.

"What is it?" Trevor put a hand on her arm. "You look spooked."

She shook her head. "All good. Just time to call it a night."

"You let us know if we can help you," Trevor said, and Ben murmured an agreement.

They broke up—Ben and Trevor heading toward Embankment together, although Trev lived south of the river, and she and Dominique were both headed west.

They sat on the bus, talking quietly, and when Dominique got off at Earl's Court, Gabriella decided to get off with her. She had to get off soon anyway and walk to the main road to catch the bus to Notting Hill, and she would rather spend more time with Dominique.

When they reached the door up to the flat over a newsagents where Dominique was sharing with a friend of her sister's, Dominique grabbed both of Gabriella's hands. "Let's meet up Saturday afternoon. Do some shopping."

"All right." She didn't have money for shopping, but she would happily tag along with Dominique.

They hugged goodbye, and as Gabriella made her way up to the main road, she realized Earl's Court was still buzzing, even though it was a Monday night.

She enjoyed the festive atmosphere, although she wondered if the noise would get old after a while if it was like this every night, and you were trying to sleep.

Notting Hill settled down after eleven.

"Want some company?" A burly man with blond-streaked hair to his shoulders flicked away his cigarette and straightened up from the wall outside a club with neon signage. She hadn't seen him lurking in the shadows and she felt her heart jump in her chest at being taken by surprise.

He stepped into the light, and shoved his hands into his trouser pockets.

His accent was Australian. Dominique was right about Earl's Court.

"No, thanks, mate. Just getting the bus." She kept walking.

"Oh?"

He swung into step with her, and she wondered how worried she should be.

"I'll walk you to your stop."

"Why?" she asked bluntly.

He gave a shrug. "Bored. My girl left the club early, and I don't feel like going home just yet. Plus, I'm always happy to escort a fellow countrywoman safely to her bus stop." He put out his hand. "Tony."

"Gabriella." She shook his outstretched hand, liking that he didn't try to hold on too long.

"From?" he asked.

"Melbourne."

"Ah. I'm from Sydney."

"A surfer?" Gabriella asked him. He looked like one, wearing a colorful woven jumper and a leather necklace she associated with the breed.

"Yeah." He shrugged. "I don't like this place. I'll be going back as soon as my girl finishes her semester at college."

"Have you been down to Cornwall? I hear there's surfing there."

"Yeah." He perked up a bit. "It was good. Cold, though." He jammed his fists back into the front pockets of his jeans, hunching his shoulders as if remembering the bite of an icy wind off the sea.

They had reached Cromwell Road, and she pointed to the bus stop. "This is me. Thanks for the chat."

"Sure." He seemed a little uncertain. "I don't like leaving you alone here."

The wind had picked up, suddenly blowing cool with the promise of rain, and Tony ducked around the back of the bus stop to light another cigarette.

Gabriella looked down the road, checking for the bus, but it was nowhere in sight.

A white van cruised past on the far side of the road, and she watched it turn up ahead and disappear.

Add white vans to the green jaguar as vehicles she needed to be wary of.

Her life was a lot more exciting that she had imagined it would be.

Tony stepped back out from behind the bus stop, drawing on his cigarette as if it were a lifeline.

"I didn't offer you," he said, patting his top pocket in invitation.

She shook her head. "Never started."

"Wise," he said. "They cost the bloody earth and they make you crook."

She grinned at him. "I miss the lingo," she said. "My friend Dominique lives 'round here, and she says it's chock full of Aussies. I hadn't realized how nice it is to hear the sweet strains of home."

Tony grinned back. "Well, happy to oblige."

Gabriella glanced down the street again and went still at the sight of the white van coming back down the road, this time on her side.

"Hey. You want a lift?" The man inside was in shadow. She just caught a glimpse of a cap pulled down over his forehead.

"No, thanks." She took a step closer to the bus stop.

"I'll get you home faster than the bus," he said. His voice was strangely low, as if he were trying to disguise it.

"She said no, mate." Tony took a step closer to the van, and with a sudden jerk, it took off.

As the van sped away, the bus rumbled up to the stop.

"Thanks, Tony. I appreciate the escort." Gabriella waited for the bus doors to swing open.

"You going to be all right?"

She gave a nod and a wave and climbed in, digging in her bag for the right change.

She looked out as the bus left the stop, saw Tony was still

standing on the pavement, head bent as he drew on his cigarette. He looked in no hurry to go anywhere.

The bus stopped all along Cromwell Road, then turned north west toward Notting Hill, squealing and jerking as it negotiated tight corners and threaded through streets crowded with cars. During one such jerk and squeal, Gabriella glanced back, and thought she saw the white van, following them.

For the first time, her uneasiness bloomed into actual fear.

She was close enough to home she could get off anywhere now, and still make it to her door in ten minutes.

She eyed the other occupants of the bus. There were a few kids upstairs, she could hear them joking and laughing. Downstairs with her there were two men who looked like they were coming off a late shift, a few couples who had probably been to the movies, and a short, round woman in a scarf and a shabby overcoat.

When it looked clear one of the couples, one of the men, and the overcoat lady were all getting off at the next stop, Gabriella joined them, slipping in the middle of the group as they disembarked.

The stop was in darkness—Gabriella could see a broken street light—and when the bus squealed to a stop, it overshot slightly, coming to a halt in front of what looked like a pedestrian path between a house and a park.

Gabriella ducked her head and took the path, tagging along behind the young couple.

The path opened out onto a street she recognized, much to her relief.

She jogged all the way home, looking behind her often.

There was no sign of the van, and when she closed the front door behind her, she leaned back against it, a little out of breath.

"Trouble, Gabby?"

She almost gave a shriek as Solomon emerged from the passage to his uncle's flat.

She glared at him. "That's the second time you've scared the living daylights out of me." She straightened up.

"What's the trouble, pet?" he asked.

She couldn't help the chuckle that escaped. "Pet?"

"That's what the tea lady at work who's from Newcastle always says," he said with a grin. "I like it."

She debated telling him; decided it couldn't hurt to have his boys keeping a look out.

"I saw a white van in Clematis Lane a while ago, and it might be involved with the killings. I thought one was following me."

Solomon took her by the shoulders and moved her out of the way, opened the door and stepped out.

She could hear him jog down the short walk to the road.

He came back more slowly. "Nothing out there now."

"I know. I think I lost it. I got off the bus ten minutes before my stop and took the back lanes here."

"How did the driver know where you live?"

"He stopped at the bus stop in Earl's Court, offered me a lift. I said no, then I saw a white van behind the bus later. It might not have been the same one," she said. "And I don't know how he found me in Earl's Court. If he did."

"But you think it's possible?"

She shrugged. "Better safe than sorry." Then she gave a huge yawn. "I'm finished. I'll see you round, Sol."

He gave a wave as she started up the stairs, and then she heard the front door close quietly as he left.

She tapped a finger to her lips as she climbed, trying to remember everything she could about the van driver. His cap had hidden his eyes, but she'd noticed in the glimpse she'd caught that he'd been smooth-shaven, and she had the impression he wasn't much older than she was. He'd been wearing a jacket, maybe denim or gray cotton, with wide lapels.

She didn't believe it was a coincidence that a white van driver had offered her a lift. He couldn't have seen Tony on his first pass and she wondered if he would have tried to get her in his van if he'd realized she wasn't alone.

Probably not.

She didn't want any more drama, but she decided she'd better let DS Archer know about the encounter in the morning.

When she reached her door, she couldn't hear anyone in the flat opposite, so either Jerome was out, or he was having a quiet night in.

She hoped he was in. It was a comfort to know he was there.

For the first time since this started, she was afraid.

chapter fourteen

DC HARTRIDGE WAS LEANING against James's car as he came out of the pathologist's office.

Patty Little's father had been waiting in the small, gray-walled corridor when he'd come out of the post mortem, and James had eventually had to leave him, crying silently over his daughter's body, in the care of Dr. Jandicott himself.

"What did Jandicott have to say?" Hartridge asked as they both got into the Wolseley.

"Miss Farnsworth was right. The victim most likely died on Saturday night, or the early hours of Sunday morning. And she didn't die in that alley. She was left there afterwards."

"She did look posed," Hartridge said. He flicked open his notepad and James caught a glimpse of neat handwriting. "The Fraud boys got back to us. They said the shell company that owns the car our first body was found in was set up by a law firm in Chelsea."

"Where?"

Hartridge gave him the address and James drove straight there. He had planned to interview Devenish, the gallery owner, about how well he knew Patty, but that would have to wait.

If they didn't get a lead on the identity of their first victim soon, he was going to have to go to the press.

The law offices were in a converted Georgian row house near the Natural History Museum, the street a smart line of white stucco walls and glossy black railings, with various personal touches in the form of pot plants on the front porch or brightly colored doors.

Messrs. Golightly and Todd, Solicitors, had chosen to keep things severe with a door as glossy black as the railings, and not a pot plant in sight.

James tried the door and it opened easily, but no one sat at the secretary's desk set in the wide hallway. With a shrug, James walked into the waiting room, just down from the desk, and found that empty, too.

However, behind one of the two doors on the opposite side of the waiting room, James could hear someone talking.

He rapped on it, then stood back.

The talking ceased immediately, and after a moment, footsteps approached.

The door opened and a man in a striped three-piece suit scowled belligerently at him. "Who the hell are you?"

James had already taken his warrant card out, and he held it up. "Detective Sergeant Archer," he said. "This is Detective Constable Hartridge. Are you Mr. Golightly, or Mr. Todd?"

He looked past the man into the room, searching for who might be with him, and saw the window was open, the net curtains blowing in the breeze.

"Has someone just escaped out of that window?" he asked. He glanced back at Hartridge, signaling him to go and check it out.

Hartridge took the hint immediately, running out the room to the front door in pursuit.

"No, they haven't." The man in the striped suit glanced at the window, then smoothed a hand down his tie nervously before turning back at James, mouth tight. "What's this about?"

"Murder, sir." James watched his pompous expression falter and his face pale. "May I have your name?"

"Edward Golightly." Golightly was not happy to have to give his name—his hold on the door jamb was tight enough to make his knuckles white.

"And the name of the man who ran when I knocked?"

"I have no idea what you're talking about." Golightly took a final look into the room, then stepped forward, forcing James back as he closed the door behind him. "Why didn't my secretary announce you? Do you have an appointment?"

"There was no secretary when we arrived, and this is my appointment." James held up his warrant card again. "Your firm set up a company that's come up in a murder enquiry, Mr. Golightly. I need the name of the client you were acting for."

"What's the company name?" Golightly fussed with his tie again, and James had the feeling he knew exactly which company James wanted information on. Someone had tipped him off, or the Fraud boys had tramped around a little too obviously and sent up a red flag with their enquiries.

"High House."

Golightly attempted a smile. "I'll need to get my secretary to look through the files. If you leave your number, I'll have her ring you when she gets back."

"No." James wasn't letting this weasel out of his sight until he had the information he needed. "You'll look it up for me, now, if you're going to pretend you don't know what I'm talking about."

"I say, who's your superior officer, because I'm going to put in a complaint." Golightly's mouth was bloodless around the edges with outrage. "This is a solicitor's office. There are questions of client privilege."

"DI Whetford is my boss," James said. "I'm sure he'll be delighted to hear from you. And I'm not asking for privileged information, I'm asking for the name of the client you set up a company for. One whose name you should have forwarded to the Companies Register, but somehow haven't gotten around to yet."

Golightly drew himself up. "Well, I'm not going to get the

information for you. I wouldn't even know where to look without Miss Carshaw."

"That's fine. I'll just use your telephone to ring up to arrange for a warrant to search the premises," James said. He moved through the waiting room to the reception area, and as he lifted the telephone handle, Hartridge burst back in, breathing heavily.

"Got away," he said, putting out a hand to steady himself on the desk. He looked over at Golightly. "I got a really good look at him, though."

Golightly wasn't able to hide the dismay on his face.

James gave a nod. "Good. We can put out a sketch, let the public know where he was last spotted and who he's associated with. It might help identify him." He began to dial.

"You will keep the name of this firm out of the press," Golightly squawked.

"Not possible, I'm afraid. I have to find who my murder victim is, and this is the best chance to do that. I have no choice." He turned away in satisfaction at the way Golightly's eyes bulged at his statement.

Just as the call was answered, Golightly darted forward and pushed down the telephone hook to cut off the call.

James cradled the hand set against his shoulder and turned slowly to face the lawyer.

There was a moment of silence between them.

"Look, I'll let you have the information you're looking for if you keep my name out of the paper." Golightly was sweating slightly. "Do we have a deal?"

"We do." James slowly put the receiver back in its cradle and watched as Golightly went back through into the waiting room.

Both he and Hartridge followed behind him as he opened the door into his office, but instead of going in, he stood in the doorway and stared. When he turned to look at them over his shoulder, his face was slack.

"He's only stolen the file, the bastard." He pointed at a

gleaming desk with nothing on it. "We were looking it over when you knocked. He's taken it."

James stared at him for a long moment as he tried to calm the fury inside him at being bested again. "Then, Mr. Golightly, let's start with who 'he' is."

chapter fifteen

DEVENISH.

The car was Devenish's.

It was Devenish who'd run when James had come knocking at Golightly's office.

James rattled the door of the gallery, and then turned to Hartridge, shaking his head. "Locked. And I don't see any lights on in there."

"We've come straight here from Golightly's. Devenish would have had to double back to his car after he ran." Hartridge put his hands on either side of his face and peered through the window into the gloomy depths. "Maybe we got here first."

James surveyed the street. "He never saw me—he ran before Golightly opened the door—but he knew you were a police officer when you chased him, I'm sure. I don't know that he'd come back here in a hurry."

"I was lying about getting a good look at him. I just noticed how on edge Golightly was when I came back in, and somehow the lie just fell out of my mouth."

"It was a good lie." James grinned at Hartridge. "It rattled him, all right. He couldn't tell us what we needed to know fast enough if it would keep his name out of the papers." He glanced into the unlit interior of the gallery one last time. "Let's go round the back. See what we can see there."

They took the alley where Patty Little had been found, coming out into a narrow laneway which James had glanced at quickly the day before, but hadn't really explored with any thoroughness.

The narrow back lane was surprisingly clean, with less litter and detritus than he was used to seeing. It was only wide enough to allow for a single car, and there was no place to stop and pull to the side or park out of the way.

The bobbies who'd searched it after Patty's body was found had come up empty-handed.

With a shriek of stiff hinges, a door set close to the corner of the building swung open into the alley, further up from where Patty's body had been placed.

Mrs. Pinter, the gift shop owner, stepped out, arms full of boxes. She gave a little cry of surprise at the sight of him and dropped them.

"Oh, it's you, Mr. Archer. You gave me quite a turn."

"Sorry, Mrs. Pinter." James came forward and picked up the boxes that had tumbled to the ground. Hartridge moved across to lift the lid of the big bin set against the wall so he could dump them inside for her.

"What are you doing back here? Looking for clues to do with young Patty's death?"

"No. We're looking for Mr. Devenish."

Mrs. Pinter patted her hair. "He went out just before lunch, so it may be he won't be back today. He does that sometimes."

"Takes a half day?" James asked.

"Well, it's not as if the gallery is particularly busy," she confided. "I have wondered a time or two if he doesn't make his money from all the rent he gets, and just keeps the gallery as a vanity project." She tilted her head toward the gallery side of the building. "He makes something from the painting restorations, I suppose. That dreadful foreign man he hired to do the work is thankfully not a morning person. Still, I don't know how it can bring in that much. He probably lives off his trust."

"His trust?" Hartridge asked.

"His father's Sir Reginald Devenish, you know? Something high up in the civil service. Department of Health, I think. Pots of money. Or, there was, before the war. I rather think death duties put a big dent in their fortune, but you wouldn't know it to look at Mr. Devenish. His mother, my friend, was a lot less flashy with their money when she was alive, God rest her soul."

"Did Mr. Devenish live with her?" James asked. "Can you give me the address?"

"Heavens, no. He lives in a flat in North London, I think, but I don't know where it is. Given how he goes about, it's probably very high end. His mother and father live near Grosvenor Square."

"Didn't you tell me you got a very reasonable rent from Devenish because of your connection to his mother?" James asked.

Mrs. Pinter leaned forward conspiratorially. "I'm quite on tenterhooks at the end of each month since his mother died six months ago, waiting for him to give me the flick, so to speak, but so far, he hasn't even mentioned raising the rent. So I have to give him credit for that, don't I?"

James murmured agreement. "You said he gets income from all the rent he gets. You're not his only tenant?"

"Oh, no, dear." Mrs. Pinter waved an arm. "He owns all the shops on this side of the street. One end to the other."

A car turned down the back lane, the tires crunching on the rough gravel. James turned to look at it, and Hartridge did the same.

"Devenish?" Hartridge asked, voice eager.

"No, it's that foreigner that does the painting restoration," Mrs. Pinter said. "He works at the back of the gallery. Night owl. He's at it from around this time of the afternoon until long after I've gone home."

How long after, James wondered? Could this man be a

possible witness to what happened—at least to the man in the car? He'd died during the work week, whereas Patty had been killed over the weekend.

The car drove past them, the driver watching them with alarm, and drew to a stop outside the gallery.

"No one else can get through," Hartridge commented. "His car is blocking the way."

"No one else uses it. The lane is only for the shops and Mr. Devenish owns them all." Mrs. Pinter tossed her hair.

"Why don't you like him, Mrs. Pinter?" James watched the man get reluctantly out of the car. He kept his head down, scurrying around the side of the vehicle to get a leather satchel from the back seat.

"He's rude. I only went over to say hello the first time he came in, and he slammed the door to the workshop in my face." Mrs. Pinter sniffed. "It runs along the whole back of the gallery and my shop, you see. Mr. Devenish took what was probably the storeroom of my shop and broke through the wall into the gallery storeroom to make it all one space. So I can hear him moving around in there, coughing and banging things about." She indicated the door she'd come through. "Mr. Devenish had to have this door put in so I could get to the bins, because there's no access to the alleyway from my shop since he bricked up my storeroom door, other than through the front, and I can't go that way with my rubbish. Not with customers coming in."

"And you say this painting restorer is a foreigner? Where's he from?"

"Germany or Austria or something." She sent the man, who was still eyeing them nervously as he unlocked the door at the back of the building, an acid look. "I must be going, I might have customers, standing out here passing the time of day. Good afternoon to you." She marched back to the door and slammed it shut behind her.

"I wanted to ask her what his name was," Hartridge said.

"We can ask him ourselves." James was already moving to the

door the man had disappeared behind. He knocked, and after a delay that made him think the man was standing just behind it, panicking, it eventually opened.

"Ja?" His accent was strong.

James held out his warrant card, and Hartridge did the same. "Detective Sergeant Archer, and Detective Constable Hartridge. We're looking for Mr. Devenish."

The man's eyes wheeled a little in his head. "I haven't seen Herr Devenish," he said. "Not for two, three days."

"And you are, sir?" James asked politely.

"Herr Fischer," he said.

"From?"

"Switzerland."

"And you work for Mr. Devenish?" Hartridge asked.

"I restore art." Mr. Fischer was fighting to stay still, James thought. As if he were willing himself to look calm, when he was anything but.

James would love an excuse to look inside the workshop, but he had no probable cause. Still . . . "Is it all right if I come in and have a look to see if Mr. Devenish is here?"

"*Nein.*" Mr. Fischer shook his head. "I don't have permission to say this is all right, you understand?"

James gave an inward sigh. "I understand." He pulled out a card. "Could you please ask Mr. Devenish to contact me urgently if you see him. My number is on that card."

Mr. Fischer scrutinized it, then gave a reluctant nod. "Of course."

"Thank you." James moved back and before he had taken one step away, the door was shut and a bolt rammed into place on the inside.

They waited until they were back in the alley before they spoke.

"Something very fishy going on, if you ask me," Hartridge said.

"Very," James agreed. "I'm not sure what, but that chap looked like he was about to faint with nerves at any moment."

"Maybe he's one of those people who had a bad time in the war," Hartridge said. "They get very twitchy around police."

"Switzerland was neutral in the war, but it's a possibility." James didn't think so, though. "More likely, Devenish is up to something, and Fischer's up to his neck in it. And somehow, that's led to two bodies been left on his doorstep."

"Do you think Devenish killed them both?" Hartridge asked.

James glanced at him. "I'd certainly like to ask him about that. But leaving the bodies outside his gallery seems a bit of a strange move. More likely he's got on the wrong side of some dangerous people, and one of them is leaving him a message."

"Like a warning, you mean?" Hartridge asked.

James gave a nod. "Or a threat."

chapter sixteen

DS ARCHER FOUND her on her rounds.

Gabriella had left a message for him during her tea break, calling him from a pay phone near a café where she often stopped for a cup of weak, disappointing coffee. She'd expected him to come back to her flat later, or leave a message for her at the traffic warden center.

He must have seen the surprise on her face that he'd tracked her down.

"I had to call in to the Yard and they told me you'd left a message. We were close by."

Clematis Lane was just down the road, and she guessed that's where he'd come from. He was accompanied by a younger officer, also in plain clothes, who he introduced as DC Hartridge.

She had just finished writing a FPN for a lorry parked on double yellows, and she tucked her ticket book into her satchel.

She was suddenly hesitant to tell him about the van. It was conjecture, but he had insisted she let him know if she felt unsafe at any point.

"You want a cuppa?" he asked her after a moment's silence.

She gave a nod, and they moved to a small café tucked back from the street. Gabriella had never gone inside before, but it was neat and smelled of pies.

DC Hartridge gave a deep, appreciative sniff. "We missed lunch," he said to Archer.

"We did." Archer turned to her. "What would you like?"

"Just coffee, if they have it. Otherwise a cup of tea." She had never taken to tea, but she realized soon after her arrival she would have to develop a taste for it. Mr. Rodney loved coffee, but he had also adopted a love for tea, she guessed to assimilate with the English, and she drank it with him.

"You sure? It's on the Met."

She shook her head. She'd brought sourdough sandwiches from home, and had eaten them over an hour ago.

When they were all settled at a table, Hartridge and Archer digging in to plates of meat pie and chips and her delicately sipping yet more weak, disappointing coffee, she finally realized she needed to stop prevaricating.

"I think a white van followed me last night."

Archer stopped with a forkful of pie close to his mouth, and set it back on his plate. "Where?"

"I was waiting for a bus on Cromwell Rd and this bloke in a white van drove past, then he turned around, came back and offered me a lift."

Archer leaned forward. "Did you see him?"

She lifted a shoulder. "He was in shadow, and he had one of those soft tweed caps pulled low over his forehead. My impression was he was in his mid to late twenties. He had a jacket on with wide lapels, and I think he was trying to disguise his voice."

"You said no?" Hartridge asked.

She nodded. "I said no. And he tried to persuade me to change my mind."

"Did he try to force you in?" Archer's gaze was fixed on her face.

She shook her head. "There was someone else at the bus stop —" no need to go into what Tony was doing there "—and he stepped forward and told him to get lost, and the man drove off very fast."

"He tried to do this with a witness right there?" Hartridge asked, astonished.

"The other man was lighting his cigarette behind the bus stop when the van drove past the first time. I don't think he saw him."

Archer gave a slow nod. "But you said you think he followed you?"

"The bus arrived just as he drove off. I got on, but then I noticed a white van behind the bus." She held her cup of coffee in both hands. "I honestly don't know if it was the same one. I got off the bus early and took some back ways to get home, and I didn't see the van again."

"You did the right thing, telling me." Archer began eating again, in a concentrated, methodical way that told her he ate when he could, because he didn't know when he was going to have a chance again.

Come to think of it, he had a lean, hungry look, even given his size. His cheekbones were sharp in his face, and he looked like he was made purely of bone, muscle and sinew.

Hartridge had already finished his meal, and he pushed his plate away with a sigh of happiness. "What do you think, Sarg?"

"How do you think he found you, to offer you the lift?" Archer asked her. The effect of his full attention was quite shocking. It was suddenly difficult to hold his gaze.

"That I can't say. That's why I'm not sure it's the same van. Unless he somehow knows I'm Australian. I *was* in Earl's Court at the time. It's called Kangaroo Valley for a reason. He could have been cruising, just in case he saw me."

Hartridge gave a snort of laughter at the Kangaroo Valley reference, but Archer gave a slow nod.

"Why not? You've interacted with Devenish, and you say he was parked opposite the gallery when you had your conversation. He could have heard your accent himself."

That's what she had also figured out, as she lay in bed the night before. It was the most likely answer, if the van really was the same one.

"So, he got lucky?" Hartridge asked.

Archer's lips twisted in a wry smile. "Why not? He seems to be on a lucky streak. We're not even close to working out who he is."

Gabriella set her half-drunk cup of coffee down. "I have to keep going on my round."

"Remember what I told you? You think something's up, you run into a shop or a house and call me." Archer looked like he wanted to reach across the table and grab her hand, but just stopped himself.

She gave a nod and slid out of the booth, and both men did the same. She left them paying at the counter, with a wave and a thanks for the coffee, and she thought Archer looked worried when he waved back.

She wasn't sleeping well, and she was very sure DS Archer had taken note of the dark circles under her eyes. She kept hearing rats scrabbling in her dreams. It made for long, miserable nights.

She stopped and waited on the other side of the street when she noticed the lorry driver had gotten back to his truck and was swearing as he pulled the FPN off his windscreen. He saw her as he started up the engine and shook his fist at her as he drove away.

Ah, well.

She should probably be grateful that her black cap with its yellow band and the black uniform made her very difficult to distinguish as an individual. No one would recognize her out of uniform.

Which was a point.

How had the white van driver done it?

And then she thought back to the night club.

Had he noticed her then?

Maybe he'd even been in the club before Patty had left, watching her?

She tried to think if anyone had stood out, but she'd been with Liz, and a lot of men had been looking at them. She would have to ask Liz if anyone had spoken to her after she left, had asked any strange questions.

She hoped the answer to that was no. The thought of someone stalking her through the streets, for just the possibility of what she'd seen, was more terrifying than the thought of finding her deserting father. Or even the sound of rats.

chapter seventeen

JAMES WALKED up the path to the door of the large Grosvenor Square house with interest. It was a substantial, imposing home.

He rang the bell, with Hartridge standing just behind him, and a maid opened it.

He introduced himself and held up his warrant card. "I'd like to speak to Mr. Devenish, please."

"Young Master Devenish? Not Sir Reginald?" The maid, who looked as if she were in her late forties, shook her head. "He hasn't lived here since he went off to university."

"Is Sir Reginald in? We are looking for Mr. Devenish's address."

"I'll just see if he's in," the maid said, looking unsure whether to shut the door in their faces or not. Eventually, politeness won out over suspicion, and she invited them to wait in the hallway.

She disappeared down a passageway, and after a few minutes, an old man came out to greet them. He was what James thought of as part of the civil service set. Tweed suit, highly polished shoes, silk kerchief in his pocket, folded just so. He looked close to retirement age, but James had a suspicion that a lot of these old men of a certain class and standing only went when they were pushed, and not a moment before. They enjoyed too much power to let go without a fight.

"New Scotland Yard, eh?" he asked, looking at James's warrant card. "What's this about?"

"We need to speak to your son, Paul. He may have information on the identity of a murder victim in a case we're investigating," James said.

Sir Reginald looked at them out of cold, watery blue eyes. "Rubbish," he said. "Paul's not involved in any murder."

"We're not accusing him of anything, sir," James said, "but we have strong evidence that the car the victim was found in is owned by your son. We weren't able to catch him at his gallery, could you give us a home address for him?"

Sir Reginald blinked at him, fussing with his jacket sleeve. "I'd have to look it up. I haven't been round to his flat very often." He slowly turned toward the long sideboard in the hallway and walked over to a black leather address book, and paged through it. "Here you go."

Hartridge bent close and wrote the address down.

"If he should get in touch with you, sir, please let him know to contact us urgently." James set his card down next to the phone.

"His lordship didn't like that at all," Hartridge commented as they walked toward the Wolseley.

"No." James wondered if it was just a refusal to believe his son was involved in anything dodgy, or whether he knew there was something going on, and didn't want to admit it.

They drove to the address Sir Reginald had given them but no one came to the door.

Devenish was nowhere to be found.

"He's got questions to answer on the first body, and about Patty," James said as they drove back to the Yard. "But we can't wait any longer. It's been a week since we found him. It's time to go to the press with a picture of the victim in the car."

It weighed on James that someone, somewhere, was missing the victim, not realizing they were dead.

And if Devenish had known all along who he was, James would make sure he was charged with obstructing an investigation. No matter how rich his father was, or how much power he wielded in Whitehall.

chapter eighteen

GABRIELLA SAW Johnny McLad's face everywhere as she walked her rounds, staring out at her from every newsagent she passed.

She hoped DS Archer found someone who knew who he was.

It had been a week since she'd found his body.

It felt like a lifetime ago.

She turned reluctantly onto Clematis Lane. There was no one parked in front of the gallery, but even so, she slowed as she approached it, nervous of crossing in front of the narrow alley between the gift shop and The Cat's Meow. The boutique had been closed since Patty died, and Gabriella wondered if she had been the only member of staff.

She had just passed the gallery's closed door, when the woman who she'd seen outside the gift shop before, studying the front window display, came flying out and almost fell down the few steps that led up to her shop.

"They're killing each other." She grabbed Gabriella's hand. "I'm so glad to find a uniformed officer. You have to help."

"I'm not the police," Gabriella said, although she'd had been mistaken for a copper more than once. "Who's killing who?"

She regretted asking the moment the words were out of her mouth.

"Mr. Fischer and Lenny are killing each other. I can hear them!"

The woman hadn't let go of Gabriella, and she tried to drag her up the stairs into the shop. After a moment's resistance, Gabriella allowed herself to be dragged.

She couldn't leave this woman in this state, even if she had no official standing.

As soon as they were inside the shop, Gabriella could hear it, too. Shouting, thumping, things breaking.

"Do you have a telephone?" Gabriella looked around for one, and the woman nodded, her head like a bobble doll, as if she couldn't stop.

"Behind the counter."

Gabriella pulled out DS Archer's card and rang the number. She left a message, because he wasn't at New Scotland Yard, but she did ask for some bobbies to be sent round, as quickly as possible.

From behind the thin wall at the back of the shop, someone gave a high-pitched scream of pain, and the woman put her hands over her ears. "Make them stop."

"Wait outside on the steps for the police. I'll go around the back." She wasn't sure if the woman even heard her, but when she made for the door, she heard her shuffling after her, so hopefully she had.

She felt a quick, hard thump in her chest and her breathing hitched as soon as she stepped into the alley.

There were still blood stains on the ground where Patty had lain, and she tried not to look at them as she hurried past. The alley ended in a tight back street with a dead end that she'd never been down before, although she'd noticed it on her rounds when she turned left out of Clematis Lane.

The powder blue Ford Prefect that had been parked in the loading zone the other day was now parked right near a door that seemed to go into the gallery's back entrance. It was blocking a black car parked a little further along.

The back door was slightly ajar, and Gabriella approached it cautiously.

While she'd been running down the alley, the screaming had stopped, but it had been replaced by quick, shallow breathing, and the sound of someone moving around, their steps crunching on what was surely broken glass.

She pushed the door open a little way and peered inside, wishing she had a weapon to protect herself. What she found was a small antechamber, with canvases stacked against a wall, and a table with some oil paints and an open bottle of turpentine standing on it.

She moved through to the next door, and what she saw inside had her momentarily astonished.

It looked like a laboratory. Long, wooden trestle tables with glass jars and bunsen burners were set out in parallel, and it smelled strange. A man walked through them, shoving equipment onto the floor as he went.

A whimper of sound and a rocking motion caught her attention and she saw a second man in a white coat, curled up on his side next to one of the tables. He was pressing a hand to his shoulder, which was bleeding through the fabric. He glanced up as she moved into the doorway, and gave a groan at the sight of her.

The other man turned at the noise. When he faced her, she saw it was the driver of the blue Ford, the delivery man who'd spoken to Patty that day with Mr. Devenish.

"Shit," he said.

"You must save me," the man on the floor panted out, in a thick accent. "He's trying to kill me."

"This isn't your business," the Ford driver said. "You're the traffic department, aren't you? What are you even doing here?"

Before she could answer that, she heard someone coming from behind her, and turned in alarm.

The sight of the tall bobby from the other day had her blowing out a breath in relief. She remembered DS Archer had called him PC Longmore.

"All right?" he asked.

She gave a quick nod. "He isn't, though." She tilted her head to the man on the floor. She switched her attention to the driver, who had gone still at the sight of the constable. "And that man is someone I think DS Archer would like to speak to."

"Is that so?" Longmore shot her a quick look of surprise. He gave the whole scene a quick look-over. "You'll have to go back round to the shop and call for an ambulance and more support for me."

Gabriella guessed from this that he'd come on his own, and he could hardly leave. The Ford driver would be out like a shot and gone as soon as the way was clear—it was in every line of his body.

She murmured her agreement and backed out, happy to be free of the strange smell and the stranger atmosphere. She jogged back down the alley to Clematis Lane, and found the gift shop owner sitting on the steps with her hands over her ears.

Gabriella stepped around her, deciding asking permission to use the phone would be a waste of time. She made the calls, and was assured some of Longmore's colleagues were already on the way.

She looked through the cupboard under the counter, found a small first aid kit, and took it with her when she went back to let Longmore know what was going on.

"I know first aid," she said, holding up the kit. "I can make a start on him before the ambulance gets here."

Longmore seemed happy for her to take the initiative, and she crouched beside the man in the white coat, careful to avoid the broken glass. "Can you take your coat off?" she asked him.

He struggled up, leaning against a table leg, and she helped him ease it off his shoulder and get his shirt unbuttoned so they could do the same with his shirt.

She was busy cleaning the jagged cut with some antiseptic wipes when a few more bobbies arrived, along with two medics.

They carried the man off, giving her a friendly nod of thanks for her efforts.

All the while, the Ford driver fumed at the far end of the room, arms crossed over his chest, refusing to come closer and be put under arrest.

Gabriella repacked the first aid kit. There was blood on her hands, but she'd been careful not to get it on her uniform. She eased past the policemen crowding the small antechamber. "I'll go return the kit and wash my hands in the shop, then I'll be off."

Longmore looked less than enthusiastic about that idea.

"DS Archer knows where to find me. I have to get on with my rounds. And you really got here just after me."

After a moment, he gave a nod of agreement and Gabriella slipped out from under the curious eyes of the other bobbies.

She washed up in the gift shop's tiny kitchenette and once again stepped around the gift shop owner sitting on the stairs, when DS Archer and DC Hartridge pulled up in the loading zone with a screech of brakes.

"Miss Farnsworth?" DS Archer called as he closed his door.

"It'll all over," she said, then couldn't help a quick grin. "Bar the shouting."

"Shouting," the woman on the steps said. "Lots of shouting."

"Did you hear what the shouting was about, Mrs. Pinter?" Archer asked.

"Some." Mrs. Pinter lifted her head. "About Patty. Lenny accused Mr. Fischer of killing Patty."

"And what did Mr. Fischer say about that?" DS Archer's voice was calm, although Gabriella could see the gleam in his eye.

"He said it was Lenny who had killed her, by being too cocky, and he needed to direct his anger at himself."

DS Archer turned to her. "What can you tell me, Miss Farnsworth?"

"PC Longmore and some other officers are arresting Lenny at the back, and the ambulance took Mr. Fischer off to hospital. Lenny stabbed him in the shoulder with a broken laboratory flask." Gabriella thought about it, then raised a shoulder. "Or, that's what it looked like." She hitched her satchel up higher on her shoulder. "I'm off on my rounds."

"Wait." DS Archer frowned. "How are you involved?"

"Mrs. Pinter grabbed me as I was passing. Fischer and Lenny were fighting in the room that runs along the back of her shop. She begged me to help, so I called you at the Yard, and when I couldn't get you there, I asked them to send some local bobbies for help, and I went round the back to see if I could do anything."

"And could you?" DC Hartridge asked when she paused.

She shot him a quick grin. "No. Fortunately PC Longmore arrived hot on my heels, and while he kept Lenny from trying to escape, I tried to do some first aid on Mr. Fischer until the ambulance arrived. Some more bobbies arrived to help get Lenny under control, and I left them to it."

"We'll need a statement," DS Archer said. "Can you come round to the Yard later?"

She gave a nod. "I'll come after my shift."

Just then, Longmore and his fellow bobbies emerged from the alley with Lenny between two of them.

He looked like he hadn't gone quietly.

"Well, I've got to be off. Cheers." Gabriella gave a wave and walked away. She decided it was the illegal parkers in Clematis Lane's lucky day, because she was moving on to the next section of her rounds.

They could park wherever they liked.

chapter nineteen

JAMES LEANED back in the uncomfortable wooden chair in the interview room, eyeing Lenny Foster as if he had all day. "So, when you accused Mr. Fischer of killing Patty, what did you mean by that?"

Lenny sniffed, rubbed his nose, then sipped at the cup of tea Hartridge had brought him, playing for time.

James gave him a slow smile. "And when Mr. Fischer said it was you who was responsible for her murder, what did *he* mean?"

Lenny sloshed a bit of tea over the rim. "I'm *not* responsible." He bared his teeth. "I suppose Fischer isn't, either. It was bloody Devenish. I told him that ignoring the warning Sam got was a mistake, given how badly that had ended for him, but Devenish wouldn't listen."

"What warning?" James didn't ask who Sam was, or his full name. He'd let Lenny talk first.

"Sam'd been warned off of the Chelsea clubs, but he had so many customers lined up, he couldn't turn the business down. And Devenish gets seventy percent, so Mr. High-and-Mighty wasn't going to put the brakes on that, was he?" Lenny shook his head in disgust.

"Warned off by who?"

Lenny lifted a shoulder. "Never saw them. Only Sam did.

Couple'o thugs selling heroin. Their boss didn't like us muscling in on his territory, even though we were selling something completely different. Didn't matter to them, 'cause most people only have enough money for one type of high."

"And what type of high are you selling?" Hartridge asked, pencil poised over his notebook.

"A perfectly legal one," Lenny sneered at them. "It's called LSD. It's used to treat psychiatric illness in micro doses."

"And Mr. Fischer is making it in that makeshift lab behind the gallery?" James asked. "And not administering it in micro doses, I'm guessing?"

"Devenish set it up. Fischer used to work for the Swiss company that held the patent, but they let the patent lapse earlier this year. It's perfectly legal to manufacture it." Lenny leaned back, suddenly smug.

"We'll look into that," James said. "Why did you choose today to attack Fischer? What was behind that?"

Lenny tapped the table with his fingertips, then sighed. "Devenish has stopped taking my calls since after Patty's body was found. I can't get hold of him, so I went round to the lab to see if I could find him or Fischer."

"And?"

"Fischer was there, in a panic, because Devenish was ignoring him, too. And I got into it with him. Though, God knows, he's right about there being plenty of blame to go 'round."

That sounded like the first sensible thing he'd said. "And what do you know about Sam? What's his full name?"

"Sam Nealy. Sam was a bastard. Seriously, he managed to get up the nose of everyone he ever met." Lenny worried his lip. "He'd come and pick up his supplies in the evening from Fischer, then I'd drive him to the clubs so he didn't have to find parking."

"What does LSD look like?" Hartridge asked. "Is it injected?"

"That's the beauty of LSD," Lenny said with a smirk. "One dose is about a quarter of the size of a stamp."

James had noticed the sheets of tiny, serrated squares when

he'd gone in to look around the laboratory. Each one had had the image of a rainbow on them. "The rainbow stickers are the product?" He had never heard of such a thing.

Lenny shrugged. "I don't know the technicalities of how Fischer does it, but yes, the punters are paying a pound for one tiny little square."

"And they what? Eat it?" Hartridge asked, frowning.

"They put it on their tongue, and then they fly." Lenny smiled.

"You partaking of your own product, Lenny?" James asked.

He flicked a dismissive hand. "I've taken it a time or two. But it's not like heroin. You don't get withdrawals. It's not addictive like that."

James would have to leave this new drug to the clubs and vice unit to sort out. He was interested in the murders.

"Back to Sam Nealy. Is he the man we found dead in the car?"

Lenny gave a nod.

"What do you know about that?"

"The night before he was found, the Tuesday? It was just a regular night. Always a little quiet on Tuesdays, but I took him out to do his usual rounds at the clubs."

"You'd drop him off afterward at his car?" James asked.

"Yeah. He usually parked in the back laneway, but a few times, Mr. Fischer needed to get out and Sam had parked him in, so Devenish told him to park in front of the gallery." Lenny lifted a shoulder. "I dropped him off at about half three that Wednesday morning. That was early. Too early for Devenish to be there. But some nights, we'd only finish around six or seven the next morning, and Devenish would be waiting for Sam, to divvy up the proceeds, like. Didn't trust Sam to have them on him any longer than he had to, the greedy bastard."

And after he'd spent some time counting his money on those mornings, Sam Nealy would come out and have a bit of argy bargy with Gabriella Farnsworth, James guessed.

"And he didn't seem worried that night? Nothing happened to make him nervous?" Hartridge asked.

"Not that night. It was business as usual. I hang around in the car near the club he's working, so he can just come out and hop in. Better'n a taxi, in case anything dicey goes down, you know? Sometimes the bouncers don't like us there, and he'd have to leave quick smart."

"But you said he'd been warned off. When was that?"

"The Saturday before he was done in. He told Devenish on Sunday and Little Lord Fauntleroy asked if the bloke was in a gang or something, but Sam didn't know. So Devenish told him to tell the next heavy who harassed him to tell his boss to talk direct to him."

There was more than a little edge to Lenny and Devenish's relationship, it seemed. Given James had also found Devenish to be condescending and too posh by half, he could see where Lenny's resentment was coming from.

"And this was three days before he was found dead?" James tried to remember Devenish's demeanor that first day he'd been questioned. He'd been jumpy, but otherwise calm.

"Yeah, but we didn't really put it together. Not right away. There were too many rozzers about, poking your noses in our business, and so we took a break for a couple of days."

"Then you started up again," James guessed.

Lenny shrugged. "Saturday's our busiest night. Patty saw Mr. Fischer driving to the gallery down the back alleyway, and she came out to give Devenish a piece of her mind. She thought Sam was killed because of the drugs, and here we were, still going about business as usual."

"She knew what you were up to?" James wished she had said something the day he'd interviewed her.

Lenny fidgeted. "She'd seen Sam in the clubs way back when we started selling the stuff, when she was out dancing with her mates, yeah? She recognized him because he'd come down the back lane while she was tidying up after closing the shop. She worked out quick enough he was selling drugs, and that they were being supplied from the gallery. Devenish sent me over to make sure she wouldn't blab, see?"

"When was this?" James asked.

"Months ago. Months and months." Lenny's head came forward, and he rubbed a hand over his forehead. "She was a ripper, Patty. Beautiful. Smart. Had a lot of go, that girl."

"And now she's dead."

Lenny lifted his head, his eyes burning in rage. "No need to remind me, copper. I know."

"I stood over her body," James enunciated every word. "I looked at her hands, bitten by rats. I told her parents the bad news while her mother wept and her father paced the floor, not knowing what to do with himself."

Lenny's mouth gaped open.

"So don't make out you're the victim here. Patty is. And I want to know why, and who did it."

For the first time, Lenny looked sick. "It was that same bastard what did for Sam. Like I said, Patty saw Fischer driving down the back lane, then saw me bringing in the supplies Fischer needs to make the stuff, and she worked out we were back to selling again. I'd already told her about Sam getting threats, and she worked out I was going to be going out—taking Sam's place. I knew the clubs he went to. I knew the lay of the land. So she tried to get us to stop. Told us to go to you lot with what we knew. But Devenish . . ." He paused, took a deep breath. "Devenish and me, we persuaded her it would be fine."

"So why was she killed, and not you?" Hartridge asked.

"I don't know." Lenny started crying, great sobs as he bowed his head. "I really don't know."

"She was last seen getting into a van outside Dance-A-Go-Go. Did you see her there?" James watched him carefully as he asked the question.

"Yeah, I was there. She told me off." Lenny's voice was hoarse with tears. "She told me I was playing with fire, selling in the same club where Sam was threatened."

"Dance-A-Go-Go was where Sam was warned off?" Well, that was a valuable piece of information.

Lenny nodded. "But no one came near me that night—at any of the clubs. I told Patty she was worrying for nothing. I told her to go home and stop fretting." He looked up with red eyes. "I could have given her a lift home, but I wanted to sell more stuff, to make up for the two days we'd paused things." He stared down into his cold cup of tea. "She only went to Dance-A-Go-Go to try to stop me. And instead, someone stopped *her*."

chapter twenty

GABRIELLA STARED after DC Hartridge in dismay.

He'd rushed off to make her a cup of tea she didn't want, and she suspected it was to keep her in DS Archer's office when she really just wanted to leave.

She fiddled with the statement she'd brought with her, having typed it up in the Kensington and Chelsea Traffic Warden Centre after work. Hartridge had looked extremely pleased to see it was already typed up, but that hadn't stopped him from trying to keep her at New Scotland Yard.

He took a long time to come back, so she started reading the front labels of the files on Archer's desk, none of which were open, unfortunately for her curiosity.

"Miss Farnsworth." Archer's surprised voice from the doorway gave her a guilty start.

"Mr. Archer." She got to her feet and held out her statement to him. "I typed it up at the office for you."

He took it, glancing down to read it as he moved around to sit at his desk. The late afternoon light coming from the window behind him illuminated the dark blond of his hair, and cast interesting shadows under his cheekbones.

She'd slid back into her chair while he read, and she waited there, perched on the edge of her seat until he looked up again.

"Thank you, this is very comprehensive."

She stood again, and he stood with her. "Have a good evening, Mr. Archer."

"James," he said.

She paused. "Better not, surely?"

Before he could answer, Hartridge appeared in the doorway, holding a mug of tea. "Here you go," he said to her, holding it out.

"Thank you." She looked down at the dark brown liquid, and tried not to grimace. "I should be going. Maybe you could have it," she said to Archer hopefully, and put it down on the desk.

"Of course." He looked amused.

"Will Mr. Fischer be all right?" she asked after an awkward pause.

"We're going to the hospital to interview him now. The doctors wouldn't have given the go ahead for an interview unless he was doing well." Archer moved around his desk and picked up his coat. "Why don't I walk you out? I'll meet you at the car, Hartridge."

The constable backed out into the corridor. "Good evening, Miss Farnsworth." He gave a little salute as he disappeared off down the passageway.

They walked down the stairs side by side, and when Gabriella glanced over at him, she realized he was watching her with a hooded expression.

"What impression did you get of Lenny when you stepped into that lab?" he asked.

"He was dismayed to see me. It was like he hadn't expected anyone to come in response to the shouting and smashing." She shrugged. "That seemed pretty short-sighted to me, like he was acting purely on emotion, smashing things up like a child."

"He claims to be upset about Patty."

"Then he should have kept her safe," Gabriella said. "I'm guessing she didn't have a thing to do with that lab, but she's the one who ended up dead in the alley. Not him. Or Fischer. Or Devenish."

"Lenny says the first victim, Sam, was approached in Dance-A-Go-Go and warned off selling the drugs he and Devenish were peddling. It might be the same person was watching Patty and Lenny the night she died, and got the wrong end of the stick and assumed she was involved. Have you ever seen anyone acting suspicious there?"

Gabriella shook her head. "It was my first time there." But Melvin would know. She could ask Solomon about it.

"I don't have the right to tell you where to go, but I'd avoid Dance-A-Go-Go until this is sorted." Archer held the door into the reception area open for her.

She stopped in the doorway, so close to him she could see the gold flecks in his gray eyes. "I appreciate the advice."

He blinked slowly, and she felt a flush rise up from her chest to burn her cheeks.

She forced herself through the door.

He stepped close to her as she walked out of the building, his shoulder rubbing hers as they squeezed past people coming the other way.

"If you see anyone following you again, or even catch sight of a white van, call me." He took her hand as if to shake it, but they both knew that wasn't what he was doing.

She gave a nod, gently pulled her hand free and, seeing the bus pull in, ran toward it with a backward wave.

By the time she sat down on the upper deck, Archer was gone.

She flexed her hand, staring down at it.

That seemed to escalate quickly, but really, it had been on a slow boil since the first day she'd sat in his office.

She leaned her forehead against the window, desperate for a bit of cool, and kept her eyes peeled for a white van.

She saw a few, but the modifications on them ruled them out. When the bus lumbered up to her usual stop, though, she stayed where she was and let it take her deeper into Notting Hill. She didn't feel like going home and making herself dinner, and she wanted to speak to Solomon about the club.

She got off a street away from the Calypso Club and enjoyed the walk there. The air was cooler, the sky a delightful red and orange.

There were plenty of times she missed the weather and the familiarity of home, but sometimes she was gripped by a thrill at being in such a bustling, cosmopolitan place, and was glad her hunt for her father had led her here.

The calypso band was in full swing when she pushed through the door, and Jerome was sitting behind the desk.

"Gabriella." He pronounced it like Solomon, in the same friendly, slightly amused tone.

Gabriella wondered what they found so funny about her or her name, but she had never detected any malice or ill will with it, so she had decided to take it as a sign of acceptance.

"I'm here for dinner, and to talk to Solomon, if he's here." She pulled out her purse and found the right amount to hand over.

Jerome took it and wrote her name carefully in the book. "Mr. Rodney's here, and Solomon might be round later."

Jerome would tell him she was looking for him, Gabriella guessed, so she murmured her thanks and went to find Mr. Rodney.

Catherine was sitting with him, and when he saw her, he waved her over enthusiastically.

"You came." Mr. Rodney beamed as he patted the chair next to him.

"I came." She smiled at both of them as she sat down. "Catherine." She was still struck at the outrageous beauty of the woman.

Catherine inclined her head regally. Rather than looking ridiculous, the movement suited her.

"Catherine has just finished her course today. We're celebrating," Mr. Rodney told her.

"Congratulations," Gabriella said. "What course?"

"Secretarial," Catherine said. "Now I can help Solomon run his business."

"I thought Solomon worked for British Transport?" Gabriella said. Although, in truth, she knew that's the impression he wanted her to have, without ever actually saying that's what he did.

"Oh, he does." Mr. Rodney sounded so proud. "But he started importing things from home, for the community. It's making enough now that he can hire Catherine to run things from a small office. Maybe, if it really takes off, he can leave BT and become an entrepreneur."

Oh, he was already an entrepreneur. She and Catherine exchanged a look, and after a moment of tension, Catherine sent her a wide smile.

She had passed some new test, Gabriella guessed.

They ate their dinner companionably, but by the time Mr. Rodney was ready to go home, Solomon had not put in an appearance.

Catherine bid them good night and went back into the kitchens to help her mother and the other women who ran the club with the clean up, and Gabriella and Mr. Rodney set off home.

They were still on Parade Street, only ten houses away from the Calypso Club, when the attack happened.

A man came out of the narrow space between two old Victorians. He was all in black, with a black cap and a black face covering, and Gabriella just caught the flash of his blade under the weak street light before he darted forward and struck out at Mr. Rodney, who always insisted on being a gentleman and walking closest to the road.

Mr. Rodney gave a soft cry, and Gabriella found her voice had frozen. She couldn't find a scream inside her.

Instead, to compensate, she attacked, shoving the man as hard as she could.

He obviously didn't expect it and staggered back, while Gabriella heard Mr. Rodney collapse to the ground behind her.

She needed to scream. There were always a few boys hanging around outside the club, and they'd come running. She needed her throat to work.

The attacker got his balance back and swore softly, squaring up to her again.

"Run, Gabby." Mr. Rodney's voice was breathless.

She would not be running. "So brave," she managed to hiss, pleased that she could actually make a sound. "Attacking an old man. What a hero."

The words seemed to genuinely throw him. He hesitated, and in that moment, she finally managed to find a scream, and as she did, she shoved him again.

Help came, but not from the direction of the club, as she'd expected.

Beyond the attacker, down the street, she saw Solomon, Melvin, and a third man, and they were running, the silent, focused run of men who weren't scared to mix it up.

Something about the focus of her gaze made the attacker glance back.

"Fuck me." He darted into the street, around Mr. Rodney, and ran away, in the direction of the club.

Solomon shouted something, Gabriella guessed an order for the boys outside the club to stop him, but she didn't really listen, she had turned and was kneeling beside Mr. Rodney.

"Where?" she asked him.

He was lying fully down on the pavement now. His hand lifted weakly, touched his side.

"Call an ambulance," she ordered the men as they reached her. "I'd say move him to the club, but I don't think that's wise." She looked up at Solomon, who was staring at his uncle with wide eyes. "If there's a first aid kit in the club, bring it to me."

Solomon flicked a hand, and Melvin and the other man ran off.

"Did he get away?" Mr. Rodney asked Solomon, trying to sound like he was fine.

"The boys didn't understand me until it was too late." Solomon sounded so reasonable, Gabriella looked up, then looked away, fast.

He was enraged.

She went to work removing Mr. Rodney's jacket, and when Solomon realized what she was doing, he crouched down beside her and helped. When she pulled the white, starched shirt up, they both drew in a breath at the cut across his abdomen.

The other man, not Melvin, arrived with the first aid kit.

Suddenly realizing the police would most likely get involved, now that the ambulance was coming, Gabriella lifted her gaze to Solomon. "Melvin wasn't here," she said.

He tilted his head. "He wasn't?"

"No." She didn't want to explain anymore than that here on the street. And not in front of Mr. Rodney.

"All right. He wasn't." Solomon glanced at the man next to him.

"Was just you and me, boss," the man said.

"George, meet Gabriella, my uncle's neighbor. "Gabriella, George."

"I can honestly say it is extremely good to meet you, George," Gabriella said, using the iodine swabs in the first aid kit on Mr. Rodney's cut.

She caught George's quick grin.

"How you holding up there, Mr. Rodney?" George asked, helping Solomon as they rolled their jackets up to use as a pillow for his head.

The ambulance arrived quickly, lights and sirens blaring, and the medics loaded Mr. Rodney up on a stretcher and left for the hospital right away.

It was a sober statement on how bad his injury was.

They even let Solomon go along with to the hospital, when he explained he was Mr. Rodney's family.

Gabriella packed up the first aid kit and began walking back to the club to return it.

George walked beside her. Maybe Solomon had told him to keep an eye on her. "You know who that was who attacked you?"

She shook her head. "I couldn't see his face. But I have some ideas about why he did it."

"And one of those ideas means Melvin might come to the attention of the coppers if they knew he was mixed up in what happened tonight?"

Gabriella nodded.

He said nothing more, but when Melvin appeared at the top of the club's steps, he motioned him down.

"Scarper before the coppers get here. You weren't here, right."

"Right." Melvin was quick on the uptake. He nodded to Gabriella.

"Thanks for the rescue, Melvin," she said. "Things were getting dicey."

He just grinned at her, and then he was gone, melting into the darkness.

Catherine stepped out and ran down the steps, and Gabriella handed her the first aid kit. "Solomon went with Mr. Rodney to the hospital."

"Someone stabbed him, Mel said?"

Gabriella nodded.

"Did you see who?"

"It was dark, he was masked up, and it happened quickly. Lucky the boys were coming up the road at the right time."

"You go to Sol at the hospital, Cat. I'll sort things here." George patted her shoulder awkwardly.

She gave a nod and ran back up the stairs.

As she disappeared inside, the police arrived.

Two bobbies on foot, and a car.

She saw the bobbies gazes flick over the tight group of boys outside the club, then George, then herself.

“I’m one of the people who was attacked,” she said, to get their attention fully on her.

“How many people were attacked?” one of the officers who’d arrived by car asked.

“Just me and Mr. Rodney. The ambulance took Mr. Rodney away. The attacker stabbed him.”

“Just the one person attacked you?” The officer had come around the car, standing closer to her, which was better than the distance he’d had before. He looked as if he expected trouble.

The Notting Hill Race Riots were still very fresh in everyone’s memories, even five years on. Gabriella hadn’t been in London then, but Mr. Rodney had spoken about them a time or two.

No one wanted a repeat.

“Yes. It was dark and I didn’t see his face. The lads might have gotten a better look as he ran past them.” She looked over her shoulder at the group of sixteen year olds who often hung out on the steps, chatting and joking.

“Did you?” the officer asked them.

“White bloke. Wearing black. That’s all I got,” one of the boys said. “He ran over to the pavement on other side of the street, and the cars parked that side were blocking him a bit. But he was wearing a mask or sommat, anyway.”

The other boys had similar things to say.

“Where did the attack occur?” One of the bobbies had also come closer, and looked more relaxed.

She showed them, walking them back down to the scene, and George came with her.

“What’s your role in this?” the officer asked him.

“George and Solomon were coming up the street toward us,” Gabriella said. “They saw what was happening and came running, and the bloke got wind of them and ran.”

“Solomon?” the bobby asked, notebook out.

“Mr. Rodney’s nephew. He went with him in the ambulance to the hospital.”

“Ah.” The last of the tension seemed to leave the officer, who introduced himself as PS Yates. "And do you know any reason why someone would attack you or Mr. Rodney?"

Gabriella paused, and Yates's eyes came up suddenly, sharp and hard.

"You do."

She lifted a shoulder. "I don't want to think it, but I'm a traffic warden, and I found the girl stabbed the other day in the alley, and since then, I think someone's been following me. I told DS Archer about it." She fished in her handbag, pulled out his card and held it out.

Once again, she had the feeling she'd completely surprised Yates. Whatever he thought she was going to say, this wasn't it.

"Right." He took the card, studied it, and handed it back.

She almost told him that if he hurried to interview Mr. Rodney, he might be able to catch DS Archer at the hospital as well, as he'd be there, interviewing Mr. Fischer. But that felt too convoluted. Like she was way too involved.

Which she was, but that wasn't PS Yates's business.

He would probably disagree.

"You've got a way to get home safely?" Yates asked.

"I'll walk her home." George hadn't said a thing until now, other than to give his name to the bobby, and he sounded amused.

When they left, she stood in a pool of shadow beside him, watching them go.

"What was so funny?" she asked.

"You," he told her. "From da way you coaxed them into relaxing in front of da big, bad, black men, to throwing all der ideas of you and Mr. Rodney stepping out together and being attacked for it out da window. I could barely keep a straight face, me."

Oh.

She started to giggle, especially at the exaggerated island accent he'd put on, and he joined her with a deeper chuckle.

"Mr. Rodney," she said, to get them serious again. "Is there a phone in the club so I can call a taxi to take me to the hospital?"

“I’d wait until tomorrow,” George told her, putting out an arm for her to slip her hand through. “Won’t be any way he could have visitors tonight, other than Solomon.”

He was right, so she took the offered arm, and let him walk her home.

Hopefully tomorrow would be less exciting.

chapter twenty-one

"DS ARCHER?"

James was just leaving the hospital, and he and Hartridge stopped at the sight of the uniformed officer hailing them.

He recognized PS Yates from the Notting Hill nick. "Yates."

"Just had a stabbing on my patch," Yates said. "A Gabriella Farnsworth—"

James was aware of a sudden drop in temperature, a sudden roaring in his ears. "Miss Farnsworth was stabbed?" He would never know how his voice came out as calmly as it did.

"Not a scratch on her. Her companion, Mr. Rodney, he's the one got hurt. Attacker ran off when he was interrupted."

The tight grip the air seemed to have on him suddenly loosened.

"Did she see who it was?" Hartridge sounded excited.

Yates was shaking his head. "He chose a really dark spot, and he wore a mask and knitted cap. I reckon he knew what he was about. She said it might be related to that Chelsea case . . .?" Yates looked a little uncertain, as if he didn't know whether to believe what she had told him.

"Yes." James sounded grim. "She's been followed. We think the man who stabbed two people over the last week and a half is nervous she saw him."

"Hell." Yates winced. "Lucky for her two blokes came along and stopped him. Sounds like he took one look at them and legged it."

"You here to interview her friend who was stabbed?" Hartridge asked.

James was relieved one of them was thinking, because he would have let Yates go in, his only thought to go straight to Gabriella.

"You want to come with me?" Yates asked.

"If he got a good look, that would be one of our best leads," James admitted.

He turned on his heel and followed Yates in.

A tall black man with dreadlocks and very sharp clothes was leaning against the wall in the corridor outside the victim's door, eyes closed, arms and legs crossed.

"Excuse me," Yates asked, looking down at his notebook. "Are you Solomon Harriot?"

Harriot opened his eyes slowly, although if James were to guess, there was nothing relaxed about him.

"I am."

"Police Sergeant Yates." Yates held out a hand, and Solomon straightened up and shook it. "How is your uncle?"

"The doctor's in with him. They patched him up. The knife didn't go too deep, but he'll have a scar." Solomon was taking them all in. "Did you speak to Gabriella?"

"I did." Yates looked down at his notes again. "Can you tell me what you saw, sir?"

"Me'n George were walking toward the club, and we saw a scuffle up ahead, and then there was Gabriella, shoving some bloke away from my uncle, who was lying on the ground." He looked across at James. "There was no shouting, you know? That was the strange part of it. And then suddenly she was shouting at him, and he sort of froze a minute, like he couldn't believe it. Then she saw us and he took one look behind him and scarpered."

"Did you get a good look at his face?" Hartridge asked.

Solomon shook his head. "I didn't. I asked my uncle if he did, but it was a really dark bit of street, you know, and he covered his mouth and nose. Bastard planned exactly where he was going to jump out."

Yates nodded. "Miss Farnsworth and your friend, Mr. Mohan, showed me where it happened. He chose the darkest stretch of road."

While they were standing there, a doctor emerged from the room, and noting Yates's uniform, started shaking his head. "Mr. Rodney is asleep. I've sedated him. He may be pretty fit for someone in his mid 70s, but you'll have to come back tomorrow morning if you want to speak to him."

They walked back out together, Solomon Harriot choosing to join them as the doctor didn't want him there, either.

"Can we give you a lift home, Mr. Harriot?" James asked. He was curious to know where the Trinidadian lived. He wondered if he was Gabriella's upstairs neighbor.

"You going to the Gate?" Harriot asked.

"The Gate?" James had never heard of that.

"What we call Notting Hill," Harriot said.

We being those who originally hailed from Trinidad and Tobago, James guessed.

"Then yes. I'd like to speak to Miss Farnsworth while the incident is fresh in her mind."

That was the truth, but he'd have gone, anyway.

Harriot accepted the offer, and they dropped him off three streets away from Gabriella's house, in front of a small, single family dwelling. A woman came out while he was getting out the car, as if she'd been watching from the front window, and pulled him into a tight embrace when he reached her.

When James pulled up outside the old converted Victorian, he looked up and saw the light was still on on the top floor.

He suddenly wished he'd made an excuse to lose Hartridge, somehow.

He climbed out slowly, aware it had been a hell of a day, and decided having Hartridge as a chaperone was probably not a bad thing.

"You been here before?" Hartridge asked.

James nodded. "Once, after she found Patty Little's body." He didn't elaborate, and led the way inside. It worried him that the front door was on the latch, and he turned the lock behind them before heading up the stairs.

He knocked softly on Gabriella's door, aware she might be jumpy after the attack.

"Who's there?" she called, and he didn't like the tremble in her voice.

"It's DS Archer and DC Hartridge." He felt she deserved fair warning he wasn't on his own like last time.

There was a moment of silence. "One moment."

He heard her walk away, and a few minutes later she opened up, clearly having changed out of her pajamas into a pair of jeans and a t-shirt. She looked rumpled and a little grumpy.

He forced himself not to look at her mouth.

"Sorry to disturb you, Miss Farnsworth," he said. For the first time since he'd bumped into Yates he looked at his watch and winced. "I didn't realize the time. But do you mind if we come in and ask a few questions?"

She drew back from the door without a word, walked over to her little round table and sat down. "Did you see Mr. Rodney? Is he all right?"

"The doctor says he's in good shape, and his nephew says there'll be a scar, but no other damage."

She bowed her head, and when she looked up, her eyes glistened. "That he got hurt at all, because of me—"

"Not because of you." James made his voice very firm. "We don't know for sure why you were attacked, but if it's to do with Patty and Sam, then it's because of Devenish and Lenny and whoever is doing this. Not you."

She drew in a deep breath. Gave a nod.

"So what can you tell me?" James sat down, leaving Hartridge to stand behind him and take notes.

"I couldn't see his face. He had on a knit cap, black clothes, and a scarf tied over his mouth. I was looking more at the knife, anyway. He was taller than me, but not extremely tall. George and Solomon," she flicked a look across the table at him, "and you, would tower over him."

"Could he have been the man who tried to pick you up in the van?" James asked.

She gave a slow nod. "He could be, but I couldn't say for sure."

"Did he say anything? Have any accent?"

She shook her head. "All he said was . . ." She glanced at him and blushed. "He swore and ran off when he saw George and Solomon." She sniffed. "I called him a coward. That threw him."

James was pleased to hear the righteous indignation in her voice. It was better than the tears.

"I pushed him, too, to get him away from Mr. Rodney. He really didn't expect that. He sort of stopped, and though I couldn't see his face, I think he was shocked."

James could well believe that.

"Then Solomon and George were running toward us, and he did a bunk."

"Can you tell me what you did after you left the Yard?" James asked. "Do you think he might have followed you, or already knew where to find you?"

"Oh." She stared at him. "I hadn't even thought of that. I took the bus from the Yard straight to the club. I nearly got off at home, but they serve dinner at the club and I didn't feel like cooking. Mr. Rodney is a member, and I have a standing invitation to attend."

"Mr. Rodney is your neighbor," he guessed.

"He used to live opposite me," she said. "But he just moved downstairs to the ground floor. Sometimes Solomon comes over to take him to the club, but sometimes I take him, and we were just walking back home when we were attacked."

So he had either followed the bus from the Yard, or he was on the bus.

James guessed he was on the bus. Maybe he had followed her from work to the Yard, and waited for her to come out.

"He had to have been following the bus." Gabriella spoke slowly, her eyes wide as she looked over at him. "I did check, but I didn't see anything."

"He knows you're aware of the white van," James said. "He might have been in another car." He decided not to suggest the possibility that he had been in the bus with her.

She leaned back, face a little pale.

She looked ready to drop.

"We'll leave you to get some sleep," he said, scraping back his chair. "I'll get the local bobbies to swing past every hour to check on the house."

She nodded, but he didn't think she really heard him.

She followed him and Hartridge to the door.

"Why does he want to kill me?" she asked. "I haven't seen his face. I can't identify him. And even if I could, it would be to say he was driving a white van. That's all."

"He obviously thinks you know more than you do," James agreed.

They left her leaning against her doorjamb, and her question niggled at James. Because she was right. Why did their suspect see her as such a threat? Unless Gabriella knew something that she didn't realize was significant.

He looked forward to asking the bastard about it in an interview room down at the Yard.

chapter twenty-two

SHE HAD A NEW ROUND.

Mr. Greenberg had switched her route with Patrick Nelson's, no reason given, but everyone could guess. And she couldn't have been happier.

She was in south Kensington, in the side streets—a nice, quiet patch. And not a green jaguar in sight.

It wasn't that much different to her old route, if she was being honest, but a whole borough over, and with a slightly less well-heeled air, although not by much.

Usually, routes were changed every two months, and a change wasn't due for another three weeks, but Patrick Nelson hadn't seemed put out by it, and given he had full seniority, being a retired copper, and would have been able to refuse without any consequences, she guessed everyone was happy.

Maybe Mr. Nelson was looking forward to finding something to help DS Archer. Getting back in the game for a bit.

Gabriella was happy to leave him to it.

She had plans to visit Mr. Rodney in hospital later, and she wanted nothing more to do with the whole affair.

She moved through her assigned streets with relief, and was even amused when she found an abandoned car on the edge of a park with slashed tires.

She rounded the front, looking for any sign of a license registration on the dashboard, and a head popped up from the back.

It gave her a start.

"Where's Mr. Nelson?" the figure asked, voice gritty as a gravel road.

"Mr. Nelson is on a different round, now." Gabriella stepped closer, saw the person on the back seat had created a nest for themselves.

"Who're you?" The demand would have been rude, but Gabriella could hear a slight tremor in the rough voice.

It was a man, she finally worked out. A small, wizened man, wrapped up as if it was the depths of winter, although in fact it was a particularly nice late summer day.

As a nod to the weather, the windows of the car had been wound down, presumably to let a cross breeze through.

"Mr. Nelson lets me stay here."

Gabriella wondered if that was true.

As if seeing the skepticism on her face, he wriggled a bit closer to the window.

"'Til they come tow the car," he amended.

What harm was it doing? Gabriella gave a nod. "I'm Miss Farnsworth."

"Teddy Roe." Teddy extended a hand covered in a filthy mitten through the window.

Gabriella shook it gently, and she suddenly felt a lot more friendly toward Mr. Nelson. Not that she'd disliked him before, but he had seemed very stern and rigid to her.

That was obviously a front.

Mr. Nelson was marshmallow inside.

"Long as I don't cause no trouble, Mr. Nelson lets me stay," Teddy said, as if to make sure she understood.

"I'm happy to keep to that arrangement, Mr. Roe."

It seemed to take him a moment to get her meaning, and then he relaxed back on the seat in a way that almost broke Gabriella's heart.

"Well, good day to you, Mr. Roe." Gabriella moved on, noticing a curtain twitching in the house closest to the park.

Friend or foe, she wondered?

Probably a friend, as Mr. Roe wouldn't have lasted long if someone had made a formal complaint.

Given the car wasn't recently abandoned, and Teddy Roe's nest looked well established, she wondered if there wasn't a conspiracy of silence in reporting the vehicle.

She was surprised Mr. Nelson hadn't said anything to her, but then, given it was his duty to report the matter, what could he say without compromising himself, and probably her into the bargain?

By saying nothing, they could both claim to have thought the matter already reported.

Nelson had taken the chance she would make the same choice as he had. She found her liking for him increased yet again.

She finished her rounds without incident, and changed and left as soon as possible, heading for Notting Hill first, to visit the small little shop tucked up next to a haberdashery that sold groceries from Trinidad and Tobago.

As she stepped inside, she wondered suddenly if Solomon owned it, then dismissed the idea. If he did, Mr. Rodney would have as much of the special Trinidadian coffee he loved so much as he wanted, whereas he coveted it, and limited himself to one special cup a day.

Perhaps it was a foolish gift, as he couldn't have any in the hospital, but she hoped it was something for him to look forward to when he got out.

The hospital was cool inside, and she found Mr. Rodney sitting up in bed, talking to Catherine when she arrived.

"Gabby!" He almost jumped out of bed, and both she and Catherine leaped forward to stop him. "You're all right?" he asked, subsiding back against the pillows in the face of their alarm.

"I'm very sorry you were attacked, but he didn't lay a finger on me."

"I was telling Catherine how you pushed him, and called him a coward." Mr. Rodney patted Catherine's hand. "She went for him, like a tigress."

Gabriella studied him as she sat down on the only other chair left in the room. "You look pretty good for someone who was stabbed."

"Not stabbed so much as slashed," Mr. Rodney said. "Not nearly so dangerous and easily mended."

"That's good." She pulled out the coffee, and handed it to him as he crowed in delight.

When the nurse came to shoo her and Catherine out, she told them the doctor would probably discharge him by the end of the weekend.

"This your trouble following Mr. Rodney?" Catherine asked as they walked out together.

Gabriella looked over at her, lifted a shoulder and nodded at the same time. "I don't understand why, but probably."

"You don't understand why?" Catherine sounded surprised.

"If it's the man who killed those two people I found, I don't understand what the motivation is. I can't identify him."

"He maybe doesn't know that." Catherine sounded less edgy. "Or it might just be someone who doesn't like seeing a white girl walking with a black man."

"That's what George said the police thought, at first." She shook her head. "But there was none of the stupid name calling that usually goes with that. He came out fast and quiet, and he went straight for Mr. Rodney, like he was getting him out of the way before he focused on me."

"Why'd you make Melvin disappear?"

Again she lifted a shoulder. "Just being overly cautious. The man who probably killed those people might also be selling drugs at Dance-A-Go-Go. If the police got wind of where Melvin works . . ."

Catherine stopped and was staring at her. "Mel needs to know this."

"I know. Can you pass it on?"

They had reached the bus stop, and Catherine nodded, but given the number of people around them, they didn't discuss it further.

Later, Gabriella got comfortable on her window seat, legs extended out in front of her, coffee in hand, and looked out of the small, open window to the street below. Birds were raising a racket, settling into trees for the night, and the golden light of sunset washed over the old, slightly ramshackle houses, lending them a glamor they didn't usually have.

There were people walking on the pavement, but no one was behaving suspiciously, or appeared to be paying unusual attention to her house.

Some children played hop scotch a few houses up, but as she watched, their mother called them in for their dinner.

Tea, they called it here.

She forced herself to acknowledge that there could be someone, clever enough not to be obvious.

She'd been thinking a lot more clearly this afternoon than she had this morning. Since Catherine's pointed questions.

Even if her attacker didn't know exactly where she lived, he had a good idea of her general area. He'd followed her bus once, and while she'd lost him, she hadn't gotten off that far from home. The second time, he'd followed her right to the club. Which meant, for everyone's safety, she couldn't go back there until this was over.

Mr. Rodney was hurt because she hadn't understood how determined this man seemed to be to kill her.

She understood now.

chapter twenty-three

JAMES PULLED up outside Gabriella Farnsworth's house and leaned back against his seat.

He closed his eyes for a moment and let himself enjoy being still and relaxed.

It was Friday night. Theoretically he was off the clock until Monday, although that wasn't going to happen.

Since Lenny had given them Sam Nealy's name, they had found Nealy's basement flat in Holland Park, and searched it thoroughly.

His landlady, the house owner who lived above, hadn't even realized he was missing. Apparently she thought it was life as usual, him working nights and sleeping days.

She had not been pleased to discover police officers at her door. It seemed Nealy had given her the impression he was a security guard, and she had actually felt safe, knowing he was on the property.

Finding his next of kin was proving harder than it should have been, and Hartridge had spent a frustrating day trying to track down his mother, the only name on his birth certificate.

The clubs and vice unit had promised to get back with some names of heroin dealers who operated in the West End, but James had the distinct feeling they were being territorial.

He held the option of calling in DI Whetford in reserve. Whetford could be counted on to beat his chest and push his way in when it came to jurisdiction, and as long as he wasn't taking a backhander from this particular heroin dealer, James could use him as a threat.

A clatter of bin lids jerked him from his thoughts, and he opened his eyes.

A man of Caribbean heritage set a metal bin on the pavement, and disappeared around the side of Gabriella's house, then came back with a second one.

As he set it down next to the first, Gabriella came out of the front door and called a greeting to him, carrying what turned out to be a rubbish bag, to put in one of the bins.

They chatted for a moment and then Gabriella went back inside, and the man went to fetch another bin.

Above him, Gabriella's light winked out, and James forced himself to get out of the car.

He had come to check on her, and it looked as if she was about to leave.

He'd managed to find a parking spot close to her front door and he came round the front of the Wolseley in time to see Gabriella emerge onto the street.

She walked away from him, into the growing shadows of dusk, and as he was about to call to her, a man stepped out from the side of the house opposite hers and crossed the road just in front of James to follow her.

He was so focused on his prey, he hadn't noticed James. He never once look around or back.

James surged after him, quiet now, focused on every detail of the man in front of him.

He had a stocky build, so possibly not the same man who'd attacked Gabriella and Mr. Rodney the night before.

Gabriella had described her attacker as wiry.

Her follower was wearing a flat cap and dark clothes, and he moved confidently. He wasn't nervous about trailing a woman in the darkening streets.

James tried to catch a glimpse of his hands, and thought there might have been a knife in his right hand, but it was difficult to tell.

The man was gaining on Gabriella, but holding back a little. The street was busy, with plenty of people coming home from work in time for dinner, a few children still playing in the road, squeezing out every second of freedom before their mothers or fathers called them in.

He was looking for a quieter place to attack, James guessed.

He wouldn't get one.

And then, Gabriella stopped and stepped up to the edge of the pavement.

James had been concentrating so much on her and her follower, he was taken surprise by the sight of a bus coming down the street on the opposite side.

Gabriella looked left, then right, for traffic, and darted across the street, waving a hand to the bus driver.

The man following her seemed to be as thrown as James was, hesitating on the pavement as he watched her run for the bus.

Before he could follow her, a massive truck drove past, blocking the road, and forcing the man to take a step back.

When the truck had finally lumbered past, the bus had pulled off.

The man's body language said he had missed his chance, and he knew it.

James couldn't arrest him for walking the streets, but he could follow him, and see where he went to. He flicked a quick glance at the bus, shuddering and squealing off down the road, with satisfaction. Gabriella was out of harm's way, and his best lead since this all began stood right in front of him, completely unaware he was even there.

The man pulled out a cigarette as he watched the bus turn a

corner, lighting it and smoking for a moment, as if contemplating his next move.

Instead of turning back, he started walking down the pavement in the same direction as Gabriella had been going before she crossed the road. James kept up a leisurely stroll behind him, glad that at this hour, with so many people leaving work, it was easy to hide in the crowd.

Unlike before, when he'd been trailing Gabriella, his mark turned back a few times, but James didn't know if that was something he did as a precaution, or whether he'd sensed he was being followed.

The drag of the day seemed to evaporate as James kept him in sight, invigorated by the hunt.

And then the mark disappeared.

James knew he had been passing a pub, and he jogged to the entrance and stepped through.

There was his prey, ordering a pint at the bar.

Relaxing, James waited for him to find a seat, and then went to the bar to order a pint himself. While he waited to be served, he looked around the place, a long, casual sweep of his gaze.

There was a free table for two near the fire that had a good view of the booth his mark had slid into, and James headed there and sat with his back to the wall.

The pub was busy and getting busier, as more and more people poured in.

There were clearly groups of work colleagues coming in together, others coming in on their own for a quiet drink at the end of the day.

He wondered what his prey was doing here.

The man drank his pint as if there was no rush.

Eventually he finished his drink and strolled off to the back of the pub to the men's, and, swallowing down the last of his own drink, James sauntered after him.

When he got into the toilet, there was no one there, and

feeling a sudden frisson of panic, James ran out, just in time to hear the door to the back alley close.

Either he'd been spotted, or it was his mark taking precautions again.

He jogged to the back, pushing open the heavy door and stepping into a dark, narrow alley, with overflowing bins to the left.

He looked toward the high street, hoping to catch a glimpse of the man, and which way he went.

There was no sign of him.

"Damn."

A movement just behind him and to the left was all the warning he got before something smashed into his head.

"Looking for me, mate?"

The words seemed to be coming from a long way off, and then they shut off altogether.

chapter
twenty-four

GABRIELLA KNEW she was being followed almost right away.

The reflection of her pursuer was clear in the side mirrors of the cars she passed. Although nothing about the way he dressed and moved was familiar, and she didn't think it was the same man who'd attacked her the night before, he was following her, and she guessed that wasn't a coincidence.

She'd kept her pace steady, glad beyond anything there were so many people out and about. If she had left a little later to go visit Mr. Rodney in hospital, she'd have been much more vulnerable.

The bus that came down the street was the wrong one, but she sensed the man getting closer, moving in, and all it would take was a sudden lull in foot traffic, and he would have his chance.

But she also didn't want to lose him.

She wanted to turn the tables.

So far she had had things done to her.

That was no longer acceptable to her.

She'd darted across the street, waving to the bus, and then, seeing her chance, ducked behind a low brick gate that fronted a neat single story house.

She crouched behind it, pleased to find it had a built-in letter-box. She lifted the flap, looking through the narrow opening into the street, and saw her follower smoking as he looked after the bus.

Then he began to move off.

She'd waited a moment before following him, aware her movement across the road might attract his attention, and then she sucked in a shocked breath as she saw DS Archer casually stroll after him.

He must have been watching her house.

She vaguely remembered him saying something about extra patrols last night, but she hadn't thought he would be doing them himself.

As she jogged across the road and fell in behind the men, she kept further back than felt right, but she was unsure what to do now she knew Archer was on the case. He was the police, and she should probably leave the field of battle to him.

But she had been so invested in following her attacker, in turning the tables, she found it difficult to let go.

She was so far behind them, she almost missed seeing DS Archer go into the pub, and slowed down even more, guessing her attacker had gone in, too.

Both would recognize her immediately if she were to go in as well, so she hung around outside, pretending to be waiting for someone.

More than one man offered to buy her a drink while she waited, but she made the excuse she was waiting for a friend to fob them off with as little fuss as possible.

Whatever they were doing in there, it seemed to take a long time.

She was about to give up when she caught sight of Archer through the window, heading to the back of the pub.

She caught her lip with her teeth, wondering what to do, when she heard the slam of a door coming from the narrow alley to her right, around the side of the pub. She had checked it out earlier, while she waited, considering it as a hiding place if both men came out.

Not knowing what else to do, she moved toward it and peered around, just in time to see a shadowy figure hit James Archer in the back of the head with a plank of wood.

He went down silently, and the man loomed over him, staring down.

He murmured something to himself, and then stepped around the detective's body, heading straight for her.

Panicked, Gabriella pulled back and looked wildly for a place to hide, but the obvious answer was inside the pub. She darted through the doorway, standing just inside and watching at the door in case he'd seen her and was coming in after her.

She'd rather know if he was on to her immediately, but when the door opened, it was a couple, arm in arm, who stepped through, and beyond them, she saw no sign of the man.

She turned, finding the back passage she'd seen Archer take minutes before, and walked down it to the back entrance.

She stared at the metal door for a moment, getting up her nerve, then pushed through it.

Archer lay on the ground in front of her, very still, and for a terrible moment she wondered if he was dead.

She crouched beside him, feeling for a pulse, and let out a breath of relief when she found it, strong and steady beneath her fingertips.

She heard a car engine, as if a vehicle was reversing into the alley, and then footsteps. She wished it could be help, but she very much doubted it.

She scuttled to the bins, crouching low in the shadows.

"I don't like this. We were supposed to get the girl, not him. Just leave him here and call it a bust." The man who spoke sounded nervy.

"We need to know why he was following me. The boss will be interested." The man who spoke was James Archer's attacker.

"I don't like any of this. Not grabbing the girl, not strange men following us." The man came closer, though.

"We came out on top, didn't we?" Archer's attacker said. "Let's get him up and into the back of the van."

He's a big'un. It'll be difficult."

The men bent, hauling Archer up between them, arms draped over their shoulders, and dragged him away.

Gabriella peered around the bins to see what they were doing, confident their focus was on getting Archer into the van, which they'd reversed as far down the alley as they could.

The engine was running, and they tossed him in the back with no care whatsoever, closed up and moved to the front, opening the driver and passenger doors.

Bloody hell.

She scrambled out from behind the bins and stood, dithering, before running to stand at the back of the van. The engine revved, and on a rush of adrenalin, she opened one of the van's double doors and slipped inside, holding it slightly open so the two men wouldn't hear it slam closed.

The motion of the van pulling off jerked it toward her, and she had to put her hand in the way to prevent it banging closed. Tears welled at the pain of it and she hoped she hadn't broken anything.

She stood, balancing as the van swayed, wedging her foot to keep the door from closing and possibly locking her and James in.

It took a moment for her eyes to adjust to the darkness inside.

James Archer lay at her feet, but otherwise it looked empty, except for a toolbox against one side.

She crouched down, still with one leg and arm extended to keep the door in place, and flipped the lid of the box open.

She withdrew a hammer and a screwdriver, holding them awkwardly in one hand, and stood again, thinking through her options.

She had surprise on her side, but she couldn't carry James Archer. He was head and shoulders taller than she was and a good deal heavier.

The van slowed and then rumbled over rough ground, making it difficult for Gabriella to stay balanced.

Finally it came to a halt, and wincing, she transferred the screwdriver to her injured hand, mind racing at what to do if the two men came round the back and opened the doors.

She had some idea of protecting James, but she wouldn't be able to fight off two men, even if both her hands were working.

Why was she waiting then? She would do James Archer no good being captured with him. Even if she just knew where he was so she could fetch help, that would be better than nothing.

She opened the door and hopped down, getting her bearings.

The van had come to a halt outside a warehouse, the road beside it chewed up from too-heavy trucks and no maintenance. There was nowhere obvious to hide, but they were parked near the corner of the warehouse, and she ran toward it, rounding the corner, and then pressed herself up against the wall just as she heard the men finally exit the vehicle.

"Fred, the back's open," Archer's attacker said, outraged.

"Don't look at me. You closed it up. Unless . . . he *is* still in there?"

"Aye, he's still there. Out cold." There was a sudden thread of worry in the man's voice. "Mebbe we hit him too hard?"

"You hit him too hard, you mean. None of this 'we' business."

"Were you there, or weren't you?"

It sounded to Gabriella as if one of them climbed into the back. "He's breathing," Fred said, voice considerably lighter. "Let's find out who he is—" His voice cut off. "Fuck me. He's a copper."

There was sudden silence.

Gabriella crouched low and risked peering around the corner. It was almost fully dark now, and it was hard to see the two men, but from their tone, they were clearly unhappy.

"The boss'll want to know about this."

"The copper ain't seen our faces. Let's keep it that way. If we have to dump him somewhere, no harm done." Fred sounded like he was trying to convince himself.

"You think a copper'll think it's no harm done to be knocked out and then dumped somewhere?" The other man didn't bother to hide his skepticism.

"Well, he won't be able to point the finger at us, not if we keep shtum." Fred jumped down from the back of the van and its axle creaked. "Let's get him into the office and go find a phone box to call the boss."

Gabriella waited while they pulled James Archer out of the van and carried him inside.

The warehouse was near the Thames. She could hear the river and the water traffic nearby. The whole place smelled of creosote and diesel, and when she lifted the hand she had pressed against the wall, it came away smudged with black dust.

No one appeared to be around, and she could just make out a chain-link fence and an open gate to the right.

They certainly hadn't stopped to open a gate when they'd driven in, and hopefully they'd leave it open when they left.

She'd been waiting less than ten minutes when the two men came out of the building, arguing in low voices. They climbed into the van and started it up, turning it in a tight circle to leave the way they'd come.

Gabriella crouched down, out of sight, and the moment the van turned left and its lights disappeared, she was up and running to the entrance.

The door was shut but not locked. She opened it cautiously and found herself in a large, dark space. The warehouse was unlit and the smell of diesel and dust was even more pronounced inside.

She opened the entrance door wide to let in what little ambient light from the city there was, and as her eyes adjusted she made out a small office to one side.

As she approached it, she saw it was made of ill-fitting wooden planks. It had a door set in the middle and a small window on one side, almost as if they'd bought a garden shed and plonked it down inside the warehouse.

They probably had.

The door to it was locked, but she had the screwdriver and the hammer, and she used the screwdriver to lever the door open.

It was made of cheap wood that cracked and buckled easily after a bit of pressure. If her hand hadn't been hurting so much, she would have been able to jimmy it even quicker.

She shoved at the door, forcing it open with a groan, and although she could see nothing within, she heard the sound of someone breathing.

"DS Archer?" she whispered. "It's Gabriella Farnsworth."

"Gabriella?" His voice was rough and sluggish.

The sound of his voice helped her find him, and she crouched down beside him. He was tied hand and foot, and when she touched his face, she realized he was blindfolded as well, the material tight across his eyes.

"Turn your head," she told him, then got to work on the knot at the back. It was too tight for her, though, especially with her damaged hand.

It would take her ages to get this off him.

She suddenly wanted to cry in frustration and worry. She stopped, lifting her head and closing her eyes, determined not to shed a tear. She took a deep breath through her nose.

"Hang on." She had made out the shape of a desk when she'd forced her way in, and she got up and opened a drawer, but with no light, it was useless. She couldn't see anything.

She'd have to risk finding a light switch.

She went back to the door she'd jimmied open and felt around for a switch. She breathed out in relief when she found one. The light that flickered to life was weak, but it was all she needed.

She could see DS Archer had struggled up to a seated position while she'd been hunting through the desk for something to help her cut his bindings, and he looked ill under the poor lighting.

She ran back to the desk and began looking through drawers, and gave an exclamation of relief when she found a pair of scissors.

"Hold still." She crouched beside him and cut off the blindfold carefully, catching a few hairs in the process. Then she went to work on the ropes.

"What are you doing here?" he said eventually, after she got his hands free and had moved to his feet.

He lifted an arm, probing the back of his head gingerly.

She glanced up at him. "I knew I was being followed, so I pretended to catch the bus and was planning to turn the tables. Except you were following the man, too." She flexed her fingers to give her hands a break, especially her left hand, which felt double its usual size.

He simply stared at her.

"Be grateful I kept at it, even after I saw you following him, or no one would know where you are right now." She went back to cutting the ropes, and finally tugged them free.

She stepped back to give him room to get to his feet, but the moment he tried, he turned his head away and groaned.

"Concussion," she told him as she crouched next to him and tucked herself under his shoulder. They finally got upright, but the detective swayed so much, Gabriella was afraid he was going to take them both down.

"Give me a moment," he gasped, and closed his eyes.

He had spiky brown lashes, Gabriella noticed. He opened his eyes, and she found herself right up beside him, looking into gray eyes that were still slightly unfocused.

"Where are we?" he asked and she turned away, looking toward the door, suddenly uncomfortable with the intimate way they were standing.

"A warehouse near the river." She began to walk, drawing him with her, and he managed pretty well, getting stronger so that by the time they reached the warehouse door, he wasn't leaning on her so much.

She looked out and thought she could hear an engine, as if a vehicle was coming toward them. "Let's get around the side of the warehouse. Come on."

He went with her willingly enough, one hand out to steady himself on the wall, the other still tucked around her shoulders.

The van came sweeping through the open gate, turning sharply as it had before to stop right near the entrance.

The entrance they hadn't closed behind them.

Damn. She hadn't had time to think of that. At least she had switched off the office light.

"Didn't you shut the door?" Fred's accusation was harsh. "I know there's no key, but you could at least shut it behind you."

"I did shut it." The other man sounded disinterested. "But the latch is probably not catching. The place is falling apart."

They closed the van doors, and Gabriella peered around the side. Neither man was in sight, and it would take them moments to see the broken door to the office, and see that James was gone.

"Get in the van," she whispered. "Now."

She left him to his own devices, running around to the driver's side and opening the door, hoping beyond hope they'd left the keys in the ignition.

They had.

A fumble of sound came from her left and she glanced over, saw DS Archer at the door. He got in just as the man who'd followed her burst from the warehouse.

Gabriella turned the key in the ignition, but it didn't catch right away, and the man pulled the passenger door open and had his hands on Archer and was hauling him out before she could try again.

She twisted the key a second time, and the engine coughed to life, but suddenly her door was yanked open, too, and Fred grabbed her with hard, bruising hands, lifting her out bodily as if she weighed nothing.

"Fuck this for a lark, mate," he said as he clamped her arms at her side. "I'm out."

chapter twenty-five

HIS HEAD FELT like someone had jumped up and down on it.

James knew he had to put that aside. Had to turn things around, somehow. Because the way things were going was not good. At all.

They were back in the van, neither of them tied up, but the man who'd hit him over the head stood wide-legged at the back, holding onto a handle above his head and blocking the door. He had a knife, and it was pointed in their direction.

It was dark in the van, and their guard had wrapped a scarf around his lower face to disguise his features. He said nothing, hanging on as the van rumbled over uneven ground.

There was a definite tension between the two men who had abducted them. One wanted to dump them on a street and let them go, the other didn't seem to know what he wanted.

The compromise they had reached had been done out of earshot, so James had no idea what was going to happen now.

The van came to a stop, although the engine wasn't switched off, and the whole vehicle rocked as the driver got out and then James heard the rumble of a retractable garage door.

He felt the dip of the van as the driver got back in and then it reversed a short way and stopped again.

A bang came through the wall from the driver's side, and their guard opened the door, revealing a dark space with a musty smell beyond. He dropped down and pointed the knife at them.

"Get down and go to the back of this garage. If you don't, or if you try to run, I'll be waiting to stick you, got it?"

The man left the doors open and stepped to the side.

Gabriella rose to her feet behind him and walked to the door, jumping down and turning with her hand out to help him.

But even that was beyond him. He scooted forward on his behind and carefully lowered his legs to the ground and stood, swaying with dizziness as soon as he was on his own two feet.

Gabriella slid under his shoulder again and helped him move away from the van, which had already started moving forward.

He just had time to see their guard, reaching up to grab a handle, and then the rumble of the door drowned out any other sound, enclosing them in darkness, until he heard the snick of a padlock being attached.

He expected it to be just as dark as the van, but somehow it wasn't. He couldn't work out how until Gabriella urged him over to a far corner and helped him sit down on what turned out to be a pile of stiff, ancient canvas covers.

"Look," she said, pointing up. "Stars."

There were indeed stars. Shining down on them from a large hole in the roof.

It was a good thing it hadn't rained for quite a few days, or James guessed the canvas sheets would have been damp as well as stiff and foul smelling.

Still, it was good to have a slice of open sky above them, and while the light of the stars was minimal, it was comforting, somehow. Less like a cell.

"Did you see where we are?" He hadn't been able to, but she was more alert than he was right now.

She shook her head. "I thought I heard buses and traffic. It took about thirty minutes to get here from the warehouse. I did see a row of garages on the other side to us just before he closed the door. I don't think we're near any houses."

So a storage facility, or garage space. There were hundreds of them dotted through the city.

Gabriella had been standing, looking up through the hole in the roof, but now she crouched down in front of him. "How are you feeling?"

"Not good." He had to be honest, because he could barely stand upright, and that meant he could do nothing to help get them out.

"Just lie still. I'll see what I can find in here."

She moved away, walking the perimeter of the garage. There was a clang of metal and he heard hopping.

"I kicked over a bucket," she whispered. She emerged beside him again, holding it. "Maybe I can get up on the roof," she said, setting the bucket upside down right beside the canvas sheets where he was lying, as close to the hole as she could get. She carefully stood on it, balancing as she looked up, and then shook her head. "Too low."

She got down, and went back to her search, but eventually she came back to the canvas sheets and sat beside him, tucking her short skirt primly beneath her. "I can't find anything in the dark."

She settled back, her face tipped up to the star-lit sky.

"Do you think Fred meant it? That he was out of this?" she asked.

"Fred?" He tried to work out if he knew who Fred was, or if the blow to his head had made him forget.

"The driver. I didn't catch the other man's name, but the driver was Fred."

"I don't know if he meant it, but we aren't tied up, and they've definitely gone." The best he could hope for was that they wouldn't be coming back, and he and Gabriella could somehow free themselves, or be able to attract enough attention that someone would let them out while the two men took their chance to disappear.

The worst case was that they had passed on his and Gabriella's whereabouts to their boss, and Mr. Big was coming to deal with them himself.

"I wish they'd dropped us at a hospital," Gabriella said. "You've got a serious concussion."

"It's not too bad." He played rugby, had had concussion before, and he knew this was bad, but he didn't like the worry in her voice.

She gave him a sidelong look, then moved around a bit, trying to get comfortable. "I guess we'll have to wait for morning to see better, and hopefully someone will be about."

"Where were you going tonight?" James asked. "Before all this nonsense? Will you be missed?"

"I was going to visit Mr. Rodney in hospital. I told Jerome, my neighbor, I was going, but he's working late. No one will be expecting me."

"But you work Saturdays, don't you?"

She gave a sigh. "Yes. I work until midday on Saturdays. Mr. Greenberg will miss me. And I was supposed to go shopping with a friend in the afternoon." She turned her head to look at him. "What about you?"

"Hartridge is expecting to meet me at the Yard tomorrow at ten." They were going to try to track Devenish down again. He had still not got in touch, and James was losing patience with him. He wondered what Hartridge would do when he failed to turn up.

"Nothing we can do about it," Gabriella said, shifting a little. Her skirt rode up higher on her thigh, and despite his pounding head, he noticed.

He closed his eyes and slid down on the canvases. "We'll find a way out. Maybe even before we're missed."

"Maybe." She sounded tired. "You don't have family in London?"

"No. I'm from Cardiff." And he was very bad at calling his parents. His colleagues would miss him long before his family realized something was wrong.

"Why did you move to London?" she asked, as the warmth of her shoulder against his, the scent of her, wound around him.

He cleared his throat. "Always wanted to join the Met." He didn't say that hadn't gone as he thought it would. He would need to know her a lot better before he admitted to that. "So what brought you all the way to London?"

She hesitated, and that was so surprising, he opened his eyes and half lifted up to look at her.

She was staring up at the stars, hands behind her head. "I came to see if I could find what happened to my father," she said.

It was such an unexpected comment, he was silent for a moment. "You don't know?" he asked carefully.

"He left my mother and me after the war, when I was six, to come back to England to deal with his deceased father's estate. Or that's what he told my mother. And she never saw or heard from him again after he got on the ship that brought him here."

"She obviously tried to find out what happened?" Of course she would have.

"Yes." She sounded tired. "She contacted the British embassy in Canberra, asking for help. She contacted the shipping company. She contacted your lot—New Scotland Yard." Gabriella lifted her shoulders. "Everyone said the same thing. There was no record of him, and he was an adult and was allowed to disappear if he wanted to."

"So when you were old enough, you decided to take matters into your own hands?" James asked.

"I've always wondered, sure." She lowered her hands, tucking them under her armpits. "But I also thought if he didn't want to get back in touch with us, I wouldn't waste my time looking for him."

"So what changed?"

"My mother met someone maybe three years ago. Gino. He's great. He loves her. She loves him. She deserves some happiness. But the priest won't declare my father dead, even though we haven't heard a word from him in sixteen years, so they can't marry. And it's killing them."

He considered the hell of that limbo. "They won't just move in together?"

She gave a snort. "I've tried that tack. Believe me. But my mother is a good Catholic, and so is Gino. Although I reckon he could be persuaded. My mother, not so much. She's stubborn as a mule. And she would never think of going against the church after the Archbishop of Melbourne supported Italian Australians during the war, when the government was interning men in other Australian states. The Italian side of my family lived more or less normal lives because of the church."

He knew internment had happened to Italian men in the UK, he hadn't realized it had also happened in Australia. He could see how being spared that would generate a great deal of loyalty. "How are you getting on with your search?"

"I've sent off for his birth certificate. I've sent off for his death certificate. I've had no luck on either count. According to the records, he doesn't exist. Or, not under the name he married my mother with, or the name he put on my birth certificate."

He could hear the fury in her voice. She had worked out her father had been living a lie the entire time he had been with her and her mother.

He thought of his own quiet, self-effacing parents. The idea of deception on this level was unimaginable.

"Did you check the ship manifest?" he asked.

"He either never got on that ship, although my mother swears she waved at him from the dock as they'd pulled out of the harbor, or he bought his ticket under another name." She turned on her side to face him. "I've requested a list of everyone who boarded that ship. And I'm going to have to go through the men of the right age one by one."

He could hear the determination in her voice.

She lapsed into silence. There was the sounds of cars in the distance, the rumble of trucks on some distant road. The yowl of a cat, and then the spitting and hissing of a cat fight, were much closer.

James let himself drift, the feeling of being stabbed repeatedly in the head easing off as his headache improved.

He had checked his watch when they'd been deposited in the garage. The florescent hands had pointed to ten o'clock.

He would rest for a few hours, and hopefully, when he was more himself, he'd figure out a way to get them out of here.

He knew his being a policeman had probably turned the tables in their favor. That, and whoever Fred was, he hadn't been up for anything more than a little kidnapping.

The other one, he was a little harder to read.

If one of them was going to tell their boss where the prisoners were, it would be him.

James hoped that if the boss did decide to take care of them himself, he would at least wait a few hours, when James felt more able to defend himself and Gabriella.

Why not hope for the best?

chapter twenty-six

SHE WOKE with her nose pressed into James's neck, breathing in the salty, spicy scent of him. It helped to drown out the musty smell of the canvas they lay on.

Sunlight, fresh and pale with dawn, touched her cheeks and she enjoyed the sensation of warmth for a moment before she raised her head.

James was watching her, his gray eyes steady as they hadn't been the night before.

She had woken him again and again through the night—every time she moved to find a more comfortable position—to check he hadn't gone into a coma.

He had insisted on covering them both with his suit jacket, and they had lain close together, the shared heat creating an intimacy that caused a definite shift in their relationship.

She knew it, and the way he was looking at her told her he knew it, too.

"Morning," he said, and she smiled up at him.

He blinked, then his lips quirked up on one side in response.

"Where's that bucket from last night?" she asked.

"Do you need to . . .?" He looked suddenly discomforted, and it took her a moment to understand what he thought.

"No. Well, yes, but not desperately. Now that it's light, I

thought I'd see if I could use it to get up onto the roof, and try to open the door on the other side."

"Oh." He looked over at the bucket. In the night, his arm had come around her, and she had fit herself flush against his side, her head on his shoulder. He didn't seem inclined to loosen his hold. "Didn't you say it wasn't high enough last night?"

"Yes." She reluctantly pulled herself away from his warmth and rolled to her feet, feeling multiple aches as she stretched.

James got to his feet more slowly, but she kept a sharp watch on him and he seemed to be all right.

He pulled the canvas they'd slept on away from under the hole in the roof, and set the bucket down directly beneath it. He looked up at the uneven break above and glanced over at her.

"I don't think I'd fit through."

She agreed, which is why she had suggested she do it. She walked over and he held out a hand, which she used to steady herself as she clambered up.

"It's not high enough."

"I'm going to put my foot on it, bend my knee, and you're going to step up onto my thigh," he said, and then did it.

Still using him for balance, she carefully stepped up, reaching up with one hand and getting it through the hole.

"Still too low," she said. There was no way she could boost herself up.

"Now you're where you are, let's try this." James put both hands on her thighs, just below her bottom, and lifted her.

All those muscles that she had admired in his arms seemed to bulge as he thrust her upward, and suddenly she was shoulder height above the roof.

She put her hands out, used her arms to propel her, and with James's help from below, eventually clambered up.

Her short skirt had ridden up around her thighs, but she dismissed the embarrassment that flared momentarily in her as she tugged it down. Much more important things to worry about than flashing her knickers, that was for sure.

"All right?" James called up.

"I think so." Although her left hand was throbbing at having had pressure on it. "I'm going to crawl across the roof." She didn't know how strong the wavy fibercrete was, and given it had collapsed in one corner, she guessed not very strong at all. So she carefully moved on hands and knees toward the front of the garage and peered down over the side.

The roof sloped upward from back to front, and the ground looked a fair distance away.

The sound of someone coughing came from her left, and she shielded her gaze against the rising sun to see an old man limping down the row of garages in blue overalls.

"Hello!" she called, waving.

He came to a stop, looking around for her.

"Up on the roof! Hello!"

Eventually he found her, but his eyesight was obviously not good, because he was frowning and squinting as he came closer, and then stopped in amazement.

"A girl on a roof."

"Yes. My friend and I were locked in the garage last night and I climbed through a hole in the corner. Can you break the padlock to get my friend out, and get a ladder for me to get down?"

"Break a padlock?" the man said, shaking his head. "I don't go around destroying other people's property."

"There's a detective sergeant of Scotland Yard injured and trapped in that garage," Gabriella said. "You'd be on the side of the law if you broke it. But if you don't want to, can you go and fetch a bobby or two to help instead?"

"The coppers?" he spat to the side.

"Can you at least get a ladder to help me down, then?" Gabriella asked, suddenly finding her patience wearing thin. She had to force herself to keep her voice calm and friendly.

"Reckon I can." He was still standing in the middle of the row, looking up at her, when Gabriella saw a man walking down toward him.

He was wearing a hat low over his eyes and a dark gray jacket. Something about him set her heart thumping and when he stopped, took a few steps back at the sight of her and the old man, then darted quickly around the back of one of the garages, she understood why.

Despite the warm rays of the rising sun, a chill went through her. She crawled back over the roof and looked down at James, who was staring up at her from below.

"He's here."

"He?"

"The killer. I think." She didn't have proof, but the way he moved, the quick jerk of surprise when he saw there was someone else there, and that she was on the roof, made her sure of it.

It wasn't a normal reaction.

"Stay on the roof." James squinted up at her, shielding his eyes from the early morning sun.

She shook her head. "Then I'm as trapped as you. And sooner or later the old man will leave, or he'll kill him, and then we'll be at his mercy."

A thump came from the front of the garage, and Gabriella crawled back over.

"Got the ladder for ye." The old man held the bottom of it. "Mind how you go."

"Thank you." She would usually have climbed down carefully, but she didn't have time for that. She scrambled down as fast as her injured hand would allow and turned to the old man the moment she was on the ground.

"Thank you for your help. I saw the man who arranged for us to be locked up here coming down the row. He's hiding behind one of those garages. He's dangerous. You need to go, right now." She looked past him, saw the man step out into the row again. "There he is."

The old man turned. "Eh?"

Gabriella didn't want to leave him here. Didn't want to leave James. But she couldn't deal with this on her own.

She turned and ran, racing to the end of the row, to the street she could see beyond.

She glanced back as she reached it, saw the man she thought was the killer coming after her.

That was good. At least he wasn't going after James, trapped inside the garage.

She heard a shout of pain, and just caught a glimpse of her pursuer shoving the old man down as he ran past.

She blindly turned right, sprinting down a road that had businesses all along it. At this time of day, on a Saturday morning, it was quiet, with no one about.

She could hear cars on a busier road up ahead, and headed in that direction.

She could also hear the pounding of boots on the pavement, and she had the terrible feeling she wouldn't make it to the main road. He was gaining on her.

She saw a park at the end of a short street to her right, and veered in that direction, thinking if she were really lucky, there might be a dog walker about. Someone to at least call to for help.

As she reached the end of the short street, she risked a glance over her shoulder, and saw the man was close. His face was terrible, his lips pulled back over his teeth as if he were snarling at her as he ran.

She bolted across the street that ran beside the park, and as she hit the grass, she saw the abandoned car, and realized this was South Kensington, and she knew this place.

Even though she didn't know quite how that knowledge would help her, it made her feel better.

She didn't call for Teddy Roe, the homeless man who was sleeping in the back of the car. He would only get hurt in a confrontation with the killer behind her.

But the lady who had stared at her from the window yesterday —she might help.

She passed the car, heard Teddy snoring within, and darted

across the street, leaping the short wooden gate, grateful it was low enough for her to do so.

She climbed the dark red steps up to the front door and rattled the knocker. "Help. I need the police."

She had committed to this action, giving herself no way to escape if the lady of the house didn't help her, so she turned to see where the man was.

He had slowed, walking across the road instead of running.

He hadn't expected her to knock on a door.

She studied him carefully, and he must have picked that up, because he dragged his cap even lower down over his forehead.

Just as he reached the low gate, the door she was leaning on opened behind her and she staggered back.

A hand shoved her to one side, so she fetched up against a wall, almost knocking a picture to the floor, and the door was slammed shut, the bolt shot.

She stared at the woman as she turned from the door. "We have to call the police."

"I heard you the first time." The woman was reed thin and in her mid to late fifties. Her eyes were sharp and glittered in the morning light. "Which station?"

"Scotland Yard." Gabriella thought about it, then shook her head. "The local bobbies can probably get to James faster. And he needs them to be fast. He's locked in one of the garages in a row close to here."

The woman went to a small table and lifted the receiver of a smart new phone, and dialed.

Gabriella listened to her cool, precise tones as she spoke. She gave her name to the desk sergeant as Ruby Everett. "Who is in danger, did you say?" She glanced over at Gabriella.

"Detective Sergeant James Archer of the Met."

The woman's eyebrow rose at that piece of information, and she relayed it. "And you are?"

"Gabriella Farnsworth." Gabriella went to the door and crouched to look through the letter flap.

There was no sign of her pursuer.

She hoped he hadn't gone back to deal with James.

"How did you know to come here?" the woman asked as Gabriella rose from her crouch.

"I saw you yesterday, and thought that you were watching to make sure I treated Mr. Roe respectfully. I'm a traffic warden, and yesterday I took over from the warden who usually does this round."

"The little girl in the black uniform with the yellow stripe on her cap." Ruby Everett gave a slow nod. "Is he gone? The man who was chasing you?"

"It looks like it." Gabriella didn't want to test it by going out, though. "Thank you very much for your help. I would be dead if you hadn't opened the door."

"You know this for sure?" Ruby Everett's eyebrows rose.

Gabriella lifted her shoulders. "I think he's killed two people in the last week and a half, and from the look on his face, I was next."

"I agree about that," the woman said, and gestured for Gabriella to follow her into a neat, well-furnished sitting room. "That's what convinced me to open up. I've seen expressions like that during the war."

Gabriella looked up sharply. She didn't suppose most Londoners had gone around looking like they were about to kill, which meant Ruby Everett had possibly been up to interesting things during the war.

"Well, I expect the police will be along after they've found your friend. They seemed excited at the mention of a detective from New Scotland Yard in trouble."

She wanted to think the man who chased her would give up, realize that the police would be called and leave before he could be intercepted, but there was something about him that told her he would push his luck.

"I'm afraid he's gone back there. He'd make it to James long before the police."

"To do what to him?" Ruby Everett asked.

"To kill him."

Ruby studied her face for a beat. Then she walked to a drawer, took out a key that was hanging around her neck inside her blouse, and unlocked it.

When she turned she was holding a revolver. "Then let's go."

chapter twenty-seven

"WHAT'S GOING ON, that's what I'd like to know."

The voice James heard through the wooden garage door sounded indignant, querulous and confused.

James thought he'd heard Gabriella running away, so this was likely the man who'd helped her off the garage roof.

Then there was the sound of running feet and the man cried out in surprise and pain.

"What's happened?" James called through the door, cursing his inability to see anything.

There was silence for a moment.

"Some bugger's shoved me as he ran past. Chasing that girl."

James's hands turned to fists where they rested against the door. The boss man, Mr. Big, was after Gabriella.

"Did she have a good lead on him?" he asked.

The old man didn't respond. He was muttering to himself, and James guessed he was getting to his feet.

He slammed his fists against the wood. "Sir! Is she going to get away?"

"I don't know, do I? They're both long gone."

Footsteps approached the door and it wobbled a little as if the old man had put his hand against it.

"You really a copper?"

"Yes." James had heard the strain in Gabriella's voice as she'd negotiated with the curmudgeon, and forced himself to keep a civil tone, as well.

"Reckon I might have a pair o' bolt cutters in the shed." He shuffled away, and James leaned back against the door, eyes closed, as he willed the old man to go faster.

This time on a Saturday morning, wherever this garage was, he doubted there would be a lot of people about to help Gabriella. And she had a killer after her.

Eventually the shuffling steps returned.

"Took a bit to find them," the old man muttered. "Got 'em now, though."

James heard the rattle of the padlock, and then suddenly the door was being lifted and he had to move away to let it roll up.

While he blinked to adjust to the brighter light, he saw an old man glaring at him from under bushy gray eyebrows.

"You look rough for a copper."

James wasn't interested in talking about his disheveled state. Someone had turned in to the row of garages from the street, walking quickly, eyes darting around, and everything about him made the alarm bells in James's head ring.

"Who's that?" he asked the old man.

The man turned, still holding the bolt cutters, and his whole body stiffened. "That's the one wot pushed me."

James tore the bolt cutters from his limp hand and moved forward, eyes going to the man's jacket for any sign of blood. If he had stabbed Gabriella, there would surely be evidence.

It was hard to get a good look at him, backlit as he was by the sun, and the moment Mr. Big realized James was out of the garage and coming toward him, he slowed, dipping his head and pulling his cap low.

James started to run, bolt cutters lifted like a club, and with a sudden, almost casual shrug of his shoulders, Mr. Big spun around, racing back toward the road.

He was gone before James even reached the end of the row.

When he reached the road, James tried to see where he'd gone, feeling lightheaded and out of breath at the exertion, angry at his own weakness. But Mr. Big was nowhere in sight.

"James." The call came from the right, and James spun, feeling even more lightheaded at the sight of Gabriella racing toward him.

She was unharmed.

She suddenly seemed to realize she was running as if to meet him in some kind of romantic embrace, and pulled herself up short, stumbling to a stop in front of him.

"I was worried he'd come back for you." Gabriella looked at the bolt cutters in his hand. "He did!"

James saw a woman walking at a more sedate pace behind her, a large handbag over her shoulder. He thought he had glimpsed her putting something that looked very much like a revolver inside it as she approached.

"This is Mrs. Everett. She called the police for me, and very kindly said she'd come with me to make sure you were alright." Gabriella turned toward the woman with a grateful smile.

They'd come armed, James realized. Armed for their own protection, and his.

He decided he would pretend he hadn't seen the gun slipped into the handbag.

"When he saw me coming at him, he ran."

"A coward," Mrs. Everett said with a decisive nod. "They always turn out to be cowards."

"Mrs. Everett saved my life," Gabriella said. "If she hadn't opened her door, he'd have got me."

Mrs. Everett looked at Gabriella indulgently, James noted with surprise, even though she had the look of a retired school mistress. Her demeanor was far more composed than he would have expected in the circumstances.

"The bobbies have arrived." She was looking beyond him, down the same street Mr. Big had gone.

James reached in his pocket for his warrant card, and was holding it out for them by the time they reached the little group.

"Mrs. Everett," one of them said respectfully, clearly recognizing the woman. "Everything alright?"

"I don't believe so, unfortunately, Constable Anders, but I think the immediate danger seems to have passed." She looked at him. "Detective Sergeant Archer may be in need of medical help."

James had been feeling more and more unsteady as he stood in the street, and he turned in surprise at her words, sure he was putting up a good enough front.

The quick movement was his undoing.

It felt as if his brain crashed against the side of his skull, and a black curtain came down over his eyes.

chapter twenty-eight

GABRIELLA DID NOT like Detective Inspector Whetford.

He leered, and spoke to her as if she were stupid.

She had already spent some time looking through a book of known criminals, but hadn't found any image that looked like Mr. Knife, although she had only had the briefest glimpse of his full face. Mrs. Everett had not recognized anyone, either, and had been sent home.

DC Hartridge stood against the wall of the interview room, head down, taking notes, his ears turning red at the tips.

They had gone over everything a few times now, and Gabriella pushed her chair back and stood.

"I'm not done with you, missy." DI Whetford leaned back in his chair, his lips pinched as he stared up at her.

"I'm sorry, inspector, but I've told you everything I can, and my hand is hurting too much now for me to concentrate on anything else." She held her hands out together, and even she winced at the purple and black bruising on her left hand in contrast to her right. It was puffy and swollen.

Whetford eyed her hand in surprise. "I didn't realize you were also injured." He spoke stiffly, as if put on the spot. "All right, I suppose we've covered most of the ground we need to. Hartridge, take her to the hospital, will you?"

"Yes, sir." Hartridge pushed off from the wall and opened the door, and, cradling her hand against her chest, Gabriella escaped.

She decided the Met might as well drive her to the hospital—it would save her bus fare—and she let Hartridge lead her to a car and help her in.

She said nothing about Whetford, and neither did Hartridge, although she had a feeling he was embarrassed by his superior.

"Have you heard any news from the hospital about DS Archer?" she asked after a long silence.

"No. The information would come to DI Whetford, and he hasn't chosen to say anything to me."

Definitely embarrassed. And not a little annoyed.

They pulled into the hospital car park and Gabriella found arriving with a police officer got her ahead of the queue.

DC Hartridge left her after she was checked in, and the doctor —who seemed harried, grumpy and tired, even though it was barely past midday—wrapped her hand firmly, telling her she was lucky not to have broken anything.

Seeing as she was there, she found Mr. Rodney's room and popped in to visit him, but he was sleeping and the nurses didn't want him disturbed, so she left a note and then went to find DS Archer.

James.

She would have to call him DS Archer in front of his colleagues, but she guessed they were on first name terms in private, now.

When she arrived at his room, she found Hartridge was visiting, and he glanced up with interest as she knocked softly and entered.

"Gabriella." James was lying in a tightly made bed, with a bandage around his head to match the one around her hand. He struggled to sit up as she came closer, pulling at the sheets.

Hartridge's eyes widened a little.

James caught sight of her hand, and narrowed his eyes. "I saw you were favoring it before, but I didn't realize you needed the hospital."

"I caught it in the van door, trying to stop it slamming closed while they were driving us to the warehouse." She lifted a shoulder. "Nothing's broken. It's just bruised."

"I don't remember that." He looked upset.

"You were unconscious at the time. There's nothing for you to remember."

There was a moment of uncomfortable silence, which Gabriella didn't like.

She had had enough of things she didn't like today. So she approached the bed, took James's hand with her uninjured one, and gave it a squeeze. "I'm glad you're all right. When do they think you'll be well enough to be released?"

"Tomorrow afternoon." He squeezed her hand back. "I'll come round when I'm out, ask you about what happened after you got down from the garage roof."

"She's been through that already, sir. With DI Whetford." Hartridge glanced at her, as if waiting for her to say something about the interview.

"Whetford?" James struggled up again, finally sitting up against the pillows. "He doesn't know anything about the case."

"He took it on himself to get involved. There's been a bit of a rumble what with a detective being kidnapped. The higher-ups don't like the sound of it."

James looked thunderous, and Gabriella realized she didn't understand the politics of New Scotland Yard, and she found she didn't care.

"You can come over and ask me anyway, if you want," she said to James. "I'm going to go home now and rest."

She nodded to Hartridge and had reached the door when James called out.

"Gabriella, how are you getting home?"

"The bus," she said.

"No." He yanked viciously at his blankets, trying to get out of the bed. "No, you're not."

"James, what are you doing?"

He had managed to free himself from the confining linen, and stood swaying in a ghastly green hospital gown, his hair standing up around his head. "This man has killed twice. And he has gone after you himself, and sent some thugs after you, then went after you again. He thinks you can identify him and he has even more reason now than before to try to eliminate you. He also knows where you live. You are not taking the bus."

"I'll take her home, sir." Hartridge's cheeks were pink.

James suddenly seemed to remember his constable was there. "All right. Thank you, DC Hartridge." He sat back down on the bed as if his legs had given way. "Gabriella, please don't go anywhere alone. This man is out to get you."

She hadn't really thought beyond getting away from the man this morning, but James was right.

At least it was past midday now, on a busy Saturday. He'd have to be brazen indeed to attack her today.

"I'll be careful." She would contact Neeky, apologize about the shopping trip, and tell her she couldn't see her for a bit. She didn't want any of her friends hurt like Mr. Rodney had been.

At least the killer didn't know about her new route.

She would have to keep it that way.

chapter twenty-nine

DI WHETFORD WAS A DIRTY COPPER, but he was also an incompetent one.

James had thought he was lazy, but now he knew his boss was also incapable of doing a good job.

It made his rise in the ranks at the Met more suspicious still. The people above him had promoted him for some reason. Now, James suspected it was because he could be counted on to keep his mouth shut and take a cut of the profits.

If his boss had thought about it for even a moment, he'd have realized Gabriella Farnsworth was in danger from the man who'd organized the kidnap of a police officer. The fact he hadn't put a constable at her door for safety was staggering.

He'd let her leave his interview room without any thought to her well being. He hadn't even, according to Hartridge, noticed her swollen hand until she brought it to his attention.

Even if he'd had no thought to her safety, he hadn't considered setting someone to watch Gabriella in case their suspect tried to kill her again, as a way to catch him. He had simply not given it any thought at all.

James walked up the path to her building, and found the door was at least locked this time. That was good, but presented a problem as to how to get her attention.

He looked around for a door bell, but the door opened and a young Trinidadian man stared out at him, eyes hostile.

"Yes?"

"DS Archer. I'm here to speak to Gabriella Farnsworth." He held out his warrant card.

"You the one got locked in that garage with Gabby?"

James blinked, then nodded. "Yes."

"Come on in, man." The door opened a little wider. "I'm Jerome, Gabby's neighbor. No worries, we got our eyes peeled for the bastard wot knifed Mr. Rodney, and his boss."

"Gabriella gave you a description of them?"

"Sure." He pointed up the stairs. "I'm doing some stuff in Mr. Rodney's flat, but Gabby's home. Go on up."

James climbed the stairs slower than usual, aware the headache that sat just behind his eyes could flare up under the slightest provocation.

The doctor told him it would take a few days before he was back to normal, and if he pushed things, it would take longer than that.

He didn't want it to take longer. He needed to be ready for whatever came next.

He was slightly lightheaded by the time he reached Gabriella's door, and he waited a few beats before he knocked.

"It's James," he said after a moment's silence.

The door swung open, as if she'd been standing right beside it, and she studied his face. "You look pale." She stepped back and he walked in after her, closing the door behind him and making sure it was locked.

It was a strange feeling, being alone with her again. As if he should take her in his arms. He didn't know if she would appreciate that, or not.

"When did you get out of hospital?" she asked.

He turned to her, found her watching him with an unreadable expression.

"Just now," he admitted. "I came straight here."

She studied him. "Surely you need a bit more time off, to recover?"

He lifted his shoulders.

She waited for him to say more, but he didn't really want to tell her his boss was useless, he was worried about her, and the thought of her unprotected made it impossible for him to return to his flat.

She sighed. "Coffee or tea?"

"Tea." Coffee was not what his system needed right now. "Do you have any?"

He hadn't ever seen her drink tea before.

"I wouldn't have offered if I didn't." She set about getting out a teapot, a charming round, fat one with flowers painted all over it.

He walked over to the dormer window, looking down onto the street. Her bedsit was up in the eaves, and there was a wide sill she had turned into a window seat, with a long cushion to sit on, and a smaller one to lean against.

James settled in to watch.

"You looking for Mr. Knife?"

He looked over at her as she brought a cup and saucer to him. "I call him Mr. Big."

"That's too complimentary," she told him, handing him his tea.

He settled back against the cushion.

"Take off your shoes," she said. "It's more comfortable with your feet up on the bench."

He lifted an eyebrow.

"You know you want to." She grinned at him. "I'll make some supper."

He sipped tea, which was strong and fragrant, and watched the street, glancing over at Gabriella as she puttered around her kitchen, putting things together with nothing more than a single electric plate and an electric frying pan.

"You look like someone who should have a full kitchen," he said.

She glanced over her shoulder. "Now that Mr. Rodney has the downstairs flat, I have the option of that. But I've enjoyed getting creative with what I have."

She put pasta into the pot on her electric plate, and then lifted the lid of her electric frying pan, stirring whatever delicious sauce was inside.

She set the small table with a candle and mismatched, charming plates and bowls, and James gave up watching the street, absolutely unable to look away as she moved around.

He was fascinated by her and her seemingly effortless ability to make everything perfect.

When she set steaming bowls down on the table and looked over at him, he got up and joined her.

"I should have brought flowers," he said.

"You should have," she agreed with a grin. "Except I don't think you expected me to feed you."

"Lucky me." He sat, diving into spaghetti and meat balls in a tomato sauce. He hadn't realized how hungry he was, and when he leaned back from the table, his plate was scraped clean.

"More?" she asked.

He shook his head sadly. "I wish I could, but I don't think I can fit in another mouthful." He stood, feeling the best he'd felt for two days. "I'll clean up, if you'll watch the street."

She hesitated, then gave a nod, walking over to curl up where he'd been sitting. He forced himself to turn away from her, imagining her curled up like that in his lap.

There would be no watching done if that happened.

He had to concentrate on this case. And then he would be calling on Gabriella Farnsworth afterward.

"Everyone Solomon knows on the street is keeping an eye," Gabriella told him. "I don't think he'll get by them."

"What's Solomon's role in this?" James had sensed the big

Trinidadian was more than he appeared, and he'd like to know what he was dealing with.

"He's Mr. Rodney's nephew, and he helps his community. He's a main part of the Calypso Club, and he's who everyone turns to if they need help. Like an unofficial mayor of the area, I suppose."

That could be true. But there was something in Solomon's eyes when he'd studied James in the hospital that said he was more than just a pillar of his community.

"He has a girlfriend?" James recalled the woman who'd come out of the house to greet Solomon when they'd dropped him off.

"Catherine."

There was a warmth in Gabriella's voice as she said the name.

"A friend of yours?"

"I don't know her well enough to call her my friend, but I like her."

He turned from the tiny sink, wiping his hands on a tea towel and then hanging it to dry from a little rail on the side of the cupboard. "All done."

She uncurled, the movement as graceful and delicate as a cat, and stood. "You should go home, James. You don't look well."

He didn't want to go home, and he didn't actually know how he would get there easily, given the way he was feeling. He was suddenly exhausted, as lightheaded as he'd been when he'd climbed the stairs.

"Let me watch just a little longer," he said. It was hard to get the words out properly. "He's more likely to try something now that it's dark."

She acquiesced with a twist of her lips and a flourish of her hand toward the window, her gaze solemn. "I'll make some more tea."

He settled back onto the seat, liking the feel of the warmth she'd left behind, and the faint scent of her on the cushion.

He heard her moving around, but he closed his eyes, just for a moment, and sank in a deep, dark hole.

chapter thirty

GABRIELLA WOKE in an instant at the faint sound outside her door.

She had slept lightly all night, aware of James just beyond the screen that shielded her bed, but this sound was from outside.

She strained her ears, trying to work out what it was she had heard, exactly.

From within the room she could hear James breathing. She had covered him with a blanket, wincing at the uncomfortable way he lay on the window bench, and had eventually gone to bed herself.

She had lain awake for a while, thinking about how they'd slept together on the smelly pile of canvas sheets in the garage—not with nostalgia, exactly—but it had been nice, lying in his arms.

There was a strange link between them, now—an intimacy that was forged out of necessity—but she knew it was more than just their forced proximity that bound them. He looked at her as if he wanted her more than he wanted to breathe. Even if his body language said he had to stay away.

She shivered at the thought. She had turned to let him know dinner was ready, and caught him staring at her.

She had wanted to forget dinner, walk over, and touch her lips to his, but there was a tightness to the way he held himself. He was careful not to touch her.

She assumed it was because she was a witness in his case, and it would have professional repercussions for him if they got involved.

That was fine with her. She could wait.

She would be interested in seeing if he came around to visit when this was over.

She guessed the answer to that would be yes. That would be her answer, also, if he did arrive on her doorstep.

She might have still been of two minds to get involved with anyone, given what she was in London to achieve, except he had held her in the garage as if she were precious.

She had never had that before.

She wanted it again.

Another soft noise came from the door, and she realized James was silent, the steady breath she'd fallen asleep to had stopped. She slid out of bed, walking on bare feet around the screen, to find him staring at the door from the window, alert and focused.

He glanced at her, put a finger to his lips.

He looked disheveled and, as Liz would say, yummy.

He stood, meeting her in the middle of the room, and she stepped close to his side. After a moment's hesitation, he slid an arm around her.

She stood still in shock for a beat, then smiled inside and hooked her own arm around his waist, pressing herself against him. He had obviously decided to let repercussions be damned.

Her door knob twisted silently, and there was the faintest of rattles, as someone tried the door.

James drew away from her, moving to the tiny kitchenette, and picked up the frying pan hanging from the hook on the kitchen wall. He flipped the handle, spinning the pan in an easy movement, then walked to the door and slid the bolt, then opened the door and swung the frying pan at the same time.

There was a sound of pain and a thud as someone hit the floor, and she saw the frying pan lift up and hit down a second time.

"What's up?" Jerome's voice sounded hoarse and sleepy. He seemed to wake up in a hurry. "Wotcha?"

"Is there a telephone in this house?" James asked, voice calm.

"Down the road, there is. At the corner." Gabriella stepped into the doorway, saw James standing over the man who James had followed into the pub—Mr. Knife's henchman.

James looked relaxed, as if the sleep on her window sill had been just what the doctor ordered. He held the frying pan loosely in his hand, but it looked like the man was down and out.

Jerome looked up at her, eyes wide, hair standing straight up from his head. "I'll go phone. Who'd you want to call?"

"If you could call PS Yates from the Notting Hill nick, that would be very helpful. Tell him DS Archer has apprehended a suspect involved in the recent stabbings and kidnap, and I require back up at this address."

"This one is involved?" Jerome lost some of the stiffness in his posture as he studied the downed man. "For sure?"

James looked over at Gabriella, and she nodded. "For sure."

"Be my pleasure." Jerome disappeared back into his flat, and for the first time, Gabriella realized he had only been wearing a pair of flannel pajama pants.

When he came back out, a minute or two later, he had pulled on sharp boots which he'd paired with dark purple pants and a tight black t-shirt. As he walked past the henchman, he kicked him with a pointy toe.

The man groaned with pain.

"Clumsy me," Jerome sing-songed as he ran down the stairs.

"You look chipper," Gabriella observed, leaning against the doorjamb.

James sent her a wide grin. "Finally I have an actual person I can arrest in this case."

chapter thirty-one

NOW THAT DI WHETFORD had had some involvement in the case, it seemed he was determined to look like he was running it.

James leaned back against a wall in the superintendent's office, arms crossed, and watched him stumble through the questions he was being asked.

Someone at Notting Hill nick had obviously alerted the press, and he, Sergeant Yates, and some of Yates's bobbies had dragged the man he now knew was Russ Holler out of Gabriella's address under the scrutiny of at least three reporters.

The number interested in the case was now many times more than that.

That made New Scotland Yard interested. Hence the call into the big boss's office.

Detective Superintendent Halberd looked up, over Whetford's head, and made eye contact with James.

"It sounds as if I should be asking questions of your bagman, Whetford. Archer?"

James straightened. "DI Whetford was busy on other business," he said. "I took the lead in the case."

"Lay it out for me."

James gave him a concise account, leaving out extraneous

details, and then leaned back against the wall as Halberd tapped his lips, watching him with interest.

So far, James had flown under the radar at the Met. He had the feeling he'd woken the dragon, and it was aware of him now.

"So this Mr. Big is still out there?" Halberd said eventually.

James gave a nod. "Russ Holler won't give him up. He's too frightened of him."

"Any way we can persuade this Lenny Foster character to talk? With the threat that he could go down for the murders of Sam Nealy and Patty Little?"

James shook his head. "He's got an alibi for Patty's death. We could make a case for Sam Nealy, but it'd be weak. And I don't think he did it."

"What about a drugs charge?" Halberd leaned forward. "They were selling narcotics in the clubs, weren't they?"

"I'd love to stick him with a drugs charge, but he might well be right about LSD. It looks like it isn't illegal."

"What about his attack on the Swiss chemist?" Whetford asked. "That's what he was arrested for, wasn't it?"

James gave a nod. "Assault is about all we can pin on him right now. And obstructing a police investigation, if we really want to go hard."

"I want to go hard," Halberd said. "Maybe he can be convinced to give us more."

James lifted a shoulder. "I don't think Lenny knows too much more. Mr. Big was their competition in the clubs. He attacked Devenish's operation by killing Nealy and then Patty Little. Now he's coming after Miss Farnsworth because he thinks she can identify him in relation to Patty's death."

"And can she?" Halberd asked.

"No. She never saw his face, and her description of the white van is too generic."

"But he thinks there's more to it?" Whetford asked.

"He has to. That's why I waited in Miss Farnsworth's flat to see if he'd make a move against her."

"And he sent Russ Holler around to kill her." Halberd said.

"Holler says not." James had only had a brief conversation with Holler when he'd come round in the hospital, before the doctors had chased him off, but Holler had flatly denied intending to kill Gabriella.

"He was just popping round to say hello?" Halberd asked.

James's lips quirked up. "He says he was told to abduct her. He had the white van parked down the street for exactly that purpose."

"Why?"

James nodded. He agreed it was a very unlikely scenario. "He says Mr. Big wanted to find out what Miss Farnsworth knows and what she's told us. Apparently Mr. Big said he'd let her go if she didn't have any information."

Halberd leaned back in disgust.

James lifted his shoulders again. What could you do with a story like that.

"What do you think?" Halberd asked.

"I think Mr. Big told him to kill her, but he knows it'll be a lot worse for him if he admits it."

"Yes." Halberd blew out a breath, and then his gaze came to rest on Whetford, sitting silently, looking more and more put out that he was being talked over. "Did he tell you Mr. Big's real name?" he asked at last.

James shook his head. "He calls him 'the boss'. Says he doesn't know his name."

"Unlikely." Halberd finally leaned back in his chair. "You can identify Holler from his abduction of you and Miss Farnsworth, though, can't you?"

"I can. He's going away for a stretch, no matter what."

"That's something at least." Halberd eyed Whetford again. "What's next, Bob?"

Whetford straightened, and suddenly looked like a man caught with his trousers down. "Next?" he said.

Halberd dismissed him, looked back to James. "How are you going to get Mr. Big?"

"I'd like to get some cooperation from Clubs and Vice, have them put some of their undercover agents into the clubs where Mr. Big was coming up hard against Devenish's crew, and see if we can find a trail back to him. Also, I'd like someone watching Miss Farnsworth."

Halberd gave a nod. "Clubs and Vice will cooperate with you. I'll make sure of it. You think he's going to try get to the Farnsworth woman again?"

"He hasn't let anything stop him going after her before," James said. "We could let it be known to the press we don't have any witnesses to Patty Little and Nealy's murders. That we're looking for the public to come forward. That might give him the message she's no danger to him."

"We surely want him to come for her," Whetford said. "It's the best way to catch him."

"Only if there's someone on her at all times. Otherwise we're setting her up without protection." James tried very hard to keep his tone mild.

Halberd's gaze flicked between them. "I agree with Bob, using her to draw him out's a good strategy, one you've already used to good effect, Archer. Make sure there's a watch kept on her flat, and that whoever's on duty knows he's dangerous and motivated."

James gave a nod. He'd known before he'd even entered the room how that would go. Whetford had been happy to bask in the glow of catching Russ Holler, and he wanted the praise to keep coming. Using Gabriella as bait was just the kind of strategy he'd have no problem with.

He watched Whetford stand and shake the superintendent's hand and stepped aside as Whetford made for the door.

"Archer."

He turned, waiting for Halberd to say his piece. The superintendent said nothing until Whetford had passed through his secretary's antechamber and was gone.

"I know, and you know, Whetford's capabilities. You make sure you are across Miss Farnsworth's protection. Don't leave it up to him."

So Halberd had not only at least some conscience, but also eyes in his head when it came to Whetford.

James inclined his head. "I intend to."

chapter thirty-two

IT WAS MONDAY MORNING, and she had rounds. Thanks to the early hour of the attack on her flat, she wasn't even late.

Gabriella had arrived at the traffic center a little early, and went straight to Mr. Greenberg's office.

He looked up at her over the top of his glasses.

"I want to explain about Saturday," she said, coming into the room. "I was . . ." She stopped.

"You were . . .?" Mr. Greenberg gestured to the chair in front of his desk.

She could feel her lips working, and she stumbled into the chair and then looked down at her hands, took a deep breath, then lifted her eyes to meet his gaze. "It sounds ridiculous. I just listened to my excuse in my own head, and I'm almost too embarrassed to tell you."

"Are you wanting to tell me you were kidnapped along with a Met detective, held overnight by a murderer and escaped?"

She leaned back in her chair, weak with relief. "Yes."

"I was worried about you, Miss Farnsworth, and given the situation lately, I called an old friend at the Met and asked if he could check if you were in any danger. I got more than I anticipated in answer." He gestured. "Your hand is injured?"

She had rebandaged it herself, badly, this morning, and lifted it up between them. "It got caught in a van door. It's only bruised, and it's my left hand, so I can still write tickets."

Mr. Greenberg studied her. "You think it's safe to go to work today?"

She lifted a single shoulder. "They've caught the man who tried to kidnap me. I don't think it's completely wrapped up—his boss is still at large—but I can't see how I'd be in danger. I can't understand why I was to begin with."

"His boss would have been the one who instructed him to go after you, surely?"

Gabriella nodded, her lips twisted in a wry smile. "Yes. The boss is still theoretically a threat to me, but he doesn't know my new route, and he must surely have the sense to keep a low profile now someone who can identify him has been taken into custody."

"You're sure? I marked Saturday as sick leave for you, and I can do the same for today." Mr. Greenberg's kindly eyes were steady on her face.

She was living by the skin of her teeth here. She couldn't afford to take sick leave if she didn't need it, in case she actually did get sick and needed it some time in the future. She didn't want to owe anyone any favors and she didn't want what was happening to make her a problem at the traffic center.

"I'm comfortable with going out." It was hard to tell who was who under the uniform, anyway. The uniform was anonymizing. Unless Mr. Knife came right up to her, he wouldn't know her.

Greenberg studied her for another moment, then gave a nod. "As you like."

She stood. "Thank you for all your help, Mr. Greenberg."

He smiled. "Keep safe out there, Miss Farnsworth."

She had every intention of doing that.

She went to change into her uniform, and found Liz already dressed and doing her hair.

Her friend eyed her as she smoothed her blonde hair into a regulation bun and clicked her tongue. "You don't half look rough, love. And you weren't here on Saturday. I was going to come looking for you if you didn't come in today."

Gabriella laughed. It felt good. "It's a long story. Come over for dinner one night and I'll tell you." She began getting into her uniform.

Liz stood, straightened her skirt, and gave Gabriella a grin. "You're on." Then her face turned serious. "I knew the man you found dead in that car. His face was on a poster I saw on Saturday night. I didn't know his name, but he was in Dance-A-Go-Go often. You want to pass that on to that copper of yours?"

"I'll tell him." Although she thought he probably already knew all that by now. She laced up her shoes and picked her hat off the hook.

"So he *is* your copper." Liz's grin had turned sly.

Gabriella huffed out another laugh. "Maybe."

"Ooh-la-la." Liz was chuckling as they left the change room and went their separate ways.

It felt good to be out. The weather was perfect—sunny and warm—and her new route was a little closer to the traffic center than her Chelsea route had been.

Despite that, her hand was throbbing like a second heart beat by lunch time and she wondered if she should take Mr. Greenberg up on using a half sick day. She was still considering it when she turned into Mrs. Everett's street and looked out for the abandoned car.

It was still there.

Mr. Nelson's connections would have led to a quick removal if he'd wanted it gone from his old route. That it was still here told her all she needed to know about things.

When she reached Mrs. Everett's house, she paused for a moment, then decided it wouldn't be a huge breach of the rules to visit. After all, the woman had saved her life.

She had just opened the gate when someone whistled to her right.

She paused, looking around.

Teddy Roe waved at her. He was crouched in the bushes that lined the park.

She turned toward him, taking a step forward, and the horror on his face stopped her in her tracks.

He waved her back, away from his hiding place.

"What's going on, Mr. Roe?" she asked.

"Someone's got Mrs. Everett," he hissed. "A postman. He delivered a package, and then he just pushed Mrs. Everett inside. I heard her scream."

Gabriella stared at him for a moment, unsure whether to take him seriously or not. "How long ago was this?"

Teddy Roe looked around wildly, and tugged at his hair. "I don't know. Not long. I can't remember exactly." He crept out of the bush and shooed her in the direction of the house. "You go get her. I'll fetch help."

He turned and lumbered down the street toward the main road, his balance slightly off.

Gabriella watched him go, forcing down the irritation that had spiraled up. He couldn't help the way he was. She would have to ask Mr. Nelson if he knew Teddy Roe's story. He seemed to be protective of him.

She turned to study Mrs. Everett's house, then walked through the open gate but didn't approach the front door. If Mrs. Everett had been attacked by Mr. Knife—who was the only person she could think of who would do something like this—then surprise was one of her few weapons.

The house took up most of the front and sides of the property, and Gabriella went down the right narrow side access to the back. It was neatly paved, and the house stood much higher than the path. She wasn't able to look into the windows, which were set above her head.

There was no sound at all from within.

She reached the end of the house and peered carefully into the back garden.

It was a lush, proper English garden—the kind that some

English immigrants to Melbourne tried desperately to replicate, despite Australian conditions. The sound of gurgling water told Gabriella there was a fountain somewhere amongst the lavender, roses and hedges.

She edged around the corner and looked for a back entrance, and found there were two.

A sturdy wooden door into what she guessed was a mud room or kitchen, and the glass doors of a small sun room, furnished in wicker with cushions in the yellow and blue of Provence.

She chose the sun room because she could see through the glass walls that there was no one in there, and breathed out in relief that the door was unlocked.

At last, once she was inside, she could hear voices.

They were low, and nothing about the tone told her there was the desperate hostage situation Teddy Roe had painted for her. She would look an absolute pillock if it turned out Mrs. Everett had pulled the postman in for a quickie, and she was about to burst in on them.

Although the tone of the conversation didn't convey high passion, either, she realized with relief.

And she was here now.

She set down her leather bag, tucking it neatly against one of the wicker armchairs, and then climbed the two stairs from the sun room into a cool, wooden-floored passageway and followed the sound of voices. She felt slightly foolish at the way she was creeping along, but she'd feel even more foolish if Mr. Knife was holding Mrs. Everett hostage.

"I can't imagine how you believe I know anything about the girl," Mrs. Everett was saying, voice icy-calm. "She ran to my door from the street, and I just happened to be bringing the newspaper in as she reached me. I saw you and that ghastly death grin you were sporting and made a decision to help her on the spot."

Gabriella's heart, already beating fast, felt like it exploded in her chest. Teddy Roe had not been mistaken.

She leaned back against the wall, listening intently. In front of her and to the right, directly opposite the open door, was a hall table with generously curved legs and a large floral-patterned vase on top.

"Death grin, eh?" The voice that responded was cultured and slightly mocking. "You stole my prey from me, Mrs. Everett. That angered me."

Mrs. Everett didn't respond.

"I said, that angered me."

She heard a sharp crack, like a hand hitting flesh.

She tried to make sense of it. This was the behavior of a madman, not a hard-nosed drug kingpin.

What would Mr. Knife be trying to achieve by beating Mrs. Everett, just because she thwarted his plans?

"I'm waiting for a sorry," he said, voice low and mean.

"You'll not get one." Mrs. Everett spoke as if she had a mouth full of marbles. "I don't know where the girl lives, all I know is her name."

"Gabriella." Mr. Knife drew her name out in a way that made the hair stand up on the back of her neck. "I know where she lives. I know where she works. I need to know her route."

"How would I possibly know that?" Mrs. Everett asked, but her voice trembled a little now.

"You're frightened for her," Mr. Knife said. "You should be frightened for yourself."

There was a sound, Gabriella couldn't quite make out what it meant, but Mrs. Everett suddenly cried out, her voice so saturated with pain, that Gabriella moved before she was even conscious of doing so.

She leaped forward, grabbed up the vase and grunted at the weight of it and the pain in her hand as she raised it over her head.

Mr. Knife was stabbing Mrs. Everett in short, sharp motions, his back to the door, and Gabriella brought the vase down on his head with all the force she could muster.

It cracked over his head and he went down with a cry, then, like a wounded animal, he began crawling away from her.

The knife, she noticed in the brief moment she glanced at him, was still held firmly in his hand.

She tugged at the thin ropes that tied Mrs. Everett's wrists to the arms of her chair, ignoring the pain in her left hand. She had one loosened enough that Mrs. Everett could pull her arm out and had moved on to the second when Mr. Knife finally managed to pull himself up to a half-seated position.

"Well, well. Here you are." His words were slightly slurred and he stared at her with blue eyes, stark against the dark red of the blood that was pouring from his scalp. He had sandy-brown hair, and he looked totally normal.

Until you looked into those eyes. Then he looked deranged.

Her fingers trembled as she tugged at the ropes, and finally she had them off.

She reached for Mrs. Everett, helping her from the chair, and she saw the older woman could barely straighten. Her clothing was slashed. Mr. Knife had gone for her sides and her chest, and blood soaked the front of her blouse.

"You better run." Mr. Knife began to pull himself up, using the window sill behind him.

Gabriella took as much of Mrs. Everett's weight as she could bear, and pulled her out into the hallway. They needed to go out the front door. The back garden was too secluded. Too private.

They needed witnesses.

They reached the front entrance just as Mr. Knife emerged from the room, knife still tightly clutched in his fist.

Gabriella stared at the two locks on the front door in dismay. She didn't even know where the keys were.

"There." Mrs. Everett spoke for the first time, her arm trembling as she pointed to a narrow door on the right, set into the passage wall just before it opened out into the front hall.

Gabriella didn't hesitate, she grabbed the handle, opened it up, and shoved Mrs. Everett inside, slammed the door behind her and turned the lock.

Mr. Knife thumped against it a moment later.

They were in the downstairs lav.

And the door was sturdy, she noted with relief. It was solid oak, and the lock was a good one.

They had water, they even had use of the facilities.

They could stay here for quite a while without too much trouble.

Mrs. Everett made a sound, and Gabriella's optimism took a dip. Mrs. Everett might not be able to stay anywhere but a hospital right now.

She gently set her down onto the wooden floor, which had a blue and white floor rug in front of the hand basin, and leant her up against the wall.

"Medical supplies?" she asked.

Mrs. Everett pointed with a blood-stained finger to the mirrored wall cupboard above the sink, and Gabriella opened it up to find it was very well stocked.

The sound of Mr. Knife throwing himself against the door again made her flinch, and then Gabriella shook it off.

"Let's get you fixed up."

chapter thirty-three

"DETECTIVE SERGEANT ARCHER?"

The question accompanied a light knock on his doorjamb.

James looked up from his desk and found two elderly gentlemen standing outside in the passageway. One was wearing a traffic warden uniform, the other a navy wool suit.

"Come in," he said, standing. "What can I do for you?"

They had to have some pull at the Met, he realized, otherwise they'd have been made to wait downstairs in Reception, and he would have been called down. Someone had let them through.

They exchanged uneasy looks.

"It's a bit of a strange one, Archer." The one in the uniform reached over his desk, hand extended in greeting. "I'm Patrick Nelson. Retired sergeant out of the White Chapel nick, now working as a traffic warden."

"Charles Greenberg," the one in the suit said, extending his own hand after James had shaken with Nelson. "I used to work out of the Met myself. I'm the head of the Kensington and Chelsea Traffic Warden Center now."

This was to do with Gabriella.

An icy hand gripped James's gut, and he invited them to sit with a sweep of his hand as he sat himself.

"Gabriella?" he asked, getting to the crux of things.

"In a word." Greenberg gave a nod. "But it's Patrick's story to tell."

James turned to the warden.

He cleared his throat. "I switched routes with Miss Farnsworth, for her safety, last week. One of the regulars from my old route, which is Miss Farnsworth's new route, found me where I usually eat lunch, with a wild story that a man had made forceable entry into a house on the route, and that he'd asked Miss Farnsworth to intervene while he went to get help."

"You went to take a look?" James was sure they'd have first gone to check before coming to him.

"I got hold of Mr. Greenberg to let him know the situation, and I met him there. It's not far from the traffic center."

"There was no sign of anything being wrong," Greenberg said. "But no sign of Miss Farnsworth, either. She was nowhere on her route."

"You rang the doorbell?"

They both nodded.

"No one answered, but I thought there was someone there just the same." Nelson held his gaze, and James could see the shrewd, cynical expression of a seasoned copper in their depths.

"You called the local nick?" James asked.

"The local coppers won't make entry just on the say so of my informant, and it's not that I blame them, but I don't think Teddy Roe would make something like this up," Nelson said. "He was part of the night crew in the war, pulling bodies from buildings that were hit in the air raids. After what he'd gone through in the Great War, that seemed to tip him over the edge. He's been homeless since the 50s, and he isn't always in the present. But he wouldn't harm a fly, and he doesn't lie."

James got to his feet.

"You're going to do something?" Greenberg looked surprised and relieved.

"Yes." He leaned over and grabbed his coat. "Let's go."

James pulled the Wolseley up next to the house where Nelson and Greenberg were sure Gabriella had gone in, and his breath caught.

The woman who'd helped Gabriella yesterday lived around here. He recognized the park.

He'd seen it from the other side, but he was sure of it—the abandoned car had stuck out in his memory.

As they all got out of the car, he looked across the roof to Greenberg. "A woman helped Gabriella yesterday after she escaped. She might live close to here."

"Helped her escape the man trying to kill her?" Greenberg asked.

He gave a nod.

"You think the attacker came back for revenge?" Greenberg suddenly looked very worried.

That made no sense, but James lifted his shoulders. "I wouldn't have said so, but this is a strange case."

He looked around, getting the lay of the land, and saw two bobbies approaching them from across the park.

He waited for them to arrive, lifting his warrant card.

"I remember you, sir," one of them said. "You were the 'tec got locked up in that garage round the corner."

James nodded, recognizing him as one of the men who'd been put on duty to guard the entrance to the laneway where the garages were built.

"This have something to do with what happened on Saturday?" the other bobby asked.

"Could be. The woman who phoned your nick for help lives here."

"Mrs. Everett," one of the bobbies nodded. "Nice lady. But we knocked and there's no answer."

"If someone is holding her captive, they'd not answer, though, would they?" Nelson said.

"I'm going to knock again." James opened the neat gate and walked up the path, climbed the steps and knocked.

There was silence within.

Nelson gave a shout, and James turned.

"I saw someone twitch the curtain, to the right."

James leaped down the stairs to look, and the curtain was moving slightly, as if falling back in place.

"Let's go round the back." He took the right hand passage along the side of the house. It was narrow but neat, and the bobbies followed behind him.

As they came round into the back garden, a man darted out of a glass door set into a sun room, and raced to the back fence.

They all ran forward to intercept him, but he was fit and quick, and he was up and over before they even reached it.

"You chase him," James ordered one of the men. "You come with me."

He jogged to the open door, stepping into the blue and yellow room, and his gaze caught on a traffic warden's black leather bag leaning against an armchair.

He ran up the few stairs into a dark passage. The bobby followed behind, his leather boots squeaking.

James stopped in the first doorway he came to, and felt that same icy hand grab him again.

It looked like a charnel house. Blood, dark and sticky, coated a chair and pooled on the floor. Shards of pottery lay all around.

"Gawd," the bobby breathed out.

"Gabriella." James called out. "It's James, are you here?" He moved to the front of the house, eyes tracking the blood drips and smears to the front door.

He turned to the left, saw a comfortable sitting room, but there was no blood in that direction.

He turned slowly, looking for where the trail led. Stepped up to the door with blood on the handle. "Gabriella."

"James?" He heard her voice and relief had him leaning against the wall.

"Yes." His voice cracked a little. "Can you open up?"

He heard the lock turn, and she stumbled out. He wanted to take her in his arms, but she turned away, pointing into what turned out to be the water closet. "We need an ambulance. Mr. Knife has stabbed Mrs. Everett."

chapter thirty-four

GABRIELLA DOZED, the sun filtering through the hospital window warming her back and shoulders, piercing some of the icy cold she had felt since she and Ruby had taken refuge in the loo. She had been holding Ruby's hand, but must have released it at some point, her hand resting beside Ruby's on the stiff white linen of Ruby's hospital bed.

The door opened suddenly, and Ruby started, half-lifting from the pillows, and Gabriella's heart began to gallop as she sat straight up in her chair.

James stepped into the room, saw he had startled them, and winced in apology.

"Just me." His voice was soft, as if not to spook them.

Gabriella cleared her throat. "Any news?"

He shook his head. "PC Wilson didn't catch him."

He looked strained, and she reminded herself he'd been in this same hospital not two days ago.

She looked down at her hand, which some kind nurse had rebandaged for her.

They were all the walking wounded.

"He's caused quite a lot of damage."

"Yes." James looked pained even admitting it. "Are you both up for an interview?"

Gabriella looked over at Ruby, who had settled back against her pillows.

She looked more alert than she had before.

"Yes." Ruby's voice was calm and steady.

James studied her a moment, then gave a nod. "Thank you. I'll fetch my constable."

He moved back to the door, murmuring to someone in the corridor.

DS Hartridge stepped in, his gaze going to Ruby, then to her. He gave a respectful nod. "Mrs. Everett. Miss Farnsworth." He lifted a notepad and a pencil.

"Tell me what happened." James took the second chair, which was neatly pushed up against the wall, and sat. He glanced at Gabriella across the bed, and then his focus moved to Ruby.

"It was so silly," Ruby said. "I was expecting a parcel today. So when the knock came, I didn't think twice. He called 'delivery' and I thought, that's wonderful, right on time."

"Right on time, as in, that's when your postman usually stops by?" James asked.

She shook her head. "No, I mean the parcel was due today, so it was on time. Mr. Hawthorne usually comes either first thing, or last thing, so that should have alerted me to something being off, I suppose."

"So you opened the door?"

She gave a nod, sharp and thin-lipped, as if she was so disappointed in herself. "The moment I pulled it open he was on me." She closed her eyes for a moment. Sighed. "It was a shock."

Gabriella reached out and took her hand again. Squeezed.

Ruby squeezed back. "He dragged me down the passage, into the morning room, and pulled some rope out the parcel he had been pretending to deliver. He tied me up with a knife pressed against my throat." She reached out a fluttering, shaking hand, and her fingertips brushed the cut there. "Then he started asking me all kinds of questions about Gabriella. About the police investigation. I told him I had no idea about any of it."

"How did he take that?" James asked.

"He seemed to find it funny. I would almost say he knew I didn't know, and it was all a game, an excuse to hurt me."

"He must have thought you knew something, or why risk taking you hostage?" James leaned back in his chair.

Ruby narrowed her eyes at him. "He didn't need a reason, Mr. Archer. Hurting me was its own reward."

James looked like he simply couldn't believe her.

"When you told him you didn't know where I lived, he told you he already knew. That all he wanted was my new route." Gabriella felt Ruby's hand tremble in hers.

"That's right. You heard that part?" She shook her head. "Of course you did. That's when you broke Aunt Violet's vase over his head."

"Aunt Violet's vase?" she said, and grimaced. "It was a family heirloom?"

Ruby laughed, the first sign of humor she'd had so far. "A horrendous, ugly family heirloom I've felt too guilty to get rid of. You saved me twice over, Gabriella."

James cleared his throat, calling their attention back to him. "He wanted Miss Farnsworth's new work route?"

"That's what he said, but he didn't actually expect me to know. I think if I had, and had given it to him, that would have been a bonus."

"I remember what he said," Gabriella said. "About being afraid for yourself. About you ruining his plans on Saturday, and how that made him angry. He was there to punish you, to hurt you because you interfered."

Ruby gave a nod. "I think so. He didn't need any more reason than that." She looked over at James. "I must also tell you that he got hold of my husband's revolver, left over from the war. I tried to get it in our struggle and he overpowered me and took it. Once he had it though, he put it in his pocket and kept on using the knife."

Gabriella looked over at James, saw he looked pained at that information, but he still didn't seem to understand what they were telling him.

"He came after me, James, even though he had to know I would have already told you everything I remembered. Even though I couldn't have seen him kill either of his victims. He came after me because he wanted to."

"That kind of behavior . . ." James shook his head. "It's out of control. We would have seen more evidence of it."

"Maybe this is the start of his spree." Gabriella lifted her shoulders.

Hartridge, who'd been lurking by the door, scribbling away as they spoke, took a step forward. "I heard back from Clubs and Vice, sir."

James glanced back at him.

"They say one of the big heroin dealers has gone quiet in the last month. A Johnny Crane. No one's seen him, and his house looks closed up. But the supplies are still getting out. And Russ Holler, the one you caught trying to get into Miss Farnsworth's flat? Clubs and Vice says he's one of Johnny Crane's men."

"But he's still under orders from someone," James said. "It's possible someone's taken over Johnny Crane's operation."

"Mr. Knife." Gabriella saw from the start both men gave that they had forgotten where they were. Who they were talking in front of.

"We can talk to Clubs and Vice later," James said, shifting back to the bed. "Gabriella . . ." he cleared his throat. "Miss Farnsworth. You entered via the sun room?"

Gabriella sent him a cheeky grin at his slip. "Yes. I heard voices inside the house and moved quietly toward them. I heard Mr. Knife stab Mrs. Everett, and I grabbed up a big vase and broke it over his head. I untied Mrs. Everett while Mr. Knife tried to shake off the effects of being hit, and we made for the front door as fast as we could, given Mrs. Everett's injuries. He had locked the front door, though, and I didn't know where the keys were, and Mrs. Everett wasn't in a fit state to tell me, so we took refuge in the lav.

Mr. Knife tried to break the door down, then he moved away, came back to threaten us with dire consequences, and then he ran." She lifted her shoulders. "Then you came."

"What dire consequences were these?" James asked, his face set.

"We couldn't hide from him. He'd get us. We would never know safety again. Blah, blah, blah."

"Blah, blah, blah?" James's eyes flashed fire, and from behind him, Hartridge seemed to go into a coughing fit.

Gabriella lifted a hand, palm up. "I choose not to be frightened by that sick bastard."

"Quite right," Ruby said. "Never let the bastards grind you down."

James stood, shaking his head. "I'm leaving a guard on your door, Mrs. Everett. Gabriella, I'll drop you home, and increase the patrols on your street."

"When they let Ruby out of hospital, I'm going to stay with her until she recovers," Gabriella said. "Mr. Rodney has Jerome to help him, so I'm free to help her."

"All right. That will save some men, if you're in the same residence. How long until they release you?"

Ruby shook her head. "Maybe tomorrow, or the day after. They can't be sure until the morning."

A plump, rosy-cheeked nurse appeared in the doorway. "That's enough, please. Mrs. Everett needs to sleep."

Gabriella squeezed her hand a final time. "All right?"

"All right," Ruby replied. "You go get some rest, yourself."

She joined James at the doorway, and Hartridge took up watch outside the door.

"I'll wait for the PC to arrive, sir," he said.

"Thank you, Hartridge." James gave a grateful nod. "He most likely won't try anything, but it doesn't hurt to be sure."

But that's where James was wrong. Gabriella shook her head. "He might very well try. It would be a boost to his ego to get into a hospital and kill her."

James followed her down the corridor toward the lifts, his gaze sharp on her face. "It would make no sense."

"It makes sense to him, because you bested him today. Stole his prey. You better watch your own back, James. He will be as angry with you as he was with Ruby Everett."

"You seem very sure," James said.

She lifted a shoulder as they waited for the lift to reach their floor. "I turned around and looked into his face on Saturday morning, and I looked into his face again earlier today. It isn't about sense to him. It's about power and control."

And right now, Mr. Knife had neither.

chapter thirty-five

HE TOOK her home and waited while she went to take a bath. The bathroom was located at the far end of the passage, and she said how pleased she'd been when she took the flat that she only had to share it with one other person.

It meant she was vulnerable, though. Coming and going from her room. He took one of the chairs from her little table and set it in the doorway of her flat, flipping through a book he found on her shelf, a fantasy novel with a saga-like plot.

When he heard footsteps on the stairs he rose to his feet, but it was Jerome who emerged from the stairwell.

"Wotcha," he said, with a nod. "Gabby all right?"

James hesitated.

"She's not?" Jerome's gaze went to the bathroom, where the sound of running water was clear.

"She had another run-in with . . ." He didn't want to call him either Mr. Big or Mr. Knife. He wanted to call him something else. "With the suspect."

Jerome flinched. "Not the one we caught this morning?"

"No. His boss."

"I need to tell Solomon," Jerome said. "He's called the boys back a bit, since we caught t'other one, you know?"

James gave a nod. It wasn't regulation, but Solomon's eyes on the street would be a good thing to have. “No one should approach him, though. He’s dangerous.”

Jerome gave a nod, but James had the feeling he wasn’t as concerned as he should be.

The sound of water stopped, and James glanced in the direction of the bathroom.

He forced his attention back on Jerome. “How is Mr. Rodney? Gabriella says you’re taking care of him.”

“He’s doing fine. Fretting over Gabby. Someone told him she was kidnapped on her way to visit him, and he’s all tied up in knots about it.”

“He’s out of hospital now?”

Jerome shook his head. “He was supposed to be, but they kept him in. He’ll be out tomorrow, maybe.”

The door to the bathroom opened, and Gabriella stepped out, cheeks pink from the heat of her bath, wearing pale pink trousers with a pink and pale green flowered top. She had put her hair up in a topknot and she was barefoot.

Jerome cleared his throat. “I’ll be movin’ along. Nice to see you, Gabby.”

“Hey, Jerome.” Gabriella flicked her towel over her shoulder. “How’s Mr. Rodney?”

“He’ll be out tomorrow.”

Her face lit up. “I’ll have to bake a cake to celebrate. Are you staying in his place, or up here?”

“Up here, but give me a knock and I’ll go down and let you in if you want to use the oven.”

She smiled her thanks and Jerome shot him a careful look and then stepped into his flat.

Gabriella moved past him, and he brought her dining chair back into the bedsit, and set it back in place.

“You hungry?” He didn’t think she would be much in the mood to make a meal, and he didn’t want to leave her, even though that was the plan. He had already organized the increased patrols.

She hesitated, then gave a nod. "Starving."

"Let's go out and eat, then."

She shot him a quick look. "Give me a moment to fix my hair." She disappeared behind the screen that shielded her bed, and a few minutes later came out with her hair brushed and loose around her shoulders, and pale lipstick on her lips.

She had a coat over her arm. "Where are we going?"

He thought of Gennaro's. Of how he'd wondered what eating at a place like that might be like. "Gennaro's?" He made it a question.

She thought for a moment. "Not too close to the action?" she asked.

He held her gaze. "Don't let the bastards grind you down."

She threw back her head and laughed at his repeat of Mrs. Everett's words earlier. "No. We won't."

Gennaro was surprised to see them.

Gabriella exchanged a few words with him in Italian, keeping it short because it was rude to speak in a language James didn't understand.

The place looked full, but unconcerned, he had a table brought through from the back, making room for them somehow, and within moments they were seated, and a waiter was offering them wine.

"I'm a beer man." James looked a little out of his depth.

She leaned over the table. "Do you like dry or sweet?" she asked.

"Dry."

She ordered a dry white, and the waiter, who had seen her talking with Gennaro, made obsequious noises and disappeared.

Gabriella grinned across at James. "Let's hope it's drinkable."

Her words seemed to put him at ease, and he grinned back.

They sipped their wine, which James claimed to like, and she helped him choose a dish from the menu, explaining what each one was.

"My grandmother is still amazed at how simple family recipes are so popular in restaurants in Melbourne, and I've had to write to her to tell her it's just the same here in London. I keep telling her she should open a restaurant of her own."

They ate pasta and spoke about their families and their lives before London, keeping away from murder and kidnap and hostage-taking.

It felt good.

The food was what she needed—a taste of home.

Gennaro came to speak to them near the end of the meal, and she reached out and took one of his hands.

"It was good?" he asked.

She nodded. "Like home."

He tapped his heart. "Then I am happy." He turned to James. "It was your idea to come?"

James nodded.

Gennaro gave a snort, but there was approval in his gaze when he nodded back. He clapped his hands, making a production out of it. "I have tiramisu. On the house for you."

The waiter appeared and put two dishes of tiramisu down in front of them.

Gabriella didn't think she had room for dessert, but tiramisu was her favorite.

James cautiously dipped a spoon in and the look on his face when he swallowed made her laugh.

"What did he call it?" James asked.

"Tiramisu."

"Yum."

"It's my favorite," she said. She savored a few spoonfuls, then gave the rest of hers to James, who was very happy to help clean her bowl.

Maybe she would make some for Mr. Rodney's homecoming tomorrow.

James came around to pull out her chair, and then she stood with Gennaro as the floor manager, a woman she suspected was Gennaro's wife, rang up their bill.

"You should be out with an Italian man," he told her in Italian. "If you don't know any, I can help you there."

She shook her head. "What's wrong with a big, strong policeman?"

"He's not Italian. And he's a policeman," Gennaro said with a shrug. "And he speaks English with a funny accent."

She smiled. "He's Welsh. And I speak English with a funny accent myself."

"You are a beautiful Italian girl, you can do this. Him, no." But he smiled back.

"I had plenty of good Italian boys to choose from in Melbourne," she said. "I didn't love any of them."

"And you love him?" Gennaro shook his head.

"No. I like him, though. A lot. It's possible one day I could love him."

"You young things these days. It's a world gone mad. You need to like people to marry them. Me," he slapped his chest, "I married Maria because my father and her father decided it. And look how happy we are."

Gabriella eyed Maria. She didn't look particularly happy. "I can see that. You are lucky."

He sighed as James stepped away from the counter. "Go, then. Go home with your big, strong policeman."

She gave him a wink. "I will."

"What was that about?" James asked as they stepped outside. He had found a parking very close by, and he opened the Wolseley's door for her.

"He was trying to persuade me I needed an Italian man in my life." She settled in and then waited for him to come round the front of the car and open his own door.

"An Italian?" He started the car, glanced over at her, and then pulled out into the traffic. "What's he got against Welshmen?"

She gave a quick laugh. "Nothing, except they aren't Italian. And he says you speak English with a funny accent."

Now James laughed. "He's got room to talk."

"I know." She looked over at him, felt a familiar annoyance rising up in her despite the lighthearted comments. "Gennaro—others like him, like my uncles—they leave the old country because they can't thrive there; they come to a new land, with new opportunities, new ways, and what do they do? They want it to go back to the old ways they're familiar with. The very ways that made it difficult to thrive in the first place."

"You've heard the story about dating Italians before," James guessed.

"Too many times to count. So I ended up countering it by saying I was half-English, too. So did they also want me to date Englishmen." She shook her head. "They did not."

"That lets me out as well. I'm no Englishman."

"No." She watched his hands clench on the wheel. "I like you the way you are."

"Good to know." He pulled up outside her house, flexed his hands and then turned to her. "Maybe when this is all over, you'd come out with me again? Not to Gennaro's."

"Not to Gennaro's," she agreed.

He kept a careful distance from her as he walked her in, even up the stairs to her door.

The very care he was taking not to touch made her feel jumpy, made her feel the tension in him.

"Make sure it's locked tight," he said, and his gaze, when it caught hers, was electric.

She gave a nod, closed the door behind her, then leaned against it as she listened to him taking the stairs back down.

She felt like she was going to come out of her skin.

She pushed away from the door and thought of what Liz would say about this.

"Ooh-la-la," she murmured, and smiled as she headed for bed.

chapter thirty-six

CLUBS AND VICE were an interesting lot.

James knocked lightly on Detective Inspector John Drummley's door, having walked through an office full of men dressed in much sharper suits than he saw in New Scotland Yard. The station, situated in the West End, near Soho, was right in the thick of the clubs and night life of the city.

"Archer?" Drummley asked. "Detective Superintendent Halberd said you'd be over."

James shook his hand and settled in to the chair opposite his desk. "It seems we have some overlapping interests."

Drummley rubbed a hand over short salt-and-pepper hair. "So Halberd impressed upon me." He let the jibe hang in the air for a moment, and then relaxed.

James relaxed as well. Getting Halberd involved to force cooperation with Clubs and Vice could have led to hard feelings, but Drummley had obviously decided to accept it without rancor.

"This new drug you found them mixing up behind that gallery? LSD? It's going to be a real headache for us." Drummley tapped his fingers on his battered desk.

"It isn't actually illegal as yet, is that right?" James couldn't remember if Hartridge had checked, or whether they'd had word from Clubs and Vice. The last few days had been a blur.

Drummley blew out a breath. "Unfortunately, that is right. I've sent a report to the Commissioner, trying to get something to Whitehall so they can change that, but right now, anyone can go ahead and distribute it, as much as they like."

"Looks like the heroin dealers aren't any happier about it than you are," James said. "And my constable says you think one of the big dealers had done a bunk or gone missing."

Drummley nodded. "John Crane. No one's seen either him, or his missus, anywhere for a couple of weeks."

"Do you have probable cause to go into his house?" James asked. "Because if he's been killed by my suspect, I'd like to know about it."

Drummley leaned back in a black leather chair that squeaked alarmingly under his bulk. "How sure are you of that possibility?"

"My man can kill. He's got no qualms about it. He was giving orders to a couple of thugs that my constable says your men have identified as working for Crane. And Crane is gone. It's possible, if not downright likely, that my man has taken over in a bloody coup."

Drummley eyed him, then glanced at the door.

James got up and closed it, sat back down.

"One of my lot's missing," Drummley said. "No sign of him. Around the same time Crane went dark, as well."

James thought he knew where this was going, but didn't want to voice it, in case he was wrong.

"He was bent." Drummley sighed as he rubbed his cheeks. "I knew it, but didn't ever catch him on anything I could prove."

"Taking backhanders from Crane?" James asked.

Drummley nodded. "I think so. If someone's gone through Crane's organization and cleaned house, and my chap happened to be getting his orders at the time . . ."

James winced. "So he could be a victim of my suspect, too."

They sat in silence for a minute.

"Mrs. Crane's sister asked the Met for help locating her," Drummley said. He pushed a piece of paper across the desk toward James. "I asked for any contact with anyone relating to the Cranes be forwarded to me. This was received yesterday morning, so it's a bit delayed, but I can use it to go knock on the door for a welfare check."

"Mind if I come along?" James asked.

Drummley hesitated, then gave a nod. "If your man is involved, you can tell us what to look for."

James rose to his feet. "There's nothing very sophisticated about him. All we need to look for is the blood."

It seemed she had a day off.

Gabriella had gone in to work, fully expecting to be given yet another new route, but instead Mr. Greenberg had put her in a taxi and sent her home.

She could come in tomorrow, he said, but he'd give her paperwork to do, not send her out on any route—new or not.

She didn't like it, but she could see he wouldn't be swayed, and so she decided to use her free time to make tiramisu for Mr. Rodney and pack a bag to go stay with Mrs. Everett tomorrow, as she was getting out of hospital the following morning.

She had the taxi drop her at the Italian shop closest to her house, and while she winced at the cost of the mascarpone, she decided she didn't care. Mr. Rodney deserved something really special.

She walked home with her shopping bags, glad of the sunshine and the clear skies. It made it seem impossible that anything bad could happen.

She turned into her street and caught sight of a constable strolling past her house. She remembered him from the night Mr. Rodney had been stabbed, and realized he must be part of the Notting Hill nick, sent to keep an eye out for Mr. Knife.

He stopped when he caught sight of her, as if he was confused at why she would be coming toward him.

She thought about last night and wondered if James had assumed she would stay at home, and whether the bobbies on patrol had thought that was where she was.

She frowned at the thought. She had work. She thought he understood that.

Like him, she had to make her own way. They had talked about their families over dinner, and she knew he had come much further than his laborer father and his mother, who was a cleaning lady.

Her own mother worked herself to the bone, getting up at 3am to start making bread and working until she fell asleep at the table on her accounts at night.

He shouldn't have assumed.

She'd half-lifted one of the bags in greeting to the bobby when there was a rustle in the bushes that edged a run-down, abandoned building a few houses down from her own, and suddenly Mr. Knife was behind her, knife to her throat.

"Good timing," he whispered in her ear. "I wanted a witness. Can't get better than the filth."

The bobby had gone very still, eyes wide.

He was young, Gabriella saw now. And he didn't know what to do.

Mr. Knife dragged her to a black car parked on the road right beside her. She could feel the strength in his hands and arms.

She'd noticed the Bentley as she'd turned onto the street. A car like that didn't belong in this neighborhood, unless it was owned by one of the slumlords who'd bought up swathes of Notting Hill, here to cast an eye over their property.

"Open the door," Mr. Knife told her.

She bent to put down her shopping, but the knife dug into her throat.

"No. Don't drop the bag."

She awkwardly opened the passenger door with two fingers.

"Get in. Careful now, keep your shopping safe."

She slid in, putting her bags at her feet.

She kept her gaze fixed on the bobby.

He had started moving closer.

Mr. Knife gave a little chuckle, and she cried out as he pressed the knife deeper into her throat.

She felt the blood, and the constable stopped dead, eyes even wider.

"Hands out." He pulled rope out of his jacket pocket, already tied into two loops. "Quickly now."

She reluctantly did so, brain racing for a way out of the problem, heart pounding as she felt the tickle of blood running down her neck. He still looked normal, she thought, shocked. Absolutely normal.

"Good girl." He pulled on the two tails of rope between the loops, and they tightened around her wrists. There was a metal ring shaped a little like a capital letter D hanging from the center loop, open on the straight edge, and he pushed her against the still-open passenger door, and hooked the ring onto the door handle, then twisted it closed.

It was something they used in rock climbing, she remembered. Her Uncle Guido often spoke about his time climbing the Alps, and she'd seen these in the photos of him standing, one foot on a rock, mountain peak in the background.

With her hands tied, she wouldn't easily be able to unscrew it.

She was attached to the car. Trapped.

He slammed the door closed, and she leaned away from it just in time to save her head being hit by the window.

He ran around the front of the car, waving the bloody-edged knife at the bobby. There was something bizarre in the action. It was almost as if he was dancing.

He jumped into the driver seat and started up the car.

The bobby ran forward, but Mr. Knife put his arm out, waving the knife in front of her face as soon as he'd put it into gear.

He roared off, and the bobby ran after them, following them until they turned off onto one of the main roads.

Mr. Knife watched in the rear-view mirror with bright blue eyes until they lost him, moving through the traffic and then turning right, toward the city.

That didn't last long, though.

They turned again, going north, into areas she wasn't familiar with, and eventually he slowed down as he approached a drive on a leafy street where the houses were set apart, and there were hedges and large trees shielding them from the neighbors.

She caught sight of a sign that said High House in dark red letters on a cream background, and Mr. Knife turned into a long driveway, hedged in on both sides for a short way, and then opening up to reveal landscaped lawns and a massive gray stone house.

How could he own something like this? she wondered.

Houses here had to go for hundreds of thousands of pounds.

One thing was for sure, the Bentley would not be remarked upon here. If it was out of place in Notting Hill, it very much belonged in these posh surroundings.

"Home sweet home," Mr. Knife said as he pulled up at the front entrance. "Sorry, but I had to let the butler go. You'll have to bring in your own bags."

She looked over at him, studying him intently. If he had lost his mind, she'd rather understand that now.

"You don't like my jokes?" he asked her, studying her back. He had full lips and a dent in his chin. He winked at her.

"Isn't a joke supposed to be funny?" she asked.

He gave a long, slow smirk. "They're funny to me."

She'd felt panicked and frightened since he'd grabbed her, now she felt pure, cold terror.

He wasn't mad at all. He was simply enjoying himself.

"Why grab me? And why in front of a police officer?"

"It was more fun this way."

He caught her horrified expression, and jabbed the knife toward her in a feint. She jerked back, trapped between him and the door, twisted by the way he'd tied her hands.

"Come on. That shopping probably needs a fridge." He got out the car and walked around to open her door. He freed her from the door and loosened one of the loops so she could slip her hand out of it. "You carry them in."

She picked them up, wondering at this focus on her shopping. Nothing made much sense to her. His behavior was so far out of her experience, she didn't know what to make of it.

The only thing she knew for sure was that she was afraid. Deathly afraid.

He waited for her to get out of the car, then walked behind her, poking her every now and again in the back with the tip of the knife.

When she reached the front door, a dark, glossy red like the lettering on the sign at the entrance to the driveway, her hands were slick with sweat, and her arms were trembling, as if the bags were too heavy to hold.

He leaned past her, one hand between her shoulder blades, the other holding keys. He opened up and then stepped back for her to go through.

She walked into a gloomy hallway. The air smelled stale, although there was a hint of wax polish and vinegar.

A staircase ran up to a second floor to her left, and in front of her was an arch, leading into what looked like a lounge with a fireplace. The room was gloomy, barely lit by what she could see was a gap in the heavy brocade curtains pulled across a set of French doors.

"Swanky, eh?" he said. "Paul Devenish was a naughty, naughty boy. Buying a place like this with ill-gotten gains."

This was the gallery owner's house.

Her heart gave a leap, and she fought back nausea. "Where is he?" she managed to croak out.

"In the garden," he said cheerfully. "I didn't want him inside, stinking up the place. He was very conveniently having a new pond dug, so I simply threw him in and covered him over with the pile of soil very helpfully piled to one side."

That's where she'd end up, too, she guessed. Unless she found a way out of this.

She stood, trying to work out what to do.

"Kitchen's this way," he said, gripping her shoulder.

He was playing a jovial role, but the bite of his fingers told a different story. She didn't understand what he wanted, why he was playing some kind of part.

She looked down at where he gripped her so hard, and after a moment, he released her.

"This way." He gave her a shove between the shoulder blades, causing her to stagger and she lost her hold on one of the shopping bags.

As the fruit and brown packages rolled across the floor, she heard him draw in a deep breath, as if struggling for control, and she went very still, one hand against the wall for balance.

It seemed to her that violence could erupt at any moment.

He was a man with very little control over his temper, and even though this mess was his fault, he would take it out on her.

The look he shot her was venomous, but he straightened and nodded tightly to the spilled items. "Pick them up and put them in the kitchen."

He stepped back, arms folded, and watched her while she bent to put the apples, the lemons and the coffee back in the bag. It was lucky she hadn't dropped the bag with the mascarpone and the Savoiardi biscuits, or it would have been much messier.

She stood and he waved impatiently to the right. She walked in the direction he indicated, turning down a passage and then through an open door into a kitchen that smelled of fried bacon and toast.

The sink was full of dishes, and there was a plate with bacon grease and crumbs on the table.

"Perhaps you could clean up, and then make whatever it was you were planning on making." He flicked his fingers.

She put the bags down on the table, and took out the tub of mascarpone. "This needs to go in the fridge."

"What is it?" He moved over and opened the fridge for her, and she saw it was nearly empty. Mr. Knife had cleaned Paul Devenish out.

"Special Italian cream for my tiramisu."

"That's what you're going to make?" he frowned. "I've never heard of it."

She shrugged.

Silence stretched between them.

"Well, you better hope I like it," he said.

"It's a complicated dish that takes hours," she said.

"I don't believe you." He leaned against the fridge with his arms crossed.

"Look it up, there are enough recipe books there." She pointed to the shelf she'd spotted on the other side of the kitchen.

He blinked at her, then moved over to the shelf.

"The Pleasures of Italian Cooking by Romeo Salta," she told him. "I've never read it myself, but I've heard of it. And I'm sure it'll have a tiramisu recipe."

He slid the book off the shelf, paged through it.

"Coffee, biscuits, eggs, booze and cream," he said. "It sounds good."

"I think so." She began stacking the dirty dishes next to the sink and then turned on the hot water tap. While it infuriated her to play maid to him, doing something helped keep her nerves at bay, helped give her space to think.

"You weren't lying. It does take a lot of time."

She didn't answer him.

"Lucky we have time."

She was afraid of that. "What is your plan?" She didn't ask him his name, even though she wanted to know what to call him. She was frightened that if he told her, that would be confirmation that he planned to kill her.

She needed to face up to reality, though. She scrubbed hard at a plate with a stubborn streak of egg yolk on it. He was going to kill her, no matter if she knew his name or not.

"The plan originally was just to take over Johnny Crane's heroin operation." He was still paging through the recipe book with interest. "That turned out to be incredibly easy to do."

It didn't sound easy to her.

"I'd worked my way up the ranks, and he trusted me, but Mrs. Crane." He shook his head and closed the book with a snap that made her flinch. "Mrs. Crane told Johnny I was a creep."

She wondered what he'd done or said to Mrs. Crane to make her say it, but Gabriella didn't ask.

"Johnny treated me a bit different after that. He didn't know I heard his missus slag me off, but he definitely believed her. I was getting less respect. And so I decided to mutiny."

He smiled as he said the word mutiny, as if it was a private joke.

"I killed a few of the boys I knew would stay loyal to the boss, then I killed Johnny. But it was Mrs. Crane that was the revelation." He moved over to where she was washing the dishes, and leaned in, too close to her.

She was glad her hands were in the soapy water, so he couldn't see them trembling.

"It was fun killing her. I hadn't realized I wanted to so much until I was actually doing it. But it was over too quickly." He drew in a sudden, agitated breath. "And Patty was even quicker."

She swallowed down the bile that rose in her throat, and turned her attention back to the sink.

"I killed Sam Nealy because it needed doing, but Patty . . ." he was still agitated. "I was in the mindset that I was killing for a purpose, but after I got Patty in the car, I remembered Mrs. C. and I was just driving around with her, drawing it out because it was going to be so good, and then Patty tried to jump out." He was quiet for a long time. "I didn't mean to stab her somewhere where she would die so quickly. I was robbed." He trailed off. "The only good thing to come out of it was me admitting I'd been lying to myself. Patty didn't need killing. Mrs. C. wasn't really necessary, either. I just wanted to do it." He smiled. "But that's not a problem I'll have with you. I'm not going to make that mistake again."

He had held the knife the whole drive, his long fingers easily holding it pressed to the gear lever as he changed gears, and he hadn't let go of it once since they'd come into the house. Now he lifted it up. "This is the knife I used. I didn't care about the knife I stabbed Sam Nealy with, he was just business. Patty, though . . . Patty should have been more. And I have great hopes for you."

chapter thirty-seven

JOHN CRANE'S house was large for London, built on a plot that had probably once contained two or three smaller single family dwellings that had been knocked down to accommodate the faux Tudor mansion James was looking at.

It was still firmly in the working class neighborhood where John Crane had grown up, a symbol of his rise for all his peers to see.

The locksmith DI Drummley had hired to open the house up stepped back from the glossy black door. "All done."

"Thanks, Pete." Drummley shook his hand and then motioned to James. "Ready?"

James nodded, glancing back to the four Clubs and Vice officers Drummley had brought along. They were standing back, talking quietly beside their cars.

The front porch was covered in newspapers, and Drummley was clearly having some trouble opening the door.

"Too many letters through the post flap," he said, then staggered back, hand over his mouth and nose, as the door finally gave way. "God."

James caught a whiff of the stench, which caught the back of his throat. He took out a handkerchief to cover the lower half of his face as he coughed, and saw Drummley was doing the same.

They shared a look and then stepped in cautiously, leaving the door wide open to help clear the air.

But there would be no clearing this air, James saw. Directly to the left of him was a formal sitting room, and a man lay dead on the floor in a puddle of unmentionable goo.

He was so bloated by decomposition, James couldn't guess who he was looking at.

"He Crane, do you think?" he asked Drummley.

Drummley gave a quick shake of his head and a lift of his shoulders in reply.

Neither of them went into the room, leaving it for the pathologist.

James moved past the door, down a wide hallway and into the kitchen. His eyes widened at the sight of another man lying dead there, too, slumped over the kitchen table.

He looked to be at a similar stage of decomposition to the man in the sitting room. He edged around the table, and stopped dead at the sight of a second man, lying on the floor.

Drummley joined him, and something changed in his demeanor at the sight of the body on the floor.

"Your Clubs and Vice man?" James asked.

Drummley didn't answer, but the horror on his face said it all. He moved away, walking into the mudroom, and gave a cry of surprise.

"Not another one?" James couldn't believe it. He carefully stepped across the kitchen to join him, and forced himself to peer into the small, tiled room that led out to the garden.

A man lay collapsed across a bench in his stocking feet, with a pair of Wellington boots beside him. He was as bloated as the other two.

"There're his shoes," Drummley said, pointing to a smart pair of leather loafers to one side.

They moved carefully back into the hall and James stood with Drummley for a moment.

"You all right to carry on?"

Drummley nodded. "Kershaw was a damned fool," he said, "but bent copper or no, no one deserves that." He coughed, putting the handkerchief back up to his mouth and nose, and then looked up at the stairs.

James processed the horror and shock of four dead bodies as he started up. He concentrated on the balustrade, which was made of a highly polished dark wood, and the carpet that ran down the middle of the steps, which had a crazy pattern on it, probably from some famous designer he had never heard of.

"Never seen anything like it," Drummley muttered as they trudged upward, and James didn't think he was talking about the decor.

This wasn't usual. This was an outrageous crime.

He heard gagging noises from the front door, and Drummley turned.

"Outside if you're going to hurl," he shouted to his people. "Outside!"

Someone muttered a response, and when James reached the top, he caught the same, gagging smell, and gave Drummley a meaningful look.

"Another one?" Drummley asked, sounding numb.

"Smells like it." James carefully pushed open the first door they came to, but it looked like it was a spare bedroom, all pale greens and lemon yellows and empty. The next door hid a bathroom, and then they came to what had to be the master bedroom.

It was a curious mix of the masculine and the feminine.

A dark maroon carpet and heavy leather furniture, with a pink frilly dressing table beneath the window. There were two dressing rooms, one off to each side, but it was the four poster bed, a fanciful affair with gauzy white curtains gathered at the corners, and a white silk canopy, which drew his eye. Or rather, the body that lay on the bed.

"Mrs. Crane?" He could barely speak. His throat felt like it had locked up.

Drummley looked from the body to him. “I think you said your suspect has no problem killing.” He waved a hand at the body. “That’s not killing. That’s something else.”

chapter thirty-eight

GABRIELLA MADE THE ESPRESSO, impressed, despite the situation, with Paul Devenish's La Pavoni espresso machine. It was beautiful, and worked like a dream.

She poured the coffee into a shallow bowl to cool, then turned back to make herself a cup.

She probably shouldn't rev her nerves up any higher, but she didn't care.

Mr. Knife watched her, leaning back in his chair beside the kitchen table. He was playing with the knife, turning it over and over in his hands.

"Why ask me to make the tiramisu?" she asked, suddenly unable to go on without knowing.

"I'm not asking you," he said. "I'm telling you."

She lifted her shoulders in agreement. "Ordering me."

He pointed his finger at her in delighted acknowledgement. "Yes."

"Why?"

He didn't answer, but she thought she knew.

The anticipation of killing was better than the actual killing. He wanted to sit there and imagine what it would be like for a while before he did it, and it was all over.

And she had to drag it out as much as possible, in case James managed to work out where she was and could swoop in to the rescue.

But that wasn't likely.

So she would have to find a way to rescue herself.

He lifted an eyebrow when she didn't pour the espresso she'd just made into the bowl like she had before, but brought the cup to her lips for a sip.

"I want a cup."

She gave a nod, turned back to the machine, and made him one, setting the cup down on the table and pushing it across to him.

He sipped it. Gave a nod. "Better than the granulated stuff."

She went to the fridge and looked inside, then stepped back. "There are no eggs."

He frowned at her, got up and walked over to the cookbook shelf, took down the Romeo Salta book again and flicked through it. Paused. "Four eggs." He looked up. "I finished them this morning."

She had long ago decided that making the tiramisu would give her time to work out an escape, but if she couldn't make it because she didn't have the ingredients . . .

Her heart felt like it was being squeezed in her chest.

"I'm having this tiramisu. I have to know how it tastes." He stood up, tapping the tip of the knife to the table. "Get in the pantry."

She turned to the door he was pointing to and walked over to it, opening it cautiously.

It was a small, dark space, with no window, and it smelled of dried thyme and something spicy, like curry powder.

She stepped inside, and the door slammed behind her, and after a moment, a key turned in the lock. He'd obviously known about the pantry and had the key handy, and the way he so quickly ordered her in told her he had planned to keep her in here if he needed her locked away.

She fumbled around, and finally found a light switch.

She knew there had to be one, there was no way anyone could find anything in here without it.

She flicked it down and a bulb came to life overhead. It was slow and weak, but it was a lot better than nothing.

She began to go through the shelves, looking for anything that could help her escape.

It was lunch by the time James got back to New Scotland Yard.

He walked straight to Detective Superintendent Halberd's office, sure that Whetford would not be in the building. He'd be out schmoozing with someone.

Halberd's secretary was gone, but Halberd's office door was open and James could hear movement. He called a hello as a warning and then knocked on the door frame.

"Archer." Halberd looked up from his paperwork. "What is it?"

His face must have been less neutral than he thought. "Five bodies found in John Crane's home, sir. Drummley of Clubs and Vice and I went in on the grounds of a welfare check, found the bodies."

"Who?" Halberd rose from his chair, his face shocked.

"We think Crane, his wife, and two members of his gang. All stabbed." Although Mrs. Crane had been butchered, rather than stabbed. "And, the fifth . . ."

Halberd must have heard something in his voice, because he went still.

"Drummley thinks it's one of his own, sir. A copper called Kershaw. Might have been in Crane's pocket."

"Hell." Halberd blew out a breath. "And you think this is your suspect? Your Mr. Big?"

It occurred to him that Gabriella's name of Mr. Knife was definitely a better one, after what he'd seen today. He nodded. "The pathologist is on the scene, and I've come back to see what my DC might have dug up for me today while I was out. Just thought I'd let you know what's happening, sir."

"And Clubs and Vice? This is going to come down on them, especially with one of their own dead. But they'll know it."

"They've turned it over to me, but I've told Drummley if he wants to look over my shoulder, I'm fine with it. Especially if I find anything that might help them."

Halberd gave a grunt. "Good. I'll let Drummley's guv'nor know."

James thought that was a conversation he was glad he wouldn't have to have, gave a nod, and turned to leave.

"Archer, this man killed five at Crane's, and another two outside that gallery."

James stopped, gave a nod. "And tried to kill Miss Farnsworth and Mrs. Everett."

"But we've never heard of him before? He's never popped up on our radar? He just appears one day, killing left and right, and no one even has his name?"

"I know it doesn't sound feasible." James couldn't believe it himself. "Unless those killings in the Crane house snapped something in him. Gave him a taste for it."

Halberd sat back in his chair. "I'll send this up the chain. The Commissioner will want to know of something this big. Whetford will no doubt want in, as well."

James knew it. "He's out to lunch, sir. I'll find him, let him know."

"I'll do it," Halberd said.

James thanked him and left, wondering why Halberd was being so helpful.

He walked up the stairs to his own office, and found Hartridge pacing outside his door.

"Did you hear?" he asked.

"Yes." Hartridge spun at the sound of his voice. "What will we do?"

"We can't do much more at the scene until the pathologist does his thing, and given the state of the bodies—"

"Bodies?" Hartridge's eyes went wide. "What bodies?"

James frowned. "The bodies we found at John Crane's house—"

"I'm talking about Miss Farnsworth," Hartridge said, voice almost hoarse.

"What about her?" James made his lips move.

"She was abducted, sir. Right in front of the PC who was watching her house. Dragged into a car with a knife to her throat."

James thought back to the state of Mrs. Crane's body, and realized his hands were in hard, white-knuckled fists.

chapter thirty-nine

THE CHEERFUL WHISTLING WAS all for show.

Gabriella knew Mr. Knife had snuck into the kitchen first to listen silently, trying to work out what she was doing in the pantry.

She had been sitting quietly, and she heard the faint scuff of his shoe on the kitchen floor, and the faint creak of the wooden floorboards when he'd snuck in.

Then she'd heard him retreat after he'd spent some time listening, and then the bang of the door, the whistling.

He was giving himself away.

His gung-ho, upbeat, aren't-I-funny demeanor was a complete lie. This wasn't a game to him.

He could also turn his anger on and off. He had lost his temper earlier when she hadn't immediately followed his order to go into the kitchen, then stood, calm and cool-eyed while she'd picked up the groceries that had spilled in the aftermath of that temper tantrum.

He was both controlling and out of control.

She didn't think she'd ever encountered anyone like him before, but she had to find a way to outwit him.

She was getting to her feet when he unlocked and opened the door in one quick move, as if to see if he could catch her out.

"I need to go to the toilet," she told him, quite truthfully.

He blinked at that, obviously not expecting it.

After a moment's hesitation, he stepped back, and gestured with his hand, which was still clutching the knife. No subtlety there.

"Maybe I should have locked you in the lav," he said.

"Maybe," she agreed. She stopped in the middle of the kitchen. "Which way?" she asked.

He pointed with the knife again, and she walked in that direction, finding a tiny alcove leading to a narrow, white water closet with a wooden door. The lock was a hook closure.

She could hear him humming just outside. It was meant to unnerve her, and it did.

She washed her hands and stepped out, and he sniffed her hair.

"Curry?" he asked.

She lifted her shoulders. "The pantry smells of it. Maybe Devenish was a fan of Indian food as well as Italian."

He pushed her ahead of him back to the kitchen, and walked to the pantry, sniffed it. Then gave a shrug as he must have smelled for himself she was telling the truth. "Get cooking."

She moved to the cupboards, pulling out bowls and a whisk, as well as a rectangular glass dish she thought would work for the tiramisu.

The carton of eggs he'd bought was on the table, along with a bottle of marsala, which had a thin layer of dust on it.

"Looks like Devenish had the booze the recipe says is best to use." He tapped the bottle with the knife then sat back down.

Again, she found the fact that she had something to focus on a great comfort. It helped to keep her hands steady.

She worked through the steps of the recipe in her head, while Mr. Knife set the Romeo Salta book on the table in front of him and glanced at it occasionally as if to check she was doing it right.

"Why me?" she asked, even though she knew she should just work quietly, to keep herself safe.

"You kept popping up. It was obvious you were the next one. Finding Sam Nealy. Watching Patty get into my van outside that club. Finding Patty." He lifted a finger for each point. "Then there you were at that bus stop, when I took a chance to see if I could find you in that place where all the Aussies live. It was fate."

She put her head down and said nothing more. Because it wasn't bloody fate. It was him.

When the tiramisu was ready to go into the fridge to set, he rose to his feet, looking down at the recipe. "Three hours." He glanced at the kitchen clock hanging near the door. "That gives us some time, Gabriella Farnsworth. Let's go into the lounge."

"Let me just get the cocoa to sift on top, and pop it in the fridge." She didn't care that her voice sounded strained. She was terrified.

He looked at the picture, gave a nod.

She walked to the pantry. She had put the cocoa right at the back. She expected him to come and watch her, and she was not disappointed.

"I can't get it." She pointed to the tin of cocoa that was clearly out of her reach. "Can I get a step?"

He reached up to get it, and when he had his arm extended, and was up on his toes, she pulled out the jar of cinnamon she'd unscrewed earlier, and threw it in his face.

He breathed it in and began to cough and choke, and he swiped at his eyes with one hand, waved the knife at her with the other.

She shoved him, hard, out of the pantry, and felt a hot slice of pain when the knife he was slashing with caught her forearm.

She grabbed the key out of the lock, jumped back in the pantry, and slammed the door, locking it and pulling out the key. She backed away from the door as she heard the sink tap running as he washed cinnamon out of his eyes.

He was still coughing and wheezing, and the water carried on running for a while.

Then there was a clunk of pipes and the taps were switched off.

"I am very angry about this." The words were soft as they came through the door. "You won't like the consequences."

She didn't say anything. She wouldn't have liked it, whatever had happened to her. If she'd simply obeyed him and gone into the lounge, she very much doubted she'd have liked that, either.

"You can't stay in there forever," he said. "And I can find a way in."

She could stay here forever, she decided. She'd rather die in here than outside by his hand. And hopefully, somehow, James Archer would work out where she was.

It wasn't impossible.

And right now, not impossible was enough.

chapter forty

"IT WAS A BENTLEY," PC Peters said. "A black Bentley. I got some of the registration." He wrote it down on his notepad and ripped the page out, handing it to Hartridge.

James glanced at him, and the bobby shrunk a little.

"There was a lot going on, sir. I was trying to get to Miss Farnsworth."

James gave a terse nod. Blaming Peters for not getting the full registration wasn't going to help anyone.

"When did she leave the house?" Hartridge asked.

"I don't know. It seems she wasn't there when I arrived. She was walking home with her shopping bags when he took her."

"And he took her right in front of you." James was still working through that piece of information. "And you think it was deliberate?"

"I was quite obviously standing there," Peters said. "If he wanted to keep her disappearance quiet, he could have taken her just around the corner and I would have carried on thinking she was safely tucked up at home."

James had thought back to what he'd said to Gabriella that evening when he'd dropped her off more than once.

He'd thought she was staying in today, but he realized now there had been no discussion about it. He had wanted to stay the night with her, and not in a professional way, and maybe that had clouded his judgement.

He felt sick about it.

"So he wanted us to know he had her," Hartridge said. "Why?"

James thought back to what Gabriella had said to him in the hospital. "He wanted to punish me. To make me feel upset and powerless, because I ruined things for him yesterday by coming to Mrs. Everett's house and disturbing him."

He should have listened to Gabriella. She had experienced this man face-to-face, and she was a good judge of character.

"That's . . ." Hartridge shook his head. "Vindictive." He paused. "And odd."

They were not dealing with anyone James had come into contact with before, that was for sure.

"So who might own a Bentley? John Crane?" He looked over at Hartridge.

"Owning a Bentley." Hartridge frowned. "That reminds me of something, but I can't remember what." He sat down at his desk and began flicking through the Crane file. "Crane owned a Jaguar. His wife owned a Mini Cooper. No Bentley."

"He could have stolen it," Peters said.

"Go look into any reported Bentley thefts," James ordered him. "If a Bentley's gone missing, it would be reported."

Peters dashed off, and James walked over to the board they had set up. "We've got everyone in this case pinned down except three. Our main suspect, Mr. Big or Mr. Knife; the man called Fred who dumped Gabriella and myself in that garage and then disappeared; and Paul Devenish, who's never come in, never got in touch again since he jumped out his lawyer's office window and ran for it."

He hadn't gotten in touch with anyone, James remembered. That's why Lenny and Mr. Fischer had ended up fighting each other in their laboratory. Devenish had gone quiet on them, and the rats had turned on each other.

"Devenish," Hartridge said. "That rings a bell."

He began digging around on his desk, pulled out another file. "You know, I sent some PCs round to his flat to follow up on him, like you asked, and a married couple were living there. He'd rented it out to them. His father must have known he'd moved when he gave us the address, surely?"

That was interesting.

And James would agree that Sir Reginald would have known his son had let his flat out. He remembered how the old codger had made a show of looking up the address.

Bastard.

"I wonder if Sir Reginald owns a Bentley? I know Paul Devenish drives a red Berkeley Sports. I saw it parked outside the gallery." James thrust a hand through his hair, trying to remember if the Grosvenor Square house where Sir Reginald lived had had a garage.

"The Berkeley Sports is a soft-top, though, sir," Hartridge said, leaning over the file. "A summer car."

A summer car? God, he was out of his depth here.

"Here it is." Hartridge jumped to his feet, thrust the file at James. "High House, that company Golightly set up for Devenish, the one that the car Sam Nealy was driving was registered to? It also owns a black Bentley."

James stared down at the list of assets. "When did this come in?"

"Yesterday, from Golightly. It's taken his secretary this long to recreate the file Devenish took with him when he ran." Hartridge lifted a hand to massage the back of his neck, then suddenly turned to scrabble through the papers on his desk. He waved the partial registration Peters had left for them in triumph. "The numbers match!"

The numbers matched. But it wasn't Devenish in the car. It was Mr. Knife.

James thought back to John Crane's house. The slaughter.

If Mr. Knife wanted to get rid of his competition, Sam Nealy was just the first hurdle. He would have wanted to cut things off at the source. And that was Paul Devenish.

He rubbed his eyes and looked back down at the list.

Went very still.

There was another asset. An address in Hampstead Heath.

"Hampstead Heath is a posh area, isn't it?" he asked Hartridge.

"Very."

"So the addresses there, they're most likely to be single dwelling houses, not flats." Nice, private, standalone dwellings. And it was called High House, for God's sake. It was probably a mansion with thick walls.

He reached for the phone.

"Who are you calling?" Hartridge asked.

"Golightly." He gave the operator instructions to find the correct number.

"You think he'll cooperate?" Hartridge asked.

"He better," James told him. "Or I'll see him in hell."

chapter forty-one

THE SOUND of gardening started up around lunch time.

Gabriella had stood up and gone to the back wall of the pantry, in the vain hope she'd hear more, but it was just the far-off sound of a lawn mower and the odd shouted comment between at least two men.

A garden service, perhaps?

This wasn't Mr. Knife's house, and he wouldn't want anyone to report a suspicious person inside, especially if they knew Devenish, so he'd need to keep quiet and go to ground.

He'd tried to batter the door to the pantry down a few times with his shoulder, but it was solid oak, and the hinges, while they groaned a little, held well enough.

They wouldn't hold forever, but she had a temporary reprieve.

"They won't hear you, if you're thinking about shouting." Mr. Knife's voice came as a sudden, electrifying shock.

He was sitting right outside the door and she had been so intent on the gardeners, she hadn't heard him.

She had already worked out that screaming wouldn't do any good. She could barely hear them, and over the mowers, she wouldn't have a chance.

But there was something in the way he spoke which made her

think he was fearful, or at least uncertain, and she suddenly remembered he had said Devenish's body was buried in the garden, where they were putting in a pond.

"Better run, hadn't you?" she asked. "They may not hear me shout, but they'll definitely call the police if they find Devenish's body. And then the house will be searched."

"They won't find it," he said, but she heard him move away.

Now would be the time for her to run, while he was distracted. There was help for her outside, and he would be somewhere in the house, probably upstairs, keeping watch to see if the gardeners discovered Devenish.

But he would have also probably locked all the entrances.

She wouldn't have a way out.

There were French doors out into the garden, though. And plenty of chairs in the kitchen she could use to smash through their glass windows.

She lay on her stomach, wincing as the cut on her forearm objected to her movement, and angled her head to see under the door into the kitchen.

There was no sign of Mr. Knife, but she honestly wouldn't put it past him to stand on the table or a chair to play games with her.

She could open up fast, check, and close again if he was there.

He wouldn't have time to get to the door if she was focused about it.

She held the big key in a trembling hand, but before she slid it into the lock, she crouched down and looked through the keyhole.

Again, there was no one there.

She needed *il coraggio*—courage—and she slid the key carefully into the lock, being as silent as she could, then pulled it open in a single twist of both the key and the handle.

The kitchen was empty.

She ran, grabbing up one of the metal-legged chairs with a thin wooden seat and back, and raced down the corridor, turned right into the lounge and then remembered there were curtains over the doors.

She yanked them open with one hand, looked over her shoulder, and seeing nothing, took a few steps back, lifted the chair up over her head, and slammed it into the glass door.

It was thick glass.

It cracked but it didn't break, and panicking, she slammed the chair into the glass again.

This time it did give, shattering outward.

She heard the sound of him, an animal noise, behind her, and she leapt through, glass shards crunching under her shoes, and a piece of glass stuck in the door frame caught at her sleeve and pulled her back slightly.

She jerked it free and ran, shouting as loudly as she could.

She didn't get far, though.

He was on her, arm clamped around her waist, hand over her mouth, dragging her back inside.

She kicked out, trying to slow him, hinder him any way she could, screaming behind his hand, and a shout from one of the gardeners gave her hope.

But he was relentless. He pulled her down the hallway, back into the kitchen, and bodily threw her into the larder.

She landed hard, winded, just in time to see him grab the key out the lock and slam the door, locking her back inside.

She'd gotten nowhere, except now she didn't control the key.

She slowly rolled onto her stomach, got her knees bent under her, and used the larder shelves to help her stand.

The mower was off now, and the gardeners were talking excitedly.

So maybe she hadn't gotten nowhere.

She heard their voices get closer, and then the sound of Mr. Knife hailing them.

How was he going to fast talk away all that? she wondered.

Mad girlfriend? Hysterical woman?

Why not? It's not as if it hadn't worked many times before.

They were talking too quietly for her to hear any longer, and she began to stockpile tin cans at the back of the larder for ammunition, and then, because she didn't have anything to lose anymore, she began to smash jars by holding onto their metal lids. The best one was a vinegar bottle that contained rosemary and chillies.

It felt right in her hand, and gave her more reach than the fatter, rounder jars.

It had broken into jagged spikes, and she reckoned she could do some damage if she stabbed him with it.

She had tried to do the smashing to one side, but it was a narrow larder, and she would have to watch the tricky situation underfoot now that she had emptied jams and pickles everywhere.

She also finally found the curry powder.

It was in a hessian sack behind a stack of pickles, and she scooped some out into a small bowl she found.

Cinnamon in his face had worked well. Curry might actually work better.

chapter forty-two

JAMES WAS ABOUT to turn into the driveway of High House when a dark green van with Bromwell's Gardening Services stenciled in pale cream on the side blocked the way, drawing up with a squeak of brakes at the sight of the Wolseley.

"Police," he said. "You've been on the property?"

The man driving blew out a relieved breath. "Glad to see you, 'n' all. Gary and me didn't know what to do, like."

"What to do?" He forced down his impatience to get moving, because there was something going on here. The two men were rattled.

"Lady threw a chair through a glass door," the man said. "Like, that's not normal. And this chap—not Mr. Devenish, some mate of his, apparently—he comes out and says how she's on drugs or sommat."

"And there's the leg." The second man in the van leaned over.

"Pipe down, Gary. There wasn't a leg." The first man shook his head.

"There was a leg. I saw it just before that chap told us we could knock off early. In the pond." Gary was not budging.

"We'll take it from here." James turned to Hartridge and he reversed the car back so the van could get past them.

"Cheers," the driver said. "Weight off my mind."

They drove off.

James and Hartridge exchanged a look.

"The Hampstead nick said they'll send some bobbies, but I don't see them now. And we don't have time to wait." Gabriella was in there. The sight of Mrs. Crane's body kept creeping into his thoughts, and he had to swallow. Hard.

He drove up the long drive, noted the Bentley parked near the front door.

He got out, went to the back of the Wolseley and opened the boot.

He took out a truncheon, handed it to Hartridge, then chose a piece of metal pipe he had somehow inherited with the car. It had a nice, hefty feel to it.

"Do we go in the front door?" Hartridge asked, his voice a little unsteady. Nerves and excitement, James guessed.

"They said a woman smashed her way out of the house through a glass door in the back. Let's go see." He headed around the side of the building and caught a sudden dart of movement, as if someone had ducked around the corner.

He adjusted his trajectory, moving away from the wall, and alerted Hartridge that there was someone there.

When he came around the corner, fast and with pipe raised, there was no one there. Whoever it was had retreated into the house, and at a fast run.

"She used a chair to smash through," Hartridge said, admiringly.

The chair lay in the garden, just outside the door, and James moved it aside. A shard of glass stuck out from the door frame, and on it was a smear of blood and a wisp of white cotton.

He didn't know that he had ever been so terrified and angry in his life.

Beyond the door was a well furnished formal lounge with leather couches and a big fireplace. The drug trade had obviously been kind to Devenish. Until he'd been murdered for it, that was.

James stepped inside and heard Hartridge behind him.

There was noise coming from deeper in the house and he jogged out of the lounge into the entrance hall, then went left, pipe loose in his hands.

The noise was clearer now.

Shouting. The sound of things being thrown.

He stepped into a kitchen, a large room with an old-fashioned Aga range to one side, and nearly tripped on a tin can lying on the floor.

A man stood to the side of a pantry door, knife in one hand, gun in another, shoulder slightly hunched as another tin can flew out at him.

He glanced at James, and the sudden malevolence that crossed his face sent a chill down James's spine.

James wondered where he'd gotten the gun, and then recalled Mrs. Everett had said hers had been stolen after she'd been attacked.

Hartridge crowded behind him. "I think I heard a car, sir," he murmured. "Might be the Hampstead bobbies."

"Get the exits covered. Make sure everyone's aware he's armed and dangerous." James kept his eyes on Mr. Knife as he answered.

Hartridge disappeared.

The man shoved his knife into a pocket, scooped up a tin and flung it with force back into the pantry, and he heard Gabriella cry out in pain.

"Come out. Now. With luck you might wriggle out of your fate a second time." He pointed the gun into the pantry, angled so he could still see James, and pulled the knife out again.

"How many times do I have to wriggle out for it not to be fate anymore? Or why isn't my fate to always escape?" Gabriella's voice was strained but calm.

The man cocked his head. "Tricky. You are tricky." He pointed the knife at James. "And you are interfering and annoying."

Gabriella was suddenly in the doorway, swinging something

down on Mr. Knife's hand holding the gun. It went off, a bullet hitting the floor, cracking the tile.

Gabriella seemed to draw back and hit out again, and the man staggered into the kitchen, still clutching the gun, looking back at Gabriella, who was standing by the door, a slim, broken bottle in her hand.

It was dripping blood.

The man looked down at his side, at the blood soaking his white t-shirt, and then lifted the gun to point straight at Gabriella.

He didn't see the swing of James's pipe coming.

chapter forty-three

SHE WAS TREATED in the back of the ambulance, sitting amongst the wailing sirens and flashing lights of the police cars.

She had a cut to her neck, which she barely remembered getting, the cut on her forearm, another to her upper arm from the French door, and the deep bruise on her collar bone when she'd caught the tin of baked beans Mr. Knife had thrown back at her.

They still didn't know his name.

She didn't really care any more.

He had been taken off to hospital already. Her upper arm was stitched, because the medic said they might as well, as it was only going to take two stitches, and then she was given a cup of tea and left to sit on the ambulance's tail gate.

She thought longingly of the espresso machine in the kitchen, and given the chaos around her, decided she might as well give it a go.

She walked into the house, which was more or less empty, as the body was out at the pond, and found the kitchen was empty, too.

She started up the La Pavoni, and was just scrounging in the fridge for milk when she heard someone enter behind her.

James leaned on the doorjamb, arms crossed over his chest, and the look on his face was hard to describe.

"I'd have thought this was the last place you'd want to be," he said.

"Devenish has a very good espresso machine," she answered, milk in hand, and added a dash to her cup. "Do you want some?"

"I think I've had enough stimulation for one day," he said.

She opened the fridge to put the milk back, and he was suddenly right behind her, hand just above hers on the fridge door.

"Is that tiramisu?"

She turned, standing very close to him. "I was going to make it for Mr. Rodney's homecoming from hospital. He made me make it for him, instead."

James frowned, as if he couldn't quite believe her.

"I'm taking it with me, by the way. It isn't evidence of anything other than Mr. Knife's weirdness. We're all going to have some. Me. You. Mr. Rodney. Jerome. Solomon, if he's in." Gabriella took the tiramisu out of the fridge, holding it in front of her defensively, and looked across at him. "Can we go home now?"

James slid a hand along her shoulder, as if to make sure she was actually there. "Let's go."

"Did you eat the tiramisu?" Ruby Everett asked as Gabriella settled her into an armchair.

"We ate it until we were sick," Gabriella said, without a trace of regret. "James said they found out Mr. Knife was someone called Colin Pratt. He was a low level thug, a stand-over man for Johnny Crane, knocking heads together to keep Crane on top of the pile when it came to distributing heroin. The police still can't believe he went from that to killing eight people and trying to kill you, me and Mr. Rodney."

"And Mr. Rodney? How's he doing?"

"He'll be fine, but it'll take him time to recover."

Ruby Everett leaned back in her chair and gave a sigh of contentment. "It feels good to be home."

A faint, almost nervous knock at the front door made both of them stiffen.

"It's Teddy Roe, Mrs. Everett. Teddy Roe."

They both relaxed.

"Let him in, Gabriella. Add another cup and saucer and he can join us for tea."

Gabriella wondered if Teddy Roe had any use for tea, but she pulled the door open and invited him in, and he seemed very pleased to be asked.

He sat, perched on the very edge of his chair, and she thought his clothes looked better than they had before. Cleaner and newer, and someone had given him access to a bath and a cut and shave.

"You're looking very dapper, Mr. Roe."

He smoothed a hand self consciously down the front of his jacket. Cleared his throat. "Mr. Nelson fixed me up, given the council came round for the car." He sounded forlorn. "Gives me a place to stay, but we have to be out by ten, and they let us back in at six in the evening."

"I've been thinking about that, Mr. Roe." Mrs. Everett set down her cup. "Would you be interested in converting the little shed in my back garden into a place to stay? There is a bathroom in there, because it used to belong to a writer who used it as a studio. There is junk in there that'll need clearing out, but it could be quite cosy, and I would feel a lot happier having someone on the property after what happened. Especially if you're happy to help me with the gardening."

"'Cause I got help," Teddy Roe said. "I went for help."

"You did." Mrs. Everett winced a little as she shifted position. "You saved us both, Mr. Roe, and if you would be so inclined to consider it, I would be very much obliged."

"What happened to him wot did it?" He nodded to the bandage on her arm.

"The police arrested him. He's in prison."

"He'll hang, then?"

"He'll hang," Mrs. Everett confirmed.

"I could go back and take a look at the shed, see if I could make do there," Teddy Roe said, scooping up a sandwich from the plate as he stood. "But I don't know much about gardening, right?"

"That's fine. I do, and if you can help me, that would work very well."

Gabriella showed him out into the back through the sun room, and watched him walk to the end of the garden.

She wondered if he realized his steps were jauntier already.

She went back into the house, made sure Ruby had everything she needed close to hand, and then left just in time to catch the bus back to Notting Hill.

"Back in the Gate so quickly?" Solomon was coming toward her as she turned onto her road.

"I'm only staying with Mrs. Everett for a week," she said. "But I forgot a few things."

"That copper, the one that's sweet on you, he going to be a problem?" Solomon asked.

She stopped, looking up at him. "Not from anything I say."

He gave a laugh at that. "Fair enough. He seems a decent sort, actually. Gave me a lift home once 'n' all." He nodded up the street. "He's waiting for you outside the house."

Gabriella waved goodbye to him and then walked a little slower toward where James leaned against the car.

He watched her approach, and she felt a flush run through her at the look in his eyes.

"What are you doing here?" she asked, clearing her throat.

He pushed off from the car. "I went round to Mrs. Everett's to visit you, but she said you'd taken the bus here. I thought I'd meet you, give you a lift back."

"Thank you."

He held the gate open for her politely. "You're back on your rounds yet?"

"I start tomorrow. Mr. Greenberg kept me on desk duty for a few days, but I'm back to the route he gave me last week, going past Mrs. Everett's place, for the next few months."

She unlocked the front door and pushed her way in, holding it open for him and then going to look for the post.

She saw a letter that made her heart leap in her chest, a letter with a shipping liner logo in one corner, and put it at the bottom of the pile. The ship's manifest had finally arrived.

Somewhere in the enclosed document was her father's real name.

She forced her thoughts away from what it could mean as she started up the steps, all too aware it could lead to yet more disappointment.

"What's happened to everyone in the case? Patty's boyfriend, Lenny, and the Swiss chemist, Mr. Fischer? Are they in trouble?"

"Fischer's being deported, as he didn't have the correct visa to work here. If Devenish had lived, he'd have been charged with illegally bringing in some of the ingredients to make the LSD from Germany. Clubs and Vice wanted to link the purchases to Fischer, but his name isn't on any of the paperwork, it was all Devenish, so he's clear of that. Devenish's father is in hot water, because it was his position in the Ministry of Health that gave Devenish the idea to start selling the LSD while it was still unregulated, and Lenny Foster, Patty's boyfriend, will be charged with assault for his attack on Fischer, but that's about all we can get him on."

James's answer took them all the way up to the top floor.

"But Colin Pratt is caught, and it is all over." She unlocked her door and felt a catch of regret that she was going to go back to Ruby Everett's. She just wanted to burrow down here, curl up on her window seat and sip coffee.

Maybe open the letter that seemed to be burning her fingers.

"Not completely over," James said, maneuvering her into the room and closing the door behind him.

Her breath caught at the way he held her, big hands spread over her shoulders.

"I hope we can have that dinner we spoke about."

She tilted her head up to him. "The one not at Gennaro's?"

"That one," he agreed.

"Maybe you can take me to a Welsh restaurant."

He paused, looking completely thrown. "I think I'd have to take you up to Wales for that," he said.

"Oh, well." She was equally at a loss.

"I'm sure it could be arranged. Or maybe you'd accept dinner made by an actual Welshman?"

"I would like that." She was holding her hands clasped in front of her, like some kind of Madonna, which made her feel ridiculous, and she stepped back. "I'll just pack." She could feel her cheeks heat as she turned away, flustered and excited at the same time.

He looked serious when she came out from behind her screen with a small bag in hand. "You're nervous."

She stared at him, dropped the bag, and lifted her hands. "Of course I'm nervous!"

He looked from her dropped bag to her hands. "Throwing your hands up. That's very . . . Italian of you."

She stepped forward and grabbed him by his jacket lapels. "And what's something the Welsh do?" she asked.

He bent his head to kiss her, and somehow, she never found out.

Look out for the next book in the Traffic Warden Mysteries, coming 2024.

also by michelle diener

Historical Fiction Novels

Susanna Horenbout series:

In a Treacherous Court

Dangerous Sanctuary (A short story - available for free, exclusively to readers who sign up to Michelle Diener's New Release Notification List)

Keeper of the King's Secrets

In Defense of the Queen

Regency London series:

The Emperor's Conspiracy

Banquet of Lies

A Dangerous Madness

Other historical novels:

Daughter of the Sky

Fantasy Novels by Michelle Diener

The Rising Wave series:

The Rising Wave (Prequel novella to THE TURNCOAT KING)

The Turncoat King

The Threadbare Queen

Fate's Arrow

Mistress of the Wind

The Dark Forest series:

The Golden Apple

The Silver Pear

Science Fiction Novels

Verdant String series:

Interference & Insurgency Box Set

Breakaway

Breakeven

Trailblazer

High Flyer

Wave Rider

Peace Maker

Sky Raiders series:

Intended (Short Story Prequel Available Free to Newsletter Subscribers)

Sky Raiders

Calling the Change

Shadow Warrior

Class 5 series:

Dark Horse

Dark Deeds

Dark Minds

Dark Matters

Dark Ambitions: A Class 5 Novella

Dark Class

Dark Class Epilogue: Free on newsletter signup

To receive notification when a new book is released and to get access to exclusive subscriber content, sign up to Michelle's New Release Notification List at michellediener.com.

about the author

Michelle Diener is an award winning author of historical fiction, science fiction and fantasy.

Michelle was born in London and currently lives in Australia with her husband and children.

You can contact Michelle through her website or sign up to receive notification when she has a new book out on her New Release Notification page.

Connect with Michelle

www.michellediener.com

acknowledgments

Thanks to Creative Paramita for the cover. Thanks as always to Claire and Jo, I am grateful for your suggestions. And thank you also to Tania H & Diane J on my reader team.

Printed in Great Britain
by Amazon

ARTILLERY

WARSAW PACT

Artillery of the Warsaw Pact

Russell Phillips

Shilka Publishing
www.shilka.co.uk

Shilka Publishing
Burslem
Stoke-on-Trent
www.shilka.co.uk

Ordering Information:

Quantity sales. Special discounts are available on quantity purchases by corporations, associations, and others. For details, contact the "Special Sales Department" at the address above.

Artillery of the Warsaw Pact/ Russell Phillips. —1st ed.
ISBN 978-0-9955133-8-9

Contents

Introduction

The Warsaw Pact (more formally, the "Treaty of Friendship, Co-operation, and Mutual Assistance") was formed on 14th May 1955. Officially, it was created in response to the formation of NATO in 1949, and the re-armament and integration of West Germany into NATO. Another, unacknowledged motive was a Soviet desire to control Eastern European military forces. The Warsaw Pact was disbanded at a meeting of defence and foreign ministers on 25th February 1991, and the Soviet Union was dissolved the following December.

The signatories of the Warsaw Pact were:

Albania
Bulgaria
Czechoslovakia
German Democratic Republic (DDR)
Hungary
Poland
Romania
Soviet Union

In 1962, Albania supported China over the Soviet Union in the Sino-Soviet split. They severed relations with the Soviet Union and ended active participation in the Warsaw Pact. In

1968, Albania protested the invasion of Czechoslovakia, and later that year they formally withdrew from the treaty.

The Soviet army, and the Russian army before it, referred to artillery as the "god of war", and was deservedly proud of the artillery arm. During the Second World War, most artillery pieces were towed, with only multiple rocket launchers being developed as mobile systems. The only self-propelled guns were tank destroyers and assault guns designed for direct fire, rather than artillery guns and howitzers intended to provide indirect fire support.

Multiple rocket launchers (MRLs) were pioneered by the Soviet Union during the Second World War, when they were officially known as Guards Mortars, but commonly known by the nickname Katyusha. The ease of construction compared to tube artillery (which requires complex tools for rifling barrels) meant that mass production was possible even after many of the armaments factories had been overrun by the German army. The relative ease of manufacture of mortars meant that they were also widely employed during the Second World War and afterwards, with very large calibre weapons being developed.

A note on armour thickness: sloping armour increases the thickness of armour that a weapon has to penetrate. The effectiveness of sloping can be calculated using the formula Teff=T/Cos(x), where T is the thickness of the armour plate, x is the angle from vertical, and Teff is the effective thickness. The increase in effectiveness for various angles is given below:

10°: 1.02
20°: 1.06
30°: 1.15

40°: 1.31
50°: 1.56
60°: 2.00
70°: 2.92
80°: 5.76

In the above list and throughout this book, armour angles are given in degrees from the vertical: so, 0° is vertical, and 90° is horizontal. In the vehicle listings, where the armour is at an angle, the effective armour thickness is listed in square brackets.

ARTILLERY VEHICLES

The Soviet Union developed several specialised vehicles for artillery command and control, and some fully tracked artillery prime movers, although artillery was more commonly towed by lorries, which would usually have all-wheel drive.

MT-LBUS

Often referred to in the West as the Artillery Command and Reconnaissance Vehicle (ACRV), this family of vehicles were developed alongside the 2S1 and 2S3 self-propelled howitzers. Variants were later developed for a range of specialised roles to support other arms. Based on the MT-LB, it shared a number of automotive components with both that vehicle and the 2S1.

The hull was of welded steel armour, thick enough to provide the crew with protection from small arms and shell splinters. The commander and driver were seated at the front, and each had a roof hatch that could be locked in the vertical position, and a large window with an armoured shutter. The driver had three periscopes, the commander one swivelling periscope. The engine was mounted behind the driver and commander. It had a torsion bar suspension with seven rubber-tyred road wheels on each side and the drive sprocket at the front.

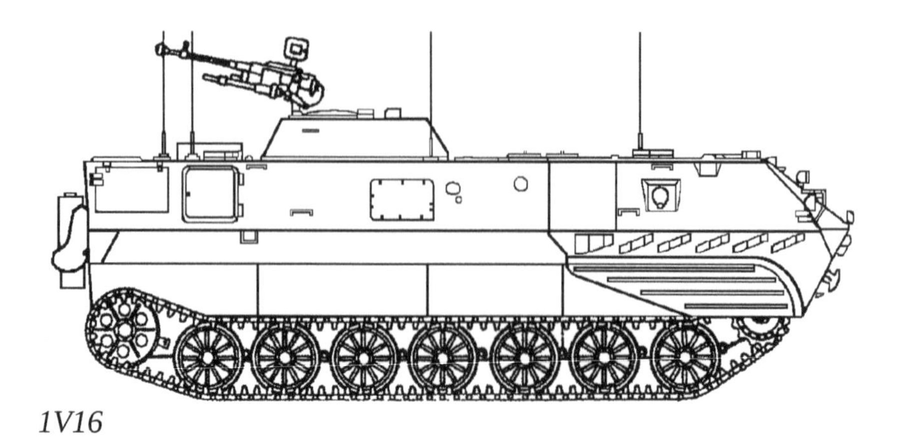

1V16

A single door was fitted at the rear, with a vision device and firing port. Roof hatches varied according to the role the vehicle was intended for. Seating was provided for seven, but the crew varied according to role, with all except the driver and commander in the rear. An auxiliary power unit was fitted, the vehicle had overpressure NBC protection, and was fully amphibious, propelled in the water by its tracks at a speed of up to 4.5km/hour. To prepare for swimming, the bilge pump was switched on, the trim vane erected, shrouds fitted to the hull side at the front, and the front road wheels were covered.

Each 2S1 or 2S3 battery had two vehicles, for the battery commander and deputy commander. The battery commander's vehicle would serve as an observation post for the commander, and the deputy commander's vehicle would serve as the battery fire direction centre. The battalion command platoon had a vehicle for the battalion commander, and one for the deputy commander, which would serve as the battalion fire direction centre.

Four variants with minor differences were used by 2S1 and 2S3 batteries. Known as the 1V12 series, they were designated 1V13 (battery fire direction centre), 1V14 (battery command vehicle), 1V15 (battalion command vehicle), and 1V16 (battalion fire direction centre). The 1V13 had a crew of six, and was fitted with a one-person cupola with vision equipment and a 12.7mm DShKM machine gun. The 1V14 had a crew of six, was fitted with whip antennas, and carried a dismountable range finder. The 1V15 had a crew of seven and was fitted with a 10m telescopic antenna, stowed horizontally on the upper left hull when in transit. The 1V16 had the same antenna as the 1V15, but was also fitted with an electronic field artillery computer.

Specifications: MT-LBus

Combat weight: 15.5 tonnes
Length: 7.48m
Width: 2.85m
Height: 2.43m
Ground clearance: 0.4m
Maximum road speed: 62km/hour
Maximum road range: 500km
Gradient: 77%
Vertical obstacle: 0.7m

Armour:
Turret: 20mm
Hull: 15mm

PRP-3

This vehicle, also known as BMP-SON, was based on a BMP-1 hull. It entered service in the early 1970s and was used with 2S1 and 2S3 units. The original turret was replaced with a larger two-man turret, fitted with two single-piece hatch covers opening forward. Each hatch had periscopes and a large optical device in front of the hatch. The vehicle had a crew of five, and the only armament was a 7.62mm PKT machine gun in the turret.

An antenna for the Small Fred battlefield surveillance radar was mounted on the rear of the turret, which was folded forward to the horizontal when not in operation. The Small Fred radar had a detection range of 20km and tracking range of 7km. There was a circular hatch and telescopic aerial on the left of the turret, toward the rear. A 90mm launcher for illumination rounds was fitted on the rear deck. Twenty illumination rounds were carried, which could be fired at ranges of 100m to 3,000m. Night vision devices and a laser rangefinder were also fitted.

PRP-4

This was a further development of the PRP-3, which entered service in the 1980s with units equipped with 2S1 and 2S3 self-propelled guns. It was designed to carry out reconnaissance of both stationary and moving targets, including low-flying helicopters, under all weather conditions, at day and at night.

Like the PRP-3, the hull was similar to that of the BMP-1, but with a larger, two-man turret, mounting a single 7.62mm PKT machine gun and optical devices. An antenna for an IRL-133-1 radar was fitted to the rear of the turret, and was folded down when not in use. The radar could detect and track MBT-sized targets at a range of 8-10km. A thermal imaging system was fitted on the left side of the turret, and an IR night vision device was fitted on the right side, along with a laser rangefinder. A man-portable laser rangefinder was carried inside the vehicle for use by dismounted teams.

An auxiliary power unit was fitted to power the extensive communications and reconnaissance equipment. Like the BMP-1, the PRP-4 was amphibious, had NBC protection for the crew, and could create smoke by injecting diesel fuel into the exhaust outlet.

Specifications: PRP-4

Crew: 5
Combat weight: 13.2 tonnes
Length: 6.74m
Width: 2.94m
Height: 2.15m
Ground clearance: 0.37m
Maximum road speed: 65km/hour
Maximum road range: 600km
Armament: 1x 7.62 PKT MG

SNAR-10

Originally thought by NATO to be an artillery location radar, the SNAR-10 (known to NATO as Big Fred) was actually a battlefield surveillance radar. Its primary role was the location of stationary and moving targets in the forward edge of the battle area.

The radar antenna was mounted on a turret fitted on the rear of an MT-LB tracked vehicle. The antenna was folded forward to lie on top of the turret when in transit, and raised for use. It could detect moving targets at ranges of up to 16km, and plot artillery projectiles at up to 10km. The vehicle also had two R-123M radios, a PAB-2A aiming circle, a power generator and a TV-240 observation device for the commander. An improved version, the SNAR-10M, was introduced in 1982.

The vehicle retained the NBC protection and machine gun turret of the standard MT-LB. Unlike the standard MT-LB, however, it was not amphibious.

Specifications: SNAR-10

Combat weight: 12.6 tonnes
Length: 6.45m
Width: 2.86m
Ground clearance: 0.4m
Maximum road speed: 62km/hour
Maximum road range: 500km
Gradient: 60%
Vertical obstacle: 0.6m
Trench: 2.41m
Armament: 1x 7.62mm PKT machine gun (2,500 rounds)
Armour: 4-10mm

ARK-1 Rys

Like the SNAR-10, the ARK-1 mounted a radar at the rear of an MT-LB tracked vehicle. It retained the MT-LB's NBC protection, but omitted the machine gun turret. In 1986, the

ARK-1M was introduced, which added a generator, mounted at the rear of the vehicle.

An artillery location radar, it had a crew of four. Mortars could be detected at ranges of up to 13km, guns and howitzers up to 8km, multiple rocket launchers up to 25km, and tactical missiles at ranges of up to 30km. It could track up to three targets simultaneously.

Specifications: ARK-1 Rys

Combat weight: 15.7 tonnes
Length: 7.62m
Width: 2.85m
Maximum road speed: 60km/hour
Maximum road range: 500km

Ya-12 & Ya-13F

Both the Ya-12 and Ya-13F entered service toward the end of the Second World War. They were identical in appearance, but the Ya-13F had a petrol engine, which was slightly less powerful than the Ya-12's diesel engine.

They were of conventional design: the engine was at the front, with the cab behind, and the cargo/personnel compartment at the rear. The suspension had five road wheels, with the idler at the front, the drive sprocket at the rear, and three return rollers. Unlike the later M-2, they had a single headlamp, mounted at the bottom left of the radiator.

Specifications: Ya-12 (Ya-13F in brackets)

Crew: 1+1
Weight: 6.5 tonnes (empty) (5.7 tonnes)
8.5 tonnes (loaded) (8.5 tonnes)
Maximum load: 2 tonnes
Towed load: 8 tonnes (5 tonnes)
Length: 4.89m
Width: 2.4m
Height: 2.2m (cab) (2.29m)
Ground clearance: 0.31m
Maximum road speed: 37km/hour (23km/hour)
Maximum road range: 290km (210km)
Gradient: 60%

M-2

Introduced after the Second World War, this was the replacement for the Ya-12 and Ya-13F. Its main distinguishing features were the two headlamps, front bumper, and higher cargo area. The Hungarian K-800 was very similar to the M-2.

The M-2 had a conventional design: the engine was at the front, with the cab behind it, and the cargo compartment at the rear. The suspension was similar to that of the SU-76, with five road wheels, idler at the front, drive sprocket at the rear, and three return rollers.

The M-2 was used to mount the Long Trough (SNAR-1) radar system.

Specifications: M-2

Crew: 1+1
Weight: 7.2 tonnes (empty)
Maximum load: 2 tonnes
Towed load: 6 tonnes
Length: 4.97m
Width: 2.82m
Height: 2.33m (cab)
Height: 2.45m (tarpaulin)
Ground clearance: 0.37m
Maximum road speed: 35km/hour
Maximum road range: 330km
Gradient: 60%
Vertical obstacle: 0.5m
Fording: 0.6m
Trench: 1.5m

K-800 (Hungary)

This Hungarian version of the Soviet M-2 entered service with the Hungarian army in the 1950s. Lighter than the Soviet vehicle, it also had a more powerful engine (130hp compared to the M-2's 110hp).

It had the same conventional design as the M-2, with the engine at the front, the cab behind it, and the cargo compartment at the rear. Unlike the M-2, the K-800's cab had a circular roof hatch. The suspension was similar to that of the SU-76, with five road wheels, idler at the front, drive sprocket at the rear, and three return rollers.

The K-800 was also built in Yugoslavia as the GJ-800. The Yugoslavian version had a different engine and the cab of the FAP lorry.

Specifications: K-800

Crew: 1+1
Weight: 6.4 tonnes (empty)
8.2 tonnes (loaded)
Maximum load: 1.8 tonnes
Towed load: 8 tonnes
Length: 5m
Width: 2.4m
Height: 2.2m (cab)
Ground clearance: 0.3m
Maximum road speed: 35km/hour
Maximum road range: 300km
Gradient: 60%
Vertical obstacle: 0.5m
Fording: 0.6m
Trench: 1.5m

AT-T

The AT-T was introduced in 1950, originally used to tow heavy artillery such as the S-23 gun, 130mm KS-30 anti-aircraft gun, and the 130mm SM-4-1 mobile coastal gun. It was later used for various towing roles, and to carry specialised loads such as radars and other electronic equipment.

The engine was under the cab floor, which had a door on each side. The cargo compartment at the rear was provided with a drop tailgate and tarpaulin cover. Fuel tanks were situated under the cargo compartment, and a winch was fitted at the back.

The AT-T was used as the basis for various combat engineering vehicles, and a fully-enclosed variant carried the Track Dish radar. A lengthened version with an extra road wheel on each side was used to carry the Long Track radar.

Specifications: AT-T

Crew: 1+3
Weight: 20 tonnes (empty)
25 tonnes (loaded)
Maximum load: 5 tonnes
Towed load: 25 tonnes
Length: 6.99m (travelling)
Width: 3.17m (travelling)
Height: 2.58m (cab)
Ground clearance: 0.43m
Maximum road speed: 35km/hour
Gradient: 60%
Vertical obstacle: 1m
Fording: 0.75m
Trench: 2.1m

AT-L & AT-LM

First introduced in 1953, the AT-L was widely used for towing anti-tank guns, tube artillery, and large mortars, until it was replaced by 6x6 lorries in the towing role. The engine was fitted at the front, with the cab behind and the cargo compartment at the rear. The cargo compartment had a drop tailgate and tarpaulin cover. The cab had a circular hatch in the right roof, and a three-part windscreen, with the outer two screens hinged at the top.

The AT-LM, introduced in 1956, replaced the original six road wheels and three return rollers with five large wheels without return rollers. The AT-L and AT-LM were used to carry electronic equipment, such as the Pork Trough and Small Yawn radars.

Specifications: AT-L & AT-LM

Crew: 1+2
Weight: 6.3 tonnes (empty)
8.3 tonnes (loaded)
Maximum load: 2 tonnes
Towed load: 60 tonnes
Length: 5.31m (travelling)
Width: 2.21m (travelling)
Height: 2.18m (cab)
Ground clearance: 0.35m
Maximum road speed: 42km/hour
Maximum road range: 300km
Vertical obstacle: 0.6m
Fording: 0.6m
Trench: 1m

AT-S

This tracked medium artillery tractor entered service in the early 1950s, towing medium and heavy artillery, such as 152mm howitzers and 100mm anti-aircraft guns. The engine was mounted at the front, with the cab behind. There was a circular hatch on the right side of the cab roof, and two doors on each side. The cargo compartment was at the rear, and had a tailgate and tarpaulin cover. As well as its primary use as an artillery tractor, it was used to mount various electronic equipment, including radars.

Specifications: AT-S

Crew: 1+6
Weight: 12 tonnes (empty)
15 tonnes (loaded)
Maximum load: 3 tonnes
Towed load: 16 tonnes
Length: 5.87m (travelling)
Width: 2.57m (travelling)
Height: 2.54m (cab)
Height: 2.85m (tarpaulin)
Ground clearance: 0.4m
Maximum road speed: 35km/hour
Maximum road range: 380km
Gradient: 50%
Vertical obstacle: 0.6m
Fording: 1m
Trench: 1.45m

Mazur D-350 (Poland)

The D-350 was developed in the 1950s, and was partially based on the Soviet AT-S. The initial prototypes were designated D-300, but production versions with a more powerful engine were designated D-350. It was used to tow anti-tank guns and artillery of up to 152mm calibre.

Of conventional layout, it had the engine at the front, cab in the centre, and cargo area at the rear. Two doors were fitted on each side of the cab, one to the front and one to the rear. The front windscreens could be opened horizontally, hinging at the top, and there was a square hatch in the forward part of the cab roof. The cargo area had a tailgate, removable bows, and a tarpaulin cover. The suspension had five road wheels, drive sprocket at the front, idler at the rear, and four track return rollers. A 17-tonne capacity winch, with 80m of cable, was fitted as standard.

Specifications: D-350

Crew: 1+8
Weight: 18.56 tonnes (loaded)
Towed load: 15 tonnes
Length: 5.81m
Width: 2.89m
Height: 2.6m (cab)
Maximum road speed: 53km/hour
Maximum road range: 490km
Gradient: 50%
Vertical obstacle: 0.6m
Fording: 0.8m
Trench: 1.45m

ATS-59

Introduced in the late 1950s as a replacement for the AT-S, the ATS-59 used a number of T-54 components. The cab was at the front, with the engine behind, projecting into the cargo compartment. The cab had a circular hatch on the right side of the roof, and a door on each side. The cargo compartment had a tailgate and tarpaulin cover.

A variant was used to tow semi-trailers carrying the SA-2 Guideline surface-to-air missile. This variant did not have a cargo compartment, instead having an attachment for the semi-trailer on the rear chassis.

Specifications: ATS-59

Crew: 1+1
Weight: 13 tonnes (empty)
16 tonnes (loaded)
Maximum load: 3 tonnes
Towed load: 14 tonnes
Length: 6.28m (travelling)
Width: 2.78m (travelling)
Height: 2.3m (cab)
Height: 2.5m (tarpaulin)
Ground clearance: 0.43m
Maximum road speed: 39km/hour
Maximum road range: 350km (500km with long-range tanks)
Gradient: 50%
Vertical obstacle: 1.1m
Fording: 1.5m
Trench: 2.5m

ATS-59G

First seen in 1972, this vehicle was initially known to NATO as the M1972. An improved version of the ATS-59, it had a redesigned cab. The cab on the ATS-59G was much larger, and of the forward control type, with the cargo compartment at the rear.

Specifications: ATS-59G

Weight: 13.75 tonnes (empty)
16.75 tonnes (loaded)
Maximum load: 3 tonnes
Towed load: 14 tonnes
Fording: 1.5m

Bumar Labedy 668 (Poland)

Based on the Soviet ATS-59G, this was used in agriculture and forestry in addition to its use as a general-purpose tractor and prime mover for artillery and anti-tank guns. It had a forward control all-steel cab, mounted over the engine. It had seating for up to five passengers in addition to the driver, with a roof hatch on the right side. The cabin had overpressure NBC protection, and could be fitted with extra defrosting equipment for use in very cold environments.

A load area behind the cab could be used to carry supplies, but could not be fitted with seats for passengers. The rear load area could be fitted with seating, or could be used for cargo. A 14.7-tonne capacity winch was fitted for recovery purposes.

SPECIFICATIONS: 668

Crew: 1+5 (plus 12 in the rear)
Weight: 13 tonnes (empty)
16 tonnes (loaded)
Maximum load: 3 tonnes
Towed load: 14 tonnes
Length: 6.28m
Width: 2.78m
Height: 2.58m (cab)
Height: 2.62m (tarpaulin)
Ground clearance: 0.42m
Maximum road speed: 39km/hour
Maximum road range: 350km (500km with extra tanks)
Vertical obstacle: 1.1m
Fording: 1.1m
Trench: 2.5m

MT-S

The MT-S was introduced in the early 1980s, but few details were ever released, and it appears to have only entered limited production. The basic chassis was derived from that used for the 2S3 Akatsiya self-propelled howitzer, which was also used for other applications, such as the GMZ minelayer.

SPECIFICATIONS: MT-S (PROVISIONAL)

Crew: 1+3
Weight: 23.5 tonnes
Length: 7.8m
Width: 3.34m
Height: 1.85m

MT-T

Introduced in the early 1980s, the MT-T used suspension components from the T-64 and a diesel engine derived from that fitted in the T-72. The cab was at the front, and the large cargo compartment at the rear, with a canvas cover. The MT-T's chassis was used as the basis for several other vehicles, including the PTS-2 amphibious ferry, MDK-3 excavator, and BAT-2 digger.

Specifications: MT-T

Crew: 1+4
Weight: 25 tonnes
Maximum load: 12 tonnes
Towed load: 12 tonnes
Length: 8.71m
Width: 3.28m
Height: 3.07m

Lorries Used as Tow Vehicles

Soviet lorry designations followed a standard formula, which began with an abbreviated form of the plant name. Before 1966, this abbreviation was followed by a number of up to three digits. The first digit related to the plant, and the second two were allotted in sequence, so that earlier designs had lower numbers.

The plant abbreviations and digits were as follows:

Gor'kiy: GAZ, first digit 0 (usually omitted)
Moscow: ZIL, first digit 1
Yaroslavl, Kremenchug: YaAZ, later KrAZ, first digit 2
Miass: Ural, first digit 3
Ul'Yanovsk: UAZ, first digit 4
Minsk: MAZ, first digit 5
Kutaisi: KAZ, first digit 6
Zaporozh'ye, Lutsk, Riga: ZAZ, first digit 9

A new designation system came into effect on 1st August 1966, although existing models kept their old designations. This new system included information on various aspects of the vehicle. The new system used the same plant abbreviation, followed by a number of four to six digits, with four being the most common.

For lorries, the first digit indicated the gross tonnage, as follows:

1: Less than 1.2 tonnes
2: 1.2 to 2 tonnes
3: 2 to 8 tonnes
4: 8 to 14 tonnes
5: 14 to 20 tonnes
6: 20 to 40 tonnes
7: Over 40 tonnes

For light vehicles or cars, the first digit referred to engine size, rather than gross tonnage:

1: Less than 1.2 litres
2: 1.2 to 2 litres
3: 2 to 4 litres
4: Over 4 litres

The second digit denoted the vehicle type:

1: Passenger cars
2: Buses
3: Lorries with sides
4: Tractors
5: Dump lorries
6: Tanker lorries
7: Vans
8: Kept for future use
9: Special vehicles

The third and fourth digits were assigned sequentially by design, usually starting with 01. Special sequences were used for ambulances, high mobility vehicles, and specially-heightened models. The fifth digit, where used, identified modifications or improvements to the basic design. The sixth digit, when used, applied to export models. A 6 denoted a standard export model, a 7 denoted models for export to the tropics. Experimental models had an E appended. This letter was omitted when the design was accepted for production.

Engines for both cars and lorries had a similar system, using three or four digits. The first digit indicated the engine's displacement and type:

1: Less than 0.75 litres
2: 0.75 to 1.2 litres
3: 1.2 to 2 litres
4: 2 to 4 litres
5: 4 to 7 litres
6: 7 to 10 litres
7: 10 to 15 litres
8: Over 15 litres
9: Gas turbine engine

The second and third were model numbers, and denoted the engine as petrol (0 to 39) or diesel (40 to 99). The fourth digit, if present, indicated modifications.

GAZ-63

The GAZ-63 was a 4x4, 1.5-tonne lorry that entered service in 1946. It remained in production until 1963, when it was replaced by the improved GAZ-63A, which remained in production until 1968. The GAZ-63 chassis was used as the basis for the BTR-40 wheeled armoured personnel carrier.

GAZ-63

The all-steel, two-seat cab was situated immediately behind the engine, with the cargo area to the rear. The cargo bay had a wooden platform, high sides, and rear tailgate. Benches were fitted, which could be folded upwards when not in use. A winch, and a tarpaulin cover with bows, could be fitted if required.

Specifications: GAZ-63

Crew: 1+1
Configuration: 4x4
Weight: 3.5 tonnes
    4.99 tonnes (loaded)
Maximum load: 2 tonnes

Towed load: 2 tonnes
Length: 5.8m
Width: 2.2m
Height: 2.25m (cab)
Height: 2.25m (tarpaulin)
Ground clearance: 0.27m
Maximum road speed: 65km/hour
Maximum road range: 650km
Fording: 0.8m

GAZ-66

The GAZ-66 was a 4x4, 2-tonne lorry that replaced the GAZ-63A, entering production in 1964. Early vehicles did not have a central tyre pressure regulation system, but this was fitted to all production vehicles from 1968.

GAZ-66

The cab was fitted over the engine, and hinged forward to give access to it. The rear cargo area had fixed sides and a drop tailgate. If required, a tarpaulin cover could be fitted, with five bows to fix it in place. Intended for use at temperatures from -50°C to +50°C, it was fitted with an engine pre-heater and cab heater as standard. Many vehicles were fitted with a winch.

Specifications: GAZ-66

Crew: 1+1 (plus 21 in the rear)
Configuration: 4x4
Weight: 4.09 tonnes
Maximum load: 2.3 tonnes
Towed load: 2 tonnes
Length: 5.92m
Width: 2.53m
Height: 2.49m (cab)
Height: 2.52m (tarpaulin)
Ground clearance: 0.32m
Maximum road speed: 90km/hour
Maximum road range: 1,400km
Gradient: 67%
Fording: 1.2m

YaAZ-214 & KrAZ-214

This 6x6 lorry was originally built at the Yaroslavl Plant from 1956 to 1959 and designated YaAZ-214. Production was then moved to the Kremenchug Plant, and the vehicle was renamed KrAZ-214. Production ended in 1967, when it was replaced by the KrAZ-255B.

The vehicle had the engine at the front, with the fully enclosed cab to the immediate rear and the cargo area behind the cab. The cargo area had a hinged tailgate, removable bows, and a tarpaulin. The vehicle had a tyre pressure regulation system, cab heater, engine pre-heater, and 8-tonne capacity winch.

Specifications: KrAZ-214

Crew: 1+2
Configuration: 6x6
Weight: 12.3 tonnes
    19.3 tonnes (loaded)
Maximum load: 7 tonnes
Towed load: 30 tonnes
Length: 8.53m
Width: 2.7m
Height: 2.88m (cab)
Height: 3.17m (tarpaulin)
Ground clearance: 0.36m
Maximum road speed: 55km/hour
Maximum road range: 530km
Gradient: 30%
Fording: 1m

KrAZ-255B

In 1967, this lorry replaced the KrAZ-214 in production, and remained in production until 1979. Of similar design to the earlier vehicle, it had a more powerful engine, leading to faster speed and better cross-country performance. The layout was the same, with the engine at the front, two-door cab behind, and cargo area at the rear. The cargo area had a tailgate, removable bows, and a tarpaulin. A cab heater, engine pre-heater, 12-tonne capacity winch, and suspension locking mechanism were fitted as standard.

Most roles originally fulfilled by the KrAZ-214 were taken over by the KrAZ-255B as it came into service.

KrAZ-255B

Specifications: KrAZ-255B

Crew: 1+2
Configuration: 6x6
Weight: 11.95 tonnes
19.45 tonnes (loaded)
Maximum load: 7.5 tonnes
Towed load: 30 tonnes
Length: 8.65m

Width: 2.75m
Height: 2.94m (cab)
Height: 3.17m (tarpaulin)
Ground clearance: 0.36m
Maximum road speed: 70km/hour
Maximum road range: 750km
Gradient: 60%
Fording: 0.85m

KrAZ-260

In 1979, the KrAZ-260 replaced the KrAZ-255B in production. It had a conventional layout, with the engine at the front, two-door cab behind, and cargo area at the rear. The cargo area had a hinged tailgate and bows to secure a tarpaulin. It had a winch mounted under the body and a lockable differential. The KrAZ-260 had an increased payload and speed compared to the KrAZ-255B.

Specifications: KrAZ-260

Crew: 1+2
Configuration: 6x6
Weight: 12.25 tonnes
    21.48 tonnes (loaded)
Maximum load: 9 tonnes
Towed load: 30 tonnes
Length: 9.01m
Width: 2.72m
Height: 2.99m (cab)
Ground clearance: 0.37m

KrAZ-260

Maximum road speed: 80km/hour
Maximum road range: 700km
Gradient: 58%
Vertical obstacle: 0.5m
Fording: 1.2m
Trench: 0.68m

UAZ-469B

A vehicle designated UAZ-460B appeared in 1960, but did not enter production. After further development, it was designated UAZ-469B. Production began in 1972, and it entered service the following year.

The engine was at the front, with a four-door crew compartment behind. The windscreen could be folded down onto the bonnet, a removable canvas top was fitted, and the tops of the

UAZ-469B

doors could be removed. A hard top was also available. Two individual seats were fitted at the front, a bench seat for three behind, and two pairs of seats facing each other at the rear. The usual load was two people plus 600kg of cargo, or seven people and 100kg of cargo.

Specifications: UAZ-469B

Crew: 1+6
Configuration: 4x4
Weight: 1.49 tonnes
    2.29 tonnes (loaded)
Maximum load: 695kg
Towed load: 600kg (2 tonnes braked)
Length: 4.03m
Width: 1.79m

Height: 2.02m
Ground clearance: 0.22m
Maximum road speed: 100km/hour
Maximum road range: 620km
Gradient: 62%
Vertical obstacle: 0.45m
Fording: 0.7m

Ural 375

Entering production in 1961, the first model of the 6x6 Ural 375 had an open cab with a canvas top. The later model could be easily identified by the fully enclosed all-steel cab, and also featured a number of automotive improvements. This was designated Ural 375D (without a winch) and Ural 375T (with a 7-tonne capacity winch). Both models had a central tyre pressure regulation system.

The cab was to the rear of the engine, with the cargo area to the rear of the cab. The cargo area had bench seats, a tailgate, removable bows, and a tarpaulin cover. A cab heater and engine pre-heater were fitted as standard.

A series of tests conducted in 1973 of a Ural 375D with a YaMZ-740 V8 diesel engine led to the Ural 4320.

Specifications: Ural 375

Crew: 1+2
Configuration: 6x6
Weight: 8.4 tonnes
    13.3 tonnes (loaded)
Maximum load: 4.5 tonnes

Ural 375D

Towed load: 10 tonnes
Length: 7.35m
Width: 2.69m
Height: 2.68m (cab)
Height: 2.98m (tarpaulin)
Ground clearance: 0.41m
Maximum road speed: 75km/hour
Maximum road range: 750km
Gradient: 60%
Vertical obstacle: 0.8m
Fording: 1m (1.5m with preparation)

Ural 4320

A diesel-powered development of the Ural 375D, production of this 6x6 lorry began in 1978. The new, more powerful engine increased payload and maximum speed, while simultaneously reducing fuel consumption and maintenance time. The main visible difference was the radiator shell, which was lengthened in front. Changes were made to various components, such as gear ratios, in order to maximise the benefit of the new engine.

Ural 4320

Specifications: Ural 4320

Crew: 1+2
Configuration: 6x6
Weight: 8.02 tonnes
Maximum load: 5.23 tonnes
Towed load: 7 tonnes
Length: 7.37m
Width: 2.5m
Height: 2.87m (cab)
Ground clearance: 0.4m
Maximum road speed: 85km/hour
Gradient: 58%
Fording: 0.7m

ZIL-157

A replacement for the ZIL-151, the ZIL-157 was in production from 1958 to 1961, with the improved ZIL-157K in production until 1966. The appearance was very similar to the earlier ZIL-151, with a slightly different cab and single rear wheels in place of the dual rear wheels of the ZIL-151.

ZIL-157

The two-door cab was at the front, immediately behind the engine, and the cargo area was to the rear of the cab. The cargo area had a wooden platform with sides, a drop tailgate, and bench seats that could be folded up when not required. Bows and a tarpaulin cover could be fitted, and a cab heater and engine pre-heater were fitted as standard. Many vehicles were fitted with a winch.

Specifications: ZIL-157

Crew: 1+1
Configuration: 6x6
Weight: 5.8 tonnes
    8.45 tonnes (loaded)
Maximum load: 4.5 tonnes
Towed load: 3.6 tonnes
Length: 6.92m
Width: 2.32m
Height: 2.36m (cab)
Height: 2.92m (tarpaulin)
Ground clearance: 0.31m
Maximum road speed: 65km/hour
Maximum road range: 510km
Gradient: 53%
Fording: 0.85m

DAC 444 (Romania)

The DAC 444 had a forward control configuration, with the cab over the engine. The steel cab had seating for up to three passengers in addition to the driver. The cab could be tilted forward to allow access to the engine. An observation hatch was fitted on the right side of the cab roof, and the spare wheel was mounted on the right side of the cab rear.

The cargo area was to the rear of the cab, and had a wooden platform, drop tailgate, removable bows, and tarpaulin cover. Folding bench seats were fitted on both sides. Optional equipment included an engine pre-heater, 6-tonne capacity winch, and a central tyre pressure regulation system.

Specifications: DAC 444

Crew: 1+3
Configuration: 4x4
Weight: 5.7 tonnes
10.7 tonnes (loaded)
Maximum load: 4 tonnes
Towed load: 5.5 tonnes
Length: 6.46m
Width: 2.5m
Height: 2.79m (cab)
Ground clearance: 0.4m
Maximum road speed: 89km/hour
Gradient: 50%
Fording: 0.65m

Praga V3S (Czechoslovakia)

Developed in the 1950s and originally built by Praga, production shifted to Avia in 1964. It had a conventional layout, with the engine at the front, the two-man, two-door steel cab behind, and the cargo area at the rear. Fuel containers could be kept behind the front bumper, and a circular observation hatch was fitted in the right side of the cab's roof. The windscreen was split, and both halves of it could be opened. The cargo area had a tarpaulin cover with removable bows, which could be stowed in the cab when not in use. Some vehicles were fitted with a 3.5-tonne winch.

Praga V3S

Specifications: Praga V3S

Crew: 1+1
Configuration: 6x6
Weight: 5.35 tonnes
10.65 tonnes (loaded)
Maximum load: 5.3 tonnes
Towed load: 5.5 tonnes
Length: 6.91m
Width: 2.31m
Height: 2.51m (cab)
Height: 2.92m (tarpaulin)
Ground clearance: 0.4m
Maximum road speed: 62km/hour
Maximum road range: 500km
Gradient: 60%
Fording: 0.8m

Tatra 138 (Czechoslovakia)

The Tatra 138 entered service in 1963, replacing the earlier Tatra 111. It had a conventional layout, with the engine at the front, two-door steel cab behind it, and cargo area at the rear, with drop sides and a drop tailgate. The military model, designated Tatra 138VN, differed from the civilian model with higher hinged sideboards, removable bows, tarpaulin cover, and a winch.

Tatra 138

Specifications: Tatra 138

Crew: 1+2

Configuration: 6x6

Weight: 8.74 tonnes

    20.59 tonnes (loaded)

Maximum load: 11.85 tonnes

Towed load: 22 tonnes
Length: 8.57m
Width: 2.45m
Height: 2.44m (cab)
Height: 3.2m (tarpaulin)
Ground clearance: 0.29m
Maximum road speed: 71km/hour
Maximum road range: 540km
Gradient: 35%
Fording: 1m

Towed Guns and Howitzers

The Soviet army showed little interest in self-propelled artillery during the Second World War. Multiple rocket launchers, anti-tank guns, and assault guns were mounted on tracked or wheeled vehicles, but development of self-propelled guns and howitzers for indirect fire didn't begin until the late 1960s.

Although towed weapons sacrificed cross-country mobility and crew protection, they were cheaper to produce and easier to maintain. The Soviets often used a single-carriage design for multiple weapons, increasing simplicity of manufacture. Towed weapons also had a measure of increased tactical flexibility. If the prime mover was destroyed or broke down, the weapon could be towed by another vehicle.

The last towed Soviet anti-tank gun to enter production was the 100mm MT-12. Development began of a 125mm towed gun, the 2A45 Sprut, but this never entered production. Both self-propelled and towed guns and howitzers, up to and including 152mm calibre, were supplied with anti-armour rounds, either HEAT, APHE (known as HESH or HEP in the West) or some version of kinetic AP.

152MM ML-20 GUN-HOWITZER

Introduced in 1938, the ML-20 replaced the earlier 152mm M1910/34, the new weapon having a considerably higher maximum elevation. The ML-20's carriage was also adopted for the 122mm A-19. Compared to the A-19, the ML-20's ordnance was shorter, fatter, and had a multi-slotted muzzle brake.

ML-20

The carriage was a box-section split-trail, originally fitted with a spoked wheel on either side of the small shield. The single wheels were soon replaced with dual solid wheels, and the solid rubber tyres were replaced with sponge rubber filled tyres. For transit, a two-wheeled limber was attached to the rear of the trail, and the ordnance was withdrawn to the rear and secured between the trails. The gun could be moved with the ordnance in place, but only for short distances and at slow speed.

The ML-20 fired variable-charge, case-type, separate-loading ammunition. HE-FRAG, concrete-piercing, chemical, HEAT, illuminating, and smoke projectiles were available. The AP-T round could penetrate 124mm of armour at 1,000m. It was normally towed by an AT-S or AT-T artillery tractor.

Specifications: ML-20

Calibre: 152.4mm
Barrel length: 4.93m
Weight: 7,270kg
    8,073kg (travelling)
Length: 7.21m (travelling)
Width: 2.31m (travelling)
Height: 2.26m (travelling)
Elevation/depression: +65/-2°
Traverse: 58° total
Rate of fire: 4 rounds/minute
Maximum range: 17,265m
Crew: 9

76mm M1938 Mountain Gun

Originally a Czech 75mm design (Skoda C5), the Soviets began licence production in 1938 as the M1938. It saw widespread service in the Second World War, and it served with Soviet mountain units during the Cold War.

The M1938 could be broken down into three loads for towing by animals or light vehicles, or into ten loads for man-packed transport. It had a split trail which could be used in a short or long leg configuration, and two pneumatic wheels. The shield

M1938

sloped back at a sharp angle, and could be removed if required. Armour-piercing and shrapnel rounds were developed, but it appears to have only been used to fire high-explosive rounds.

Specifications: M1938

Calibre: 76mm
Barrel length: 1.63m
Weight: 785kg
  1,450kg (travelling)
Height: 1.35m (0.76m without shield)
Elevation/depression: +65/-5°
Maximum range: 10,100m

122MM A-19 CORPS GUN

Introduced just before the Second World War, this was a development of an earlier gun, mounting the same recoil system and ordnance on a new carriage which allowed greater elevation. The carriage was the same as that fitted to the 152mm ML-20. The A-19 could be distinguished from the ML-20 by its longer, thinner barrel, and a counterweight in place of the ML-20's muzzle brake.

A-19

The carriage was a box-section split-trail, originally fitted with a spoked wheel on either side of the small shield. The single wheels were soon replaced with dual solid wheels, and the solid rubber tyres were replaced with sponge rubber filled tyres. For transit, a two-wheeled limber was attached to the rear of the trail, and the ordnance was withdrawn to the rear and secured between the trails. The gun could be moved with the ordnance in place, but only for short distances and at slow speed.

The A-19 fired variable-charge, case-type, separate-loading ammunition. HE-FRAG, concrete-piercing, and AP-T rounds were available. The AP-T round could penetrate 160mm of armour at 1,000m. It was towed by an AT-T, AT-L, ATS-59, or

AT-S artillery tractor, or a KrAZ-214 6x6 7-tonne or Ural 375 6x6 4.5-tonne lorry.

Specifications: A-19

Calibre: 122mm
Barrel length: 5.65m
Weight: 7,250kg
8,050kg (travelling)
Length: 7.87m (travelling)
Width: 2.46m (travelling)
Height: 2.27m (travelling)
Elevation/depression: +65/-2°
Traverse: 58° total
Rate of fire: 5-6 rounds/minute
Maximum range: 20,800m
Crew: 8

122mm M-30 Howitzer

The M-30 entered service with the Soviet army in 1939, and was the standard Soviet and Warsaw Pact divisional howitzer until it was replaced by the D-30. Each motorised rifle division had two battalions, and each tank division had three battalions. In both cases, each battalion had three batteries of six howitzers.

The split-trail carriage was identical to that of the D-1 152mm howitzer. The top half of the shield sloped to the rear, and the centre section slid upwards to allow for elevation. The howitzer could be fired without spreading the trails, but traverse was limited to 1.5° in that case. Each trail had two spades: a fixed one for use on hard surfaces, and a hinged one for use on soft

M-30

ground. Maximum towing speed was 48km/hour, and it was normally towed by a Ural 375 6x6 4.5-tonne lorry or MT-LB multi-purpose tracked vehicle.

The M-30 fired variable-charge, case-type, separate-loading ammunition. HE-FRAG and HEAT warheads were available, both of which could be fired by the newer D-30. In the 1980s, Poland upgraded some M-30s to improve their direct fire capability, designating the new weapons wz 1938/1985.

Specifications: M-30

Barrel length: 2.8m
Weight: 2,450 kg (travelling order)
2,450 kg (firing position)
Length: 5.9m (travelling)
Width: 1.98m (travelling)
Height: 1.71m (travelling)
Ground clearance: 0.33m
Elevation/depression: +63.5/-3°
Traverse: 49° total
Rate of fire: 5-6 rounds/minute

Sustained rate of fire: 1.5 rounds/minute
Range: 11,800m max, 630m effective (HEAT)
Crew: 8
Unit of fire: 80 rounds

152mm M-10 Howitzer

Introduced into service just before the Second World War, the M-10 remained in service with the Soviet army until the 1950s, and saw service with the Romanian army throughout the Cold War. Its weight made it difficult to manoeuvre, and so a new carriage was developed. This new carriage, and the addition of a double-baffle muzzle brake, resulted in the D-1 howitzer.

The upper part of the M-10's shield sloped to the rear and had chamfered corners. The carriage had dual rubber-tyred road wheels, and there was a limber, which also had rubber-tyred wheels. The recoil system was under the barrel, with the counter-recoil system above. Elevation controls were on the right, traverse on the left. The normal tow vehicle was an AT-S artillery tractor.

Ammunition was variable-charge, case-type, separate-loading. HE-FRAG, concrete-piercing, chemical, HEAT, illuminating, semi-AP, and smoke rounds were available.

Specifications: M-10

Calibre: 152.4mm
Barrel length: 3.7m
Weight: 4,150kg
4,550kg (travelling)
Length: 6.4m (travelling)
Width: 2.1m (travelling)

M-10

Height: 1.9m (travelling)
Elevation/depression: +65/-1°
Traverse: 50° total
Rate of fire: 4 rounds/minute
Maximum range: 12,400m
Crew: 7

76MM ZIS-3 DIVISIONAL GUN

Introduced in 1942, this was the latest in a long line of 76mm artillery pieces. The ordnance was used as the main armament in the SU-76, although the limited elevation in the vehicle restricted the range compared to the towed gun.

The carriage was the same split-trail carriage used on the 57mm ZIS-2 anti-tank gun, with tubular trails. A double-baffle

ZIS-3

muzzle brake reduced recoil to allow the larger gun to operate on the relatively light carriage. A vertical shield was fitted, and the carriage had two rubber-tyred wheels.

Ammunition was of the fixed type. HE-FRAG, AP-T, HVAP-T, and HEAT rounds were produced. The HE-FRAG round had 710g of TNT. The AP-T round could penetrate 61mm of armour at 1,000m, or 69mm at 500m. The HVAP-T round could penetrate 58mm at 1,000m or 92mm at 500m. The HEAT round could penetrate 120mm at any range.

It was towed by a BTR-152 APC, GAZ-66 4x4 2-tonne lorry, or a ZIL-157 6x6 2.5-tonne lorry.

Specifications: ZIS-3

Calibre: 76mm
Barrel length: 3.46m
Weight: 1,116kg (travelling)
Length: 6.1m (travelling)

Width: 1.65m (travelling)
Height: 1.38m (travelling)
Elevation/depression: +37/-5°
Traverse: 54° total
Rate of fire: 15-20 rounds/minute
Maximum range: 13,290m

152mm D-1 Howitzer

Introduced in 1943 to replace the 152mm M-10 howitzer, this used a strengthened version of the carriage and recoil system of the 122mm M-30 howitzer. The ordnance was the same as the 152mm M-10, fitted with a new double-baffle muzzle brake. It was lighter than the earlier weapon, and fired the same ammunition.

The carriage was a riveted box-section split-trail. The shield sloped to the rear at the top and included a section in the middle that slid upwards to allow the weapon to elevate. The recoil system was under the barrel, with the counter-recoil system above. Elevation controls were on the right, traverse on the left. It was normally towed by an AT-S artillery tractor, at speeds of up to 48km/hour. Two spades were fitted to each trail: a fixed one for use on hard ground, and a hinged one for use on soft ground.

Ammunition was variable-charge, case-type, separate-loading. HE-FRAG, concrete-piercing, chemical, HEAT, illuminating, semi-AP, and smoke rounds were available.

Specifications: D-1

Calibre: 152.4mm
Barrel length: 4.21m

D-1

Weight: 3,600kg
3,640kg (travelling)
Length: 7.56m (travelling)
Width: 2m (travelling)
Height: 1.85m (travelling)
Elevation/depression: +64/-3°
Traverse: 35° total
Rate of fire: 4 rounds/minute
Maximum range: 12,400m
Crew: 7

57mm ZIS-2 Anti-Tank Gun

Adopted for service in 1943, this combined the carriage of a 76mm ZIS-3 divisional gun with the ordnance of a 57mm M1941 anti-tank gun. Superficially similar to the ZIS-3, it could be differentiated by the longer, thinner barrel, without a muzzle brake.

ZIS-2

Originally it was fitted with a straight-topped shield that could be folded forward, but after the Second World War many were fitted with a new shield with a wavy top, and some had fittings for an infra-red night vision device ahead of the shield.

The ammunition was interchangeable with that for the 57mm Ch-26 and ASU-57. HE-FRAG, AP-T, and HVAP ammunition was available. The AP-T round could penetrate 96mm at 1,000m or 106mm at 500m. The HVAP round could penetrate 95mm at 1,000m or 140mm at 500m. It was normally towed by a BTR-152 or a GAZ-63 4x4 2-tonne lorry.

Specifications: ZIS-2

Calibre: 57mm
Barrel length: 4.16m
Weight: 1,150kg

Length: 6.8m (travelling)
Width: 1.7m (travelling)
Height: 1.37m (travelling)
Elevation/depression: +25/-5°
Traverse: 56° total
Rate of fire: 25 rounds/minute
Sustained rate of fire: 10-15 rounds/minute
Maximum range: 8,400m
Crew: 7

100MM BS-3 ANTI-TANK & FIELD GUN

The largest towed anti-tank gun of the Second World War, the BS-3 was developed from the 100mm B-34 naval gun and entered service in 1944. It saw some service in the Second World War, in both the anti-tank and field gun roles. In the anti-tank role, it was a very powerful weapon, able to penetrate 170mm of armour at 1,000m. In the field gun role, it was less powerful than the 122mm A-19, but was more mobile and had a higher rate of fire. It was later replaced in the anti-tank role by the D-48 and then the T-12.

It had a shield to give some protection to the crew, a standard box-section split trail, and a double-baffle muzzle brake. Distinguishing features included dual tyres on the carriage wheels and stowage boxes on the front of the shield. The ammunition used by the BS-3 could also be fired by the KS-19 AA gun, the T-54 and T-55 tanks, and the SU-100 assault gun. Usual tow vehicles were an AT-P armoured artillery tractor or Ural 375 6x6 4.5-tonne lorry.

BS-3

Specifications: BS-3

Calibre: 100mm
Barrel length: 6.07m
Weight: 3,650kg
Length: 9.37m
Width: 2.15m
Height: 1.5m
Elevation/depression: +45/-5°
Traverse: 58° total
Rate of fire: 8-10 rounds/minute
Maximum range: 21,000m
Crew: 6

85mm D-44 Divisional Gun

The 85mm D-44 was developed during the Second World War as a replacement for the 76mm ZIS-3 divisional gun. Although it was developed during the war, it was not deployed until after the war ended. The barrel was a development of the 85mm gun used in the T-34/85 tank, and was virtually identical to the 85mm KS-12 anti-aircraft gun. It used fixed ammunition, which was interchangeable with that used by the SD-44 and the Czech M-52 field gun. Penetration was up to 180mm (using HVAP-T ammunition) of vertical standard armour plate at 1,000m.

A small wheel near the end of one trail made it easier to manoeuvre the weapon into position. An infra-red night vision device could be fitted to the shield. In this configuration, the gun was designated D-44-N.

The SD-44 was a variant of the D-44 with a small petrol auxiliary propulsion unit. Initial models were conversions of standard D-44s. The engine was mounted on the left trail, with fuel and ready-use ammunition carried in the trails. The engine drove the two carriage wheels, with a small castor wheel just behind the spades being used to steer. The weapon could be driven at up to 25km/hour, and could still be towed if required. It was developed for the airborne forces, and each airborne division was issued with 18 guns in three six-gun batteries.

Specifications: D-44

Calibre: 85mm
Barrel length: 4.7m
Weight: 1,725kg

D-44

Length: 8.35m (travelling)
Width: 1.78m (travelling)
Height: 1.42m (travelling)
Elevation/depression: +35/-7°
Traverse: 54° total
Rate of fire: 15-20 rounds/minute
Maximum range: 15,650m
Crew: 8

152mm M-18/46 Howitzer (Czechoslovakia)

At the end of the Second World War, there were many German 15cm Feldhaubitze 18 (15cm sFH 18) howitzers in Czechoslovakia. With the decision to standardise on Soviet ammunition, they were re-bored to allow them to fire standard Soviet 152mm rounds, as used by the M-10 and D-1. A large square shield and double-baffle muzzle brake was added, and the weapons were designated M-18/46.

The M-18/46 fired variable-charge, case-type, separate-loading ammunition. Semi-AP, HE, and HEAT rounds were available. The semi-AP round was originally developed for naval use, with a larger HE warhead than the normal APHE round, and an effective range of 510m.

The M-18/46 had a standard split-trail, box-section carriage, with a limber. Normal tow vehicle was an AT-S medium-tracked artillery tractor.

Specifications: M-18/46

Calibre: 152.4mm
Barrel length: 4.88m
Weight: 5,512kg
    6,304kg (travelling)
Length: 8.28m (travelling)
Width: 1.71m (travelling)
Height: 1.71m (travelling)
Elevation/depression: +45/-0°
Traverse: 60° total
Rate of fire: 4 rounds/minute
Maximum range: 12,400m
Crew: 7

85mm M-52 & M52/55 Field Gun (Czechoslovakia)

The 85mm M-52 was the Czech equivalent of the Soviet 85mm D-44, and fired the same ammunition. A slightly modified version, the M-52/55, was also developed. Both could be fitted with an infra-red night vision device.

In appearance, it was similar to the 100mm M-53. The M-52 could be differentiated by the shield's wavy top, tubular rather than box-section trails, and the lack of castor wheels. Unlike the M-53, the sides of the shield did not slope to the rear.

It had a double-baffle muzzle brake and a conventional split-trail carriage, with tubular trails and two rubber-tyred road wheels. The usual tow vehicle was a Praga V3S 6x6 5-tonne lorry, which could tow it at speeds of up to 50km/hour (10km/hour cross-country). Effective direct fire range with HVAP-T ammunition was 1,150m.

Specifications: M-52 (M-52/55 in brackets)

Calibre: 85mm
Barrel length: 5.07m
Weight: 2,095kg (2,111kg)
2,130kg (travelling) (2,168kg)
Length: 7.52m (travelling)
Width: 1.98m (travelling)
Height: 1.52m (travelling)
Elevation/depression: +38/-6°
Traverse: 60° total
Rate of fire: 20 rounds/minute

Maximum range: 16,160m
Crew: 7

152mm D-20 Gun-Howitzer

Developed soon after the Second World War, the D-20 used the same carriage and recoil system as the 122mm D-74 field gun. The D-20 could be distinguished from the D-74 by the shorter, thicker barrel and larger double-baffle muzzle brake. Like the D-74, the D-20 was first seen in public during the 1955 Moscow May Day Parade. The gun in the 2S3 Akatsiya self-propelled howitzer was a development of the D-20.

D-20

The shield had a sliding centre section to allow the barrel to be elevated, and the top section could be folded down to reduce overall height. When in action, the D-20 was positioned on a firing pedestal, allowing it to be quickly traversed through a full 360°. For transit, the pedestal was inverted and secured forward of the shield. The carriage was a split box-section trail, each trail having a spade and a castor wheel at the end. For transit, the spade was folded underneath and the wheel on top of the trail. It was towed by an AT-S artillery tractor or a Ural 375 6x6 4.5-tonne lorry.

The gunner's position was to the left of the ordnance. He was provided with a PG1M sight for indirect fire, and an OP4M sight for direct fire. Ammunition was case-type, variable-charge, separate-loading. HE-FRAG, AP-T, CP, chemical, HE-RAP, HEAT, illuminating, smoke, and nuclear ammunition was produced. The nuclear round had a 0.2kT yield, and the HE-RAP round increased range to 24,000m.

Specifications: D-20

Calibre: 152.4mm
Barrel length: 5.2m
Weight: 5,650kg
    5,700kg (travelling)
Length: 8.69m (travelling)
Width: 2.4m (travelling)
Height: 1.93m (travelling)
Elevation/depression: +63/-5°
Traverse: 360° total
Rate of fire: 5-6 rounds/minute
Maximum range: 17,410m (24,000m with RAP)
Crew: 10

122mm D-74 Field Gun

The D-74 was designed to meet the same requirement as the 130mm M-46. The M-46 was considered superior, because it fired a heavier projectile to a longer distance. Nonetheless, the D-74 entered production. Most of the weapons were exported, but it saw limited service in the Soviet army, and was first observed by the West during the 1955 May Day Parade in Moscow.

It used the same carriage as the 152mm D-20 gun-howitzer. The centre section of the shield slid upwards to allow the barrel to be elevated, and sloped slightly to the rear. When in action, the D-74 was positioned on a firing pedestal, allowing it to be quickly traversed through a full 360°. For transit, the pedestal was inverted and secured forward of the shield. The carriage was a split box-section trail, each trail having a spade and a castor wheel at the end. For transit, the spade was folded underneath and the wheel on top of the trail.

The D-74 fired variable-charge, case-type, separate-loading ammunition. HE-FRAG, APC-T, illuminating, and smoke charges were available. The usual towing vehicle was a Ural 375 6x6 4.5-tonne lorry.

SPECIFICATIONS: D-74

Calibre: 122mm
Barrel length: 6.45m
Weight: 5,500kg
5,550kg (travelling)
Length: 9.88m (travelling)
Width: 2.35m (travelling)
Height: 2.75m (travelling)
Elevation/depression: +45/-5°
Traverse: 58° total
Rate of fire: 6-7 rounds/minute

Sustained rate of fire: 1.3 rounds/minute
Maximum range: 24,000m
Crew: 10

130MM M-46 FIELD GUN

Accepted for service in 1950 and first seen by the West in the 1954 May Day Parade, this weapon was ballistically similar to 130mm guns used by the Soviet navy. When travelling, a mechanism on the right trail drew the barrel back to reduce the overall length, and the spades were removed and fitted on top of the trails. The split-trail carriage was provided with a limber.

Damaged Iraqi M-46

The barrel had a pepper pot muzzle brake, with the recoil system mounted under the barrel and forward of the shield. The OP4M-35 direct fire sight had x5.5 magnification, and an APN-3 night sight was fitted, which could be used in active or passive modes. The M-46 fired case-type, variable-charge, separate-loading ammunition.

The long range and high accuracy of the M-46 meant that it was often used in the counter-battery role. It was towed by an AT-S or ATS-59 artillery tractor at speeds of up to 50km/hour.

Specifications: M-46

Calibre: 130mm
Barrel length: 7.6m
Weight: 7,700kg
8,450kg (travelling)
Length: 11.73m (travelling)
Width: 2.45m (travelling)
Height: 2.55m (travelling)
Elevation/depression: +45/-2.5°
Traverse: 50° total
Rate of fire: 5-6 rounds/minute
Maximum range: 27,150m
Crew: 8

76.2mm Mountain Gun (Romania)

Specifically developed for the needs of Romanian mountain troops, this gun could be towed by a vehicle or horse team, or quickly disassembled into loads to be carried by eight pack animals. It had a crew of seven: commander, aimer, breech operator, loader, fuse handler, projectile handler, and charge handler. When towed, it could be brought into action within a minute. When carried by pack animals, it took six to eight minutes to be brought into action. The gun could fire smoke and HEAT, as well as standard high-explosive ammunition. When firing HEAT, maximum range was limited to 1,000m. The gun was fitted with a telescope with x3 magnification.

Specifications: 76.2mm Mountain Gun

Calibre: 76.2mm
Barrel length: 1.18m
Weight: 722kg
Length: 2.45m (travelling)
3.1m (in action)
Width: 1.33m (travelling)
2.65m (in action)
Height: 1.66m
Elevation/depression: +45/-15°
Traverse: 50° total
Rate of fire: 25 rounds/minute
Sustained rate of fire: 1.3 rounds/minute
Maximum range: 8,600m
Crew: 7

130mm SM-4-1 Coastal Gun

Development of the SM-4-1 began in May 1944, with factory testing in 1948 and 1949. Government testing took place in 1950 and 1951, with service acceptance in October 1951. Initially, it used the Moskva-TsN fire control system and ZALP-B radar. These were considered too inaccurate, and so work on a new fire control system and radar began in 1950. The new Burya-MT-4 fire control and Burun radar were accepted into service in 1955. The new system was designated SM-4-1B.

SM-4-1

The carriage had two axles, each with four rubber-tyred road wheels. The axles were removed when in action, and four stabilisers, two on each side of the carriage, were extended and staked to the ground. In transit, the stabilisers were mounted on the front of the shield. The slightly curved shield had a centre section that could be removed to facilitate elevation of the ordnance. The 130mm barrel had an unusual muzzle brake and a travel lock. The SM-4-1 ammunition was not interchangeable with the M-46 field gun or KS-30 anti-aircraft gun.

APHE and HE rounds were available. The APHE round could penetrate 250mm of armour at 1,000m. Usual deployment was four-gun batteries with a radar fire control system, giving it an all-weather capability. It was normally towed by an AT-T heavy tracked artillery tractor.

Specifications: SM-4-1

Calibre: 130mm
Barrel length: 7.6m
Weight: 16,000kg
19,000kg (travelling)
Length: 12.8m (travelling)
Width: 2.85m (travelling)
Height: 3.05m (travelling)
Elevation/depression: +45/-5°
Traverse: 360° total
Rate of fire: 5 rounds/minute
Maximum range: 29,500m

100mm M-53 Field Gun (Czechoslovakia)

Developed in the early 1950s to fulfil a similar role to the Soviet 100mm BS-3, the M-53 could fire the same ammunition. It could not, however, fire the 100mm T-12's ammunition. Like the BS-3, it could be used in both the field gun and anti-tank roles.

It had a double-baffle muzzle brake, and a large diameter APN-3-5 infra-red night vision device could be fitted over the rear part of the barrel. Usual tow vehicle was a Tatra 138 6x6 12-tonne lorry, and effective anti-tank range was 1,000m.

It was visually similar to the Czech 85mm M-52 as well as the Soviet BS-3. However, the M-53 had a box-section split-trail carriage rather than the M-52's tubular trails. It had single road wheels instead of the BS-3's double wheels, and the shield had a straight top and sides that sloped to the rear, unlike the M-52. It also had a castor wheel at the end of each trail to assist in deployment.

Specifications: M-53

Calibre: 100mm
Barrel length: 6.74m
Weight: 4,210kg
4,280kg (travelling)
Length: 9.1m (travelling)
Width: 2.61m (travelling)
Height: 2.61m (travelling)
Elevation/depression: +42/-6°
Traverse: 60° total
Rate of fire: 8-10 rounds/minute
Maximum range: 21,000m
Crew: 6

180mm S-23 Gun

Developed in the early 1950s from a naval weapon, this was first seen by the West during the 1955 May Day Parade in Moscow. Western intelligence initially believed it to have a calibre of 203mm, and so referred to it as the 203mm gun-howitzer M1955. This error was corrected after examples were captured by the Israelis.

When in action, the S-23 was supported on a base. When in transit, the base was retracted under the carriage and the barrel was traversed to the rear and attached to the trails. The carriage had split, box-section trails and four large rubber tyres filled

S-23

with sponge rubber. The long barrel had a pepper pot muzzle brake.

The S-23 fired bag-type variable charges. The HE-FRAG projectile weighed 88kg, with 10.7kg of TNT. The concrete-piercing projectile weighed 97.5kg, with 7.35kg of TNT. A rocket-assisted HE projectile was also available, which weighed 84kg and had 5.62kg of RDX and aluminium.

Specifications: S-23

Calibre: 180mm
Barrel length: 8.8m
Weight: 21,450kg
Length: 10.49m
Width: 3m
Height: 2.62m
Elevation/depression: +50/-2°
Traverse: 44° total
Rate of fire: 1 rounds/minute
Maximum range: 30.4km (43.8km with RAP)
Crew: 16

85mm D-48 Anti-Tank Gun

Originally seen by the West during the 1955 Moscow May Day Parade, the D-48 was initially mis-identified as a 100mm weapon. It was replaced in Soviet anti-tank formations by the T-12 in the mid-1960s, and NATO did not realise its mistake and reclassify the D-48 as an 85mm weapon until the 1970s.

The D-48 had an impressive performance, achieved by necking down 100mm ammunition to accept a new 85mm projectile. Ammunition included AP, HVAP, and HE rounds. Estimated penetration at 1,000m was 190mm with AP, 240mm with HVAP.

It had a very long barrel with a multi-perforated muzzle brake, mounted on a split-trail carriage with two wheels and a shield. A single castor wheel was fitted to assist in bringing it into and out of action. For transit, the breech was clamped between the trails. An infra-red night vision device could be fitted. It was towed by either an AT-P armoured artillery tractor or Ural 375 6x6 4.5-tonne lorry.

Specifications: D-48

Calibre: 85mm
Barrel length: 6.49m
Weight: 2,350kg
Length: 8.72m (travelling)
Width: 1.59m (travelling)
Height: 1.89m (travelling)
Elevation/depression: +35/-6°
Traverse: 54° total

Rate of fire: 15 rounds/minute
Maximum range: 18,970m
Crew: 6

57MM CH-26 AUXILIARY-PROPELLED ANTI-TANK GUN

The Ch-26 mounted a shorter version of the Ch-51M gun from the ASU-57 self-propelled anti-tank gun on a new split-trail carriage, fitted with an auxiliary propulsion unit. It could fire the same ammunition as the ASU-57, and like that vehicle was developed for use by airborne divisions. The two-cylinder petrol engine was fitted on the right side of the shield, with fuel stored in the hollow trails. The driver's seat was at the end of the trails, facing rearwards. A single road wheel was lowered to the ground before driving. A pair of boxes were fitted behind the driver's seat, containing ready-use ammunition, and an infra-red sight was often fitted on the shield. It was towed by a BTR-152 APC or driven under its own power at speeds of up to 40km/hour.

SPECIFICATIONS: CH-26

Calibre: 57mm
Barrel length: 4.07m
Weight: 1,250kg
Length: 6.11m
Width: 1.8m
Height: 1.22m
Elevation/depression: +15/-4°
Traverse: 56° total
Rate of fire: 12 rounds/minute

Maximum range: 6,700m
Crew: 5

98mm Model 93 Mountain Howitzer (Romania)

Like the 76.2mm gun, this was developed for the Romanian mountain troops. It had a conventional split-trail carriage, but unusually, the rear half of each trail folded upwards and lay on top of the front half when in transit. The trails were then locked together, using a locking pin that had a towing eye included. A small rubber-tyred wheel was mounted under the lock to assist with deployment.

When in action, a spade at the end of each trail helped to absorb recoil, and stakes could also be driven into the ground through the rear part of the trails if required. The carriage had two rubber-tyred wheels and a pair of handbrakes, used when positioning. Elevation and traverse were both manual, with the controls fitted on the left side. Sights for both direct and indirect fire were also fitted on the left side of the weapon. A small shield was fitted to give the crew some protection. The barrel had a multi-baffle muzzle brake, and ammunition was of the separate-loading type. HE and HEAT rounds were available.

It was normally towed by a DAC 444 4x4 2.5-tonne lorry, which also carried the crew and ammunition. It could be quickly disassembled into three loads, each of which could be transported on a carriage towed by a horse.

Specifications: Model 93

Calibre: 98mm
Weight: 1,500kg

Length: 4.25m
Width: 1.65m
Height: 1.7m
Elevation/depression: +70/-5°
Traverse: 40° total
Rate of fire: 6 rounds/minute
Maximum range: 10,800m
Crew: 8

100mm T-12 & MT-12 Anti-Tank Gun

The T-12 was developed as a replacement for the D-48 anti-tank gun, and was the first smoothbore anti-tank gun to enter service, in 1961. The decision to adopt a smoothbore barrel led to improved HEAT performance, higher muzzle velocity, and longer barrel life than an equivalent rifled barrel. The kinetic energy penetrator was very long and thin, further improving penetration. Production of an improved version, the MT-12 (also known to NATO as the T-12A), began in 1970. This had a new improved carriage, which was less prone to turning over whilst being towed. Both models had sights for indirect fire and direct fire, but indirect fire range was limited by the maximum elevation of only 20°. The T-12 was normally towed by a lorry, the MT-12 by an MT-LB.

The crew of six consisted of commander, towing vehicle driver, gunlayer, loader, and two ammunition numbers. The barrel had a perforated muzzle brake, and was clamped to the trails when in transit. The loader had to open the breech manually to load the first round, after which a semi-automatic loading system would open and close the breech, so that the loader only had to load

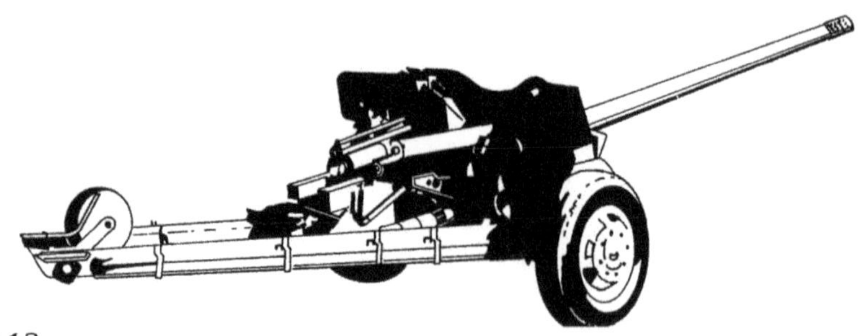

T-12

shells. Image intensifier night sights were fitted. A shield gave the crew some protection from small arms fire and shell splinters.

The T-12 and MT-12 both fired APFSDS, HEAT, and HE ammunition. The APFSDS round had penetration of 230mm at 500m, 140mm at 3,000m. The HEAT round could penetrate 350mm. From 1981, the MT-12 was able to fire the new AT-10 Stabber laser beam-riding ATGM, which had a maximum range of 4,000m and penetration of 550mm. The laser designator was mounted on a tripod to one side of the gun.

Specifications: T-12 (MT-12 in brackets)

Calibre: 100mm
Barrel length: 6.3m
Weight: 2,750kg (3,050kg)
Length: 9.48m (9.65m) (travelling)
Width: 1.8m (2.31m) (travelling)
Height: 1.57m (1.60m) (travelling)
Elevation/depression: +20/-6°
Traverse: 27° total
Rate of fire: 14 rounds/minute
Towing speed: 60km/hour (70km/hour) (road)

15km/hour (25km/hour) (cross-country)
Maximum range, APFSDS: 3,000m
HEAT: 5,995m
HE (indirect): 8,200m
Crew: 6

122mm D-30 Howitzer

The D-30 entered service in the early 1960s, as a replacement for the M-30. Compared to the M-30, the D-30 had greater range and could be rapidly traversed through 360°. The main armament of the 2S1 was based on the D-30 ordnance.

D-30

Later production models, with several improvements, were designated D-30M. The D-30M had a double-baffle muzzle brake; a square, rather than round, baseplate; a towing lunette; and changes to the cradle, carriage, and recoil system.

In transit, the D-30 was towed muzzle-first, with the three trails of the carriage under the barrel. To deploy, two of the trails were spread so that the three trails were equidistant, and the firing jack was raised, then the trails staked into position.

The D-30 fired variable-charge, case-type, separate-loading ammunition. Some D-30 ammunition was compatible with the M-30, but it also fired a non-spinning HEAT-FS round. As well as HE-FRAG and HEAT-FS, it could fire illuminating, leaflet, flechette, and incendiary rounds.

Specifications: D-30

Calibre: 122mm
Barrel length: 4.88m
Weight: 3,150kg
    3,210kg (travelling)
Length: 5.4m (travelling)
Width: 1.95m (travelling)
Height: 1.66m (travelling)
Elevation/depression: +70/-7°
Traverse: 360°
Rate of fire: 7-8 rounds/minute
Sustained rate of fire: 1.25 rounds/minute
Maximum range: 15,400m
Crew: 7

76mm GP Mountain Gun

First reported in 1966, this was designated M1966 in the West, though it was sometimes referred to as the M1969. It had a split trail, split shield, and a short 76mm calibre barrel with no muzzle brake. The trails could fold sideways, and one was fitted with a small wheel to facilitate handling. Sights for direct and indirect fire were mounted to the left of the barrel. The axles could be lowered or raised to adjust the height of the gun, and it could be disassembled for transport.

A variety of ammunition was available, including HE-FRAG, HEAT, HVAP, and AP-T. In addition, it could use ammunition produced for the 76mm ZIS-3 Divisional Gun. The HEAT warhead could penetrate 300mm of armour. Maximum rate of fire was 15 rounds per minute, and 100 rounds per hour could be sustained. It was towed by a Ural 375 6x6 4.5-tonne or GAZ-66 4x4 2-tonne lorry.

SPECIFICATIONS: GP

Barrel length: 2.8m
Weight: 780 kg
Length: 4.8m (travelling)
Width: 1.5m (travelling)
Height: 1.4m (travelling)
Elevation/depression: +65/-5°
Traverse: 50° total
Rate of fire: 15 rounds/minute
Crew: 7

152MM 2A36 GIATSINT-B FIELD GUN

Development of the 2A36 began in 1968, to satisfy a requirement for a 152mm gun to replace the 130mm M-46. The new gun was to be used in both towed and self-propelled versions, the towed version's primary purpose being counter-battery fire.

The self-propelled gun became the 2S5 Giatsint-S, and the towed gun became the 2A36 Giatsint-B. Surprisingly, the two types did not fire the same ammunition, though they shared ballistic characteristics.

Full-scale production began in 1976, but it was not shown in public until 1985. It was towed by a KrAZ-260 6x6, KrAZ-255B 6x6 or Ural 4320 6x6 lorry, or a tracked artillery tractor such as an AT-T, AT-S, or ATS-59.

The gun was fitted with a multi-slotted muzzle brake, and had sights for both direct and indirect fire. Elevation and traverse were both manual, and an armoured shield provided some protection to the crew. A hydraulic rammer was fitted, with a manual backup. In the firing position, the front was supported on a circular jack under the forward part of the carriage. Each trail had a spade, with extra-large spades available for use on soft ground.

The usual projectile was HE-FRAG, which could be fused for high explosive or fragmentation effect. A rocket-assisted version was available, which extended the range to 40km. AP-T projectiles were available for use in direct fire against armoured targets, as well as smoke, concrete-piercing, and incendiary. The ammunition was not backward-compatible with older 152mm artillery systems.

Four braked wheels and an improved suspension allowed faster towing speeds and improved cross-country mobility compared to earlier towed artillery pieces.

Specifications: 2A36 Giatsint-B

Barrel length: 8.2m
Weight: 9,800 kg (travelling)
 9,760 kg (firing)
Length: 12.92m (travelling)
 12.3m (firing)
Width: 2.79m
Height: 2.76m
Ground clearance: 0.48m
Elevation/depression: +57/-2.5°
Traverse: 50° total
Rate of fire: 5-6 rounds/minute
Range: 27km (40km with RAP)
Crew: 8
Towing speed: 80km/hour (road)
 30km/hour (cross-country)
Unit of fire: 60 rounds

152mm Howitzer M1981 (Romania)

Developed in Romania, this had a box-section split-trail carriage. A castor wheel was fitted to each trail leg to facilitate bringing the weapon into action, and these rested on the trails when in transit. A circular firing pedestal was fitted, which would be inverted and secured ahead of the shield for transit. When deployed, the pedestal in conjunction with the castor wheels allowed rapid transit through a full 360°. A large double-baffle muzzle brake was fitted, with a circular ring around the barrel immediately behind the muzzle brake, giving the weapon a distinctive look.

The M1981 fired separate-loading ammunition. HE, HEAT, leaflet, and illuminating rounds were available. Maximum range was 24,000m with HE.

130MM GUN M1982 (ROMANIA)

This was mounted on a split-trail carriage very similar to the Romanian 152mm M1985, with a similar top carriage, shield, and recoil system. The ballistic characteristics were similar to the Soviet M-46, though it appears to have been independently developed.

The barrel had a double-baffle muzzle brake. When deployed, it rested on a circular firing jack under the front of the carriage, and a pair of spades at the end of the trails. For transit, the firing jack was swung through 180° and locked under the barrel. It fired separate-loading ammunition, which could also be fired by the Soviet M-46.

SPECIFICATIONS: M1982

Calibre: 130mm
Barrel length: 6.85m
Weight: 6,150kg
    6,200kg (travelling)
Length: 10.8m (travelling)
Width: 2.59m (travelling)
Height: 2.65m (travelling)
Elevation/depression: +45/-2°
Traverse: 58° total
Rate of fire: 7 rounds/minute

Maximum range: 27,150m
Crew: 7

152mm Gun-Howitzer M1985 (Romania)

Developed in Romania, this had a split-trail two-wheeled carriage which was very similar to the Soviet D-20. The Romanian weapon had a longer barrel, leading to a longer range. Each trail had a castor wheel to assist in bringing the weapon into and out of action. When deployed to fire, the castor wheels rested on top of the trails. In action, the weapon was supported on a circular firing jack at the front of the carriage and a pair of spades at the rear of the trails. HE-FRAG and APC-T ammunition was available.

Specifications: M1985

Calibre: 152.4mm
Barrel length: 8.03m
Weight: 7,500kg
 7,550kg (travelling)
Length: 11.17m (travelling)
Width: 2.53m (travelling)
Elevation/depression: +57/-5°
Traverse: 50° total
Rate of fire: 2-4 rounds/minute
Maximum range: 24,000m

152mm 2A65 Howitzer

Introduced in 1987 and initially designated M1987 by NATO, this was the towed version of the gun fitted in the 2S19 self-propelled gun. It fired the same ammunition, and could also fire older ammunition used by the D20 towed gun-howitzer and 2S3 self-propelled gun-howitzer. It had a conventional split-trail carriage, with castor wheels at the ends of the trails to help when bringing the gun into action. These were swung around to sit on top of the trail when in action. In the firing position, the weapon rested on spades at the rear of the trails and a firing jack at the front.

The barrel had a double-baffle muzzle brake, and the weapon also had a semi-automatic breech, spring-operated ram, hydraulic counter-recoil, and a liquid-cooled recoil brake. Elevation and traverse were manual, with two speeds. Sights were fitted for direct fire and indirect fire, and pneumatic brakes were fitted.

SPECIFICATIONS: 2A65

Calibre: 152.4mm
Weight: 7,000kg
Elevation/depression: +70/-3.5°
Traverse: 54° total
Rate of fire: 7 rounds/minute
Maximum range: 24,000m
Crew: 8

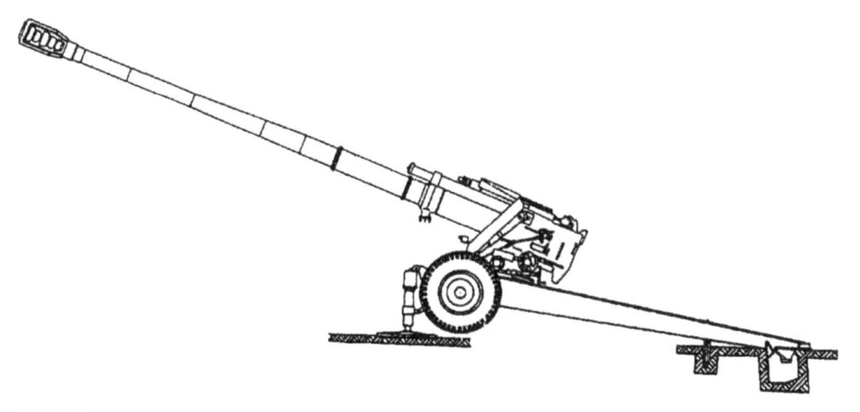

2A65

Self-Propelled Guns, Howitzers, and Mortars

During the Second World War, little interest was shown in self-propelled artillery, with only multiple rocket launchers (commonly referred to by the nickname "Katyusha") being developed as mobile systems. The only self-propelled guns were tank destroyers and assault guns designed for direct fire, rather than artillery guns and howitzers intended to provide indirect fire. Development of self-propelled guns, howitzers, and mortars started in the late 1960s, probably helped by the removal from power of Khrushchev, a firm proponent of missiles and rockets.

SU-76

In 1942, the Soviet army had an urgent need for a tank destroyer, and the SU-76 was hastily developed to meet that requirement. First used in combat in early 1943, it was found to be inadequate for the anti-tank role, and so was repurposed to infantry support. Over 12,000 vehicles were built, but production stopped in 1945.

The chassis was a longer and wider version of that used on the T-70 light tank, armed with a modified version of the ZIS-3

76mm divisional gun. Originally, it had engines on either side of the hull and a fully-armoured fighting compartment. This was not a success and only a few were built. The design was changed to have engines mounted in tandem and a partially-armoured fighting compartment, creating the SU-76M.

The hull was of all-welded construction. The driver sat at the front centre, with a single-piece hatch cover and a periscope. The engines were mounted in tandem on the right side of the hull, toward the rear, with the fuel tank to the left of the driver.

The open-topped fighting compartment was at the rear of the vehicle. A tubular frame allowed a tarpaulin cover to be fitted to give protection against inclement weather. Access was via a single door in the rear, and firing ports were fitted on either side of the fighting compartment. The commander had a vision port to the right of the armament, with the gunner's sight to the left of the gun.

The 76mm gun was mounted to the left of centre, and had a double-baffle muzzle brake. Elevation and traverse were both manual, and it fired the same types of ammunition as the PT-76 light tank. 60 rounds of ammunition were carried, and during the Second World War many vehicles carried a 7.62mm machine gun for use against aircraft.

The SU-76 did not have NBC protection, night-vision equipment, or an amphibious capability.

Specifications: SU-76M

Crew: 4
Combat weight: 11.2 tonnes

SU-76M

Length: 5.0m
Width: 2.74m
Height: 2.1m
Ground clearance: 0.3m
Maximum road speed: 45km/hour
Maximum road range: 360km
Gradient: 47%
Vertical obstacle: 0.65m
Armament: 1x 76.2mm gun (60 rounds)

Armour:
Hull glacis: 25mm @ 30° [Effective: 29mm]
Hull nose: 35mm @ 60° [Effective: 70mm]
Superstructure front: 25 @ 27° [Effective: 28mm]
Superstructure side: 12mm @ 17° [Effective: 13mm]
Mantlet: 14mm
Lower hull side: 16mm
Hull rear: 15mm
Belly: 10mm

ISU-122

Like the heavier ISU-152, the ISU-122 was based on the IS-2 tank chassis. The armament was mounted in an armoured superstructure at the front, with the engine and transmission at the rear. The main armament, an 122mm A-19S gun, was mounted to the right of centre, with the driver seated to the left. Elevation and traverse were both manual. A 12.7mm DShKM machine gun was mounted on the roof for anti-aircraft use. Long-range fuel tanks were fitted on the sides of the hull, at the rear.

The A-19S was a development of the towed A-19 gun, and had a rate of fire of three rounds per minute. HE-FRAG, concrete piercing, and AP-T rounds were available. The range of the HE-FRAG round was reduced by the gun's elevation to 13,400m.

In 1944, the original ISU-122 was replaced in production by the ISU-122S. This was armed with a 122mm D-25S gun, a development of the D-25 used in the IS-2, IS-3, and IS-4 heavy tanks. An improved breech compared to the A-19S meant that the rate of fire was increased to six rounds per minute. An MSh-17 gun sight was fitted for direct fire. Unlike the ISU-122, the ISU-122S had a double-baffle muzzle brake.

Specifications: ISU-122S

Crew: 5
Combat weight: 46.5 tonnes
Length: 6.8m (10.1m including gun)
Width: 3.07m
Height: 2.47m

ISU-122

Ground clearance: 0.46m
Maximum road speed: 37km/hour
Maximum road range: 150km (306km with long-range fuel tanks)
Gradient: 60%
Vertical obstacle: 1m

Armament:
1x 122mm D-25S (30 rounds)
1x 12.7mm DShKM MG (250 rounds)

Armour:
Hull glacis: 110mm @ 70° [Effective: 322mm]
Mantlet: 90mm
Upper hull sides: 90mm

Hull top: 25mm
Hull rear: 22-64mm
Belly: 19mm

ISU-152

Almost identical to the earlier SU-152, the ISU-152 was based on an IS-2 chassis, whereas the SU-152 was based on the KV-2. The 152mm ML-20S gun, a development of the ML-20, was mounted in an armoured superstructure at the front of the vehicle, to the right of centre. The gun was shorter than the one fitted on the ISU-122, and had a multi-baffle muzzle brake.

ISU-152

The driver was seated to the left of the main armament. Hand rails were fitted on the outside of the vehicle to allow infantry to be carried into action, and a 12.7mm DShKM machine gun was mounted on the roof for anti-aircraft use. The very limited on-board ammunition store of only twenty rounds meant that frequent resupply was required. Elevation and traverse were both manual, and the maximum elevation of the gun limited the range of the HE-FRAG round to 9,000m. Long-range fuel tanks were fitted on the sides of the hull, at the rear.

Specifications: ISU-152

Crew: 5
Combat weight: 46.5 tonnes
Length: 6.8m (9.05m including gun)
Width: 3.07m
Height: 2.47m
Ground clearance: 0.46m
Maximum road speed: 37km/hour
Maximum road range: 150km (306km with long-range fuel tanks)
Gradient: 60%
Vertical obstacle: 1m

Armament:
1x 152mm ML-20S (20 rounds)
1x 12.7mm DShKM MG (250 rounds)

Armour:
Hull glacis: 110mm @ 70° [Effective: 322mm]
Mantlet: 90mm
Upper hull sides: 90mm
Hull top: 25mm
Hull rear: 22-64mm
Belly: 19mm

2S1 Gvozdika

The first prototype 2S1 vehicles were built in 1969. It was accepted for service in 1970 and began volume production in

1971. The hull was made of welded steel, based on the automotive components and running gear of the MT-LB. The driver sat at the front with the engine behind him, and the turret and fighting compartment at the rear. Within the turret, the commander sat on the left, with the gunner below and in front of him, and the loader to the right. The gun had sights for indirect and direct fire.

2S1 Gvozdika

The main armament was a 2A31 122mm howitzer, based on the D-30 towed howitzer. It had a fume extractor and double-baffle muzzle brake, and a remote-controlled lock on the hull to fix the barrel in place during transit. A rate of fire of 5-8 rounds per minute could be maintained for a protracted period. 40 rounds of ammunition were carried in the vehicle, the usual load being 32 HE, six smoke, and two HEAT-FS. Standard practice during a fire mission was for ammunition to be supplied from outside the vehicle. When firing HE, the gun had a maximum range of 15.3km. The HEAT-FS warhead could penetrate around 460mm of standard steel armour. Chemical and HE-RAP ammunition was also available, the latter extending the maximum range to 21.9km.

The 2S1's suspension could be adjusted to make the vehicle shorter, a useful feature when transporting by air. The standard tracks were 400mm wide, but like the MT-LB, 670mm wide tracks could be fitted for use in snow, swampy ground, etc. The 2S1 had NBC protection, infra-red driving lights, and a small infra-red searchlight on the commander's cupola. It was fully amphibious, propelled in the water by its tracks. Before entering the water, a bilge pump was switched on, shrouds were fitted to the hull front, water deflectors were lowered at the rear, the trim vane was erected at the front of the hull, and covers were fitted around the engine air intakes. Only 30 rounds could be carried when swimming; any excess had to be removed before entering the water.

Specifications: 2S1 Gvozdika

Crew: 4 + 2 in ammunition carrier
Combat weight: 15.7 tonnes
Length: 7.26m
Width: 2.85m
Height: 2.287m
Ground clearance: 0.4m
Maximum road speed: 61.5km/hour
Maximum road range: 500km
Gradient: 77%
Vertical obstacle: 0.7m

Armament: 1x 122mm 2A31 howitzer (40 rounds)

Armour:
Hull: 15mm
Turret: 10-20mm

2S3 Akatsiya

Production of the 2S3 started in 1970, although it was not accepted for service until late 1971. The hull was based on an improved version of the SA-4 Ganef chassis, with a more powerful 520hp engine, upgraded track and suspension. The hull was welded steel, with the driver in the front to the left, the engine to his right, and the turret at the rear. The commander was seated in the left of the turret, the gunner forward and below him, and the loader on the right. The gun had sights for direct fire as well as indirect fire.

Main armament was a 2A33 152mm howitzer. Almost identical to the D-20 towed howitzer, it was fitted with a fume extractor and travelling lock, which was remotely operated by the driver from his seat. Traverse and elevation were powered, though manual controls were also provided. 33 rounds of ammunition were carried in the rear of the hull. Normally, ammunition was supplied from outside the vehicle and passed in through hatches in the rear, the internal ammunition being reserved for immediate use. HE-FRAG ammunition was most commonly used, though HEAT-FS, HE-RAP, AP-T, illuminating, smoke, incendiary, flechette, and scatter mine ammunition were also available. Maximum range was 18.5km with conventional ammunition, 24km when firing HE-RAP.

2S3 Akatsiya

A 7.62mm PKT machine gun was mounted on the commander's cupola. This could be aimed and fired by remote control from inside the turret. The 2S3 had NBC protection, infra-red driving lights, a small white light/infra-red searchlight mounted forward of the commander's hatch, and a self-entrenching blade at the front of the hull. It did not have an amphibious capability.

The 2S3M, introduced in 1975, increased the on-board ammunition load to 46 rounds, 12 of which were in a rotating carousel to facilitate faster loading. The 2S3M1, introduced in 1987, added a data terminal connected to the battery commander's vehicle, allowing fire commands to be instantly displayed in the fire vehicles. It also had an improved sight and new laser-guided, rocket-assisted projectiles were available.

Specifications: 2S3 Akatsiya

Crew: 4 + 2 in ammunition carrier
Combat weight: 27.5 tonnes
Length: 7.7m (8.4m including gun)
Width: 3.25m
Height: 3.05m
Ground clearance: 0.45m
Maximum road speed: 60km/hour
Maximum road range: 500km
Gradient: 60%
Vertical obstacle: 0.7m
Trench: 3m

Armament:
1x 152mm 2A33 howitzer (33 rounds, 2S3M/M1: 46 rounds)
1x 7.62mm PKT MG (1,500 rounds)

Armour:
Hull: 15mm max
Turret: 20mm max

2S4 Tyulpan

Introduced in 1970, the 2S4 mounted a 240mm breech-loading mortar on a tracked vehicle based on the GMZ minelayer chassis. The mortar, complete with baseplate, lay along the length of the vehicle when in transit. To deploy, the mortar was rotated around a hinge at the rear of the vehicle, so that it came to rest facing away from the vehicle to the rear, with the baseplate on the ground. Elevation was from +45° to +80°, with 8° of traverse.

© Vitaly V. Kuzmin

2S4 Tyulpan

Four men were carried in the vehicle, though a total of nine were required to load and fire the mortar. Twelve mortar bombs were carried in the vehicle, and a small hand-operated crane was fitted to the rear to facilitate loading. The mortar had a rate of fire of one round per minute, and could fire HE, chemical, and nuclear rounds. The 240mm mortar was the first Soviet artillery piece to be equipped with nuclear ammunition.

The vehicle hull had welded steel armour, with the driver at the front left and the engine to his right. To the rear of the driver was the commander, who was provided with a raised cupola, on which was mounted a 7.62mm PKT machine gun. The vehicle provided NBC protection for the crew while they were inside, though they had to exit the vehicle to operate the mortar.

Specifications: 2S4 Tyulpan

Crew: 4 + 5 in ammunition carrier
Combat weight: 30 tonnes
Length: 8.5m
Width: 3.2m
Height: 3.2m
Ground clearance: 0.46m
Maximum road speed: 50km/hour
Maximum road range: 500km
Gradient: 65%
Vertical obstacle: 1.1m
Armour: 15-20mm

Armament:
1x 240mm mortar (12 rounds)
1x 7.62mm PKT MG

2S5 Giatsint-S

In 1968, development began on a new 152mm gun, which was intended to be used in both towed and self-propelled versions. Production of both towed (2A36) and self-propelled (2S5) guns began in 1976. The 2S5 had a welded steel hull, and a self-entrenching blade was mounted on the front. The engine was at the front right of the vehicle, and could use diesel or aviation fuel. The vehicle provided NBC protection when sealed, though the gun could not be operated from inside the vehicle.

The driver sat to the left of the engine, and was provided with day and passive night periscopes. The vehicle commander sat behind the driver in a slightly raised superstructure with a cupola, on which was mounted a 7.62mm PKT machine gun and

2S5 Giatsint-S in firing position

a white light/IR searchlight. The machine gun could be operated from within the vehicle. The three remaining crew members were seated in a compartment at the rear of the vehicle, entering via a ramp at the rear. They were provided with periscopes, but these periscopes did not have any night-vision capability.

The 2A37 152mm gun was mounted on the vehicle roof in an open mount at the rear, and had a multi-baffled muzzle brake. Sights for direct and indirect fire were included, and a travelling lock was used when in transit. A large spade was deployed at the rear of the vehicle before firing, to provide extra stability.

The gunlayer sat to the left of the gun, and had a simple shield to his front. 30 projectiles and charges were carried in the rear of the vehicle. The projectiles were in a carousel and the charges were in three rows of ten on a conveyor belt. Maximum rate of fire was five to six rounds per minute.

Specifications: 2S5 Giatsint-S

Crew: 5
Combat weight: 28.2 tonnes
Length: 8.33m
Width: 3.25m
Height: 2.76m
Ground clearance: 0.45m
Maximum road speed: 63km/hour
Maximum road range: 500km
Gradient: 58%
Vertical obstacle: 0.7m
Trench: 2.5m
Armour: 13mm

Armament:
1x 152mm 2A37 gun (30 rounds)
1x 7.62mm PKT MG

2S7 Pion

In the late 1960s, a requirement for a large calibre self-propelled gun was issued. The calibre was not specified, and after studies of various calibres, 203mm was chosen and the 2S7 entered service in 1975. The hull was welded steel, with the driver seated at the front left, and the engine in the front right. When travelling, the commander and gunner were seated in the driver's compartment. The remaining four vehicle crew members were seated to the rear of the engine (another seven crew were carried in the ammunition vehicle). An entrenching blade was fitted to the front of the hull, and an SA-14 surface-to-air missile system was carried.

2S7 Pion

The 203mm gun was mounted on top of the hull at the rear of the vehicle, with a manually operated travel lock fitted on the hull. A large spade was mounted at the rear, which was used to stabilise the vehicle before firing. Gun traverse and elevation was powered, though manual controls were provided for emergency use. Indirect and direct fire sights were provided for the gunner, who sat to the left of the gun when in action.

The standard HE-FRAG ammunition had a maximum range of 37.5km. Rocket-assisted ammunition was available, which increased maximum range to 47.5km. Concrete-piercing, nuclear, and chemical ammunition was also available. Four rounds were carried on the vehicle, with more ammunition normally carried on a lorry. An ammunition-handling system allowed a rate of fire of two rounds per minute. The vehicle had night-vision equipment and provided the crew with NBC protection when they were inside.

The 2S7M entered service in 1983. This variant carried eight rounds of ammunition on board, had improved durability, and new communications facilities that allowed firing data to be transmitted directly to the gun from the battery commander.

Specifications: 2S7 Pion

Crew: 7
Combat weight: 46.5 tonnes
Length: 13.12m including gun
Width: 3.38m
Height: 3m
Ground clearance: 0.4m
Maximum road speed: 50km/hour
Maximum road range: 650km
Gradient: 40%
Vertical obstacle: 0.7m
Trench: 2.5m
Armour: 10mm
Armament: 1x 203mm 2A44 gun (4 rounds, 2S7M: 8 rounds)

2S9 NONA

The 2S9 entered service in 1981, mounting an 120mm gun/mortar in an armoured turret on a BTR-D armoured personnel carrier. Like the BTR-D, it was amphibious, air-droppable, and had NBC protection. It could be used in the indirect and direct fire roles, with HEAT warheads available to provide an anti-tank capability.

2S9 Nona

The driver sat in the front centre of the hull, with the commander in the front left. The gunner and loader sat in the turret, the gunner on the left, the loader on the right. The turret had limited traverse of 35° either side of directly ahead.

Main armament was a 2A51 120mm gun/mortar, with a rate of fire of six to eight rounds per minute. It could fire HE, HE-

RAP, white phosphorous, smoke, and HEAT rounds. Maximum indirect fire range was 8.8km with standard rounds, increased to 13km with rocket-assisted projectiles.

Specifications: 2S9 Nona

Crew: 4
Combat weight: 8.7 tonnes
Length: 6.02m
Width: 2.63m
Height: 1.9m
Ground clearance: 0.1m - 0.45m
Maximum road speed: 60km/hour
Maximum road range: 500km
Gradient: 60%
Vertical obstacle: 0.5-0.8m
Trench: 2m
Armour: 16mm
Armament: 1x 120mm 2A60 gun/mortar (25 rounds)

2S19 Msta

The 2S19 entered production and was accepted for service in 1989, as a replacement for both the 2S3 and 2S5. The suspension and running gear were based on those of the T-80 MBT, while the engine was the same as that fitted to the T-72 MBT. The driver's compartment was at the front, the turret extended over the centre and rear of the hull, and the engine was at the rear. The turret and hull were welded steel, and a self-entrenching blade was fitted at the front of the hull.

2S19 Msta

Main armament was a 2A64 152mm howitzer, which had a fume extractor, double-baffle muzzle brake, and travelling lock. Indirect and direct fire sights were fitted. The gun could fire HE-FRAG and smoke projectiles to a range of 24.7km. Turret traverse and gun elevation were powered, with manual controls for use in an emergency. 50 rounds were carried in the vehicle, though ammunition was normally supplied from outside the vehicle.

A 12.7mm NSVT machine gun and small searchlight were fitted to the roof of the turret, in front of the commander's hatch. Both could be operated remotely from within the vehicle. The 2S19 had NBC protection and passive night-vision equipment. Six smoke grenade dischargers were mounted on the turret, three on each side. A smokescreen could also be generated by injecting diesel fuel into the exhaust.

Specifications: 2S19 Msta

Crew: 5
Combat weight: 42 tonnes
Length: 7.15m (11.92m including gun)
Width: 3.38m
Height: 2.99m
Ground clearance: 0.44m
Maximum road speed: 60km/hour
Maximum road range: 500km
Gradient: 47%
Vertical obstacle: 0.5m
Trench: 2.8m
Armour: Unknown, but proof against small arms and shell splinters

Armament:
1x 152mm 2A64 howitzer (50 rounds)
1x 12.7mm NSVT MG (300 rounds)

VZOR 77 Dana (Czechoslovakia)

This wheeled 152mm self-propelled gun-howitzer was developed in the late 1970s, and entered service with the Czech army in 1981. It had an eight-wheeled chassis based on components of the Tatra 813 8x8 lorry, rather than the more usual tracked chassis. The Tatra 813 had been shown to have a good cross-country capability, but wheeled chassis were much cheaper and easier to maintain than comparable tracked systems.

Since the Dana operated some distance behind the lines, tactical mobility was less important than on front-line vehicles.

The driver sat in the front compartment on the left, with the commander to his right. A large, fully enclosed turret was in the centre, with the engine at the rear. Armour was sufficient to provide protection against small arms and shell splinters. A central tyre pressure regulation system and power steering were both fitted.

The driver and commander had roof hatches and windscreens with armoured shutters. Each also had two firing ports, one to the front and one to the side. The commander operated the communication system and was provided with a night sight. The driver operated the turret locking system and stabilisers.

The 152mm gun-howitzer was fitted with a muzzle brake, and could fire the same ammunition as the Soviet 2S3 Akatsiya, as well as Czech-made ammunition. The vehicle had a fully automatic loading system, which loaded the projectile and the separate charge, and could operate at all elevations. Single shot or fully automatic fire modes could be selected by the gunner.

The Dana took two minutes to prepare for firing after coming to a halt, and required one minute to prepare to move off after the last round had been fired. Hydraulic jacks were lowered before firing to ensure a stable platform. Sights were provided for direct fire as well as indirect fire. Up to 60 rounds of ammunition could be carried, but road speed was reduced if more than 40 rounds were carried.

The turret was made up of two distinct parts, with the weapon mounted externally between them, ensuring that no fumes could enter the interior. The turret could only rotate through 225°. Each side of the turret had access doors, roof hatches, and vision devices. The gunner and loader operator were in the left half of the turret, with the ammunition handler, who set the fuses, in the right half.

A 12.7mm anti-aircraft machine gun was fitted to the turret roof on the right side, and could also be used in the direct fire role. An NBC system was fitted as standard.

Specifications: VZOR 77 Dana

Crew: 5
Combat weight: 29.25 tonnes
Length: 11.16m
Width: 3m
Height: 2.85m
Ground clearance: 0.41m
Maximum road speed: 80km/hour
Maximum road range: 740km
Gradient: 60%
Vertical obstacle: 0.6m
Trench: 2m

Armament:
1x 152mm gun-howitzer (40 rounds, or 60 rounds with speed reduced to 70km/hour)
1x 12.7mm NSV MG

Mortars

During the Second World War, the Soviet Union made extensive use of mortars. The simpler construction of the smoothbore barrels used by mortars, compared to the rifled barrels of tube artillery, meant that mass production could be continued after armaments factories were overrun by the Germans. Even in peacetime, the large armies of the Warsaw Pact valued the ease of production that mortars offered.

A single mortar bomb had more explosive than a howitzer shell of the same calibre, albeit with inferior accuracy and shorter range. Mortars gave infantry commanders indirect fire support under their own command, able to stay with the infantry they supported. The Soviet Union developed mortars of very large calibres, up to 240mm. The very long barrels of the large calibre weapons mandated the use of unconventional breech-loading mechanisms, since it was simply not possible to load at the muzzle.

50mm M-38, M-39, M-40 & M-41

In the late 1930s and early 1940s, the Soviet Union developed a range of light 50mm mortars. All were conventional muzzle-loaders, but only the M-39 used variable elevation to adjust range. The others were always fired at an angle of 45 or 75 degrees. A sleeve around the base of the barrel opened or closed a number of gas ports. The more that were open, the more propellant gas was evacuated to the atmosphere, reducing propellant power and thus range. All fired HE ammunition only.

The M-38, M-39, and M-40 had base plates and bipods, but the M-41 dispensed with the bipod, having only a baseplate. An interesting variant of the M-40 was developed which had three barrels, the extra two mounted alongside the centre barrel. A lanyard was pulled to drop the bombs in all three barrels simultaneously. This variant was produced in very limited numbers, and does not appear to have been a success.

Specifications: M-40

Calibre: 50mm
Weight: 11.5kg
12.25kg (travelling)
Elevation: 45 to 75°
Traverse: 5.5° total
Maximum range: 800m

Specifications: M-41

Calibre: 50mm
Weight: 10kg
12kg (travelling)
Elevation: 45 to 75°
Traverse: 12° total
Maximum range: 800m

82MM M-36, M-37, M-41, M-43, & "NEW" M-37

The first Soviet 82mm mortar was the M-36, which was very similar to the US 81mm M1 mortar. The design of both weapon and ammunition was conventional, the ammunition having a primary cartridge and six increments. HE and smoke ammunition were available, and three types of sights were used: the MP-1, the MP-82, and a simple aiming circle inclinometer.

The M-37 was a modified M-36, with a circular baseplate instead of the original rectangle.

The M-41 was an attempt to improve the mobility and performance of the M-37. Instead of the conventional bipod and yoke, the M-41 had a long column supported by two short legs. At the end of each bipod leg was a very short axle, to which a wheel could be fitted. For transit, the bipod was folded along the barrel and clamped to the baseplate. The wheels would then be attached, so that the mortar could be towed. The M-41 was not a success, offering only slightly better mobility than the M-37, with significantly inferior firing stability and ballistic performance.

The M-43 was a continuation of the attempt to improve mobility that began in the M-41. It was basically the same, but the wheels were not detachable. This was also not a success, and so production was discontinued in favour of continued M-37 production.

The "new" M-37 was an M-37 with a lighter tripod and baseplate. A device was fitted to the muzzle to prevent a second round being loaded before the first had left the muzzle.

Specifications: M-36

Calibre: 82mm
Barrel length: 1.29m
Weight: 57.3kg
Elevation: 45 to 85°
Maximum range: 3,100m

Specifications: M-37

Calibre: 82mm
Barrel length: 1.22m
Weight: 56kg
Elevation: 45 to 85°
Traverse: 6° total
Rate of fire: 15-25 rounds/minute
Minimum range: 100m
Maximum range: 3,000m
Crew: 5

Specifications: M-41

Calibre: 82mm
Barrel length: 1.22m
Weight: 52kg
58kg (travelling)
Elevation: 45 to 85°
Traverse: 5° total
Rate of fire: 15-25 rounds/minute
Maximum range: 2,550m
Crew: 5

107MM M-38

This was a scaled-down version of the 120mm M-38, and produced after that weapon. Being lighter and smaller, it was intended for animal transport and use by mountain troops. The complete weapon was carried on a two-wheeled trolley.

Two different HE projectiles were available, one "light" and one "heavy". The light one weighed 7.9kg and could be fired to a range of 6,300m. The heavy one weighed 9kg and could be fired to a distance of 5,150m.

SPECIFICATIONS: M-38

Calibre: 107mm
Barrel length: 1.67m
Weight: 170kg
340kg (travelling)
Elevation: 45 to 80°
Traverse: 3° total
Rate of fire: 15 rounds/minute
Minimum range: 800m
Crew: 5

120MM M-38

A very successful design that formed the basis of a scaled-down 107mm weapon for mountain infantry, the M-38 was much more mobile than most mortars of its size. For transit, it was lifted onto a two-wheeled carriage, which could be towed by any suitable vehicle. Alternatively, it could be broken down into three loads for animal transport. Firing could be accomplished by either dropping the bomb onto a firing pin, or by using a trigger device. During the Second World War, the Germans used large numbers of captured M-38s, and copied it to create their own 120mm mortar.

Specifications: M-38

Calibre: 120mm
Barrel length: 1.86m
Weight: 280kg
Elevation: 45 to 80°
Traverse: 6° total
Maximum range: 6,000m

120mm M-43 (120-PM-43)

An incremental improvement on the very successful M-38, this had longer shock absorber cylinders. It retained the same style of baseplate and the tubular two-wheeled carriage. Like the earlier weapon, it could be easily broken down into three loads for pack transport. It fired a 15.4kg projectile to a maximum range of 5,700m, slightly less than the M-38's maximum range.

Specifications: M-43

Calibre: 120mm
Barrel length: 1.85m
Weight: 274.8kg
500kg (travelling)
Elevation: 45 to 80°
Traverse: 8° total
Rate of fire: 12-15 rounds/minute

Minimum range: 460m
Maximum range: 5,700m
Crew: 6

120MM 2B11 SANI/2S12

The 2B11 was a developmental improvement of the M-43. Better materials and a redesigned carriage led to a significant reduction in weight. The basic design, however, was unchanged, retaining the smoothbore barrel resting on a conical baseplate, supported by a bipod connected via a recoil buffer mechanism. The muzzle had a system to prevent double loading.

The 2B11 was normally carried fully assembled on a two-wheeled carriage, with the baseplate attached and the bipod above the barrel. The mortar was normally carried on the back of a GAZ-66 4x4 2-tonne lorry, which had special fittings for carrying the mortar. If required, the lorry could also tow the mortar, although the carriage's very light weight limited it to short moves at slow speed. The combination of mortar and lorry was designated 2S12, and the lorry also carried the crew and a supply of ammunition.

If necessary, the mortar could be disassembled into barrel, tripod, and baseplate, for transport by pack animal. Ammunition included HE-FRAG, smoke, illumination, and incendiary bombs.

SPECIFICATIONS: 2B11 SANI

Calibre: 120mm
Weight: 210kg
    297kg (travelling)
Elevation: 45 to 80°

2B11 Sani

Traverse: 10° total (56° total by moving bipod)
Rate of fire: 12-15 rounds/minute
Minimum range: 460m
Maximum range: 7,180m
Crew: 5

160MM M-43 & M-160

The M-43 was introduced during the Second World War to provide infantry divisions with a weapon that could produce a great deal of high explosive, without making significant demands on manufacturing resources.

The long barrel meant that breech-loading wasn't feasible. Instead, the barrel pivoted around trunnions close to the centre of the barrel. The M-160 replaced the wartime M-43. It was virtually identical in design, but was heavier, with a longer barrel and much greater range. The M-43 fired a 40.8kg bomb; the M-160 a 41.5kg bomb.

SPECIFICATIONS: M-43

Calibre: 160mm
Barrel length: 3.03m
Weight: 1,170kg
1,270kg (travelling)
Elevation: 45 to 80°
Traverse: 25° total
Rate of fire: 3 rounds/minute
Minimum range: 630m
Maximum range: 5,150m
Crew: 7

SPECIFICATIONS: M-160

Calibre: 160mm
Barrel length: 4.55m
Weight: 1,300kg
1,470kg (travelling)

Elevation: 50 to 80°
Traverse: 24° total
Rate of fire: 2-3 rounds/minute
Minimum range: 750m
Maximum range: 8,040m
Crew: 7

240MM M-240

First seen by the West at a Moscow parade in 1953, it was given the designation M1953. Tactical limitations, including needing a long time to prepare for either action or transit, meant that it was replaced by the 2S4 where possible once the latter system came into service.

The M-240 was breech-loaded, and had a frame with shock absorbers and a two-wheeled carriage. The sights were carried separately, and only fitted when firing. The shock absorbers protected the sights from the vibrations caused by firing. A boom was fitted to provide firing stability, and a pair of winches were fitted to assist with changing from firing to travelling configuration.

Elevation was from 45° to 65°, which translated into a minimum range of 800m and maximum range of 9,700m. Sights, elevation, and traverse gears were all mounted to the left of the barrel, which had a removable towing lunette at the muzzle. It was normally towed by an AT-P, AT-L, or AT-S, with the crew of 11 carried on the tow vehicle. Ammunition and other equipment were carried on separate vehicles.

The mortar had to be deployed on firm ground for firing. To prepare for firing, the towing lunette was removed, the baseplate lowered to the ground and packed with earth. The barrel was moved to a horizontal position for loading. Time to prepare for action was at least 25 minutes, and preparing to move took almost as long.

The 240mm F-864 mortar bomb weighed 131kg, with a 32kg warhead. It was transported to the mortar on a two-wheeled trolley, and loaded by a team of five. Two men on each side used large grips to lift the bomb, while the fifth man was at the rear, keeping the bomb steady. Rate of fire was around 1 per minute.

In the 1980s, a laser-guided projectile was developed, which could be fired by both the M-240 and 2S4 mortars. Although it was successfully trialled in Afghanistan, it never entered volume production.

Specifications: M-240

Calibre: 240mm
Barrel length: 5.34m
Weight: 4,150kg
Length: 6.51m
Width: 2.49m
Height: 2.21m
Elevation: 45-65°
Traverse: 18° total
Rate of fire: 1 round/minute
Maximum range: 9,700m
Crew: 11

82MM 2B9 VASILYEK

Introduced in the early 1970s, the Vasilyek was an 82mm automatic mortar capable of both direct and indirect fire. The complete system was known as the 2K21 and included a transport vehicle based on the GAZ-66 4x4 2-tonne lorry. The mortar was carried under a canvas cover on the cargo area. Two ramps were fitted to assist with loading and unloading.

2B9 Vasilyek

A variable-charge system was used in the indirect fire role, with up to three charges used when firing at high angles. A separate, fixed charge was used in the direct fire role. The mortar had a water-cooled barrel for sustained fire, which allowed a sustained rate of fire of 120 rounds per minute.

Although it could be muzzle-loaded like a traditional mortar, it was normally breech-loaded using a clip containing four rounds, which could be fired in two seconds. These rapid bursts of fire meant a greater quantity of explosive landing on the target in a shorter time, increasing the shock effect. When operating in a sustained fire role, the loader could link the first clip with following clips during firing, forming a continuous belt.

HE-FRAG and HEAT rounds were available. The HE-FRAG round weighed 3.1kg, and the HEAT round could penetrate 100mm of standard armour. The weapon was mounted on a wheeled carriage with a split trail. Traverse was 60°, 30° either side, with elevation from -1° to +85°.

In Afghanistan, some Vasilyeks, with their wheels removed, were mounted on the rear deck of MT-LBs. An improved version, the 2B9M, entered service in 1983.

Specifications: 2B9 Vasilyek

Weight: 645kg
Length: 4.12m (travelling)
Width: 1.58m (travelling)
Height: 1.18m
Elevation/depression: +85/-1°
Traverse: 60° total
Rate of fire: 170 rounds/minute
Sustained rate of fire: 120 rounds/minute
Maximum range: 4,270m
Crew: 5-6

120mm 2B16 Nona-K Gun/Mortar

The 120mm 2B16 combined the characteristics of a gun and mortar, in a weapon system that had no Western equivalent. It was listed as a howitzer in the Conventional Armed Forces in Europe Treaty, possibly because of its unique nature. The 2B16 was the towed version, the 2S9 a self-propelled version mounted in a turret on a BTR-D chassis. Developed in the 1970s, the 2B16 entered service in 1986.

2B16 Nona-K

The 2B16 had a split-trail carriage. Each trail had a spade and a castor wheel to facilitate bringing the weapon into action. For transit, the trails were locked together, then the upper assembly was rotated over the trails and locked into place. The usual tow vehicle was a GAZ-66 4x4 2-tonne lorry, which would also carry the crew and some ammunition. It could be towed short distances by a UAZ-469B 4x4 695kg light vehicle.

When deployed for action, the wheels were raised clear of the ground and the weapon rested on a circular baseplate. The weapon itself was the same 2A51 as mounted in the 2S9, firing the same 120mm ammunition. It had a rifled barrel and a large double-baffle muzzle brake to reduce recoil. A shield provided some protection to the crew from small arms and shell splinters.

It could fire HE, HE-RAP, white phosphorous, smoke, and HEAT rounds. Sights were provided for both direct and indirect fire.

Specifications: 2B16 Nona-K

Calibre: 120mm
Weight: 1,200kg
Length: 5.9m
Width: 1.79m
Elevation/depression: +80/-10°
Traverse: 60° total
Rate of fire: 8-10 rounds/minute
Maximum range: 8,700m (12,800m with RAP)
Crew: 5

82mm 2B14 Podnos

Developed in the early 1980s, the 2B14 was a completely new design, rather than an evolutionary development of existing designs. It was used by airborne, special forces, and light infantry units.

The general design was a conventional, bipod-mounted, smoothbore, muzzle-loaded mortar. A device to prevent double loading was available, but not normally used. Modern materials and maufacturing methods led to a reduction in weight compared to the earlier M-37. It could be broken down into loads small enough for it to be carried by the four-man crew.

2B14 Podnos

Specifications: 2B14

Calibre: 82mm
Weight: 41.88kg
Elevation: 45 to 85°
Traverse: 8° total (360° on baseplate)
Rate of fire: 24-30 rounds/minute
Minimum range: 80m
Maximum range: 3,200m
Crew: 4

Czech Mortars

The Skoda works in Czechoslovakia produced a number of mortar designs during and after the Second World War. Some of these were rather unusual, such as the 305mm design, development of which stopped at the end of the war. The B24 was an 120mm design that saw service with at least some Warsaw Pact armies. A short version, for use by airborne and mountain troops, was produced in 1948, and fired the same ammunition as the B24.

The M-48 and M-52 were both 82mm designs, with performance comparable to the Soviet M-37, and firing the same ammunition. They could be broken down into three loads for transportation.

Recoilless Guns

After the Second World War, recoilless guns had a brief period of prominence. They offered the possibility of firing a large calibre projectile to a good distance. The low muzzle velocity meant that kinetic-energy AP rounds were of no use, but chemical-energy warheads such as HEAT were effective at any speed. The combination of a large calibre recoilless gun firing HEAT warheads resulted in a potent and relatively light anti-tank weapon. They became largely obsolete with the introduction of anti-tank guided missiles, which offered greater accuracy at longer range.

82mm SPG-82

The SPG-82 entered service at the end of the Second World War. It had a long barrel with a flared muzzle and a small two-wheeled carriage. A sizeable shield protected the crew from the back-blast of the rocket-propelled rounds, but did not provide protection from enemy fire. Normally fired from the carriage, it could be dismounted and fired from the shoulder, if a second man helped to support the weight.

The SPG-82 could fire HE and HEAT ammunition, both of which weighed 5kg. Two sets of iron sights were fitted, one for each type of ammunition.

Specifications: SPG-82

Calibre: 82mm
Weight: 38kg
Length: 2.15m
Maximum range: 200m (anti-tank)
700m (HE)
Armour penetration: 230mm
Crew: 2

82mm B-10

This was a smoothbore recoilless gun that fired a fin-stabilised projectile resembling a mortar bomb. For transit, it was carried on a two-wheeled carriage. A bar was fitted to the muzzle to allow it to be dragged into position. For firing, the carriage was removed and the tripod was lowered from beneath the barrel, although it could be fired from the wheeled carriage if necessary.

It was fitted with an optical sight, but the sight had no range-finding capability. It was gradually phased out of use by most Soviet units from the early 1960s, but remained in use with the parachute battalions of the airborne divisions for some years after. HEAT and HE ammunition were available, weighing 3.6kg and 4.5kg respectively.

B-10

Specifications: B-10

Calibre: 82mm
Weight: 87.6kg (travelling)
Length: 1.68m (travelling)
Rate of fire: 6-7 rounds/minute
Maximum range: 400m (anti-tank)
4,500m (HE)
Armour penetration: 240mm

107mm B-11

Introduced alongside the B-10, which was supplied to battalion anti-tank platoons, the B-11 was issued to regimental anti-tank companies. Like the B-10, it was a smoothbore weapon, fitted with a two-wheeled carriage for transit. Normally fired from a tripod, it could be fired from the wheeled carriage in emergency, at the cost of reduced accuracy.

B-11

Primarily intended for anti-tank use with a HEAT round, it also had sights for indirect fire with an HE round. Like the B-10, it was gradually phased out of use by most Soviet units from the early 1960s, replaced with 57mm anti-tank guns as an interim measure until SPG-9s were available. The HEAT and HE rounds weighed 9kg and 13.6kg respectively.

Specifications: B-11

Calibre: 107mm
Weight: 305kg (travelling)
Length: 3.31m
  3.56m (travelling)
Rate of fire: 6 rounds/minute

Maximum range: 450m (anti-tank)
6,650m (HE)
Armour penetration: 380mm

73MM SPG-9 KOPYE

Introduced in the late 1960s, the SPG-9 was a light anti-tank gun mounted on a tripod, with a four-man crew. Light enough to be carried by two soldiers, it could also be towed on a small two-wheeled carriage or mounted on a vehicle. A lighter version, the SPG-9D, could be carried by one man, and was used by air assault and airborne units. The PGO-9M optical sight was provided for direct fire, but PGO-K9 optical sights and PGN-9 night sights were also available. A device sometimes seen above the barrel was initially thought by NATO to be a spotting rifle, but was later confirmed to be a sub-calibre training device.

Afghan soldiers loading an SPG-9

The SPG-9 fired fin-stabilised HEAT and HE-FRAG ammunition. The propellant charge was contained in an extension behind the folded fins, and fell away from the rest of the projectile after leaving the muzzle. A rocket motor inside the projectile ignited twenty metres from the muzzle, accelerating the projectile to full velocity. This combination produced a high muzzle velocity of 435m/s and a final velocity of 700m/s. The HEAT round could penetrate 400mm of armour, at a maximum range of 1,300m. The HE-FRAG round had an explosive charge of 753g of TNT, with a range of 4,500m.

Specifications: SPG-9 Kopye

Calibre: 73mm
Weight of launcher: 47.5kg
Weight of tripod: 12kg
Length of launcher: 2.11m
Height of launcher: 399-900mm
Elevation: 25°
Maximum range: 1,300m (direct fire)
4,500m (indirect fire)
Armour penetration: 400mm
Crew: 4

82mm T-21 Tarasnice (Czechoslovakia)

The T-21 was a smoothbore gun firing fin-stabilised ammunition. It was mounted on a pair of small-diameter steel wheels. It could be fired while mounted on the wheels, or while held on a shoulder. It was also seen mounted on OT-62 armoured personnel carriers. Only used in the direct fire role, it fired a 2.13kg HEAT warhead.

T-21

Specifications: T-21 Tarasnice

Calibre: 82mm
Weight: 17.3kg
20kg (travelling)
Length: 1.47m (travelling)
Maximum range: 457m
Armour penetration: 228mm

82mm M-59 & M-59A (Czechoslovakia)

The M-59 and M-59A were virtually identical, being differentiated only by the M-59A's radially finned section over the chamber, which helped to dissipate heat. They had a carriage with two rubber-tyred wheels, and could be towed behind an APC (commonly the OT-810). They were also observed mounted on or carried inside OT-62 APCs. A bar across the muzzle allowed two men to tow the weapon using a harness. HEAT and HE warheads were provided, and they were used in both direct and indirect fire roles. A ranging rifle could be utilised when they were used for direct fire.

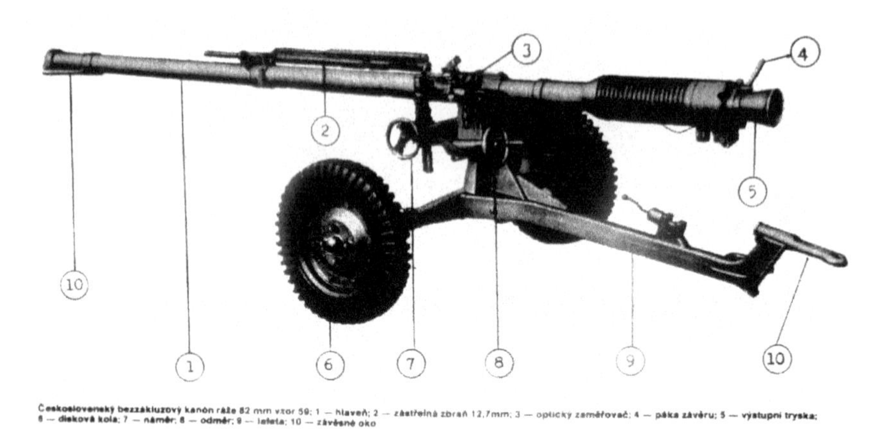

M-59A

Specifications: M-59 and M-59A

Calibre: 82mm
Weight: 385kg
Length: 4.6m (travelling)
Maximum range: 1,200m (direct fire)
    6,657m (indirect fire)
Armour penetration: 250mm

Multiple Rocket Launchers

The Soviet Union pioneered the use of self-propelled multiple rocket launchers (MRL) during the Second World War, when they were officially known as Guards Mortars, but commonly known by the nickname Katyusha. The ease of construction compared to tube artillery (which requires complex tools for rifling barrels) meant that mass production was possible even after the Germans overran many of the armaments factories. The ability to deliver a large quantity of explosive in a short time made them ideal for laying down suppressive fire to minimise the effectiveness of enemy anti-tank systems and artillery.

Most multiple rocket launcher systems were mounted on lorries or other vehicles. This allowed them to move immediately after firing to avoid counter-battery fire, a significant problem given the large launch signature and long time to reload. The few towed systems sacrificed this advantage in order to save weight, facilitating their use in airborne units.

BM-24

The BM-24 entered service in 1951. It had a crew of six and mounted twelve 240mm rockets on an elevating launcher with limited traverse. Elevation and traverse was manual, and two stabilising jacks had to be lowered before launch. The launch frames were arranged in two rows of six, mounted on the rear of a ZIL-151 6x6 chassis. Steel plates were fitted above the cab and fuel tanks to protect them from the blast when the rockets were fired. The system could fire two types of HE rocket: the M-24F with 27.4kg of explosive, and the M-24FUD, which had a lighter payload of 18.4kg but extended the range from 6km to 10.6km. It could also fire MS-24 and MS-24D rockets, fitted with chemical warheads.

BM-24

In 1956, a new rocket, the MD-24F, was introduced. This had a maximum range of 17.5km.

The BM-24T variant entered service in 1956. It used the AT-S artillery tractor as the base for the launch vehicle, and was issued to tank divisions, with the wheeled BM-24 going to motor rifle divisions. The BM-24 had open frame launchers, the BM-24T enclosed tubes.

Specifications: BM-24 Vehicle

Weight: 9.2 tonnes
Length: 6.71m
Width: 2.32m
Height: 2.91m
Maximum road speed: 65km/hour
Range: 430km
Number of launchers: 12
Reload time: 3-4 minutes
Traverse: 140°
Elevation: 0 to +65°

Specifications: BM-24T Vehicle

Weight: 15.24 tonnes
Length: 5.87m
Width: 2.57m
Height: 3.1m
Maximum road speed: 35km/hour
Range: 380km
Number of launchers: 12
Reload time: 3-4 minutes
Traverse: 210°
Elevation: 0 to +45°

Specifications: BM-24 Rocket

Rocket calibre: 240mm
Warhead weight: 46.9kg
Rocket length: 1.18m
Rocket weight: 112.5kg
Rocket range: up to 17.5km, depending on rocket type

BMD-20

Development of a 200mm rocket for what was to become the BMD-20 started in 1945. Several changes to the requirements led to delays. Trials were carried out in 1951, and the BMD-20 entered service in 1952, mounting four 200mm rockets in a single row on the back of a ZIL-151 6x6 chassis. Two jacks were lowered before firing to improve stability of the launch platform. The rockets were housed in open framework tubes on a manually operated mounting with limited traverse. The rockets had 30kg HE-FRAG warheads and a maximum range of 19km.

Specifications: BMD-20

Weight: 8.7 tonnes
Length: 7.2m
Width: 2.3m
Height: 2.85m
Maximum road speed: 60km/hour
Range: 600km
Rocket calibre: 200mm
Number of launchers: 4
Warhead weight: 30kg

Rocket length: 3.11m
Rocket weight: 91.4kg
Rocket range: 19km
Reload time: 10 minutes
Traverse: 200°
Elevation: 0 to +50°

BM-14

The BM-14 (also known as BM-14-16) entered service in 1952 as a replacement for the wartime BM-13. It had sixteen 140mm rockets, in two rows of eight, on a mounting with limited traverse. Elevation and traverse was manual, and the mounting was fitted on a ZIS-151 6x6 chassis. A remote firing mechanism was provided, allowing the operator to fire the rockets from up to 60m away from the vehicle. Initially only HE-FRAG warheads were available, but smoke (WP) and chemical warheads were introduced in 1955. Later models used ZIL-157 (BM-14M) and ZIL-131 (BM-14MM) chassis in place of the original ZIS-151.

BM-14

In 1959, the BM-14-17 was introduced, which had 17 launch tubes on a GAZ-63A 4x4 chassis. A towed variant, the RPU-14, was produced for use with the airborne forces. This had 16 tubes in four rows of four, mounted on a carriage similar to that used by the D-44 85mm gun. It was replaced by the BM-21V.

Specifications: BM-14-16 Vehicle

Weight: 8.2 tonnes
Length: 9.92m
Width: 2.3m
Height: 2.65m
Maximum road speed: 60km/hour
Range: 600km
Number of launchers: 16
Traverse: 200°
Elevation: 0 to +52°

Specifications: BM-14-17 Vehicle

Weight: 5.3 tonnes
Length: 5.41m
Width: 1.93m
Height: 2.24m
Maximum road speed: 65km/hour
Range: 650km
Number of launchers: 17
Traverse: 210°
Elevation: 0 to +47°

Specifications: BM-14 Rocket

Rocket calibre: 140mm
Warhead weight: 18.8kg

Rocket length: 1.08m
Rocket weight: 39.6kg
Rocket range: 9.8km
Reload time: 4 minutes

BM-25

The BM-25 entered service in 1957, and had six liquid-fuelled 255mm rockets in open-frame launchers. The launchers were mounted in two rows of three on a KrAZ-214 6x6 chassis. Before firing, two stabilisers were lowered and armoured shutters were fitted over the windscreens. A tarpaulin normally covered the launch assembly while in transit.

Specifications: BM-25

Weight: 18.15 tonnes
Length: 9.82m
Width: 2.7m
Height: 3.5m
Maximum road speed: 55km/hour
Range: 530km
Rocket calibre: 250mm
Number of launchers: 6
Rocket length: 5.82m
Rocket weight: 455kg
Rocket range: 30km
Reload time: 10-20 minutes
Traverse: 6°
Elevation: 0 to +55°

BM-21 Grad

Developed during the mid-to-late 1950s, the BM-21 entered service in 1963, with the designation BM-21 (known in the West as BM-21a). Each division was equipped with a battalion of 12 launchers, and each army or front had three battalions. In wartime, all battalions were to be increased in size to 18 launchers.

BM-21 Grad

The launch vehicle was based on a Ural-375D 6x6 chassis, fitted with an elevating, rotating assembly on the rear bed, carrying 40 launch tubes in four rows of ten. The launch assembly was rotated forward for travelling. Stabilisers were fitted to each side of the vehicle at the rear and were lowered to the ground before firing. The cabin contained all the equipment needed to prepare and fire the rockets, which could be fired individually, in a salvo, or by selective ripple. A remote-control unit was provided, allowing the crew to fire the rockets from a distance of up to 60m from the vehicle. Initially only HE-FRAG warheads were available, but incendiary and chemical warheads were subsequently developed.

Later, the Ural-4320 6x6 chassis was used as the base vehicle, and this variant was given the designation BM-21-1. This version also had an automated fire control system and a satellite navigation system.

In 1969, the BM-21V was developed for use by airborne forces. This was much lighter, mounting a 12-tube launcher on a GAZ-66B 4x4 chassis. Like the BM-21, two stabilisers had to be lowered before firing, and rockets could be fired individually or in a salvo. In order to facilitate air transport and dropping by parachute, the cab was collapsible, the steering wheel was telescopic, and the doors and windscreen could be removed. There were tie-down points for attaching the vehicle to a pallet for dropping by parachute.

The BM-21b Grad-1 entered service in 1976 as a lightweight, regimental-level system for use in independent MRL batteries. The basic arrangement was the same as the original BM-21, but with 36 launch tubes (the lower two rows had eight tubes each instead of 10) mounted on the rear of a ZIL-131 chassis. This variant fired a different rocket with shorter range but more effective warhead (the HE-FRAG warhead was preformed, and the incendiary warhead carried more incendiary elements).

Specifications: BM-21 Grad

Weight: 13.7 tonnes
Length: 7.35m

Width: 2.69m
Height: 2.85m
Maximum road speed: 75km/hour
Range: 480km
Rocket calibre: 122mm
Number of launchers: 40
Warhead weight: 19.4kg
Rocket length: 3.22m
Rocket weight: 77.5kg
Rocket range: 20.5km
Reload time: 10 minutes
Traverse: 180°
Elevation: 0 to +55°

Specifications: BM-21b Grad-1

Weight: 10.5 tonnes
Length: 6.9m
Width: 2.5m
Height: 2.48m
Maximum road speed: 80km/hour
Range: 525km
Rocket calibre: 122mm
Number of launchers: 36
Warhead weight: 18.4kg
Rocket length: 2.87m
Rocket weight: 66kg
Rocket range: 20km
Reload time: 10 minutes
Traverse: 180°
Elevation: 0 to +55°

BM-27 Uragan

Development of the BM-27 was completed in 1975, and it was accepted for service in the same year. It was sometimes mistakenly referred to as the BM-22 in the West. It was deployed in regiments (three battalions) or brigades (four battalions) at army or front level. Each battalion had 12 launch vehicles, but in wartime would receive an extra six. Each battalion had a Kapustnik-B automated fire control system, comprising a commander's vehicle based on the BTR-80 chassis, a chief of staff vehicle based on a Ural-4320 chassis, three battery command vehicles based on BTR-80 chassis, and three battery senior officer vehicles based on the Ural-4320 chassis. The Kapustnik-B included systems for reconnaissance, initial battalion orientation, location fixing, weather reconnaissance, ballistic tracking, communications, and data transfer.

The BM-27 launch vehicle was based on the same ZIL-135LM 8x8 chassis as the FROG-7 tactical ballistic missile. The crew compartment was not armoured, but did provide NBC protection. 16 tubes were arranged in three rows on an elevating mount at the rear with limited traverse. The top row had four tubes, while the lower two rows had six tubes each. Launch preparation and firing equipment were in the cab, where the operator could choose between firing a full salvo or individual rockets. Before firing, two stabilisers were lowered and a steel shutter was fitted over the windscreen.

The 9T452 transloader vehicle was based on the same chassis as the launch vehicle. Each one carried 16 rockets in two stacks, either side of a hydraulic crane fitted in the centre of the rear

BM-27 Uragan

deck. For loading, the launcher was traversed to one side and put into the horizontal position.

SPECIFICATIONS: BM-27 URAGAN

Weight: 20 tonnes
Length: 9.63m
Width: 2.8m
Height: 3.23m
Maximum road speed: 65km/hour
Range: 570km
Rocket calibre: 220mm
Number of launchers: 16
Warhead weight: 51.7kg
Rocket length: 4.83m
Rocket weight: 280kg
Rocket range: 35km

Reload time: 20-30 minutes
Traverse: 60°
Elevation: 0 to +55°

BM-30 Smerch

Development of the BM-30 started during the late 1970s, and the system entered service in 1987. The launch vehicle was based on the MAZ-543A 8x8 chassis, with a 12-round elevating, rotating launcher. The launch tubes were arranged as a row of four on top, with a pair of 2x2 blocks underneath, one on each side of the elevating assembly. Two stabilisers were fitted, which had to be lowered before firing. The cabin contained the launch preparation and firing equipment. The rockets could be fired individually or as a salvo. Each launch vehicle had an associated 9T234-2 transloader vehicle, based on the same MAZ-543A chassis, with 12 reload rockets and a hydraulic crane to facilitate loading.

BM-30s were organised into batteries of four launchers, with three batteries to a battalion. Each battery had a command vehicle and a staff vehicle, both based on the KamAZ-4310 6x6 chassis. These vehicles contained communications equipment, digital computers, and the Vivariy automated fire control system.

The rockets had a flight-control system to allow them to correct their trajectory in flight, leading to greatly improved accuracy, claimed to be 0.21% of range. High explosive and cluster munition warheads were available.

BM-30 Smerch

Specifications: BM-30 Smerch

Weight: 43.7 tonnes
Length: 12.1m
Width: 3.05m
Height: 3.05m
Maximum road speed: 60km/hour
Range: 850km
Rocket calibre: 300mm
Number of launchers: 12
Warhead weight: 92.5kg
Rocket length: 7.6m
Rocket weight: 800kg
Rocket range: 70km
Reload time: 36 minutes
Traverse: 60°
Elevation: 0 to +55°

BM 9A51 Prima

The BM 9A51 was developed in the early to mid-1980s, and entered service in 1987. It was primarily assigned to divisions, in battalions of 12 vehicles, which would be expanded to 18 vehicles in wartime, but was sometimes found at army or front level in place of the BM-21.

The BM 9A51 used the same Ural-4320 6x6 chassis as the BM-21-1, but mounted 50 launch tubes in a rotating, elevating mount on the rear. The tubes were arranged in five rows of 10, within a box structure. Two stabilisers were fitted on the sides, toward the rear, which had to be lowered before firing. Aiming and launching could be controlled from within the cab, or from outside the vehicle, using a remote-control unit. 72 reloads were carried on a 9T232M transloader vehicle, also based on the Ural-4320 chassis. Reloading took around 10 minutes.

The BM 9A51 could fire the same 122mm rockets as the BM-21, but a new rocket, the 9M53F, was developed specifically for it. This rocket had a HE-FRAG warhead that separated and descended below a small parachute, then detonated several yards above the ground. The combination of air burst and near-vertical descent due to the use of a parachute resulted in a wider blast radius than the more usual ground burst. If required, the fuse could be set to enable conventional operation, with the warhead remaining with the rocket and detonating on contact with the ground.

Specifications: BM 9A51 Prima

Weight: 13.9 tonnes
Length: 7.35m
Width: 2.43m
Height: 2.68m
Maximum road speed: 85km/hour
Range: 990km
Rocket calibre: 122mm
Number of launchers: 50
Warhead weight: 26kg
Rocket length: 3.04m
Rocket weight: 70kg
Rocket range: 20.5km
Reload time: 10 minutes
Traverse: 58°
Elevation: 0 to +55°

RM-51 (Czechoslovakia)

The RM-51, sometimes referred to as the RM-130, entered service with the Czech army in 1956. It mounted 32 rockets on the back of a Praga V3S 6x6 lorry in four rows of eight. The 130mm rockets were spin stabilised, and the launcher had to be traversed to one side before firing, since the unarmoured cab had no protection from back blast. Stowage boxes for spare rockets were fitted on either side of the hull, under the launcher.

The standard version was used by Czechoslovakia and exported to Bulgaria, Cuba, and Egypt. The Austrian army used the RM-51 launcher mounted on Steyr 680 M3 6x6 lorries, and

RM-51

the Romanian army used it mounted on Soviet ZIL-151 or ZIL-157 lorries.

Specifications: RM-51

Weight: 8.9 tonnes
Length: 6.91m
Width: 2.31m
Height: 2.92m
Maximum road speed: 62km/hour
Range: 440km
Rocket calibre: 130mm
Number of launchers: 32
Warhead weight: 2.3kg

Rocket length: 0.8m
Rocket weight: 24.2kg
Rocket range: 8.2km
Reload time: 2 minutes
Traverse: 240°
Elevation: 0 to +50°

RM-70 (Czechoslovakia)

First observed by the West at a 1972 parade, the RM-70 was based on a Czech Tatra 813 8x8 lorry. It had the same launcher as the Soviet BM-21 at the rear of the vehicle, but unlike the Soviet vehicle, an extra set of 40 rockets was carried between the launcher and the cab, to allow for rapid reloading. The cab was fully armoured, providing the crew with protection from small arms fire and shell splinters, and the Tatra chassis provided much better cross-country capability than the Ural-375D 6x6 chassis used by the BM-21. A central tyre pressure regulation system was fitted, allowing the driver to adjust the tyre pressure according to the ground being crossed.

An improved version, the Mod 70/85, was introduced in the mid-1980s. This used the more modern Tatra T815 VNN 8x8 chassis, with the same launcher and reloads. The cab was not armoured, but it did have a central tyre pressure regulation system and NBC protection for the crew of four.

Specifications: RM-70 (RM-70/85 in brackets)

Weight: 25.3 tonnes (25 tonnes)
Length: 8.8m (9.6m)
Width: 2.55m (2.53m)
Height: 2.96m (3.03m)
Maximum road speed: 75km/hour (60km/hour)
Range: 1,100km (1,000km)
Rocket calibre: 122mm
Number of launchers: 40
Warhead weight: 19.4kg
Rocket length: 3.22m
Rocket weight: 77.5kg
Rocket range: 20.5km
Reload time: 35 seconds
Traverse: 125° left, 70° right
Elevation: 0 to +55°

140mm RPU-14

Designed for use by airborne troops, the RPU-14 mounted sixteen 140mm rocket tubes, in four rows of four, on a simple two-wheeled, split-trail carriage. Normally towed by a GAZ-66 4x4 lorry, eighteen were issued to each Soviet airborne assault division, organised into a battalion of three batteries. It was later replaced by the BM-21V, which was based on a GAZ-66B chassis.

The RPU-14 fired the same spin-stabilised rocket as the Polish WP-8 and the widely deployed BM-14-16 and BM-14-17 lorry-mounted MRLs. The same rocket, mounted on a single-round tripod launcher, was supplied to some guerrilla forces. High explosive and smoke warheads were used.

RPU-14

Specifications: RPU-14

Calibre: 140mm
Barrels: 16
Weight: 1,835kg (loaded)
Length: 4.04m (travelling)
Width: 1.8m (travelling)
Height: 1.6m (travelling)
Elevation/depression: +48/0°
Traverse: 30° total
Crew: 5
Rocket calibre: 140mm
Warhead weight: 18.8kg
Rocket length: 1.08m
Rocket weight: 39.6kg
Rocket range: 9.8km
Reload time: 4 minutes

140mm WP-8 (Poland)

The WP-8 mounted eight 140mm rocket tubes in two rows of four on a simple two-wheeled, split-trail carriage. Like the Soviet RPU-14, it was designed for use with airborne troops, specifically the Polish 6th Pomeranian Air Assault Brigade. The brigade had a battery of six WP-8 launchers and two batteries of D-30 howitzers (twelve in total) in its composite artillery battalion.

WP-8

The WP-8 fired the same spin-stabilised rocket as the Soviet RPU-14 and the widely deployed BM-14-16 and BM-14-17 lorry-mounted MRLs. High explosive and smoke warheads were used. It could be towed by a light vehicle, the UAZ-469 being commonly used.

Specifications: WP-8

Calibre: 140mm
Barrels: 8
Weight: 687.6kg (loaded)
Length: 3.29m (travelling)
Width: 1.63m (travelling)
Height: 1.2m (travelling)
Elevation/depression: +47/-12°
Traverse: 28° total
Crew: 5
Rocket calibre: 140mm
Warhead weight: 18.8kg
Rocket length: 1.08m
Rocket weight: 39.6kg
Rocket range: 9.8km
Reload time: 2 minutes

Tactical Ballistic Missiles

When Khrushchev came to power following Stalin's death, he ordered major cuts in conventional forces, as he intended to rely on nuclear missiles for defence. The new leader was a great believer in the relatively new technology of missiles, and this led to greater use of missiles throughout the Soviet military, as it was easier to secure funding for missile systems than for gun systems. Under Khrushchev, the Soviet Union sought to build up its nuclear missile forces at all levels, from tactical systems to intercontinental ballistic missiles.

FROG-1

The first two vehicles of the FROG (Free Rocket Over Ground) series, the FROG-1 and FROG-2, entered service in 1955. The FROG-1 carried a rocket with a solid fuel engine and a maximum range of 25.7km. It could be fitted with a tactical nuclear warhead or a 1,200kg HE-FRAG warhead. The launch vehicle was based on a modified IS-2 tank chassis.

Specifications: FROG-1

Vehicle weight: 36 tonnes
Vehicle length: 9.33m

Vehicle width: 3.07m
Vehicle height: 3m
Vehicle road speed: 30km/hour (41km/hour without a rocket)
Vehicle road range: 150km
Missile length: 10.2m
Missile diameter: 612mm
Missile weight: 3,200kg
Missile range: 25.7km
Missile CEP: 700m

FROG-2

The FROG-2 had a non-amphibious chassis based on that of the PT-76 light tank. It carried a solid fuel powered rocket with a maximum range of 17.5km. The rocket was fitted with a conventional high explosive warhead.

FROG-2

Specifications: FROG-2

Vehicle weight: 16.4 tonnes
Vehicle length: 9.4m
Vehicle width: 3.18m
Vehicle height: 3.05m
Vehicle road speed: 20km/hour (40km/hour without a rocket)
Vehicle road range: 250km
Missile length: 9.01m
Missile diameter: 324mm
Missile weight: 1,760kg
Missile range: 17.5km
Missile CEP: 770m

FROG-3/4/5

The FROG-3, FROG-4 and FROG-5 were given different designations by NATO, but were in fact the same system, with different warheads on the rockets. They entered service with the Soviet army in 1960, under the designation 2K6 Luna. The chassis was based on that of the FROG-2. The vehicles weighed 18.8 tonnes and had a maximum speed of 40km/hour. The rockets could be fitted with HE-FRAG (FROG-3), chemical (FROG-4), or tactical nuclear (FROG-5) warheads.

The launch vehicles were reloaded from ZIL-157 6x6 lorries, each towing a trailer with two reload rockets, and a separate crane lorry to lift the rockets onto the launch vehicles. Each launch vehicle had a crew of 11.

FROG-3

SPECIFICATIONS: FROG-3/4/5

Vehicle weight: 18.8 tonnes
Vehicle length: 10.5m
Vehicle width: 3.1m
Vehicle height: 3.05m
Vehicle road speed: 40 km/hour
Missile length: 10.6m
Missile diameter: 540mm
Missile weight: 2,280kg
Missile range: 45km-61km depending on warhead
Missile CEP: 800m

FROG-7

In 1964, a new missile system was accepted for service, designated FROG-7a by NATO. This was a solid fuel powered rocket mounted on a wheeled TEL vehicle based on the ZIL-135LM 8x8 chassis. A range of different warheads were available. As well as high explosive, chemical, and nuclear warheads, a leaflet-dispensing warhead was produced. An air-mobile version, with the rocket mounted on a self-propelled trailer, did not got past the prototype stage. The FROG-7b entered service in 1968, with improvements to the rocket and a longer warhead, increasing rocket length from 8.95m to 9.4m. Cluster munition warheads, with 42 HE bomblets, were available for the FROG-7b. There were three types of nuclear warhead for the FROG-7: the AA-22 and AA-38 had selectable yields of 3, 10 or 22kT; and the AA-52 had a selectable yield of 5, 10, 20 or 200kT. The HE warhead carried 450kg of explosive.

FROG-7

Unlike previous vehicles, the FROG-7 TEL had an on-board hydraulic crane for loading rockets. Reloads were carried on a similar vehicle, with three rockets on each. It took around 15-30 minutes to prepare to fire, and around 20 minutes to reload.

Maximum flight time was around 160 seconds, with the engine burning for 7-11 seconds.

Specifications: FROG-7 (FROG-7B in brackets)

Vehicle weight: 19 tonnes
Vehicle length: 10.69m
Vehicle width: 2.8m
Vehicle height: 3.35m
Vehicle road speed: 65 km/hour
Vehicle road range: 650 km
Missile length: 8.95m (9.4m)
Missile diameter: 0.5m
Missile weight: 2,432 - 2,450kg
Missile range: 70km
Missile CEP: 400m

SS-1 Scud

The SS-1b Scud A entered service in 1957. Unlike the FROG series, it employed gyroscopes to provide a rudimentary guidance system. Guidance commands were only issued during powered flight and the missiles were unguided once the rocket ran out of fuel, after around 80 seconds. This resulted in poor accuracy, especially at longer ranges. The SS-1b was carried on a TEL vehicle with a tracked chassis derived from the IS-3 tank. Maximum range was 150km.

The SS-1c Scud B entered service in 1961, initially mounted on the same TEL vehicle as the SS-1b, though in 1965, a new wheeled TEL based on the MAZ-543 was introduced. This model had an improved rocket with a new engine. Maximum range was

SS-1c Scud B

increased to 300km, and accuracy was improved. Nuclear, chemical, and HE warheads were available. The launch sequence could be controlled from the TEL, but was normally done from a command vehicle. Time to prepare and launch was around one hour.

Specifications: SS-1b Scud A

Vehicle weight: 38 tonnes
Vehicle length: 12.5m
Vehicle width: 3.2m
Vehicle height: 3.32m
Vehicle road speed: 37km/hour
Missile length: 10.7m
Missile diameter: 0.88m
Missile weight: 4,400kg
Missile range: 180km
Missile CEP: 3km

Specifications: SS-1c Scud B

Vehicle weight: 29 tonnes
Vehicle length: 13.58m
Vehicle width: 3.02m
Vehicle height: 3.7m
Vehicle road speed: 70km/hour
Missile length: 11.25m
Missile diameter: 0.88m
Missile weight: 5,900kg
Missile range: 300km
Missile CEP: 450m

SS-12 Scaleboard

The SS-12 Scaleboard was the longest-ranged ballistic missile to serve with the Soviet ground forces. It entered service in 1969, mounting a single missile inside a container on the same MAZ-543 chassis as the SS-1c Scud B. In 1979, a new missile, the SS-12M Scaleboard B (initially known in the West as the SS-22) began to replace the original missiles. The TEL was the same, but accuracy was improved. Under the terms of the 1987 INF Treaty, these missiles were destroyed between August 1988 and July 1989.

Specifications: SS-12 Scaleboard (SS-12M in brackets)

Vehicle weight: 30.8 tonnes
Vehicle length: 13.15m
Vehicle width: 3.02m

SS-12 Scaleboard

Vehicle height: 3.5m
Vehicle road speed: 70km/hour
Missile length: 12.78m
Missile diameter: 1.01m
Missile weight: 9,800kg
Missile range: 800km (900km)
Missile CEP: 750m (370m)

SS-21 Scarab

The SS-21 Scarab entered service in 1976, as a replacement for the FROG-7. The TEL was a six-wheeled vehicle with amphibious capability and NBC protection for the crew, with the missile contained in a temperature-controlled unit until launch. The missile was powered by a solid fuel rocket motor, and was guided throughout the entire flight. The crew could perform all tasks related to targeting and launching the missile from within the cab. High explosive, chemical, and nuclear warheads were available, with the AA-60 nuclear warhead having a selectable yield of 5, 10, 20 or 200kT. In 1989, the Scarab B was introduced, with a longer range and better accuracy. A separate transloader vehicle carried two additional missiles, and had a crane for loading missiles onto the launch vehicle.

SS-21 Scarab

Specifications: SS-21 Scarab (Scarab B in brackets)

Vehicle weight: 18.15 tonnes
Vehicle length: 9.48m
Vehicle width: 2.78m
Vehicle height: 2.35m
Vehicle road speed: 60 km/hour
Vehicle road range: 650km
Missile length: 6.4m
Missile diameter: 0.65m
Missile weight: 2,000kg (2,010kg)

Missile range: 70km (120km)
Missile CEP: 160m (95m)

SS-23 SPIDER

The SS-23 Spider entered service in 1980, replacing the SS-1c Scud B. The TEL vehicle was based on the 8x8 BAZ-6944 chassis. It had NBC protection for the crew and was fully amphibious, propelled in the water by a pair of water jets. When in transit, the missile was contained within the vehicle. The crew did not need to leave the cab to prepare and launch the missile, which took around 5-10 minutes.

The missile had a single solid fuel rocket motor, with inertial and active radar terminal guidance, providing a high level of accuracy. It missile was difficult to intercept, and the high level of accuracy meant that use against moving or hardened targets was feasible. A transporter-loader was based on the same chassis, and carried a single reload missile with a loading crane. High explosive (450kg), chemical, submunition, and nuclear (AA-60, as used on SS-21) warheads were available.

When the INF Treaty was signed in 1987, the United States claimed that the SS-23 was covered by the treaty, since they had estimated the range to be at least 500km. The Soviet Union maintained that maximum range was less than 500km and that the system was therefore not covered. None the less, as a gesture of goodwill, all existing systems were destroyed and work on an improved version was cancelled.

SS-23 Spider

Specifications: SS-23 Spider

Vehicle weight: 24.7 tonnes
Vehicle length: 11.76m
Vehicle width: 3.13m
Vehicle height: 3m
Vehicle road speed: 70 km/hour
Vehicle road range: 700km
Missile length: 7.5m
Missile diameter: 0.9m
Missile weight: 4,500 - 5,000kg
Missile range: 50-480km
Missile CEP: 30-150m

Glossary

AA: Anti-Aircraft
AP: Armour-Piercing
AP-T: Armour-Piercing Tracer
APC: Armoured Personnel Carrier. An armoured vehicle used to transport infantry, usually lightly armed and armoured
APC-T: Armour-Piercing Capped Tracer
APFSDS: Armour-Piercing Fin Stabilised Discarding Sabot. A type of kinetic energy anti-tank round, usually fired from smoothbore guns
APHE: Armour-Piercing High Explosive. Known in the West as HESH (High Explosive Squash Head) or HEP (High Explosive, Plastic), it had a thin metal outer shell containing plastic explosive. On impact, the plastic explosive squashed against the target before exploding.
ATGM: Anti-Tank Guided Missile
CEP: Circular Error of Probability. A measure of accuracy, the CEP was the radius of a circle within which 50% of projectiles would fall
CP: Concrete-Piercing
HE: High Explosive

HEAT: High Explosive Anti-Tank. A form of chemical energy anti-tank warhead, it fired a jet of super-heated molten metal into the target.
HEAT-FS: High Explosive Anti-Tank, Fin-Stabilised. A HEAT round stabilised by fins rather than by spin imparted from a rifled barrel. Usually fired from smoothbore guns.
HE-FRAG: High Explosive Fragmentation
HE-RAP: High Explosive — Rocket Assisted Projectile. A HE projectile with a small rocket motor to boost range
HESH: High Explosive Squash Head. A form of chemical energy anti-tank warhead, particularly favoured by the British army
HVAP: High Velocity Armour-Piercing
HVAP-T: High Velocity Armour-Piercing Tracer
Lunette: A ring used to attach a weapon to a vehicle for towing
MBT: Main Battle Tank
MRL: Multiple Rocket Launcher
Muzzle brake: A device fitted to the muzzle of a gun to redirect propellant gasses, reducing recoil
NBC: Nuclear, Biological, and Chemical
RAP: Rocket Assisted Projectile. A projectile with a small rocket motor to boost range
TEL: Transporter, Erector, Launcher. A vehicle on which one or more missiles were transported, and from which the missiles were launched
WP: White Phosphorous

Image Credits

GAZ-63: Vitaly V. Kuzmin (CC-BY-SA 4.0)
GAZ-66: High Contrast (CC-BY)
KrAZ-255B: LutzBruno (CC-BY-SA 3.0)
KrAZ-260: Vitaly V. Kuzmin (CC-BY-SA 4.0)
ZIL-157: ShinePhantom (CC-BY-SA 3.0)

ML-20: Vitaly V. Kuzmin (CC-BY-SA 3.0)
M1938: Сайга20К (CC-BY-SA 3.0)
A-19: Balcer~commonswiki (CC-BY-SA 3.0)
M-10: Kovako-1 (CC-BY-SA 3.0)
D-1: Alex Zelenko (CC-BY-SA 4.0)
D-44: Michael Rivera (CC-BY-SA 4.0)
D-20: ShinePhantom (CC-BY-SA 3.0)
SM-4-1: ShinePhantom (CC-BY-SA 3.0)

ISU-122: Taw (CC-BY-SA 3.0)
ISU-152: Vitaly V. Kuzmin (CC-BY-SA 4.0)
2S1 Gvozdika: Vitaly V. Kuzmin (CC-BY-SA 4.0)
2S3 Akatsiya: Vitaly V. Kuzmin (CC-BY-SA 4.0)
2S4 Tyulpan: Vitaly V. Kuzmin (CC-BY-SA 4.0)
2S5 Giatsint-S in firing position: Parutip (CC-BY-SA 3.0)
2S7 Pion: Vitaly V. Kuzmin (CC-BY-SA 4.0)

120mm 2B16 Nona-K Gun/Mortar: Smell U Later (CC-BY-SA 3.0)
120mm 2B11 Sani/2S12: Vitaly V. Kuzmin (CC-BY-SA 4.0)

82mm 2B14 Podnos: Vitaly V. Kuzmin (CC-BY-SA 4.0)
82mm B-10: Pibwl (CC-BY-SA 3.0)
107mm B-11: Zala (CC-BY-SA 4.0)
82mm T-21 Tarasnice (Czechoslovakia): Bukvoed (CC-BY-SA 3.0)
82mm M-59 & M-59A (Czechoslovakia): Jozef Kotulič (CC-BY-SA 4.0)

BM-24: Bukvoed (CC-BY-SA 3.0)
BM-14: (CC-BY 3.0)
BM-30 Smerch: Vitaly V. Kuzmin (CC-BY-SA 4.0)
RM-51: Tourbillon (CC-BY 3.0)
140mm RPU-14: Vlad (Военный музей) (CC-BY-SA 3.0)
140mm WP-8 (Poland): Kerim44 (CC-BY-SA 4.0)

FROG-3: Leonidl (CC-BY-SA 3.0)
FROG-7: Vitaly V. Kuzmin (CC-BY-SA 4.0)
SS-12 Scaleboard: Vitaly V. Kuzmin (CC-BY-SA 4.0)
SS-21 Scarab: Gulustan (CC-BY-SA 3.0)

Digital Reinforcements: Free Ebook

To get a free ebook of this title, simply scan the code below, or go to www.shilka.co.uk/dr and enter code WPAR34.

The free ebook can be downloaded in several formats: Mobi (for Kindle devices & apps), ePub (for other ereaders & ereader apps), and PDF (for reading on a computer). Ereader apps are available for all computers, tablets and smartphones.

About Russell Phillips

Russell Phillips writes books and articles about military technology and history. His articles have been published in Miniature Wargames, Wargames Illustrated, and the Society of Twentieth Century Wargamers' Journal. Some of these articles are available on his website. He has been interviewed on BBC Radio Stoke and The Voice of Russia.

To get advance notice of new books, join Russell's mailing list at www.rpbook.co.uk/list. You can leave at any time.

For a full listing of Russell's books, go to www.rpbook.co.uk/books.

Find Russell Phillips Online

Website: www.rpbook.co.uk
Twitter: @RPBook
Facebook: RussellPhillipsBooks
Goodreads: RussellPhillips
E-mail: russell@rpbook.co.uk
Join Russell's mailing list: www.rpbook.co.uk/list

Index

Lightning Source UK Ltd.
Milton Keynes UK
UKHW012011160322
400166UK00002B/761

9 780995 513389